PRAISE FOR GAYLE ROPER

Autumn Dreams

"*Autumn Dreams* takes readers on a delightful off-season vacation to the Jersey shore of my childhood—complete with an ocean view and a delicious menu of characters. Cassandra and company face more than one stormy night before this romantic mystery concludes with a sunny splash. Enjoy the trip!"

LIZ CURTIS HIGGS, BESTSELLING AUTHOR OF
BOOKENDS AND *BAD GIRLS OF THE BIBLE*

"When Gayle presses her peopled pen, a cast of heart-lively folks emerge. Colorfully arrayed in real-life pressures, you'll recognize their struggles and feel their emotions. My greatest challenge was not to peek ahead, but I didn't want to 'awaken' from this *Autumn Dream.*"

PATSY CLAIRMONT, WOMEN OF FAITH SPEAKER AND
AUTHOR OF *STARDUST ON MY PILLOW*

"Gayle Roper has written another wonderfully entertaining book with characters that endeared themselves to me in the first few pages and a neatly woven theme that shows the wisdom of waiting on God's perfect timing. *Autumn Dreams* was my third 'season' in Seaside and I can't wait to return for the winter."

DEBORAH RANEY, RITA AWARD-WINNING AUTHOR OF
AFTER THE RAINS AND *A SCARLET CORD*

"Gayle Roper spins a memorable tale of romance and intrigue, embellished with a cast of heartwarming characters armed by faith and united by love against a threat to one of their own."

LINDA WINDSOR, AWARD-WINNING AUTHOR OF
ALONG CAME JONES AND *DEIRDRE*

"Master of romantic suspense Gayle Roper has delivered another winner in *Autumn Dreams*. Real characters with all their flaws and all their baggage fill the pages of this well-written book. Once you pick it up, you will not be able to put it down until you have come to the dramatic end!"

"I loved the first two books in Gayle Roper's series. Now she's done it again—wielding her powerful pen, creating captivating and compelling characters, a page-turning plot, and stirring action that inspires me to say, 'More! More!' I'm so glad this isn't the end. Write number four quickly, Gayle!"

Summer Shadows

"Once again, Gayle Roper shows herself to be a master at creating compelling characters."

"Suspenseful drama, sweet romance, and breezy seaside setting…Gayle Roper's *Summer Shadows* is ideal for summer reading."

Spring Rain

"*Spring Rain* is a heartwarming love story that doesn't shy away from tackling tough subjects like homosexuality and promiscuity. Ms. Roper handles them with grace and compassion, never compromising the hope-filled truth of God's Word while giving us a bang-up tale of romantic suspense!"

—⁂—

NOVELS BY GAYLE ROPER

The Decision
Enough!

SEASIDE SEASONS:

Spring Rain
Summer Shadows
Autumn Dreams

THE AMHEARST MYSTERIES:

Caught in the Middle
Caught in the Act
Caught in a Bind

Autumn Dreams

SEASIDE SEASONS BOOK THREE

GAYLE ROPER

Multnomah® Publishers *Sisters, Oregon*

AUTUMN DREAMS
published by Multnomah Publishers, Inc.

© 2003 by Gayle G. Roper
International Standard Book Number: 1-59052-127-7

Cover image by Photonica

Unless otherwise indicated, Scripture quotations are from:
The Holy Bible, New International Version © 1973, 1984 by International Bible
Society, used by permission of Zondervan Publishing House
Other Scripture quotations are from:
Holy Bible, New Living Translation (NLT)
© 1996. Used by permission of Tyndale House Publishers, Inc.
All rights reserved.

Multnomah is a trademark of Multnomah Publishers, Inc.,
and is registered in the U.S. Patent and Trademark Office.
The colophon is a trademark of Multnomah Publishers, Inc.

Printed in the United States of America

For information:
MULTNOMAH PUBLISHERS, INC. • P.O. BOX 1720 • SISTERS, OR 97759

Library of Congress Cataloging-in-Publication Data

Roper, Gayle G.
   Autumn dreams / by Gayle Roper.
       p. cm. — (Seaside seasons; bk. 3)
   ISBN 1-59052-127-7
     1. Single people—Fiction. 2. Baby boom generation—Fiction. 3. Parent
and adult child—Fiction. 4. Adult children of aging parents—Fiction. I. Title.

   PS3568.O68A97 2003
   813'.54—dc21

                                           2003004145

03 04 05 06 07 08 09—10 9 8 7 6 5 4 3 2 1 0

For Chuck,

the best of the good guys,

with love and respect.

—∞—

Special thanks to Bobb Biehl of the Masterplanning Group International (www.masterplanning.tv or www.masterplanninggroup.com) for his great tips on how Dan would approach business and management matters. Anyone who says, "At about five this morning, I thought of something Dan would do, but I didn't call" is someone who understands that Dan and Cass are "real" and that I like to sleep. It's a privilege to share Aylen Lake with you and Cheryl, to say nothing of dinner at Wilno Tavern or the Madawaska Valley Inn.

Thanks to Peg Fulton of Parkside Bed & Breakfast, 501 5th Street, Ocean City, New Jersey, who shared not only her Bed & Breakfast with us, but also gave me invaluable information, insights, and stories about running a Bed & Breakfast at a shore resort. She also arranged for our tour of the New Brighton Inn Bed & Breakfast which became the prototype for SeaSong.

And to Claire Gallagher, who was gracious enough to read *Autumn Dreams* in manuscript form and give me her opinion of Jenn and Jared. With no teens of my own anymore, Claire was a wonderful and much-needed help.

Slowly, steadily, surely, the time approaches
when the vision will be fulfilled.
If it seems slow, wait patiently, for it will surely take place.

HABAKKUK 2:3, NLT

One

"AUNT CASSANDRA."

Two words. Four Syllables. Utter despair.

Cass Merton looked at her sixteen-year-old niece, Jenn, the drama queen, seated across the breakfast table. She was regal, demanding, and very full of herself.

Whatever possessed me to think I could do this? Cass wondered. What did she know about raising the beautiful Jenn and her hulking eighteen-year-old brother, Jared? After two months of *in loco parentis,* she was ready to ship them off to their mother and father in Saudi Arabia and fie on the dangers. Certainly the risk to Cass's own sanity was more real than the uncertain threats of Islamic terrorists.

Jenn's face crumpled, and Cass braced for whatever was coming next.

"Everybody's going!" She was a study in distress. "It's all they've talked about all week. Please, Aunt Cassandra, I can't be left out."

"I'm not going," Jared said around a spoonful of Cheerios.

Jenn ignored him. She opened her eyes wide, going for the innocent look. "Don't you trust me, Aunt Cassandra?"

Cass was impressed in spite of herself. Jenn changed tactics like a chameleon changed colors, and each time she had the look down pat.

"Trust is not the issue, Jenn." Cass thought she sounded the epitome of reason as she petted Glossy Flossie, who lay half on the table, half on Cass's place mat. The old black cat spent most of her time on the back of the sofa in the family sitting room, never going into the public rooms, but when Cass relaxed in the kitchen after breakfast, Flossie always joined her. The cat arched her neck for a better scratch under her ancient chin, her purr rumbling through the room. "Wisdom and obedience are my concerns."

"I knew it." Jenn pouted. "You don't trust me."

Cass watched her niece in fascination. How did the girl look so adorable with that lower lip stuck out beyond the tip of her nose? Whenever Cass pouted—which wasn't often these days, since almost-forty-year-old women weren't allowed to pout—all she ever looked was infantile.

"You're an idiot, Jenn." Jared took his cereal bowl and juice glass to the sink. He rinsed them both and put them carefully in the dishwasher. He tossed the empty Cheerios box in the trash, the fourth he'd consumed this week. "Aunt Cassandra's right about this one."

Jenn spun to her brother, pout forgotten. Now the delightful rosy color in her cheeks and the becoming sparkle in her Elizabeth Taylor eyes were caused by anger. "Butt out, Jared. If I wanted your opinion, I'd have asked for it."

"You never ask for it," Jared said with a calm that irritated Jenn further. "And believe me, you need it."

"Like someone like you knows from popular!" Jenn's voice dripped with scorn.

"Jenn!" Cass was appalled.

Jared just smiled sadly. "At least I'm smart enough to know a party the cops are going to bust before the night's over."

Cass swallowed. She hadn't thought about a raid. Certainly she'd been worried about underage drinking, the scourge of too many adolescent parties. And Derrick Smith, the party's host, she didn't trust an inch. She just hadn't thought as far as the police. Cops at the door of her B&B, escorting a belligerent and/or weeping Jenn home in the middle of the night. Now there was something that would be great for business as well as create a marvelous memory for the girl. Or Jenn in a holding cell in the company of who knew what unsavory women, waiting to be bailed out. Cass shuddered.

"Like Derrick'd let the party get out of control," Jenn scoffed.

Jared looked at her with a mix of pity and bewilderment. "Wise up, Jenn. Derrick will be the drunkest one there."

Jenn stared, flabbergasted. "He will not!"

Jared shook his head. "For a smart girl, you can be awfully dumb."

"I am not!"

"Yes, you are," Jared said, placing his paw of a hand on her shoulder. He towered over her by ten inches. His eyes were full of sympathy.

"Smart or dumb?" Cass wasn't certain she was following the conversation. "Which?"

"Both." Jared slid his arms into his green letter jacket with the big gold *S* on the back. "Almost as smart as me—"

Jenn blew a raspberry at him.

"—and much, much dumber." He opened the back door and walked through, automatically ducking. "Later, Aunt Cassandra." He sketched a little wave.

Jenn tossed her shining auburn hair over her shoulders with a loud snort of disbelief. Her perfectly polished green fingernail with little gold stars shining on the lacquered surface jabbed in the direction of her brother. "Are you going to let him talk to me like that?"

How many thousands of dollars does a ticket for immediate travel to Saudi Arabia cost? I might be able to afford two if I cash in my IRAs, providing the penalty isn't too steep.

Jenn grabbed her purse and book bag and stalked toward the door. "I'm going to that party tonight!"

Cass stepped in front of the girl. "You aren't going tonight."

Jenn blinked up at her in surprise and took a step backward. Cass made herself as tall as she could, though she doubted size would intimidate Jenn, who was too used to her father and brother, to say nothing of her three uncles and grandfather, giants all.

"You tell Derrick that he can come here if he'd like to," Cass said, all reason and generosity, "but you are not going to his house."

The drama queen struck an appalled pose. "Don't tell me you believe Jared?"

"Only because I already checked things out for myself."

"What?" Horror and disbelief filled Jenn's face. "You checked? How?"

"Derrick's parents will be away for the weekend. The party will have no adult supervision." Cass watched the girl's eyes narrow as she took in that piece of news. "Jenn, you are not going."

"Please, Aunt Cassandra. Please."

Cass expected Jenn to drop to her knees and grab the hems of her jeans any minute now. Instead she restrained herself and dropped a green-nailed hand onto Cass's arm.

"I mean, think about how special it is for a sophomore to be invited to a senior's party as his date."

Like that bit of cajolery would sway a thinking adult. "No."

The anger returned. "What if I defy you?"

It was Cass's turn to blink. Didn't the girl know you weren't supposed to tell people ahead of time that you planned to defy them? Not that she herself had ever defied anyone, but she'd grown up with four older brothers who had had no trouble at all ignoring the rules if they felt the situation called for it. As the daughter of Cass's third brother, Tommy, the king of defiers, Jenn came by her rebellious tendencies naturally.

Cass stared Jenn in the eye. "If you flout me, I'll come and get you."

"What?"

"I'll march into the house calling your name. I'll tell everyone I've come for you because it's past your curfew. I'll call all the boys 'handsome' and the girls 'honey.' I'll grab your hand and hold it while I drag you outside."

Jenn blanched. "You *wouldn't*."

"I would. And I'll bring Uncle Hal and Uncle Will along for good measure. Maybe Aunt Ellie and Aunt Lucy too."

Jenn was obviously shaken at the thought of her two huge and very voluble uncles, their petite but extremely mouthy wives in tow, crashing Derrick's party, though she struggled not to let her distress show. She sent Cass what was supposed to be a scathing look. "Why not fly in Uncle Bud and Aunt Jane too?"

Cass nodded. "Not a bad idea. Colorado's not that far from New Jersey. Maybe your mom and dad could even come home for the weekend. Then we could have a family reunion at Derrick's."

With a snort Jenn stomped out the door and off to school, doubtless planning to make all her teachers pay for Cass's uncooperative spirit.

Cass sighed. Tommy was on a one-year business assignment in Saudi Arabia doing something he had never bothered to explain to Cass, whether because it was some sort of secret government mission or because he deemed her too dumb to understand, she wasn't certain.

He and Rhonda were due back in the States at the end of August. Cass glanced at the calendar hanging on the wall by the family phone. Friday, October 18 today's date read. Cass sighed again. It was going to be a long year.

She gathered up Jenn's juice glass and small plate, brushing the toast crumbs off the table onto the floor. It needed to be swept anyway. She wiped off the tiny table stuffed in one corner of her cramped kitchen, taking care not to bother Glossy Flossie who still slept on the place mat. As she whipped the broom around the room, Cass reviewed the coming busy weekend, smiling with satisfaction that her bed and breakfast would be filled.

Later today, nine guests were due at SeaSong, eight for the weekend and one for an indefinite stay. She didn't have many guests who booked for an unspecified amount of time, and certainly she couldn't accept someone like that in high season. But it was fall, and the later it got, the fewer reservations there were. This guest's presence wouldn't cost her income like it might in the summer if she had to turn away a definite future booking because he might still be here.

He was to have the second-floor front left, the premier room with an actual view of a wedge of the ocean two blocks away. There was a small private balcony off the room where the guest could enjoy the brine-scented breeze that blew almost constantly from the water. If the current run of Indian summer days continued, he could sit outside and bask in the sun's kiss for hours.

Cass grinned. She sounded like she was writing brochure copy again. *Enjoy the sun's kiss on your own private balcony at SeaSong, Seaside's premier B&B.*

The family phone rang. Cass stared at it. What had Jenn for-gotten today? She answered cautiously.

"Cassandra? This is Mrs. Martin."

Cass's heart sank at the sound of the high, slightly shaky voice of the old woman. There was only one reason for Mrs. Martin to be calling at this hour—or at any hour. "Mom?"

"She's sitting in my living room right now." Mrs. Martin made a tsk-tsk sound. "She's come looking for Elsie."

Cass closed her eyes. "I'll be right there."

"Don't rush. She's calm for the moment, drinking a cup of tea."

Cass grabbed her red sweater, her keys and purse; patted Flossie quickly as she rushed past; and raced to her car parked in the paved area off the back alley. What was she going to do about Mom? And where was Dad, for heaven's sake?

Oh, Father God, what do I do?

Thankful that her parents lived only a few blocks from SeaSong, Cass turned the corner onto Scallop Street, a residential neighborhood full of small, cozy retirement homes set back five blocks from the ocean. All the houses were neat and tidy, all lawns small with healthy but unimaginative plantings, all except her parents' home where mums, marigolds, and petunias still bloomed in clusters of lush color while a clematis vine with small, sweetly scented white flowers climbed the porch rail.

She pulled up in front of her parents' white clapboard home and hurried up the walk past the porch planters of still glowing if slightly leggy red geraniums. Maybe Mom had come home. She opened the front door. "Dad? Mom?"

"I'm in the kitchen, Cassandra," her father answered. "Come on back."

Cass walked through the jam-packed living room where flo-ral-covered chairs too big for the space sat cheek and jowl with a monster plaid sofa that could be pulled out into a queen-sized bed, had there been room to open it. The clutter and colors always made Cass shudder. Home décor had never been Mom's strong suit, and recently that shaky skill had deteriorated even more.

"I can't give up my treasures," Mom had said when she and Dad moved into the small Seaside house from the much larger one in the Gardens at the north end of the island where they had raised Cass and the brothers. Mom had not only held on to almost everything, but she'd added considerably to her stock courtesy of all the garage sales she faithfully attended.

"Look at this beautiful vase." Or picture or little statue. "I thought of you as soon as I saw it."

Somehow a matador on black velvet didn't seem the perfect gift to Cass, though her lack of enthusiasm never deterred her mother. Sleazy treasures appeared mysteriously in her antique-filled B&B. After years of trying to convince her mother that plastic flowers and little gnomes with their noses chipped didn't go with SeaSong's decorating scheme, she'd given up. She couldn't deal with the flood of tears that filled Mom's pale blue eyes at the criticism.

Instead, she rounded the knickknacks up after Mom left. Since Mom never remembered what she'd put where, the only price Cass paid for her lack of appreciation for her mother's eclectic taste was a back room full of atrocious oddities. She'd have a garage sale of her own if it weren't so bad for business. Tacky. Plebian. When you aimed to be the best in the county, maybe even the state, and when you had guests paying a considerable sum for the privilege of staying at SeaSong, such things mattered.

"Where's Mom?" she asked her father as she walked into the kitchen, bright with sunshine and the yellow and white color scheme. The yellow was so brilliant and the paint finish so shiny that Cass invariably got a headache every time she spent more than fifteen minutes in the room.

Dad sat at the kitchen table and barely looked up from the papers he was playing with. "I don't know. Upstairs, I guess."

She looked at his bent head. He had beautiful white hair, thick with barely any receding at the hairline. His slim mustache matched his hair, and he kept it carefully clipped. When he was younger, she'd always thought he looked like Errol Flynn, though she never told him so.

"Those people involved in movies are in league with the devil," was one of his favorite lines as she and the brothers grew up. To be compared to one of the hedonists, even a handsome, swashbuckling one, would have insulted him. Instead she told him he looked like Walter Cronkite, the Most Trusted Man in America.

Right now he was bent over a collection of sweepstakes envelopes and forms. They were his latest passion, and she shook her head at the waste of time they entailed. But what else should an eighty-year-old man do?

Cass left him and started upstairs to the two small bedrooms, his and hers. Dad snored so much Mom refused to sleep in the same room. He in turn refused to talk to the doctor about easing the affliction.

"She's just a grouchy old lady," he'd say. Then he'd grab her and kiss her, a real smackeroo, he called it. She in turn would punch him softly in the stomach as she preened under his love.

Cass had always wanted a man to love her as her father loved her mother. Ardently. Faithfully. It was one of life's sorrows that it had never happened for her.

"Mom?" Cass peered into her mother's rose room, the bed with its rose quilt neatly made and covered with every rose, pink, magenta, or crimson pillow Mom ever found at a garage sale. No one was there.

Cass peered into her father's room, stark in its lack of amenities. Cass often wondered if he was unconsciously reliving his Army days during the Good War, the glory days when he accomplished great feats. If it weren't for the blue paint and the plain blue quilt, the room would look like a barracks.

She rushed downstairs. "I'll be back," she called, though she doubted Dad heard. When he was filling out the forms for all those prizes he was convinced he would win, he heard nothing. She hurried across the street. A straw wreath sporting some well-weathered dried flowers and a bedraggled scarecrow hung on Mrs. Martin's front door. The scarecrow's hair, made of Spanish moss, reminded Cass of Mrs. Martin's permed curls. Cass raised her hand to ring the bell, but the door opened before she had a chance.

"She's in here." Mrs. Martin, a solidly built woman who should really buy her clothes a size or two larger, stepped back for Cass to enter. "She didn't want to go home just yet. She's convinced Elsie's coming to my house today."

Cass shared a sad look with Mrs. Martin, a young thing at a mere seventy-two. Mrs. Martin was as aware as Cass that Aunt Elsie had been dead for over ten years.

Charlotte Merton sat primly on Mrs. Martin's floral sofa, look-ing pleased as could be to have the opportunity to wait in such a pleasant place for her sister. Her face was carefully made up, her cheeks a soft pink, one eyebrow carefully drawn, the other a bit too heavy for her fragile bone structure. Her soft perm made her hair stand out like dandelion fluff, and when she saw Cass, she smiled sweetly.

Cass smiled back as her heart caught. Mom's eyes behind her trendy specs were glassy and vague. Where had the intelligent, wise woman Cass so admired gone? Who was this stranger in her mother's body? "Hello, Mom."

Mom blinked, and the vagueness diminished. "Cassandra Marie! How wonderful to see you, dear." She set her cup of tea carefully on the end table beside her. The powdered sugar dough-nut in her hand was liberally dusting both her chin and the navy blouse she had on. "Would you like a cup of tea while we wait for Elsie? She should be here any minute."

"Would you like some tea?" Mrs. Martin asked, clearly uncer-tain what she should do in light of her neighbor's strange behavior.

Cass gave Mrs. Martin an appreciative look but shook her head. "Thanks, but no. Mom and I have to get home." She held out a hand to her mother.

Mom waved her away. "If we leave, we'll miss Elsie."

"Mom, I think that if Elsie comes, she'll come to your house, don't you? I don't think she knows Mrs. Martin."

Mom looked at Mrs. Martin in surprise. "Is that right? You don't know my sister? I thought everyone knew Elsie."

Mrs. Martin shook her head. "We never met."

"Oh." Mom stood, befuddled. "How sad. Elsie is a lovely per-son. When we were young, people always said she was the brainy one and I was the pretty one. It took Lew to figure out that I was both pretty and bright." She simpered, like a child might. It both broke Cass's heart and grated across her nerves.

Mom took her teacup and drained it in one great swallow. She carefully set it on its saucer, picked up her napkin, and carefully blotted her lips. Unfortunately, the action missed most of the sugar on her chin.

Cass took her mother's arm and gently led her outside. Her eyes met Mrs. Martin's, and she nodded her thanks to the woman.

Mrs. Martin, her eyes sad, nodded back.

Reminder: Never let Mrs. Martin move from Scallop Street.

"You've got some sugar on your chin, Mom." Cass pointed as they walked to the street.

"Oh, dear." Mom brushed at the offending powder. "Is it gone? I don't want Lew to see me looking sloppy. He always says I'm the best looking girl in Seaside."

Cass nodded, knowing her father often made that very comment. How she wished someone would say wonderful things like that about her.

Mom stopped at the curb. "Oh, Cassandra Marie, look!" She clapped her hands like a girl. "There's Elsie's car, right in front of our house." She giggled. "Imagine. You were right."

Cass glanced at the only car sitting at the curb in front of her parents' home. "That's my c—" she began.

She got no further. Mom pulled free and dashed into the street, waving her arms. "Elsie, dear, here I come."

"Mom! Watch out for the car!"

Two

Even if he hadn't had his car windows lowered to enjoy the crisp, salt-tanged air, and even if he hadn't heard the shout of the woman in the red sweater, Dan Harmon would have been aware of the old lady charging into the street. How could he miss her?

Her halo of white curls shone in the sunlight and her navy blouse fluttered as she gave her geriatric impression of a sprinter. Her gait might be a bit creaky, but she made surprisingly good time for someone who barely lifted her low-heeled shoes when she ran.

Dan pumped his brakes and slowed to a stop.

The old lady stopped too, right in the middle of the street. She threw her arms wide. "Elsie, dear!" she called in an impressive roar for someone her age. "Here I am. Where are you?" A great smile curved her lips. "I knew you'd come."

Dan blinked. The old lady didn't know he was here, a mere five feet from her. Even if she was hard of hearing and couldn't perceive his engine idling, shouldn't she feel the heat that poured from it through the hood?

The woman in the red sweater and jeans rushed from the curb where she'd been frozen. "Mom!" He could see strain in her face. Well, if his mother went around dashing into the street screaming for Elsie, he'd probably feel stressed too.

The woman took the old lady firmly by the arm. "Come on, Mom. Out of the middle of the street." She gestured toward Dan. "We're holding up traffic."

The old lady glanced at Dan, looking thoroughly surprised to see him. Then she grinned broadly and wiggled her fingers in a coy wave.

He nodded and smiled back. When she was young, she must have been one of those cute women that young men flock to, the ones who seem helpless and make all males want to protect them. Even now she was a cute old lady. Not too smart apparently, but cute.

"He's handsome, Cassandra Marie," she said loudly enough for the whole neighborhood to hear. "Ask him his name."

While Dan grinned at the outrageous comment, Cassandra Marie turned as scarlet as her sweater and shook her head. He hoped she wasn't disagreeing with her mother's assessment of his looks but rather with the order to ask his name. He glanced in the rearview mirror to assure himself that he hadn't sprouted a second head since he left New York City early this morning.

His dark red hair had barely receded and was silver only at the temples. He wore dark sunglasses that concealed his navy blue eyes. He was proud that he didn't yet need glasses and that he had all his own teeth, though there was enough silver amalgam in his mouth to fund a small country. At forty-four, he still had more than his share of women asking his name, though usually not under orders from old ladies.

He studied Cassandra Marie, a tall woman, five ten or five eleven, big-boned though not fat, with long, long legs. She stood between her mother and his fender, a protective presence, though he wasn't sure whether she was protecting her mother from the car or him from her mother. Or maybe herself from the need to look at the man her mother thought handsome. All he saw for the moment was her blond ponytail held back with a fat red ribbon. Then she glanced at him, and he saw strong brows that sheltered worried looking hazel eyes.

"The handsome ones always like Elsie," the old lady said as Cassandra Marie turned from the car and tried to pull her from the street. "It makes me mad sometimes." She shot Dan a dirty look, and he felt like protesting his innocence. He'd never even met Elsie.

Slowly, slowly the women moved toward the curb while Dan impatiently waited for the road to clear. Not that he had anywhere special to go. It was just that sitting still made him antsy.

The old lady stopped in the narrow slice of road between Dan's car and the one parked against the curb. She looked at Dan and pointed. "This is Elsie's car."

Uncertain whether she expected a response, he nodded, but she had already turned away. She scanned the front yard of the house where flowers bloomed in profusion.

"Now where's Elsie?"

Dan had been wondering exactly the same thing. With all the shouting, shouldn't she have heard?

"That's not Elsie's car, Mom," Cassandra Marie said as she dragged her mother around the red car and toward the curb. "It's mine."

The old woman eyed her daughter stubbornly. "Elsie has a red car."

"Yes, Aunt Elsie had a red car." Cassandra Marie helped her mother step up onto the curb. "But hers was a Dodge. Mine's an Accord. See?" She pointed to the insignia on the trunk. "A Honda Accord."

Clearly the old lady wasn't buying it. "Looks like Elsie's Dodge to me."

The road was clear, it was time to go, but Dan hesitated a minute longer, not quite trusting the old lady to stay where she was. Apparently, Cassandra Marie didn't have much confidence in her mother either because she kept a firm hold on the woman's navy-clad arm.

"Elsie, Elsie, Elsie," the old lady chanted. "Where are you?" She turned to Cassandra Marie. "Where is she?"

Something in the woman's childlike singsongy voice made Dan's nerves contract.

"Why do you think Aunt Elsie's coming over today?" Cassandra Marie's voice was kind, but Dan noticed she didn't answer her mother's question.

The old lady looked disgusted. "Because she called, of course."

Cassandra Marie stilled. "She called?"

Dan recognized real distress, and things began to make sad sense.

"That's what I said," the old lady snapped as she began to stalk up the front walk past the mums and marigolds. She spun and pointed a finger at her daughter. "Sometimes, Cassandra Marie, I worry about you."

"And I worry about you, too, Mom."

Dan just bet she worried. She turned and flicked a small wave in his direction, offering a distracted smile as a thank-you for his patience. The small smile lit up her face, and he saw what a pretty woman she could be. He smiled back and nodded as he pulled away.

Just how long had Elsie been dead?

Poor Cassandra Marie. Poor Mom.

A picture of his own mother formed in his mind. She was about the size of Cassandra Marie's mother, but there all similarity ended. His mom could be the Over the Hill Gang's national poster child for mental health, strength of character, and common sense.

"Dan!" she'd said when he told her he was storing all his belongings and going to Seaside indefinitely. "Are you feeling quite well?"

The thought flitted through his mind that she could make a case for him being as bad as Cassandra Marie's mom, totally out of touch with the real world, looking for that which was long past finding. Not that she'd ever say anything like that even if she thought it. She was too committed to being positive in her outlook. What she had said when she got over the shock of his drastic realignment of his life was, "Go with God, Danny. Go with God."

He sighed as he drove south a few more blocks, then turned the next corner and found himself a block from the bay. A wooden barrier constructed of railroad ties blockaded the end of the road so no one could drive off into the water of Great Egg Harbor. He pulled up to the barrier and climbed out of his silver BMW.

The steel blue bay stretched before him, reaching from his feet to the distant mainland. To his right he could see the Ninth Street Causeway; to his left was the Thirty-fourth Street Bridge. Fading away on either side of him were homes, condominiums, and apartment complexes whose main entrances were on the street but whose living areas all faced the water. Most of the residences had gigantic decks filled with colorful patio furniture and overflowing planters, miniscule lawns lovingly tended, and docks sticking out into the water, boats bobbing alongside.

Not bad, he thought as he took in the vista that the owners and renters enjoyed daily. *Not bad at all. I could live with this.*

Even on this fall Friday, several boats plied the bay—some fancy white speedboats with high pilot bridges gleaming in the sunlight; some no-nonsense aluminum fishing boats with raised seats and men serious about their sport; some sailboats, sheets apuff in the breeze.

He squinted into the sun diamonds sparkling on the water. Maybe he should get himself a boat.

He watched a sleek Cigarette boat roar by, its wake crashing against the barricade on which he stood. What did you do on such a powerful motorboat on a bay this small? Somehow he couldn't picture the driver—pilot?—going fishing, not with that gold jewelry he had draped around his neck. Did he plan to just drive around to impress people, especially the beautiful woman draped over the seat? Or did he plan to go out onto the ocean? He was heading that way.

A catamaran with sails the colors of the rainbow caught his eye. It, like the speedboat, was heading for the inlet that opened into the Atlantic. Sailing in the ocean—or was it on the ocean?—now there was a challenge. Maybe he should get a sailboat. At least there was more to sailing than turning a key and steering.

All he knew was that he didn't want one of those little aluminum boats. It wasn't size or money or trying to impress people. It was fishing itself. While he loved seafood, he disliked fishing. All that sitting and waiting. And waiting. He shook his head. He was just too impatient. He was more than happy to pay other people for catching the flounder and blues while he enjoyed the results.

Of course, there was sport fishing for the big catches like blue marlin. That took stamina and skill. Not that you did that kind of fishing at Seaside. Such activity would involve a big trip to someplace like Baja California. He waited, but the idea raised not even the smallest spark of interest.

Instead, his stomach loosed a rushing tide of acid, and he swallowed against the fear that hovered just behind his heart, the dread that nothing would raise a spark of interest for him ever again.

He took several deep breaths to calm himself. He'd figure it out. Eventually. That was why he was in Seaside.

He turned his back on the men and women traversing the bay, telling himself he wasn't jealous. Well, he wasn't, at least of their boats. He could have any one of them if he wanted. In fact, he could buy all of them if he wanted. It was the fact that they had a specific goal for today that he envied.

Catch my limit.

Impress the babes.

Sail the Atlantic.

For some reason he thought of Cassandra Marie, the lovely blond Amazon with the dippy mother. Even she had a goal—get Mom off the streets before she hurt herself.

Never before had Dan *not* had a plan for his day. Even yesterday he'd had a plan—pack his duffel for Seaside and get the keys to the couple who were subletting his apartment indefinitely. Say good-bye to life as he knew it.

Well, then, maybe today's goal could be to say hello to life as it was going to be. He nodded, strangely comforted that he wasn't floating in freefall after all. In the last two years, he and God had had many talks about what his life should look like. They even agreed on the ultimate goal.

He should seek God's will.

Unfortunately, that knowledge didn't much help a compulsive, overachieving pragmatist like himself. Too abstract. Too lacking in something he could wrap his hands and mind around. Oh, he knew that the chief end of man was to love God and enjoy Him forever, but when he tried to imagine what that meant, especially the enjoying God part, and how he should accomplish it, his mind was as blank as an unused ledger and a lot more useless.

The unknowns of waiting for understanding terrified him, and if he felt he had any choice, he wouldn't be in Seaside uncomfortably anticipating who-knew-what.

He climbed back in his car and continued driving around the island. At the far south end he parked and walked through the little state park and onto the wide beach. No people were nearby, just ocean unbroken to the horizon and sand that persisted on sifting over the edges of his loafers, making uncomfortable little mountains in his shoes.

He'd forgotten about sand's ability to go wherever it wanted—in your shoes, in your food, in your bathing suit, up your nose. As he slipped off a shoe, turned it over, and dumped the offending sand, the insight he'd first had two years ago slammed into him again.

His life had been and was as insignificant as the stream of sand blowing away in the ocean breeze. Sure, he was extremely successful, and his company, the Harmon Group, had enjoyed an exceptional reputation. In leading THG, he'd piled up a considerable fortune for himself. But on 9/11, as he watched the Twin Towers come down from less than a block away, as he'd raced with everyone else from the great black cloud that threatened to swallow them whole, as he crouched behind a car and tried to protect himself and some unknown woman by wrapping his suit coat about their heads, he'd known with utter clarity that money was only money.

"What good is it for a man to gain the whole world, yet forfeit his soul?"

Dan slipped his shoe back on and walked along the water's edge, the moist sand giving under his loafers, the water that saturated it seeping through the seam between sole and leather upper. He didn't care. What were wet feet compared to an empty life?

God, I can't do this! Forty-four is too old to have no specified future.

A new thought seized him. What if he'd idealized Seaside, built it up in his mind as the place to find answers? What if he had decided God called him here, and he'd made a grave misjudgment?

An incoming wave broke over his foot, soaking his sock and leaving a watery residue in his loafer. Shaking his head, Dan turned and walked back to his car. He climbed in, took a deep breath, and turned the key. Time to visit the place that had brought Seaside to his mind as a possible destination, the place that gleamed like a beacon lighting his way home: Seaside Chapel.

As he pulled up beside the cedar shake structure, he was struck by how small it was in spite of the addition of a classroom wing. As a boy he'd thought the place enormous. Now that he was six four and then some, a man of the world, sophisticated, and enamored with the truly big, the church appeared little and quaint.

He sat for a few minutes, waiting for the disillusionment to creep in and ruin his fond memories. With relief he noted that, if anything, his heart warmed, and the images in his memory brightened.

He saw his mother, clad in the shorts she usually wore only in the house, running from her car to the church before anyone saw her to arrange flowers for the Communion table. He saw his father standing behind the pulpit, well-worn Bible in hand, preaching his heart out. He saw the single stained glass oriel window that sat high in the wall behind the pulpit where the morning light flooded through, washing over Jesus as He knelt, hands folded on a rock, praying. Glass a lighter shade of blue than most of the sky showed the Father's blessing being poured onto His only Son.

As a boy Dan had studied that picture Sunday after Sunday as his father preached. Finally, curiosity driving him, he asked, "Why is Jesus taking a shower?" In all the years he'd listened to his father and his Sunday school teachers, he'd never heard the shower story.

When his parents stopped coughing like they were suddenly seized with a virulent strain of pneumonia, they explained about God's blessing flowing onto Jesus. Dan had nodded sagely, but he'd never stopped looking for the showerhead at the picture's edge.

Was the window still there, hung high in the paneled wall? Maybe now he was old enough to spot the showerhead. He grinned to himself.

The announcement board on the front lawn told him that someone named Paul Trevelyan was pastor now. What would it feel like to see this unknown man in a pulpit where he'd only known Dad dressed in his black suit, white button-down shirt, and either his red or blue tie no matter how hot the weather?

He took a deep breath and sat up straight. *Forget the past, Harmon. It's today and tomorrow that need your attention.* His agitation about his unknown future still unsettled his usually cast-iron stomach, but as he drove away, he felt a little less grim.

When Dan pulled up to the corner that held SeaSong in its embrace, he was impressed in spite of himself. In fact, it looked even better in real life than on its website, which was not always the way it went.

The place was a wonderfully restored Victorian of three stories with a nifty turret that wrapped one corner of the top two stories. It was painted a soft gray with darker gray, navy, and crimson detailing and white railings and window frames. Deep crimson, rose, and pink mums bloomed in profusion across the front of the house and in pots on the porch. A small but immaculately kept side lawn ran between SeaSong and its neighbor, with a slate path curving invitingly to a sitting area under a mature copper beech.

He climbed the front steps and let himself into a small lobby where an antique walnut grandfather clock against the right wall bonged three times. Check-in time.

A small registration counter sat perpendicular to the interior stairs, and a young woman in a navy sweatshirt sat behind it. Dan opened his mouth to speak to her, but something about the way all her attention was fixed on the phone in her hand stopped him. She held the receiver halfway to her ear while her fingers hovered uncertainly above the number pad.

In a sudden rush she punched several digits, then paused, a look of panic rolling over her face. She slammed the receiver down, holding it in the cradle with both hands as though she expected it to jump up and attack her. Then her shoulders slumped, and a tear slid down her smooth cheek. She reached up and brushed it away with a sleeve, then brushed again as another escaped. She sighed and rose.

Trouble in River City? Dan cleared his throat so she'd know he was there.

She started at the sound, freezing for the slightest minute as if she'd been caught doing something terribly wrong.

He smiled at her, hoping to relieve whatever made her so nervous. How old was she? Maybe twenty? She had the wonderful glow of youth about her, but true maturity hadn't yet arrived.

For some reason he thought of Cassandra Marie. True maturity. A woman in her prime. Many might think this pretty girl with her dark ponytail and brown eyes outshone Cassandra Marie, but for Dan's money, the tall, leggy blonde won hands down. Undoubtedly, fashion mavens would say Cassandra wore a few too many pounds, but he disagreed. Cassandra was a real woman.

The girl behind the counter blinked once, twice, and suddenly she smiled too brilliantly at him through her tears. "Hello! Welcome to SeaSong. Let me get Cass to help you." She turned and fled—there was no other word for it—through a swinging door at the back of the lobby.

Dan shrugged and stepped into the common room on his right to wait. The room was filled with several pieces of furniture so old and so well cared for that he knew they must be valuable antiques. He eyed a rose velvet sofa that looked very uncomfortable. What was it with people and antiques? He'd never understood the pull. It was the one modern piece, a navy recliner that screamed, "Sit in me and lean back!" that made him feel comfortable.

He was about to sit when the small library just off the common room caught his eye. Someone had spent hours on the woodwork, the exceptional detailing and clean lines, but what impressed Dan the most was the uncanny imagination that had made such a small space so beautiful. He ran a hand over the satiny finish of the wood as he flashed a quick look at the eclectic collection of titles that lined the shelves. He was reaching for a book on sailing when a warm voice said, "Hello. Welcome to SeaSong. I see you've already found our library."

He turned and blinked as he found himself facing Cassandra Marie for the second time today. She held out her hand and smiled broadly. "I'm Cass Merton, the innkeeper."

When Dan realized she did not recognize him, he was amazed at how disappointed he felt.

Three

Cᴀss ᴜɴʟᴏᴄᴋᴇᴅ ᴛʜᴇ third-floor room in the turret and stepped back to let Mr. and Mrs. Harvey enter ahead of her. She followed them in, enjoying their looks of pleasure as they studied the attractive room. The walls were a soft apricot wash, the rug a deep pile cinnamon, and the quilt a floral in apricot, soft yellow, cinnamon, and several shades of green. The antique dresser held a pot of deep cinnamon mums, and the watercolors over the bed were shore birds standing in a marsh turned an autumnal gold, umber, and apricot.

After showing them their fully renovated private bath with its one-piece shower stall and fluffy apricot towels, she excused herself and went back to the registration desk. Only two more couples to come. They wouldn't arrive until close to nine, so she went through the swinging door behind the desk into the private part of SeaSong, the part that was home.

She still had to pinch herself frequently when she thought of the miracle of owning SeaSong. All during her growing-up years she had watched the building slowly fall into disrepair as the Eshelmans, the elderly couple who owned it, could no longer maintain it. Somehow, though, they continued to rent rooms in the summer in spite of the neglected appearance of the place.

"They must charge awfully low rates," she told her parents.

While she was in college, Cass worked two blocks over as a waitress at the Ocean House. She biked past the old place twice daily. Then as a new teacher at Seaside High, Cass parked across the street from the old Victorian. Often at the end of a trying day filled with recalcitrant students, she'd stop and stare at the house, always seeing it as it could be, not as it was. Renovated, painted, refurbished, it could rival any house in the state. She was sure of it.

Slowly the idea of creating a bed-and-breakfast from the old derelict grew, and with it grew the tantalizing idea of trading her teaching career for one in hospitality. How much would the old house cost to buy? How much to renovate? What would she do with it if given the chance? She bought books on restoring old houses; she read and studied how-to booklets from Home Depot; she figured costs and saved every penny. She designed cozy bedrooms and began haunting antique stores and estate sales, making careful purchases.

But she told no one. She knew what the brothers would say after they picked themselves up off the floor where they'd fallen when weak with laughter. The idea of their baby sister having such a pipe dream was ludicrous. She knew her parents could never help her financially and might not even support her outrageous scheme. She might stand five ten in her stocking feet and weigh twenty-five to thirty pounds too much, but her family still saw her as a little girl to be humored and guided away from her own foolish whims.

So secretly, especially on nights when grading one more essay would make her scream, Cass made plans.

When she had unexpectedly acquired the great white elephant of a house, everyone held the same opinion about what she should do with it.

Sell it.

"You'll make a bundle," the brothers said. "The land is worth hundreds of thousands."

"Wow! What a killing you're going to make," her fellow teachers said. "That land is a gold mine."

They were right, of course. Every inch of land in a small island resort like Seaside had an incredibly high monetary value. But it wasn't the land that held Cass's imagination, nor the money it could bring. It was the big, derelict house two blocks from the sea, the house that made her sing every time she remembered that, miracle of miracles, it was hers. So it became her SeaSong.

"I'm keeping it," she told everyone and moved in despite the gasps and groans and words of wisdom advising against such an action.

"I've been praying about this for a long time, and it's what I want to do. Why not? I'm single, strong, and motivated."

"You're nuts." No one except the brothers was impolite enough to actually say the words, but she knew what they all thought. She also didn't care.

Using the house and lot as collateral, she secured a sizeable loan and went to work. She hired men to put on a new roof, electricians to rewire the house and bring it up to code, and plumbers to modernize existing bathrooms and make new ones until each room had its own private facility. She met with a landscaper about making the most of the small corner lot, drawing up plans that she followed herself. She sanded woodwork and painted walls until her arms ached, prowled the entire state for furniture, and searched for and tried out countless recipes for what she hoped would become her signature gourmet breakfasts. And every night as she soaked out the stiffness in the Jacuzzi tub in the second floor turret room, she planned and dreamed. And prayed.

Thank You, God. Thank You! Help me do this right.

By the time the first summer arrived, the second- and third-floor turret rooms were repaired, repainted, and refurbished, their bathrooms renovated and fully modernized, and Cass rented them out. Because town laws and regulations prohibited building during the high tourist months—those who were the town's lifeblood must not have their vacation rest disturbed by the pounding of hammers and the whir of saws—Cass could do nothing over the summer but learn the skills of an innkeeper. She found to her delight that she loved the very act of hospitality.

"Welcome to SeaSong," she'd greet each person. "I am so glad you've chosen to spend your vacation with us."

At first the use of the plural pronoun was strictly the royal we. She did everything herself, wearing herself to the bone, but she'd never been happier. When fall came and she didn't return to teaching, she felt not a twinge of regret. She was too busy creating the best B&B in the state of New Jersey. Today, more than ten years later, her rooms were booked months in advance and for top dollar. Even the brothers, much as it pained them, had to agree that she'd done all she'd hoped and more.

She hummed as she entered her sitting room, a small, cozy area with a pair of overstuffed love seats that had been her grandmother's, a small screen TV and VCR, a maple rocker nowhere near as fine as the antique one up front in the common room, and a moderately sloppy desk crammed with all the nitty-gritty of running her inn. This room was where she and Flossie spent most of their free time.

The other private room on the first floor, separated from the sitting room by a wide arch, was her kitchen. Fitted out with an oversize refrigerator, two ovens and a stove, as well as a small table that seated four, it was more than ample for the gourmet breakfasts she prepared and served each morning. As one of the few innkeepers who hadn't gone to continental breakfasts, not even during the week, Cass was justly proud of her inn's reputation for fine eating.

A narrow staircase that had once been for servants ran from the kitchen to the two bedrooms directly above. For the next year one of these bedrooms belonged to Jared; the other, Cass's own, to Jenn. Cass now slept in the walk-in storage closet tucked under the guests' staircase and opening into the kitchen.

Pressed against one wall of the little closet/bedroom was a single bed so narrow Cass knew she'd roll right out if there were anywhere to roll. Against the opposite wall was a disreputable-looking dresser whose drawers could only be pulled open if Cass knelt on the bed out of the way. Even then they couldn't be pulled out all the way in the limited space. In fact, Cass found the easiest way to get in and out of bed was to climb over the footboard, ducking the whole time so she didn't bump her head on the slanted ceiling of the stairwell. The only other piece of furniture was a tiny night table crammed between the dresser and bed. It was so small there was room for only a lamp on its surface. Cass's Bible and any books she was reading lay on the floor.

Cass wandered into the kitchen and stared at the cluttered table. Jenn had not yet cleared from dinner nor done the dishes, her responsibility each night.

"I have to what?" she'd said when Cass first talked about what living with her would be like.

"She's worried about her nails," Jared explained with that mix of condescending disbelief and amused affection he often had for his little sister.

"Jared and I will bus ourselves," Cass said. "You are responsible for your own dishes and the general cleanup."

"And what will you two be doing while I slave in the kitchen?"

Biting her tongue because she understood that Jenn was not happy about leaving her own home, her own life, for a year, Cass said gently, "I'll be running SeaSong and cooking all our meals."

"And I'll be working around the place doing all kinds of things that need doing, especially grounds." Jared made a scissor movement with his fingers as if he were trimming the shrubs.

"Yeah, but you get paid," Jenn protested, referring to the fact that Jared had worked the past two summers for Cass, primarily but not exclusively on grounds.

"Rest assured, you will not be penniless." Cass smiled at her disgruntled niece.

Looking at the present mess, Cass was tempted to withhold Jenn's allowance, but she was already so far in Jenn's doghouse that she knew she wouldn't. She would, however, find Jenn and set her to work.

Cass found the girl on the porch swing, legs drawn up, her head on her knees.

"Jenn."

There was no answer, but Cass was certain the drama queen knew she was there.

"Jenn."

"What?" The word quivered in the air, abrupt and caustic.

Cass sighed. Teenage angst could be very wearing. "Your dishes are still on the table, and the kitchen's a mess."

"Like I care."

Cass leaned against the porch railing and forced herself to speak pleasantly. "Come on, toots. Enough with the moping. When things need to be done, they need to be done."

"So *do* them."

Cass felt her temper quicken. *The kid is unhappy because her life has been upended,* she reminded herself. *And then there's the party and Derrick.* Cass was studying her feet, trying to decide what to say next, when Jenn straightened up and pointed a green-nailed finger straight at her.

"It's all your fault!"

Cass blinked. She bent and peered into the common room. Fortunately it was empty. Family arguments made for bad PR. She turned to Jenn. "Well, granted I cooked the dinner and therefore dirtied some of the things awaiting you, but I don't think it's worth an accusation in that tone of voice."

"I'm not talking about the dishes," Jenn shouted. "I'm talking about Derrick!"

Automatically Cass put her finger to her lips. "Shh, Jenn! The guests. I'm sorry about the party, but—"

"Ha!" Jenn interrupted. "Like you really care. But it's not the party." Tears began rolling down her face.

What was it with some teenage girls and their emotions? She didn't remember behaving like Jenn, but then she suspected that by the time Jenn was forty, she wouldn't remember acting like this either.

"So you're not upset about the party anymore?"

Jenn scowled fiercely through her tears. "Of course I'm upset about the party." She sniffed, swallowed, then swiped at her cheeks.

It is the party. It's not the party. It is the party. Cass stuffed her hands into her jeans pockets. Ten more months. Her headache intensified.

"Hey, Aunt Cassandra." Jared walked around the side of the house, followed by his bosom buddy Paulie. "We're going over to Paulie's for some pizza and some videos."

"You just ate dinner," Cass said.

Jared and Paulie, both over six feet tall and still growing, looked at each other and shrugged. "So?"

Hollow legs. "When will you be home?"

"Ten, eleven. I won't be late. I've got to get a good night's sleep 'cause of the game tomorrow."

"You coming to see us, Ms. Merton?" Paulie asked.

"Wouldn't miss it for the world."

Satisfied, the boys lumbered off into the gathering darkness, hulking figures in their jeans and sweatshirts.

Jenn stared after her brother and Paulie. "Why'd you let him go without checking with Paulie's mom?"

"How do you know I didn't check?" Cass asked, dodging a direct answer. Now definitely wasn't the time to tell the girl that she had more confidence in Jared's choice of friends than hers.

Jenn sighed. "Paulie's mom better never go away for the weekend and leave Paulie home alone."

"Why not? Paulie's a good kid."

"He's totally nuts."

"Not totally nuts, Jenn. Different." And maybe a little bit nuts, Cass admitted to herself, but in a fun way, not a dangerous one. She would never forget the day this past summer when she'd gone outside and found Paulie, here to keep Jared company as he mowed and groomed the lawn and shrubs, trying to make a topiary out of one of her yew bushes by the front porch.

"It's a dragon," he told her with pride. "Those branches sticking up are the spikes on his back. There's his body. See?"

Try as she would, all she saw was a denuded shrub stripped of its pride and purpose. A pile of deep green, very healthy branches littered the lawn. She shook her head. Only Paulie. She had to admit though that the burning bush she'd purchased to replace the beyond-salvaging yew looked great about now with its brilliant red foliage.

Cass studied her moping niece. "So, if you're not upset about the party, what's the problem?"

"There is no party."

No party should fix everything, shouldn't it? "And this is bad?"

"Yes!" Jenn jumped to her feet. The light streaming through the glass of the front door showed Cass a beautiful young face with eyes wide in desperation. "Derrick won't speak to me because it's all my fault!"

"It's your fault there's no party?"

"Well, it's not mine, really, even though Derrick treats me like it is. It's yours!"

"Mine?" Cass pointed to herself.

"You. Called. His. Mom." Jenn spit out each word. "She had a fit. Derrick got in big trouble for even thinking about having people over when they weren't home."

"I should hope so." Cass decided Derrick might be a problem, but his mother sounded like a fine woman.

"But he blames me. And all because you called!"

"Jenn, you know I didn't call to make trouble for you. Just the opposite."

The girl made a disbelieving sound.

Cass tried again. "I don't think it's very nice of Derrick to blame you. It doesn't make me think very highly of him."

Wrong thing to say. Worse than wrong. Jenn leaped to Derrick's defense with all the fury of a mother bear defending a helpless cub.

"Don't you diss Derrick. Don't you dare! He's the hottest guy in the senior class! And he liked me." She started to cry. "He liked me!"

Cass pushed herself away from the rail. "And just like that he stops?" She shook her head. "How can he go from liking the nicest girl in the sophomore class to not liking her just because she has an interfering aunt? That's pretty bad."

"You don't understand!"

"I understand that he has no class. What do you want with someone like him, Jenn? You're beautiful. You're sweet. You don't need to yearn over someone who doesn't even value how special you are."

"Oh, puh-lease. Don't bother with flattery. It won't help."

Cass could tell that by the tone of Jenn's voice. Still she tried again. "Do you think Jared would ever treat a girl like Derrick has treated you? Do you think he'd blame her for something that clearly wasn't her fault?"

Jenn blinked. "You're using my brother as an example of how a cool guy acts? My *brother?*"

"Jared's a great guy."

Jenn snorted. "I hate to say this, Aunt Cassandra, but you don't know from cool."

"Maybe not, but I know from common decency."

"You don't understand," Jenn repeated. "He liked *me*." She pointed her green nail at her own chest. "Me!"

Cass shook her head. "If he truly liked you, he'd have treated you differently."

"You just don't get it, do you?"

Cass opened her mouth to respond, but Jenn rushed on.

"What am I thinking! Of course you don't get it. Of course you don't understand. How could you? You're just a dried-up old maid!"

Cass's head snapped back as if she'd been slapped. She stared at Jenn as a mix of shock and pain swirled through her gut, black ribbons of anguish twining about her heart. Without a word she turned on her heel and grabbed for the front doorknob. She missed but the door opened anyway, and unable to check her momentum, she crashed into the chest of Dan Harmon, the guest in the second-floor turret.

"Sorry," Cass muttered, rocking back on her heels. She made to step around him. In the background she heard Jenn's horrified voice. "Aunt Cassandra, I'm sorry! I didn't mean it! I didn't!"

He steadied her with a hand on her elbow as they both ignored Jenn. "Are you okay? I'm not a very soft wall."

She couldn't make herself look at him. How long had he been standing there? What had he heard? Her face burned. She had broken one of her cardinal rules of innkeeping: Never have a private conversation in a public area. Vacationers did not want to get involved with the host family's problems when they were trying to escape their own.

"I'm fine," she whispered to his third shirt button. "Excuse me."

And she ran like the dried-up old maid that she was.

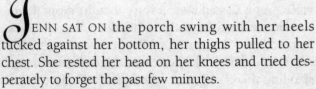

Four

$\mathcal{J}$ENN SAT ON the porch swing with her heels tucked against her bottom, her thighs pulled to her chest. She rested her head on her knees and tried desperately to forget the past few minutes.

She had never felt so ugly.

She blinked back tears of self-loathing. What was the point of working so hard every morning to make herself look good, to make certain her hair was just right, her makeup perfect, her outfit the latest, her nails just so, when inside she was vile and just plain nasty?

Derrick hated her.

Aunt Cassandra hated her.

That new guest guy hated her.

And she couldn't blame them. At this moment she hated herself.

She saw the looks on each of their faces as clearly as if she were still with them. Derrick's angry, accusing face. Aunt Cassandra's hurt, sad face. The new guest guy's look of disbelief and disdain.

She wasn't certain which one hurt most. Well, not the guest guy because she didn't know him. Still, she cringed when she remembered his unspoken condemnation. He'd turned and looked after Aunt Cassandra when she ran away, clearly concerned over her distress. Then he looked back at her. He hadn't said a word—like, what right did he have anyway? But he consigned her to some lowly immature adolescent worm status.

A worm. That's what she was, a worthless, crawl-on-your-belly worm. She sighed and fought the tears. Her throat ached from the effort.

Derrick had stalked up to her in the hall first thing that morning and said loudly enough for everyone to hear, "What's the matter with you, girl?"

She smiled at him. "Nothing, now that you're here."

He sneered. "Don't get all cute with me!"

For the first time she realized he wasn't looking at her with that approving light in his eyes. Rather, the sparks flying from his gaze meant anger, and she flinched. She also became aware that all the chatter and rush that usually filled the hall had gone silent. It was like one big held breath as everyone waited to hear what came next.

"What's the matter?" she asked, trying to keep her voice from shaking.

"Like you don't know."

"I don't." She felt desperate.

"Then you're dumber than I thought."

As everyone snickered, she stared over his shoulder at the clock on the wall because she couldn't bear the scorn on his face.

"You told your aunt, and she called my mom!"

A collective gasp rang from the attentive audience.

Jenn blanched. "I didn't realize it was a secret."

"Does anyone," he shouted to their audience, "have a copy of *Life Skills for Dummies*? Jenn needs a copy big-time."

Her visions of enduring love crashed about her feet like a building imploding, and she thought she would choke to death on the clouds of dusty pain swirling about her.

Oh, Aunt Cassandra, how could you?

"Party, Derrick?" he said in a falsetto voice Jenn could only assume was an imitation of his mother. "You were going to have a party while we were gone? Didn't we tell you no party? Didn't we? And just what kind of party, Derrick? Booze? Girls? Drugs? Well, just forget it, Derrick."

How, Jenn wondered, could you feel the heat of mortification and the chill of rejection at the same time?

He—and everyone else in the hallway—glared at her.

"Needless to say, no one at my house is going anywhere this weekend, including me."

Her eyes flew to him. "You're grounded? But you didn't do anything yet."

His sneer reappeared, and she cringed. Sally Jameson tittered, and Derrick sent her an approving glance.

"I'm sorry, Derrick," Jenn whispered. "I didn't mean to get you in trouble."

But he was gone, walking down the hall with the blond and bouncy Sally.

Suddenly the hall was alive with mocking laughter, with girls whispering behind their hands, with guys mentally crossing her off their lists. She would certainly have died of mortification if Jared hadn't grabbed her elbow and led her down the hall.

"Don't let them know you're upset," he said, his face impassive. "That's what Coach always tells us. 'Don't let the other team know you're vulnerable.' Or 'Don't let them know you don't know what to do. If you act like you're fine, they'll believe you are.'"

Puh-lease. A football pep talk? She swallowed again and yet again to keep a sob from erupting. *Just what I need.*

But she had been so glad for Jared's support. Not every brother would be willing to help a worm in need. He walked her to her first class and sent nutty Paulie to walk her to her second one. After that she was on her own. Never had the school day seemed so long.

Tonight wasn't going much better. She dropped a foot to the porch floor and gave the swing a push. She grabbed one of the pillows Aunt Cassandra heaped on the swing and hugged it to her stomach.

It was all her parents' fault. If they were here, all these problems never would have happened. Saudi Arabia! For a year!

When her father first told her about the transfer, she'd been uncertain about living in a foreign country, especially one as strange as Saudi Arabia. Why couldn't Dad get assigned to someplace like England? At least she could speak the language, and William and Harry were so cute. Maybe she could even meet them if the family went to live there.

But Saudi Arabia? Who wanted to meet some prince in a head scarf? What if he wanted to stuff her in some harem? Didn't they marry daughters off young over there?

Dad had smiled benignly, interrupting her thoughts. "But we've decided that it isn't safe to take you kids along, considering today's political environment."

"What?" She couldn't believe her ears. Not take her and Jared along? Abandon them? Without even talking to them about it? And who cared about today's political environment anyway?

Her mother—the mother who always stood up for her and let her get away with pure, unadulterated murder—smiled sweetly. "We know you'd rather stay here in Seaside."

No! No, I wouldn't, she thought, even though Saudi Arabia scared her. *Families live together.*

"I want to go with you." She looked at Jared who sat slouched on the sofa, his long legs stretched out in front of him. "Don't you want to go too?"

He shrugged. "I don't know. It's my senior year coming up. I'd hate to miss it."

"So be a senior the following year. Or you could homeschool." She turned desperate eyes to her parents. "Even better, I bet they have schools in Saudi Arabia, don't they? I mean ones that teach in English? Jared could take his senior year there."

Her parents started shaking their heads before she even finished speaking. Jared shook his head too. "They don't play football in Saudi Arabia."

What was it with boys and football? "So play soccer or whatever it is they play over there."

Jared just looked at her, and she knew a traitor when she saw one.

She pleaded, begged, and cajoled, but her parents' minds were made up. They were going away and leaving her behind for a whole year. "What do Jared and I do?" she finally asked in a defeated tone.

At first the idea of living with Aunt Cassandra had sounded cool. She loved to visit SeaSong, and whenever she stayed the night, Aunt Cassandra treated her like one of her special guests. She served her the same gourmet breakfasts, put the same chocolates on her pillow each night, and gave her the blue bedroom decorated like a girl's fairy tale bedroom. In short, Aunt Cassandra made her feel like a princess.

Well, that was then; this was now. She pushed the swing again. Now she was expected to work for her keep.

"*Help Brenna with those beds, Jenn, please.*"

"*Table five needs some more coffee, Jenn. Remember to smile, please.*"

"*Pull the towels out of the dryer and fold them before they wrinkle, please, Jenn.*"

Like saying *please* made the orders palatable.

Mom might have run off with Dad for a year, but one thing about Mom: She never asked Jenn to do housework. That's what the cleaning lady was for.

But at SeaSong, Aunt Cassandra treated Jenn like *she* was the cleaning lady. One day she even made Jenn clean toilets! *Toilets!* Why the woman even bothered to hire Brenna when she had Jenn to kick around was one of life's mysteries.

A car pulled up at the curb, breaking into Jenn's sad thoughts. A man and a woman climbed out, and Jenn turned her head away.

"Oh, John, look!" the woman said as she stood at the curb. "It's even more beautiful than its pictures. I'm so excited."

Paying guests, and happy ones at that. Just what Jenn needed. She jumped off the swing, leaving it shivering and squeaking on its chains. She rushed to the front door, only to stop short at the sight of the registration desk and the door beyond it. Aunt Cassandra had a telepathic feel for arriving guests and would be coming through that door any second. Making a quick decision, Jenn turned, raced down the front steps, passing the new guests coming up as she ran down.

The woman, all cheer and goodwill, smiled at Jenn as they passed. "Hello."

Jenn ignored her. She was in no mood to be pleasant and inn-keeper-y. She raced around the side of the house, in the back door, through the kitchen, and up the back steps to her room. Sanctuary. She glanced at her CD player. She wished she had the nerve to put on some really wild, hard rock and crank it full volume. That'd show Aunt Cassandra what she thought of her and her interference and her sacred SeaSong. Instead, Jenn threw herself on her bed—Aunt Cassandra's bed—and had a good cry over the wretchedness of life.

She cried a long time.

$\mathcal{A}$S DAN DOUBLE knotted the laces on his running shoes, he peered out one of his windows. Nice Saturday morning. Sunny, brilliant blue sky. He wondered what the temperature was. If he were going to stay here any length of time, he'd have to get a thermometer to hang outside the window. Granted, he could use the Weather Channel either on the TV or online, but nothing beat the real thing.

For want of the real thing, he flicked the TV on and learned the temperature, at least in Atlantic City, was fifty-two. Not bad. Not bad at all.

He grabbed his ratty running sweatshirt, the one that read NO BRAND in large letters and I REFUSE TO WEAR THEIR NAMES UNLESS THEY WEAR MINE in smaller letters. He slipped outside and walked around the side of the building to the backyard to do some stretching exercises. As he walked, he glanced up at the line of windows that formed the enclosed porch where later that morning he and the other guests would be served a full breakfast. None of that continental breakfast stuff for SeaSong. Cassandra Marie Merton served full breakfasts all year long.

Thinking about her brought a thoughtful frown to his face. Last night when she'd literally run into him, her face had been taut with hurt, her huge hazel eyes blinking hard to hold the tears at bay. Not that he blamed her. He'd heard what the girl—spoiled, nasty kid—had said.

"Of course you don't understand. How could you? You're just a dried-up old maid!"

Talk about hitting below the belt, especially when the beautiful Cass was anything but dried up.

He wanted to hug her, to comfort her, to tell her—what? He tried to think of something to say that would help her feel better, something that would take that haunted look off her face. Nothing had surfaced. He was as dry as an abandoned well.

He'd grimaced slightly, trying to remember the last time he offered anyone comfort. Another waterless well. Was it a matter of his not knowing how to comfort or a matter of being too busy too long to even notice when someone needed it? Neither option said anything positive about his character.

When the distraught Cass disappeared into the back of the house, the part he assumed was for the family, he turned to the girl in the swing and glared. If he couldn't make Cass feel better, he could make the girl feel bad. He was more than surprised when the girl gasped at his expression and her face crumbled. She dropped her head to her knees to hide from him.

Feeling as though he'd kicked a puppy, albeit one with a nasty bite, he drove off to his solitary dinner. Several times while he ate, his mind wandered from the book he brought along to the scene on the porch, but it wasn't the kid's distress he saw. It was Cass's. The same vision continued to plague him when he wandered aimlessly down the boardwalk, when he came back to his room and watched an old Clint Eastwood cowboy movie on TV, when he lay in the haze between sleeping and waking.

Each time he wished he'd been smart enough to help. Even now in the fresh light of a new day as he clamped first one knee, then the other to his chest, he tried to think of what he might say the next time he saw her.

Just ignore the kid. She's just jealous and spiteful.

Oh, yeah. Beat up on the kid. That'd impress Cass.

Pay no attention. She's too blind to recognize true beauty when she sees it.

He grimaced. A bit over the top, but didn't women love compliments? And he really meant it about the beauty part. Just looking at Cass was a pleasure. He rolled his head around on his neck, knowing he'd never say anything about how beautiful she was. He hadn't the courage. Still, there had to be something comforting that wouldn't embarrass either of them. He just needed to think harder, though why he was worrying about her was anyone's guess. He barely knew her. Who had time for such nonsense?

You've got nothing but time, another voice muttered. *Nothing but time stretching as far as your imagination can see.*

And just like that, the panic opened up again, this time in the form of a giant chasm gaping at his feet, huge, yawning, bottomless. A cold sweat drenched him, and his breath came in gasps.

So I have nothing but time, he told himself as he took deep, steadying gulps of the cool morning air. *So what? I'm just on a prolonged vacation. That's all.*

He didn't believe himself. Vacations were supposed to be fun times, not days spent in an agony of uncertainty and fear, feeling useless and powerless. He put his hand out to support himself against the sycamore tree, waiting for the panic to pass, praying for it to pass.

The back door flew open. He jumped, looked up, and blinked in surprise as Cass Merton rushed out in a pair of running shorts and shoes. Her hair was pulled carelessly back in a ponytail. Her sweatshirt read Out of My Way; I'm Running.

She began stretching without noting him lurking behind the sycamore, and as he watched her, the black void at his feet slowly disappeared. His feet rested on solid ground again.

Her face was clear of last night's hurt, but there were violet stains under her eyes, as if she'd passed a sleepless night.

"Good morning," he said.

She stopped dead, her arms over her head, and gave a little bleep of alarm. As she lowered her arms, he noted that her left hand ring finger was bare. No hulking husband? Hard to believe.

"Sorry." Dan held up a hand as he came out from behind the tree. "I didn't mean to startle you." He stopped in the center of the small courtyard behind SeaSong.

"Good morning, Mr. Harmon." She gave him a stiff smile, and her cheeks reddened. Probably embarrassed as she remembered last night.

"Do you run regularly?" It was inane, but it was all he could think to say. The comfort well was still dry.

"I try for four times a week." She smiled again, more naturally this time. "Sometimes I even make it, like this week." She bent at the waist to adjust a sock. "It's summer that gives me difficulty."

"A full house and a load of work?"

She nodded. "But it's hardly something I can complain about."

They pulled their feet up behind them, touching their heels to their bottoms, stretching their thigh muscles. There was something pleasant about warming up with her, about finding her an exercise enthusiast like himself. Somehow the vision of her running off in one direction and him in the other seemed foolish.

"Where do you like to run most?" he asked as he released his foot.

She shrugged. "The high school track." She pointed to the south, and Dan could make out the school itself rising above the trees a block away. "The boardwalk, though not in high summer. Too crowded."

"Where are you heading this morning?"

"I think just over to the track. I've still got a lot to do for breakfast, and Brenna's not due until seven-thirty."

Cass started an easy jog toward the high school, and Dan fell in beside her. She didn't seem to mind.

"Brenna's the girl on the porch?" he asked

Color stained Cass's cheeks again. "No. That's Jenn, my niece."

He nodded. "Fifteen?"

"Sixteen. And a drama queen if ever there was one." Cass gave a rueful smile. "The funny thing is that I used to be her favorite aunt."

"But not anymore?" It was more statement than question.

"Not since I started imposing discipline. She and her brother, Jared, are living with me this year while their parents, my brother Tommy and sister-in-law Rhonda, are on overseas assignment for Tommy's company."

"Where are they?"

"Saudi Arabia."

"Ah." There was a moment of silence where all he heard was their breathing. "My brother and sister-in-law live overseas too."

Cass glanced up at him. "Where?"

"France. They're missionaries." He waited for the usual start of disbelief. Most people he knew couldn't fathom someone being a missionary.

"Really? How wonderful!"

He blinked. She'd surprised him.

"You must be proud of them."

Dan nodded. He was proud of Andy. It took a lot of courage to adopt another country as your home, to adapt to another culture, to raise your kids away from their heritage and homeland, away from family and friends.

"How long have they lived in France?"

Dan did some quick math. "Eighteen years."

"Where?"

"A little town called Cognin."

"Is it a picturesque little town?"

"I don't know."

Cass looked at him in surprise as they crossed the street, heading for the baseball diamond and the track beyond. "You don't know?"

Dan heard something he couldn't quite define in her voice. "No, but it looks pretty in their pictures."

"Haven't you ever been to visit?"

Dan shook his head. "Too busy."

"To visit your brother?"

This time he identified the disbelief and censure without any trouble.

"What do you do for a living that's so demanding?" she demanded.

"I conduct due diligence on companies."

"You do what?"

"I vet companies to see if they're safe for my clients to invest in."

"And vets can't take vacations?"

"I'm not a vet."

"Or maybe you're not successful enough to afford the trip."

He turned, ready to defend himself, but he saw she knew very well that he wasn't a vet and that he could afford the trip. After all, he was paying for the most expensive of her rooms indefinitely. He relaxed.

"Who's the pretty girl at SeaSong with light brown hair that she wears in a pony tail? Big brown eyes? She was behind the registration desk when I arrived."

Cass looked at him, one eyebrow raised. "The brothers do that."

He frowned. "What brothers? Do what?"

"My brothers. Change the subject when it gets too hot." And she took off around the bases of the ball diamond.

He raced after her, but he never quite caught up. She stepped where home plate would be if the field were prepared for a game. "Yes!" She did a little dance as he jogged in place beside her. "I always wanted to play on the boys' team in high school, but my family, especially the brothers, didn't want me to."

"How many brothers?"

"Four, and all older." She grinned at him, a delightful, impish curve to her mouth. "They didn't want me to play because they knew I was better than they were."

"A little cocky here, aren't we?" he asked as they jogged off the baseball field.

She shrugged. "I can't help it if I'm good. And the girl at SeaSong is Brenna."

"Ah. She was making a phone call when I saw her, or at least almost making one. And I could swear she was about ready to cry."

Cass grabbed at a clip holding her hair back on the side and reinserted it to catch a piece of soft blond hair that had fallen on her neck.

"Ready to cry, huh?" She looked thoughtful. "I haven't figured Brenna out yet. You know how you find these kids who are much too smart to be doing whatever job they're doing?"

Dan nodded. He'd used a couple of bike messengers in New York who were like that—brilliant kids who for some reason didn't want the responsibility of a regular job.

"That's Brenna. She's worked for me since the middle of August when the summer kids began disappearing to return to college. She showed up at my door one morning, said she was new in town, and did I need a chambermaid. She's reliable and willing to do anything I ask, and she never complains. But something's wrong. Or at the very least, something's not right."

They stepped onto the track, and Cass began to run in earnest. Her long legs ate up the ground, and Dan dropped back to watch her.

"I bet you love to beat the boys, don't you?" he yelled to her.

She slowed and glanced over her shoulder. "Any time I can." And she was off again.

She was one of those women who obviously loved physical activity, not because it was fashionable or healthful, but because it was fun. He bet she was accomplished in several sports. Yet she didn't move like a jock. She had a grace that made her movements smooth and flowing, a pleasure to watch.

Maybe being unemployed and shiftless wouldn't be so bad if he could follow her around all day.

Shiftless. Ah, dear Lord, I can't stand the thought!

As they walked briskly back to SeaSong, they were both puffing pleasantly. Dan was used to slowing his gait for women, but Cass had no trouble keeping up with his long strides. Her cheeks were rosy from exertion, and wisps of hair had fallen free to cling to her damp neck. He had trouble keeping his eyes off her.

They stepped up onto the curb at SeaSong, and Cass stopped. Dan pulled up too.

"Hey, Mr. Carmichael," Cass called as she waved to an old man standing in front of the battered house next door.

Mr. Carmichael looked up from his study of the scraggly yews fronting his decaying porch. "Cassandra," he said with no enthusiasm.

"Ready to sell yet?" Cass asked.

"Never." He pointed his finger at her. "And never to you, missy."

Cass grinned. "I love you too, Mr. Carmichael." But as she turned away and walked toward the back of SeaSong, she sighed.

Dan looked at her, intrigued. "Do you really want to buy his house?" It was small and ramshackle, far beneath the glorious standards of SeaSong.

"I'd like to renovate it."

Dan stepped back and studied the house next door again. It was the equivalent of a dirty, wizened street person with its peeling paint, missing porch spindles, and ragged lawn. He hurried to catch up with her. "But it's a disaster."

"Now. Still, it's better than SeaSong was when I got it."

Dan looked at the beautifully painted and landscaped SeaSong. "You're kidding."

She shook her head. "Absolutely falling down."

"You certainly hired some very capable people to make the transformation. SeaSong's beautiful, both inside and out."

She stopped and faced him, hands on her hips. "Why do you say that?"

"That SeaSong's beautiful?" he asked, lost. "Because it is."

"Not that."

He knew from her tone that he'd stepped in a mess, but he couldn't figure out what he'd said that upset her. "You mean my comment about hiring capable people?"

She nodded, her eyes narrowed at him.

Surprise jolted through him. "You actually did all the work yourself?"

"With occasional help from the brothers."

Dan was afraid his face showed too much amazement, but he couldn't help it. He looked up at the roof, the high windows, thought about the beautifully restored woodwork in the library, his sleek, modern bathroom and beautiful bedroom.

"Except for the roof," she qualified, obviously trying to be completely truthful. "I don't do roofs. Or plumbing or electrical wiring. But painting, plastering, sanding, varnishing, decorating— all me."

He looked at the third floor with its scalloped shingle siding. "Impressive."

She followed his line of vision. "Cherry picker."

"What?"

"I rented a cherry picker for the painting, both general and the detailing."

He got vertigo just thinking about it.

She looked at him and apparently read his look of distaste for the task as disbelief. She shook her head in such a way that it was obvious she found him wanting. She gave a sad smile and a half-hearted wave. "See you at breakfast," and she was gone.

But he didn't see her at breakfast. All he saw were Brenna of the big brown eyes who smiled politely as she poured his coffee and Jenn, the drama queen, who wouldn't look him in the eye.

After polishing off the delicious warm grapefruit sweetened with brown sugar, the egg casserole laced with cheese and ham, and the freshly baked scones with lemon curd and clotted cream, he wandered back to his room. He stood in the turret and stared into space. Now what should he do with himself?

The lost feeling threatened him again, but he fought against it. He couldn't let himself panic every time he felt bored or wretched. After all, he had survived 9/11, unlike so many of his business connections. He had come away from the experience with nothing but a ruined suit, raspy breathing, the echoes of screams that still haunted him in the night, and a vision of collapsing steel and concrete that never faded.

For years before that infamous day all he'd thought about was business, business, business. Somehow, though he never intended it to be so, God had gotten lost as he found success. Not that he ever said, "I don't believe anymore, God. Get out of my life." It was more, "I'm so busy being successful that I don't have time for You, Lord."

"Love the Lord *your God with all your heart and with all your soul and with all your strength."*

He rested his forehead against the window. That's why he was here. To learn to love God. When he'd felt God pulling him to sell the Harmon Group and take time to reevaluate, he never expected it to be so painful. So frightening.

He took a deep breath and forced himself to stand up straight. For want of a better idea, he pulled out his laptop and wrote Andy the longest e-mail he could ever remember writing him. When Dan reread it before hitting send, he was surprised at how full of Cass it was. He almost erased it and started over, but then he thought about how much his sister-in-law would like teasing him about Cass, and he sent it electronically winging across the Atlantic.

Next, he went on-line and checked the figures from Wall Street as of closing Friday. He made a quick e-trade on a generic brand pharmaceutical company he had investigated just before he closed his business, and he made himself several thousand dollars. He wondered if the client he had researched this pharmaceutical company for found it as profitable as he did. He sighed. He'd probably never know because he'd never see the client again.

The phrase "footloose and fancy free" struck him. To be that unencumbered had never appealed to him, and now here he was, his feet loose and his fancy as free as it ever would be. He shuddered.

Then he thought of Andy again. He could make an e-trade for his brother. Of course, Andy had no portfolio. He barely had enough money for living expenses. But why should that be a problem? Dan had more than enough.

Taking the money he'd made for himself that morning, he set up a new account in Andy and Muriel's names, investing the money on their behalf. Then he put five thousand in each of three separate accounts, one for each of Andy's three kids. When it came time for college expenses, only a year or two away for the oldest child, Uncle Dan would have grown a sturdy nest egg, mature and ready for use.

He sat back, immensely pleased with himself. Why had he never thought to do such a thing before? He glanced at his watch. He had been busy trading for twenty-one minutes. At this rate the day would fly past. Hah!

At eleven there was a knock on his door. He answered, filled with the ridiculous hope that it would be Cass who needed to ask him something, anything. Instead, it was Brenna who asked, "When would you like me to clean your room, Mr. Harmon?"

Oh. He blinked. *I need to leave.* "I'll just go—" He twirled his hand vaguely because he had no idea where he'd go. "I'll be back sometime after lunch. Is that all right?" He grabbed a pair of sunglasses and his jacket and dashed down the stairs, feeling as if he were a terrible inconvenience.

He hit the sidewalk frowning. He'd stayed in hotels all over the country, no, all over the world. Why had he never felt so dispossessed before?

Ah. I never stayed in my room during the day before.

He'd always had plans, purpose, a *raison d'être*.

He wandered to the boardwalk as a default destination, crossed it, and went down onto the beach. Today he wore walking shoes, and the sand didn't pour in as readily as it had yesterday. He walked for several blocks in the hard sand left by the receding tide, head down, hands in his pockets. Was he a fool or a very wise man to have closed the Harmon Group and come to this little town? Could he ever survive the inactivity, the boredom?

He came to a cluster of shell fragments lying along the tide line, some aberration in the rushing waves depositing significantly more in this one place. They were all broken, even the heavy clam shells and the sturdy black mussels, some pieces pounded to fragments smaller than a tack head. Shattered they were, just as he was, smashed by the pounding waves of a relentless, unfeeling ocean.

Are You like the ocean, Lord? Are You trying to break me?

"Be still, and know that I am God," a voice that sounded remarkably like his father whispered in his ear. "Wait for the LORD; be strong and take heart and wait for the LORD."

Dan stared at the horizon where it faded into the sky. Wait patiently. The very thought was so antithetical to his personality that he almost gagged.

I don't know how to wait patiently, Father. I've never done it in my life. I'm a doer, Lord, a Type A of the first magnitude. The prospect of sitting on my hands waiting scares me witless.

He waited for another impression, preferably a comforting one that told him how wonderful he was for following God this far, and now that he'd proven his obedience, he could go back to work. Nothing came. Sighing, he walked to the boardwalk and grabbed a hamburger in one of the snack shops.

When he deemed he'd been gone long enough, he walked slowly back to SeaSong. Why, he didn't know. There was nothing to do there. In fact, why was he in a B&B to begin with? Why not an oceanfront suite at a big motel on the beach? He could certainly afford it. More room. A better view.

He shook his head. Somehow he knew SeaSong was the place for him. How he knew, he couldn't explain. He, pragmatic, realistic, and show-me to the core, just knew.

Cheers off to his left drew his attention. A football game was going on over at the high school. He veered in that direction. Only the second day in Seaside and he was already desperate enough to attend a high school football game where he knew none of the players. Unbelievable. He handed the man at the gate his money and went in.

On the far side of the field a line of girls in skimpy red and white uniforms were yelling, "Defense! Defense!" as they shook their pom-poms and bounced on their white tennies. On this side of the less-than-stellar but real turf, a line of girls and two boys in green and gold jumped and cheered as a player in a green jersey streaked down the field, the football clutched against his body. The stands closest to him erupted. The green shirt was brought down by a flying tackle from a big kid in red and white, and the other side cheered.

He glanced up at the frenzied crowd, trying to remember when he'd last been that enthusiastic about any game, let alone a high school one. Of course, he had season tickets for the Knicks, the Jets, and the Yankees and enjoyed taking clients to the games; it was good business. Certainly he enjoyed the games more when his teams won, but he never felt the emotional involvement of these fans.

He turned back to the field and watched as a kid in a green jersey raced across the goal line. Score one for the home team.

He glanced at the cheerleaders doing cartwheels and looked up into the stands at the screaming crowd. How small town and unsophisticated.

Then he saw Cass, jumping up and down next to a huge guy wearing a green and gold football jersey over his sweatshirt. She turned to the big man, a huge smile lighting her wonderful face, and he wrapped her in a hug. She kissed his cheek.

Dan turned and left. He could do without high school football.

Six

WHERE WAS SHE?

Tucker asked himself that same question every day, had asked himself every day for almost a year. Where was she? Or better yet, where was her body?

He stared out the back French doors to the sparkling pool and the manicured lawn beyond, all the way to the sharp drop-off at the edge of the property. In the distance he could see greater Los Angeles spreading for miles. At night the view looked like a fairy city, its lights winking at him. Now it looked like the clogged metropolis it was with a layer of smog sitting on it like a loathsome, yellow gray toad. It was a wonder any of them could breathe.

He wandered out into the yard, ducking so he didn't crack his head on his stepmother's hanging plants at the edge of the patio. He hated those plants, but Patsi ignored his complaints just as she ignored most everything else about him.

The few occasions he'd managed to get her to notice him recently had all been when he'd bumped his head on one of the baskets and sworn mightily. Today it was a hanging fuchsia that clobbered him.

"One day I'm going to throw all these things over the bank!"

She looked at him with her eyes wide in that ingénue look of innocence that had gotten her minor movie parts when she was young but which now sat very poorly on the face of a fifty-year-old woman. "Tuck, you watch your language. And just because you've gotten tall is no reason to take the plants down."

Personally he couldn't think of a better one. He reached up for the huge fuchsia he'd just cracked his head on.

"Don't you dare!" she said with a trace of her old spunk. "You just need to duck. Besides, Mary Lou and Belinda have hanging baskets on their lanais."

"Patio, Patsi."

"Lanai, Tuck."

"Keeping up with the Joneses, Patsi."

"Too big for your britches, Tuck."

He blinked. They were having an almost normal conversation. Then he watched as the blanket of depression settled on her again. Her face went slack, her eyes lost their fire, and she became a shell. It had been like that ever since Sherri disappeared. Every day Patsi sat on her lanai, staring, weeping, doing nothing except eating her heart out.

He shook his head in disgust and wandered across the lawn to the white split-rail fence. Bending, he climbed through.

"I'm on the wrong side of the fence, Patsi," he taunted. "I can feel the cliff crumbling under my feet as I speak."

She didn't even move.

Patsi had made the gardener install the split-rail fence shortly after they moved here. "I'm so afraid someone will fall over," she said, looking at Sherri who at the time was only two to his seven.

As Sherri got older, she pulled a white chair so close to the fence that she sat with her feet propped on the bottom rail each evening, watching the lights blink on in the distance.

"It's a fairyland," she said. "Quick and bright and free of tarnish. Just like people should be."

Tuck never ceased to marvel at his stepsister's idealism. "People are like the real L.A., Sherri. Ugly. Dark. Black with tarnish. The lights are just illusion."

She shook her head, her rose-colored glasses firmly in place. "I like my view better."

Idiot girl. Her chair wasn't there anymore, of course. Patsi had made the gardener put it away.

"I can't stand to look at it, all empty and forlorn," she said, tears streaming down her cheeks. That was back when all she did was cry.

Now all she did was stare. And pray. The praying gave him the willies worse than the staring.

Tuck threw himself down on the ground so his head peered over the edge of the drop. It was a long way down to the rocks clustered at the base of the raw dirt cliff. It fascinated him to look down there and wonder what it would feel like to fall. Sometimes he thought that since the cliff was undercut so badly, making a mildly curved C, all he had to do was lie here long enough, and the dirt beneath him would give way. All over California, cliffs, houses, and occasionally people were sliding down hillsides in the rain. Why not him?

He reached to his right and grabbed a large pebble that sat in the untended area this side of the fence. He stretched his hand out over the abyss and dropped the stone. It plunged straight down until it hit the vertical wall where the cliff curved back out. The stone made a great bounce before it hit the wall again and began rolling, rolling until it hit the rocks.

"Tucker, get back here."

He turned and saw his father standing at the fence. The man was trim from all his time playing racquetball, and his jawline was still taut though he, like Patsi, was in his fifties. Even in jeans and a black t-shirt, he looked like money, but the money didn't hide his tension. His knuckles were white where he gripped the top rail.

"You know how Patsi worries about someone falling."

Tuck climbed to his feet, looking back at Patsi on the patio. She stared vacantly, aware of nothing. "She doesn't look worried to me, Dad." Though he always thought of his father as Hank, he took care to call him Dad. "At least she's not worried about me."

His father turned and glanced back at his wife. As he did so, Tuck was struck by the amount of white hair Hank suddenly had. Tuck frowned. The idea of his father being old was somehow unsettling. Not that he and Hank had a relationship or anything. It was the fact that Hank was the money machine, and Tuck didn't want to lose access to his personal golden goose.

Or share.

He lowered his head so Hank couldn't read his face.

Wherever Sherri is, she'd better be dead.

Seven

CASS PULLED TWO pans of her made-from-scratch sticky buns from the oven and upended them on a wire rack to cool a bit. She slid the three quiche Lorraines she had baked earlier that morning into the oven to rewarm. The bran muffins and cranberry-orange bread went into the microwave to warm. Into her large blender she poured orange juice and two bananas and hit frappé.

Brenna walked into the kitchen through the swinging door that opened onto the dining porch just as Cass poured the beverage into a cut glass pitcher.

"I put the granola, yogurt, and fresh fruit on the serving hutch," she said. "The coffee's ready, and the tea water is hot. I've got the basket of herbal and regular teas all arranged. There's a cream pitcher, sugar, Equal, and Sweet'N Low on each table. I pulled a couple of daisies from a couple of the tables' bouquets because they were looking a bit droopy. Did I forget anything?"

"Milk, real cream, and the artificial creamers?"

Brenna turned from the refrigerator with a tray of the items in her hand. "Done."

Cass smiled. "When you take them out, ring the breakfast bell, will you? It's eight-thirty."

"I hope they don't all come at once. I hate having to serve everyone at the same time. Someone always has to wait."

"They've got an hour time frame. I think some will make it a lazy Sunday."

"I hope."

For the next hour and a half, Cass was busy in the kitchen keeping the food coming as the various guests appeared. Brenna and Jenn, much to Jenn's obvious disgust, circulated among the guests and offered the breads and beverages. Then it was all over for another day. Sated guests wandered from their tables, mingled in the common room for a few minutes, then disappeared to their private rooms. Cass began filling the dishwasher. She also filled the sink with hot, sudsy water for the cut glass and the gold-edged dishes. She glanced at the clock. Ten. If she moved quickly, she'd just have time to grab a bite and change her clothes for church.

But where was Brenna with the rest of the dirty dishes? From the size of the pile resting on the counter many pieces were still missing. Cass pushed open the swinging door into the dining room. No Brenna. No Jenn either, but that wasn't a surprise. She undoubtedly took off as soon as the last guests left their tables. Hopefully she was upstairs getting ready for church.

Cass dropped back into the kitchen, then pushed open the swinging door to the registration area—and found Brenna. She opened her mouth to say something to the girl when she was struck by Brenna's unnatural stillness. Tension vibrated from her. As far as Cass could tell, Brenna was staring at the registration desk. She tried to see around the girl to see what was holding her in thrall, but for once her height didn't help her.

Then Brenna reached for the phone.

Cass watched as she put the receiver to her ear. The faint, melodic tones of the number buttons drifted in the air. Brenna twisted and stared blankly out the side window as she waited for the call to connect. Then without saying a word, Brenna slapped the receiver back on the cradle. She remained motionless for several seconds, one hand holding the phone, the other pressed over her mouth. Then she turned her face into her shoulder and swiped her cheek on her shirt. Tears?

Cass recalled Dan's words: *"She was making a phone call when I saw her, or at least almost making one. And I could swear she was about ready to cry."*

Cass stepped back into the kitchen, her hand on the door to

keep it from making any noise as it slid shut. She returned slowly, thoughtfully to her dirty dishes. What a mystery Brenna was.

A few minutes later as Cass slotted a piece of antique Limoges china with its pink flowers and gold banding into the dish rack to dry, the door from the dining porch shot open, and Brenna came in with a loaded tray.

"They loved the sticky buns," she said brightly, just like she hadn't cried in years. "They're all gone."

Cass studied her. No sign of weeping except maybe the slightest redness around her eyes. "Then it's a good thing I held back some for our breakfast."

"You held back some what?" Jared asked as he thudded down the stairs and into the kitchen, bringing the aroma of his pine-scented aftershave to mingle with the breakfast fragrances of cinnamon, cheese, and bacon.

"Sticky buns." Cass held out a Corelle dish with six on it. Jared smiled and reached. "And you can only have two!"

He stopped and shook his head. "Aunt Cassandra, Aunt Cassandra, what have I done to deserve such cruel punishment?"

"If you don't like it, you can get out the Cheerios. You know where they're kept."

"I already had some earlier, remember?"

"Then you don't want any quiche?" She shot him a teasing glance. Jared was so easy to have around. What had happened to that family niceness gene when it came to Jenn?

"I guess I can force a piece or two to fill in the holes."

Even Brenna laughed as he loaded his Corelle with two pieces of quiche, two sticky buns, and two large serving spoonfuls of leftover fresh fruit.

"Wouldn't want it to go to waste," he said.

"Personally, I don't know why it doesn't go to waist." Cass put her hands on her rounded hips. "Just looking at that plateful makes my clothes feel tighter."

It was a rush, but Cass and the kids made it to church on time. Immediately Jared and Jenn left her to sit with their friends, and Cass slid into the pew beside her parents. One of the nice things about fall was that getting to the worship service was again a regular part of her life. The frantic summer schedule often made attending impossible. Between cooking and serving breakfast, checking out the weekend guests and readying their rooms for incoming folks, high season Sundays passed in a blur of activity.

But weekday guests were scarce now, and the rush to prepare for them immediately was unnecessary. The beds that needed changing and the baths that needed scrubbing could wait until tomorrow. The only guest remaining for the week was Dan Harmon, who had left SeaSong on some errand about nine this morning, not that she'd noticed, and Brenna had cleaned his room and bath already.

Cass sat back in her pew and mentally put her feet up. She sank into the warm anticipation of worshipping. When Paul or whoever wrote Hebrews encouraged the early believers not to forsake getting together, he knew what he was talking about. Personal devotions were great, but nothing took the place of joining with other believers.

She glanced at her parents. Dad had on his gray slacks, white shirt, and navy blazer. Every Sunday it was the same outfit, winter or summer.

"It's classic," he'd said. "And I don't have to think about what to wear."

"You just like uniforms," Cass told him. "If not your postal uniform anymore, then your Sunday one."

He shrugged. "I've got five neckties. That's one for each Sunday of the month, even on five-Sunday months. That's as much variety as I want. Of course, when I win one of the sweepstakes, I think I'll buy a sixth tie, maybe even a black suit, what with all the funerals we have to attend these days."

This morning, sitting straight in his pew, he looked alert and full of life. So did Mom. Cass studied her mother with care. Her blue tweed suit over a blue shell was neat and tidy. Her curly hair was well combed and her eyes sparkled as she reached across Dad to squeeze Cass's hand.

"Good morning, Cassandra Marie." Mom smiled. "How are you today? It's good to see you. It's been so long. You keep too busy at SeaSong."

Cass smiled back and nodded. Mom, she realized, didn't remember seeing her on Friday. Which meant she didn't remember the search for Aunt Elsie either. Was that good or bad? As the congregation stood to sing with the worship team, Cass felt the familiar desperation Mom often invoked these days.

Oh, Lord, what should I do? How can I stop these attacks?

The most frustrating thing about Mom's periodic descents into senility was that the brothers claimed that Cass was the one with the problem.

"Come on, Cassandra," Tommy said in August at the picnic Will and Lucy held as a bon voyage party for him and Rhonda. "Mom's as sharp as ever."

Will and Hal stood beside him and nodded. "Nothing wrong with Mom," they agreed.

"Guys, she got lost and couldn't remember her way home! She had to ask for directions."

"Haven't you ever gotten lost?" Tommy said, clearly unhappy with the conversation. "Ease up, Cassandra."

"Not coming home from the grocery store I've shopped in for almost fifty years," Cass retorted.

But the brothers weren't listening anymore. They were edging away to jump in Will's pool.

The fact that the brothers didn't see what was so obvious to her wasn't what annoyed her most, though it definitely bothered her. A bunch of ostriches, all of them. What really irked her was the condescending manner in which they let her know she was the one with the problem, not Mom.

If only she could turn to Dad for help, but he was so consumed by his sweepstakes that Mom could run around the neighborhood naked, and he'd never notice.

Cass sighed. She loved her family dearly, every single one of them, but there were times they drove her crazy.

A shuffle in the pew ahead caught her eye. In surprise she noted Brenna and her boyfriend, Mike, taking a seat. Brenna looked pretty in a pink shift, but Mike, a young man who was more bones than flesh and who looked like a younger Lyle Lovett, was decidedly uneasy. He kept fidgeting and clearing his throat. At one point, Brenna reached back and patted his shoulder. He managed to stand still for all of two minutes.

"Hey," Dad whispered in an aside subtle enough to be heard all over the small sanctuary. He pointed to Brenna. "Isn't that—"

"Yes," Cass interrupted brutally, thankful that the singing almost hid his voice. She patted his hand and applied herself to the service. Even though she sang much of the time with her eyes closed to better focus on the Lord, she couldn't help noticing that Brenna seemed to know all the songs. Just as obviously Mike didn't. Cass also couldn't help observing that Brenna sang through tears, a great wash of them pouring down her lovely face. Now it was Mike who patted Brenna on the shoulder, his solicitude sending a little shaft of envy zinging to Cass's heart. What was it like to have a man care for you like that?

Forgive me, Lord. You're enough. You always have been and You always will be.

Pastor Paul Trevelyan spoke, and as always Cass wished the elders would get with it and ask Pastor Paul to take the position at Seaside Chapel permanently instead of on the interim basis under which he now served. He was such a nice, capable young man.

Cass winced. *Young man.* Did that say a lot about her age or what? He was maybe ten or twelve years younger than her own almost forty. A mere kid, all unlined face and unflagging energy. Well, someday he'd reach the advanced age of forty, too. Of course, by then she'd be fifty. She sighed silently.

As Pastor Paul closed the service in prayer, Cass was aware of movement in front of her. She glanced up to see Brenna and Mike sneaking out. She was disappointed because she had hoped to talk with the couple and maybe get more of a feel for the puzzle that was Brenna.

As she followed her parents down the center aisle, Cass beckoned to Jenn and Jared, who were talking with their friends. Jared nodded and said prompt good-byes. Jenn made believe she didn't see her and kept on talking.

Cass shook her head. *What am I going to do with her?*

As she walked out the front door, Cass was surprised to see Dan Harmon talking with Pastor Paul. Interesting. It became more interesting still as Pastor Paul turned to her. "Did you know that your guest's father used to pastor here at Seaside Chapel?"

Now there was an unexpected piece of information. "Really?" She tried to recall a Harmon. "When?"

"About thirty to thirty-five years ago," Dan said. "Just for the summers. At that time, the Chapel only held summer services."

"Ah." Cass smiled. "We didn't come to the Chapel then. We didn't start coming until the services were year round."

As Dan nodded, Mom reached around Cass and held out her hand.

"Hi, I'm Cass's mother." Dan took her hand, a startled look on his face. "Nice to meet you, Mrs. Merton."

Cass noticed Dan's surprise. Much as she hated to admit it, she noticed most things about Dan. She looked at Mom again. Nothing was out of place. She was the perfect picture of a sweet older lady. Happily her conversation today was quick and lucid.

"How are you enjoying your stay at SeaSong?" Mom asked.

While Dan made polite noises about SeaSong, Cass longed to slink away. Even when Mom's conversation made sense, she was always unpredictable when she spotted a potential man for her unattached daughter. Often she made Cass feel like she was standing on the auction block, and Mom would let her go at a rock-bottom price to anyone who made an offer.

Mom reached out and slid her arm through Cass's, halting any escape attempt. Cass forced herself to smile and tried not to wonder how Dan saw the two of them together—her tiny, cute mother and her towering, lumpy self.

Pastor Paul wandered off to talk to some other visitors at the same time Will and Lucy Merton walked up.

"More Mertons," Mom said, and happily introduced Dan.

As Dan shook Will's hand, he said, "I think I saw you at the football game with Cass yesterday."

Cass looked at Dan in surprise. He was at the game? She hadn't seen him, but then she had been pretty absorbed in watching Jared and Paulie and the rest of the team.

"Great game, wasn't it?" Will asked. "Jared played really well."

While Dan nodded noncommittally, Mom laid a hand on his arm. "We're all going out for lunch. Won't you join us?"

Cass flinched, but Dan didn't seem to realize he was being wooed, pursued, courted. In fact, he looked pleased. "Thank you. I'd like that."

"Good." Mom smiled with evident satisfaction as she patted his arm.

Cass groaned inside. She'd seen that smug look on her mother's face too many times before.

Mom, please, no matchmaking. He's our guest at SeaSong, for Pete's sake.

"Where are you going?" Dan asked. "I walked this morning, so I don't have my car. I'll have to get it and meet you."

"Oh," Mom said, momentarily nonplussed. Then she grinned craftily. "That's no problem. Cassandra Marie can drive you, can't you, sweetie?"

Cass had read her mother correctly. The lady'd sized Dan up and come to the conclusion that he was an excellent prospect for saving Cass from permanent, previously inevitable spinsterhood. Funny how she'd done that at both her mental best and worst.

Cass smiled at Dan in spite of the sharp sword of potential embarrassment that hung directly over her head, suspended by the slender thread of Mom's erratic mind. "You can fight Jared for the front seat."

"I'm riding with Uncle Will and Aunt Lucy and the cousins," Jared said.

"Me too." Jenn stood close by her brother, eyeing Dan warily.

Cass nodded, accepting the inevitable. Dan and her. Together. Alone. What an awful situation. She bit her lip to keep from grinning.

With Dan at her side, she walked to her car, noticing that he made her feel small, a rare and wondrous experience. When he held the door of her red Honda for her, her heart tripped at the courtesy. She couldn't recall the last time a man had done that. Certainly the brothers never thought to.

Dan climbed into the passenger seat, and suddenly the car seemed crowded. She couldn't remember when or if she had ever been so aware of a man. Because she felt so drawn to him and wanted to lean toward him, she pressed against her door. Because she wanted him to feel drawn to her, she became reserved and shy, her mind completely blank.

"Does your family go out like this every week?" Dan asked as they pulled onto the road.

She nodded and cleared her throat to get rid of the breathless feeling he gave her. "Usually we do. Mom loves to get us together."

"Nice family tradition," he said, smiling, and Cass caught herself staring. He had a wonderful smile. She forced her eyes back to the road just in time to hit the brakes at the light at Ninth Street. Dan braced himself with his hand on the dash and said, "Oops."

Cass studied the traffic signal with an intensity usually

reserved for a microbiologist studying a new strain of virus in the electron microscope. She knew her face was scarlet.

"When we were all younger," she said in a rush, "Mom made a traditional Sunday dinner with roast beef and browned potatoes, carrots and onions—the works—every week. I think of that as the family tradition. Going out to eat is her substitute since cooking a big meal every week has gotten to be too much work. It makes her too nervous."

A new and unpleasant thought grabbed her like a boa constrictor wrapping around its victim. Had Mom gotten to the place where she couldn't remember how to make the big dinner? Or maybe she could no longer manage the logistics of it, getting it all cooked correctly and finished at the same time? Cass's breath whished out. Either alternative was a bad sign, one that had been staring her in the face for months. She just hadn't known how to interpret it.

"You're fortunate to have your family so close." Dan's voice was wistful.

"Yes, I am." Problems and all.

"When Dad couldn't take the job here at the Chapel full-time, we moved to Indiana. He and my mother still live there, though he's retired now."

"Why didn't he take the Chapel position?" If he had, she would have grown up knowing Dan. Strange thought.

"Money."

"Money?" Cass looked at him, surprised.

Dan grinned. "Sounds crass, doesn't it? It isn't really. Dad had been an engineer for several years before he felt God calling him into the ministry. Those years in seminary depleted his savings, and the Chapel, being very small, couldn't pay enough to feed a family of four. So it was Indiana."

And I never met you until a few days ago.

Silence fell, and Cass became increasingly uncertain. As far back as she could remember, she had felt tied in knots around men. Or at least men she liked. When the brothers brought home friends she didn't like, she was fine. Conversation was easy, teasing, comfortable. In a business setting, she was fine. She was supposed to be in charge, she knew what was expected of her, and her strong personality showed to advantage when she ran SeaSong or led the meetings of the Seaside B&B Guild.

It was social situations and interesting men that undid her.

And, without question, it was all the brothers' fault.

Without meaning to, they had made her so self-conscious that she couldn't relax and act naturally. She knew that at almost forty she should be beyond such a reaction, but that didn't change the audiotapes that ran through her mind every time she was around someone she liked.

"*I love you, chubby tubby.*"

Hal, six years her senior, called that to her every night when she went to bed right up until the time he married little, slim, elegant Ellie, a model for petite clothes. If Cass were within reach as he said the endearment, he'd pinch an inch. Or two or ten.

Cass had been twenty when Hal and Ellie walked the aisle, and she'd been a bridesmaid in a hot pink dress with a flounce at the bosom. Not only did the dress make her resemble a drunk's traditional pink elephant, but the color ate her fair complexion whole. All Ellie's little, dark-haired friends looked lovely as they walked the aisle. She'd died a million deaths as she followed with her pasted-on smile. As she reached the front of the church, Hal had glanced at her and winked.

"I love you, chubby tubby." And he'd smiled sweetly before turning his attention back to Ellie.

Tommy, four years her senior, always teased her about her height. "Come on, Cassandra. Stop that growing. You're going to be bigger than all the boys. Who's going to want an Amazon with a big bottom for a girlfriend?"

Who indeed? When she was in junior high and all the boys came to her knees and her baby fat still quivered, she realized how true Tommy's comment was. She was growing up to be a monster. The fact that he took to calling her *BB* for big bottom didn't help her self-confidence any. When the other brothers picked up on it, she flinched every time she heard it but knew she couldn't complain. If they knew how it bothered her, they'd use it twice as much.

At least Bud didn't say anything derogatory. He just looked at her and shook his head and married another lovely munchkin.

The funny thing was that she knew the brothers loved her. They constantly pummeled each other both physically and verbally as they grew, and they treated her like one of them, hitting her as much as they slugged each other, calling her names as easily as they insulted each other. She never minded the punches and gave as good as she got. The names, however, eroded her confidence a bit more every time she heard them.

"I should have been a boy," she had sobbed to her mom one day in tenth grade, her little mother who now barely came to her shoulder.

Mom reached up and patted her gently on the cheek. "Don't worry, Cassandra Marie. God knows what He's doing."

Cass wasn't certain whether it was the lack of conviction in her mother's voice or the fact that God seemed to be keeping silent about the whys of what He was doing, but either way her height and girth shadowed her life like a jail term trailed a reformed thief.

When she'd come out to run yesterday morning and found Dan, her first horrified thought was, *He's going to see my legs!* The second was, *And I never did lose that extra weight!*

She had immediately turned their run into a competition. If she looked on him as a challenge, she could deal with him. All her life she'd loved to win, and that meant beating all kinds of people in all kinds of situations. She'd simply added Dan to that list. Run faster. Control your breathing better. Beat him.

But sitting here in the car with him was different. Now she was supposed to chat and be sociable. Now she had to be charming. She shivered.

"Does your mother have a twin?" Dan asked suddenly.

"What?" Cass was jerked from her introspection by his question.

"A twin. Does your mother have one?"

Cass shook her head as she pulled into a parking space near Dante's at the Dock. "Whatever made you ask that?"

"She doesn't seem like the same lady at all." He waved his hand in Mom's direction as she walked to the restaurant door.

Cass pulled the key from the ignition and dropped it in her purse. "The same lady as what?"

Dan reached for his door handle. "But you called her Mom both times. Certainly you don't have two moms even if they act nothing alike."

Cold prickles traveled the length of Cass's spine. "That was you Friday?" she asked in an appalled whisper. "That gray car?"

He nodded. "Silver. They call it silver."

She glared at him. "Like it matters."

"Yeah." Dan nodded and sighed. "Like it matters."

It helped a bit that he seemed to understand that car color was nothing compared to a mother's encroaching senility, but it tore her heart that he had seen Mom at her worst. She managed a tight smile in spite of the tears that gathered. "We'd better get in there."

"Hey," Dan said, frowning. "I didn't mean to upset you."

She blinked the tears away. "Don't worry about it. I'm really not upset at you. It's Mom. She's always been so dynamic, so strong, so much fun. Then suddenly she became someone totally different, a stranger." She swallowed. "It's hard."

Dan ran a finger across the dust on the dashboard. "Does she realize what's happening?"

Now there was an interesting and scary question. What would it feel like to know you were losing your mind? "I don't know. She's never said. Fortunately, she doesn't seem to remember you and the car and Friday, so she thinks she just met you. She'd be mortified if she knew you'd seen her in that condition."

"It's our secret," Dan assured her.

Cass nodded and climbed out into the crisp autumn sunshine. He walked beside her up the walk. He held the door, and she passed through. She felt the heat of his hand at the small of her back as he directed her to the noisy family group the hostess had wisely seated in the corner, all the kids at one table, the adults at another.

Dante's was unusual in that it had a family side and a fancy side, the menu and prices differing significantly. The Merton party was on the family side. Somehow their waitress made sense of everyone's orders and which meal should be on which check. Cass couldn't decide whether she was more embarrassed or pleased when Dan insisted that Cass's meal was his treat.

"Does that mean us, too?" Jared called from the neighboring table, pointing to himself and Jenn.

"Sure," Dan said. "Why not?"

"But, Dan—" Cass started, looking at the handsome man seated next to her.

"Cassandra Marie," Mom interrupted from her seat across from Cass. "You must never argue with your young man in public."

Her young man? "But Mom—"

"Why," she continued, smiling sweetly but looking alarmingly vague, "Jared is taking care of his girlfriend very nicely. Let—" She looked at Dan, obviously at a loss for his name.

"Dan," he supplied.

Mom nodded. "Dan. Of course. Let Dan take care of you."

Cass looked at her mother. "Jared's girlfriend?"

"Certainly. That lovely girl sitting beside him. I forget her name."

Cass felt tears again prick her eyes. The lovely girl sitting next to Jared was Jenn.

Mom had forgotten her own granddaughter.

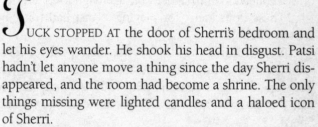

Eight

TUCK STOPPED AT the door of Sherri's bedroom and let his eyes wander. He shook his head in disgust. Patsi hadn't let anyone move a thing since the day Sherri disappeared, and the room had become a shrine. The only things missing were lighted candles and a haloed icon of Sherri.

He crossed the pale yellow carpeting to the windows with their yellow and blue floral drapes. The view was similar to that in the backyard, L.A. in all its glory. He could just imagine Sherri sitting here on the window seat staring at the city lights, a smile curving her lips as she dreamed her sweet dreams.

She had been so optimistic it gave him stomach cramps just thinking about her.

He turned from the window and began one of his frequent but secret forays about the room. What would he do this time? Steal something? Break something? Ruin something?

Part of the fun of invading his stepsister's domain was the surprise of suddenly realizing what was the right thing to do this time. It was almost mystical, the fine certainty that stole over him and caused the hair on the back of his neck to stand erect. He'd smile. The family princess was about to suffer significantly more discomfort than a pea beneath her pile of mattresses.

The first time he'd experienced this *knowing,* he was nine. Four-year-old Sherri had been in the kitchen being fed by their cook. Hank was still at work, of course, and Patsi was at one of her unending meetings, keeping the world safe from predators who killed whales and baby seals and dolphins.

He'd been curious to see how the little princess lived, so he prowled the room, at first just looking. Then he poked into her drawers, fascinated by all the miniature clothes. Her closet held more dresses than most children's departments, and her toy box was filled to overflowing with any toy a little girl could desire. The lower shelves that ran around the walls held games and the higher ones a collection of designer dolls too high for Sherri to reach.

"These dolls aren't for playing," Patsi had told Sherri. "They are too valuable."

Tuck studied the dolls with their pink cheeks and rosy mouths, their curling hair and magnificent outfits. Why would a girl want dolls she couldn't play with? A pretty doll with brown hair that hung to her waist caught his eye. She reminded him of Sherri.

And the *knowing* zinged through him.

He grabbed the glorious doll from the shelf. While she smiled sweetly, vacantly at him, he took Sherri's pink plastic little-kid scissors and chopped her hair off. Silken curls fell to the floor, and he smiled. He hacked and hacked until only a couple of inches of now ugly, uneven hair remained. He very carefully set the doll, the shorn hair, and Sherri's scissors on her bed. Then he pulled her desk chair over to the shelf where the doll had stood.

He stood back and studied his crime scene. He grinned. He skulked down the hall to his room where he played a computer game with the sound muted. He wanted to hear when the doll was discovered.

He wasn't disappointed. Patsi screamed in distress, then anger as she upbraided her darling daughter for such a vile act. Sherri was in hysterics as she pleaded her innocence, and all the designer dolls disappeared for safekeeping in spite of Sherri's tears.

For fifteen years he kept up his subtle torture of his stepsister. A much-loved stuffed animal would be found lying in the sodden grass after a rain or floating in the pool, ruined. A favorite article of clothing would develop a mysterious stain. A CD acquired a scratch that warped the music. A report for school inexplicably disappeared from the computer.

At first Sherri ran to Patsi or Hank about every little thing, and they scolded her for her carelessness. Then he became aware that no one suspected Sherri any longer, and he relished this turn of events because it made the game that much more interesting. Get in, do the deed, and get out undetected. He was twelve when Hank took him to a child psychologist, the first in a long line of shrinks of all kinds and philosophies.

Like they would ever persuade him to give up that *zing*.

The years he was away at college were probably a relief to Sherri, but they were hard on him. He'd learned to like wielding the power of emotional pain. He had to make do with vacations and summers. Then she went away for the whole summer, first as a camper, then a counselor. He missed her terribly. How could he hurt her when she was gone? He still prowled her room, he still plotted, but he yearned for the immediate satisfaction of her distress.

His most daring act occurred the night before she came home from camp the summer before she disappeared. He crept into her room and attacked Happy, her parakeet. Before that night he'd only damaged inanimate objects. But, oh, the *zing* in upping the ante.

When she came home, she found the bird flopping in his cage with a broken back.

He still smiled over that one. As she wept on Patsi's shoulder, it was as if her tears had washed over him in a fragrant waterfall, comforting him. Even Hank's glares and Patsi's looks of disbelief, all aimed at him, hadn't upset him. No proof.

And then, not too long after, Sherri had disappeared.

He missed the pain.

Nine

*T*UESDAY AFTERNOON CASS was dusting in the common room when she heard the melody of the phone buttons being punched just around the corner at the registration desk. She walked to the doorway and there sat Brenna, the phone clamped to her ear. Again she was staring out the side window at nothing. Again her face was etched with equal parts pain and sorrow, and her eyes swam with tears.

As Cass watched, she couldn't help wondering why the girl was using the office phone when she had a cell phone of her own. Cass had seen her use it countless times, usually talking with Mike. The only thing she could think was that Brenna didn't want the number to show on her bill—which would also be Mike's bill if they had a joint plan. If she called from SeaSong, no one—certainly not Mike and probably not Cass herself—would notice one or two or even half a dozen extra calls since she paid a flat rate for SeaSong's 800 number.

Was Brenna trying to keep secrets from Mike? All kinds of questions about how he and Brenna were getting along raced through Cass's mind. When she'd hired Brenna, she hadn't known the young woman was living with her boyfriend. By the time she found out, Brenna had proven to be an excellent worker, and Cass couldn't see letting her go over the issue, even though she didn't approve of cohabiting. Once she'd actually talked to Brenna about it.

"Why don't you guys get married if you're living together?"

"Married?" Brenna looked surprised at the suggestion. "But I'm only twenty."

"What about the idea that sex and marriage are supposed to go together, and you shouldn't have one without the other?"

Brenna wrinkled her nose as if she smelled something bad. "I've heard that."

Cass waited for the *but*. Brenna didn't disappoint.

"But no one follows that old-fashioned idea anymore."

At least not many. "I do."

Brenna just looked at her, and Cass realized that in Brenna's eyes her singleness was proof that she was wrong. If she put out a little, Brenna was too polite to say, she wouldn't be climbing alone into the rinky-dink bed under the stairs every night.

"I'm a Christian, Brenna, and I want to do things the way the Bible says to. And the Bible says wait."

Brenna nodded. "I know that." She set her jaw. "I just didn't want to."

"Has living with Mike made you happy? Filled all the holes inside?"

"Were you ever in love with anyone, Cassandra?" Brenna asked, ignoring the question.

Interesting question. "I don't know. I was almost engaged to a guy once a long time ago, but he decided he loved a little redhead who came to my elbow. At the time I thought my heart was broken. Now I wonder."

"Did you sleep with him before the little redhead came along?" Brenna folded her arms, waiting for the truth.

"Brenna!"

"Hey, you brought up the subject."

True. "No, I didn't. He was a Christian too, and we both felt the same way about being chaste."

"You're an anachronism, Cassandra." Brenna reached over and patted her hand. "But you're a great boss."

Cass smiled at the girl to show she understood Brenna meant nothing nasty with the old-fashioned crack. "All I'm trying to be is an obedient Christian."

"Um." Brenna frowned. "Don't you get lonely all on your own?"

Cass thought of the many times she and the Lord had talked about that very topic.

"Yes, I get lonely, but I know that the Lord should be enough."

"Sounds good, Cass, but the Lord can't hug you. I'll take Mike any day." And Brenna had disappeared into the next room to strip the bed.

But it seemed everything might not be hunky-dory in Brenna and Mike's little paradise. She was clearly bothered, obviously struggling with—what? Cass had no idea. All she knew was that Brenna no longer automatically smiled when she spoke of Mike, and she didn't call him on her cell a million times a day. She seemed more solemn and preoccupied. Add secret, teary phone calls, and Cass thought she saw the handwriting on the wall.

As she watched Brenna on the phone, curiosity about the person at the other end wiggled actively in Cass's brain with all the energy of a pup wagging a greeting. Ruthlessly she made the nosiness sit and stay as she backed into the common room to give the girl privacy.

The minutes spun out as Cass dusted the rocker, the escritoire she'd gotten at an estate sale in Haddonfield, and the Federal style fireplace with its collection of antique candlesticks, all with candles, ready for a summer electrical storm or a fall hurricane to knock out the lights.

She found herself straining to hear Brenna's voice. However, Brenna didn't speak. She didn't say a single word. Strange. Very Strange. Dial a number, but don't talk to whoever answers?

Concerned, Cass walked openly into the front hall where Brenna could see her.

She could also see Brenna clearly, and Cass's breath caught at the tears bathing that lovely face. Instinctively, she held out a hand. "Brenna?"

The girl dropped the phone into the cradle and spun. "I'm sorry!" she blurted, her voice quavery. "I'll pay; I promise I will."

Cass shook her head. "I'm not concerned about that. I'm concerned about you. Are you all right?"

Brenna backed toward the swinging door behind her. "I'm fine. Really."

"Honey, fine people don't cry. Maybe I can help?"

"I'm fine," Brenna repeated as she backed through the door. The tears continued to run down her cheeks. "Never felt better." A shaky laugh drifted through the whishing air as she let go of the door and fled.

Cass was thoughtful as she went back to her dusting. She was wiping down the books on the lower shelves in the library when Dan walked in carrying a novel.

Cass stood, telling herself that what she felt was simply an innkeeper glad to see a guest. "Having a good day?"

He shrugged. "Not too bad."

A short silence ensued while Cass tried to think of something to say. Dan walked to the shelves and slid the novel into a slot. He cleared his throat. "I told Brenna to tell you how good the omelet was this morning. Did she?"

"Yes, she did. Thanks."

Dan scanned the shelves. "Um."

"Remember you told me you saw her make an almost phone call?"

He looked at her over his shoulder and nodded.

"She just made another one, only this time I think she held on long enough for a connection."

Dan turned to face her. A sly grin slid over his face. "You can usually tell there's a connection because people say interesting things like hello."

She raised an eyebrow at him. "They do? Well, that's the weird part." She stuffed her dust cloth into her jeans pocket. "She didn't say anything. When I walked to the registration desk, she slammed the phone down and bolted."

Dan leaned against the bookshelves, looking thoughtful. "Why would she make a call and say nothing?"

"Good question. And she was crying, really crying."

"Ah." He nodded sagely as if that information answered all their questions. Then he shook his head. "I don't get it."

"I can't figure her out either. I just hope she comes to work tomorrow."

"She wasn't mad that you saw her, was she?"

"No. Just incredibly sad and embarrassed." Cass reached over and pulled a novel from the shelf. "Here. Read this one by Harry

Kraus. You'll like it. It's a mystery about a man trying to create a new identity for himself."

He took the book even as he looked at her strangely. "I haven't read as much fiction in my whole life as I've read since I got here!"

"It's good for you. Relaxes you."

"It makes me tense. I keep feeling I should be doing something worthwhile."

"Reading's worthwhile."

"Fiction?"

"Sure. It lets you see life as it could be or should be. At least the novels that offer hope do. The bad guys get caught. The lovers get together. The quest is solved. Besides, Jesus told stories."

Dan looked intrigued. "The parables. I never thought of that. And don't worry about Brenna. She'll show."

Cass sighed. "I just wish I could help her."

Dan put his novel down on a shelf and moved closer to Cass. "I know you're worried about her. It speaks volumes about you that you care so much for someone you've only known a couple of months. But if she won't let you get close, there's nothing much you can do, at least for now."

Cass frowned. It was almost as bad as one of the brothers patiently explaining something beyond her understanding.

Dan saw the frown. "Come on." His voice was light, teasing. "You know I'm right."

Cass pulled out her dust cloth and swiped at a few more dustless books, then stood staring at their spines. He was right, and she did know it. "I hate it when I can't fix things."

"Are you telling me you're a control freak?" He sounded appalled.

She glanced up, ready to argue, and saw his grin. She couldn't help but grin back.

"Have dinner with me tonight."

She couldn't hide her surprise even as she tried to tamp down the pleasure his invitation brought.

"Please. I'm so tired of eating alone I could scream."

"Oh." Of course. It wasn't that he was dying to have dinner with her. It was more that she was the only person he knew. She was merely a hedge against another night of boredom. She gave a mental shrug. So what? A dinner with Dan was a dinner with Dan. "What time?"

"You have to feed the kids, don't you?"

"You mean they aren't invited?"

Dan looked momentarily startled. Then he caught on to her wide-eyed innocent act. "Cute. Is seven okay?"

At six-thirty Cass put the kids' meal on the table. She'd thought Jared would never get home from football practice. She had time for a quick shower and a general spruce-up before she met Dan in the lobby. She reached in her cubbyhole of a bedroom and grabbed her robe off the back of the door. She started up the stairs to the family bathroom.

Her private line in the kitchen rang, and sighing, she answered.

"Cassandra Marie." Mom's voice was full of tears.

"Mom! What's wrong?" Had something happened to Dad?

"It's Elsie."

Cass's stomach clutched. *Oh, Mom!* "What's wrong?"

"She's up in the attic above the garage, and she won't come down. I've called her and called her, but she won't come down. And I can't figure out how to get to her."

"Oh, Mom, she can't be up there." Hopelessness swept Cass. "She's been dead for several years. Don't you remember?"

"What?"

"Aunt Elsie died a long time ago."

"She—she did not." Cass could hear the horror in her mother's voice. "Not Elsie. She's in the garage attic. I can hear her moving."

"Mom, where's Dad?"

"Who?"

Cass blinked. Mom remembered her daughter but not her husband? "Dad. You know, Lew."

"Oh, you mean that handsome Lew Merton?"

"Yes, that's who I mean. May I speak to him?"

"Let me see if he's come to visit."

"Mom, he lives there."

"With Elsie and me? I would think not. It wouldn't be proper."

Cass blinked against her tears, aware that Jared and Jenn were watching her with concern. "Just find him for me, okay? I need to talk with him. Try the kitchen."

"Okay. Don't go away." And she hung up the phone.

"Mom!" Cass called, but the line was dead.

"What's wrong?" Jared asked, rising.

Cass stared at the receiver still in her hand. "Aunt Elsie is in the garage attic."

"What? That's nuts."

"Apparently not to Mom." She slapped the phone in its cradle. "I've got to go over there right away." She looked distractedly for her purse and keys. When she grabbed them, her hands shook.

"Isn't Grandpop home?" Jared asked.

"I don't know." She rubbed her forehead. "Mom didn't seem to realize they were married, let alone if he was there."

"You shouldn't go over there alone." Jared's brow was furrowed with concern. "Call Uncle Will."

Cass shook her head. "He lives off island. It'll take him much longer to get there than me. And Mom called me."

"Then I'll go with you." He started for the steps. "Just let me get my jacket."

Cass's heart swelled. What a great kid. "Oh, Jared, you don't have to come along."

"You can't go alone." He repeated, clearly incensed at the very idea. "Who knows what you're going to find."

"Aunt Elsie?" muttered Jenn.

"Funny. Very funny." Jared launched himself upstairs for his jacket.

"Do you want to come too?" Cass asked Jenn. "Or do you want to stay here?"

Jenn pushed back in her chair. Varying emotions flashed over her face: reluctance, uncertainty, guilt, but the primary response was fear. "I'll stay here."

Cass couldn't blame her. She was afraid of what she would find too. "No problem. I just don't know when we'll be back."

"What about Mr. Harmon?" Jenn asked as Jared thundered downstairs.

"Uh-oh! Dan!" Cass raced into the front hall and called, "Dan! Dan!"

He appeared at the top of the stairs in his stocking feet, buttoning his shirt, tucking it in his jeans as he hurried down to her. "What's wrong, Cass?"

"My mom just called." Her voice broke. "I have to go over there."

"It's like Friday?"

Cass nodded.

He turned and started back upstairs. "Let me get my shoes, and I'll go with you."

She stared at him, immensely moved. "Thanks, but you don't have to. Jared's coming."

"Of course I have to," he surprised her by saying. "Now you get your car, and I'll be out back in a minute."

Nodding, Cass ran to the garage on the alley, Jared on her heels. While she appreciated Jared's accompanying her, it was Dan's coming along that made her feel she might be able to cope after all.

"Sit in the back, Jared." She slid into the driver's seat. "Dan's going with us."

"Okay." The relief in his voice matched her own feeling of reprieve.

When they pulled up in front of the neatly landscaped house on Scallop, the smoke alarm was blaring and two old men stood on the sidewalk in the dark trying to decide what to do.

"I don't see no smoke," one said to Cass as she scrambled out of the car.

"I smell it," the other said. "But I don't see any fire."

"We'll check it out," Dan called as he followed Cass up the walk, Jared loping behind.

"Mom?" Cass called, making for the kitchen and the smoke alarm. "Where are you?"

She heard no answer and half expected to see both parents on the floor, overcome by fumes of some kind. What she found was an empty room and a pan on a stove burner with a high flame under it. Billows of smoke rose from the burning hamburgers in the pan, little tongues of flame leaping in the grease. All this was overlaid with the terrible fumes from the pan's melting Bakelite handle. A gray haze clung to the ceiling, swirling around the alarm.

"Man, these things are annoying," Dan said as he pried the casing open and released the battery.

Cass grabbed a tea towel, wrapped it about the handle of the smoldering pan, and rushed toward the back door. "Jared!"

He beat her by a step, pulling the door open for her. She went out into the backyard, holding the pan as far from her body as possible. Still, waves of heat, acrid fumes, and smoke enveloped her, making her eyes water. How much longer before the little flames licking the hamburgers would have jumped the pan, and there would have been an actual fire? Shivering at the thought, she set the pan in the dirt at the edge of the garden where it wouldn't fry any vegetation. Dan was right behind her with a pot of water to douse the charred mess.

"Hey, don't use water," Jared called as he ran to them. "It's a grease fire. Use baking soda." He stuffed a box of it into Dan's hand. "I found this in Grandmom's cupboard." In no time the flames were smothered. Cass stood back and stared at the mess for a minute, then went searching for her parents while Dan and Jared opened the front and back doors and several windows to help clear the smoke.

She found both Mom and Dad upstairs in Mom's pink bedroom, arguing over Elsie.

"They're up here," she called to Dan and Jared from the landing at the top of the steps. The two hurried upstairs and stood behind her in the bedroom doorway.

"Can't you hear her?" Mom asked Dad, unaware of the three arrivals. She rested her hands on the wall that adjoined the garage. "There! *Charlotte! Charlotte! Get me out!* Lew, we've got to help her!"

"Charlotte," Dad said, his face a mass of worry wrinkles. "Stop this. Please! Elsie's not there. She's dead!"

Mom glared at Dad. "That's what Cassandra Marie said, but you're both wrong. I know it." Her voice quivered, and her face crumpled. "Elsie'd never die and leave me." She turned back to the wall. "Hold on, Elsie. I'll save you."

Cass wanted to cry. Her clever, intelligent mother! "Mom," she said, her voice loud to get her parents' attention.

They both turned in surprise, noticing for the first time that they had company.

"Cassandra Marie," they both said, coming to her with open arms.

"And Jared." Dad veered off to shake Jared's hand.

"And look, Lew. Cassandra Marie's brought her boyfriend. Isn't that nice?" Mom patted Dan on the arm.

Dan smiled warmly. "Hello, Mrs. Merton. It's good to see you again."

"Have you eaten yet?" Mom asked him, apparently as taken with his smile as Cass was, apparently snapping back to real life at the sight of him. Them.

"None of us has eaten," Cass said.

"None of you? Well, we'll fix that. Lew, let's call that seafood place—oh, what's its name?—and get flounder dinners brought in." She turned to Dan, concern clear on her face. "You do like flounder, don't you?"

"Very much."

"Good." She put her hand in the crook of his elbow and led him from the room. "Fried or broiled?"

Cass reached out as her father started from the bedroom and caught his arm. "Wait a minute, Dad."

He stopped and looked at her with a question.

"Jared, go down and help Grandmom order what we need from Campbell's, will you?"

"Yeah," Dad said. "Don't let her call the order in. Who knows what we'll get if she does it."

Jared thumped downstairs, calling, "Grandmom, I want fried flounder with french fries and coleslaw."

Cass sat on her mother's bed. She patted the place beside her. "Sit here, Dad. We need to talk."

"Not now." He edged toward the door. "Dinner—"

"—will be at least a half hour." Cass crooked her forefinger to call him to her.

He came reluctantly, his shoulders slumping, his step dragging. He dropped to the bed and stared at the floor. Hopelessness sat like a pall about him. "She's only like this part of the time, Cassandra. Most of the time she's fine." He looked at her, his eyes suddenly fierce. "Most of the time she's fine!"

"Dad, she left food cooking on the stove over a very high flame. Didn't you hear the smoke alarm?"

"Food on the stove?" He looked stricken. "That was my fault, not hers. She forgot to make dinner, so I was cooking some hamburgers when she started yelling about Elsie. I had to come up to calm her."

"What would have happened if there'd been a fire?" Cass's blood turned cold as she thought of them trapped upstairs, fumes rising, overcoming them.

"Well, there wasn't." Dad stood. It was obvious that as far as he was concerned, the conversation was over. "Your mother and I are fine, Cass. We don't need or want your help." He strode from the room, flicking the light out as he went.

Cass sat in the darkness, her arms wrapped about herself to try and stem the chill that crawled over her like flies over a carcass.

Oh, Lord, what are we to do? Should we get someone to live in and care for them here? Should they go to a home? How much longer before Mom needs full-time care? Can they afford it? Can the brothers and I help? How much can I afford? And how do I get the brothers to see what's going on here? How do I get them to help?

"Aunt Cassandra." Jared stood hesitantly in the bedroom door. "We ordered the food. Grandmom wants to drive to get it—"

Cass's blood stopped in her veins.

"—but I told her I would. I said I needed the driving practice."

"Good thinking." Cass fished in her jacket pocket and pulled out her keys. She tossed them to him. "My purse is on the counter in the kitchen. Take the cash you need."

Jared nodded and turned to go. He paused and smiled sadly. "You know, we can't let her behind the wheel anymore."

Cass pressed her hand to the pounding pain between her eyes. "I know, but how do we stop her?"

Jared shook his head, having no more answers than she did.

Cass continued to sit alone in the dark after he left. Alzheimer's? The very thought gave her the shakes.

Dad was clearly in denial about how serious Mom's problem was becoming. No wonder the brothers didn't see any trouble. They all shared Dad's tendency to paint the world as they wanted it to be, and they had the skills and intellect to make that approach work most of the time. But this time reality wouldn't cooperate.

Dimly she heard footsteps on the stairs, but she didn't move. Moving took too much energy.

Dan stopped in the doorway, a huge silhouette backlit by the hall light. "Are you okay?"

His quiet concern slid over her like a soothing salve on a wound. She felt her headache take two steps backward, the constriction about her heart ease. "Sure." She tried to smile but was amazed to find herself crying instead. She swiped at her eyes, trying to stop, trying to regain control. The more she tried to stop, the harder she sobbed.

"Ah, Cass." He came to her, took her hands, and pulled her to her feet.

"I'm sorry!" She sniffed and looked for a tissue box. She saw none. She sniffed again. "I never cry." She wept harder.

He pulled her close and wrapped his arms around her. He rested his cheek against her hair. "Shh, Cassie. It's going to be okay."

No, it wasn't. She knew it, and so did he. She threaded her arms about his waist and washed his shirt with her tears.

Ten

𝒲HEN THEY GOT back to SeaSong a few minutes after ten, Dan was totally drained. He couldn't imagine how Cass felt.

"Alzheimer's," Jared said as they sat in the quiet dimness of the garage after the silent trip home.

Cass turned to look at his shadowy figure in the backseat. "Could be. Certainly dementia of some kind."

"My dad always said you were overreacting."

Cass's voice was rueful. "Tell me something I don't know."

"I'm sorry." Jared sounded guilty as he stuck his hands in his jacket pockets.

"Don't apologize for your father, Jared." She reached back and patted his knee. "And thanks for your help tonight. You were great."

"Yeah." He reached for the door, opened it, and light flooded them. "I'll e-mail him about tonight. I'll tell him." He climbed out and walked slowly to the house.

"It's hard for him to see his grandmother like that," Cass said.

"They're close?"

"Mom's always been a wonderful grandparent. Dad too. They have the kids for sleepovers at Camp Grand, named for Grandmom and Grandpop. They have the out-of-town grandkids in for a month each summer. Everybody gets great birthday gifts and their own personal night out with them. Oh, Dan." She choked on a sigh. "This is so hard."

Dan's heart broke a little for her. He slid out of the car and walked around to the driver's side. Cass still sat behind the wheel. He opened the door and held out his hand. She took it, and he helped her out. He kept her hand as they walked to the house, wishing he could somehow make her pain go away, but knowing he couldn't. They went in the back door, across the darkened kitchen to the door that led to the shadowy public hall.

Dan released her hand and took hold of her shoulders. "I want you to get a good night's sleep now." He knew he sounded like an idiot, like his mother, in fact, but he persisted. "Tomorrow things won't look quite so bleak."

She nodded, smiled weakly, and raised one hand to rest it on his. "Thank you." Dan felt another piece of his heart break. At least this time he'd done better than the other night. He'd gone with her, hugged her, offered her verbal comfort even if he didn't have a solution to offer her.

Maybe there's hope for me yet, Lord.

"Good night, Dan." Still wearing her sad smile, she waved him through the door. He walked to the stairs.

Lord, help me help her. Please. I'm still not good at this, as You know, but someone's got to be there for her. She's there for everyone; let me be there for her.

The whoosh of the swinging door opening again caused him to turn.

Cass stood there, her face shadowed, but when she spoke, her voice was strong. "I almost forgot. I was going to ask you if you wanted to have breakfast with us in the mornings instead of sitting on the sunporch in solitary splendor."

"Really?" He stared at her, thinking how nice that invitation was and how special that she remembered to issue it after the night she'd just had.

She misunderstood his hesitation. "But of course you don't have to," she hurried to say, gesturing with a hand like she was waving the invitation away. "It's no trouble to serve you in there. It's just that you'd said—"

"I'd love to eat with you." He meant every word of it. He hadn't realized how much of a people person he was until this week when he had no one to share his table. Company at breakfast would somehow start the day off with sunshine, regardless of the weather. Of course, lunch and dinner still loomed, but two meals alone were so much less boring than three.

She hurried on as if she hadn't heard him. "The kids eat at about seven-fifteen so they can leave for school in plenty of time. I know it's earlier than I serve in the dining room, but you get up early anyway. And I'll make the same things for you I'd make if you ate in there." She pointed toward the sunporch dining area.

"Cass, I'd love to eat with you guys." He didn't really care whether the kids were there or not. Not that he minded the kids, of course, but she was the draw with her lovely hazel eyes and soft blond hair. "And you don't have to make me special dishes. I'd be happy with cereal or toast. That's what I usually eat." Unless he had a business breakfast.

"Oh, no. You're our guest. You're paying for a nice breakfast."

"I'm used to cereal. Cheerios. Special K. Raisin Bran."

"Cheerios are Jared's favorite."

"We men stick together."

"Jenn likes yogurt."

"I think not."

"Wimp."

They smiled at each other.

"See you at breakfast." A flick of her hand, and Cass was gone.

When Dan reached his room, he fired up his laptop and logged on to Google. In the topic line he typed Alzheimer's. Shazaam! Several thousand sites that could tell him more than he wanted to know about this specific form of dementia. The more he read, the worse he felt for Cass and her family.

As a progressive, degenerative disease of the brain and nervous system, he read, Alzheimer's begins in small bites, usually seen in memory loss, and increases over time until it completely disables a person. It attacks the parts of the brain that deal with memory, thought, and language—the parts that make people the unique individuals they are. It is incurable, and though there is a genetic type, most cases are random and unpredictable.

After reading for over an hour, he signed off and got ready for bed. His mind whirred with thoughts, and he knew he had to calm it down if he was ever to sleep. He thought about a late movie on TV but decided he didn't want the noise or the ads. He'd read the novel Cass had given him.

He searched the room twice before he remembered he had left it in the library during the afternoon. Muttering under his breath at his own memory loss, he pulled on his jeans and crept downstairs as quietly as he could. The only light was a weak one on the registration desk, offering just enough light to keep him from tripping. He cut across the common room and into the library. Sure enough, there was the book, sitting right where he had left it.

He turned and almost fell over Cass who appeared in the library door with a suddenness that startled him. Even as he reached to steady them both, a watch-it snarl from the furball lying like a baby in her arms warned him to keep his distance.

Dan stepped back. "Who's your friend?"

"This is Glossy Flossie, my little sweetheart." Cass smiled down at the spineless lump in her embrace.

"She sounds more like a little grouch to me."

Cass kissed the cat's head and rubbed her ears. "Don't let the mean man upset you, Flossie." She looked up at Dan and gave him an impish smile. "He's not all bad."

Dan felt inordinately pleased. He leaned closer, prepared to befriend the animal for Cass's sake, when Flossie showed her canines. Dan backed up. "If she treats all your guests like she treats me, no wonder you keep her hidden."

"I don't keep her hidden. She's shy."

He looked doubtfully at the black cat. Flossie hissed. "Right. Shy."

Cass ran a soothing hand down the cat's back. "Easy, sweetheart." Flossie began to purr. "She's old and doesn't feel too well."

Dan nodded like the large-dog man he was. Cats always made him antsy. They were too secretive. Give him a lab or a retriever, even a boxer or a Dane, any day. Open, affectionate, straightforward in spite of noses that prodded in unacceptable places.

"What brings you down here in the middle of the night?" Cass indicated the library.

He held out his book. "I left it this afternoon. What about you? Having trouble sleeping?"

She nodded. "I'm all jittery inside. I thought I'd come look for something to read to make my eyes heavy. I want something light and airy." She smiled ruefully. "I want to escape."

"Can't say I blame you." He reached behind her, ignoring Flossie's snarl, and flicked on the light.

Cass squeezed her eyes. "Too bright!"

He flicked it off.

"Better," she said and walked over to a shelf of paperbacks. She was wearing a fuzzy bathrobe of some dark shade that had looked deep blue in the brief flash of light. She squinted, trying to read the titles in the dimness. She pulled a book with a garishly colored cover, studied it a minute, and returned it to the shelf.

She turned, her hand still resting on the shelf. She just stood, staring beyond him, lost in thought. He saw her expression and knew the thoughts were melancholy.

"I'm losing my mother." Her voice shook. "Right before my eyes she's dying as surely as if she had cancer or some terrible physical condition."

He reached for her hand, squeezed it tightly, and pulled her to the red velvet love seat in the common room. Flossie growled her disapproval, but Cass let him lead her anyway. She sat, and he sat beside her, continuing to hold her hand.

"You know," he said, "they can diagnose Alzheimer's, not definitively but with high probability. Right now the only way they know for certain is studying the brain postmortem."

She nodded. "The thought of a diagnosis scares me silly— which is in itself silly because, diagnosis or not, she's going to continue to deteriorate." Sorrow shadowed her face more deeply than the night.

He gave her a halfhearted smile that was meant to be comforting, then looked away. He had another topic to broach with her, but he didn't think now was the best time.

"What?" she said, pulling her hand free to stroke Flossie. "What other terrible things did you learn?"

He shook his head. "It's not about the Alzheimer's. It's something different. It can wait."

"Dan." She poked him in the ribs, surprising him and making him jump. "Tell me what it is that's bothering you."

"It can wait until tomorrow."

"Now, Dan. Please."

He hesitated. He leaned forward, resting his elbows on his knees, and studied the carpet intently. In the stretching silence he heard the steady drone of Flossie's purr as Cass continued to stroke her. Head, neck, shoulders, spine. Head, neck, shoulders, spine. He'd purr too, if someone did that to him.

"I'll set Flossie on you if you don't talk," she threatened.

He glanced at the black, furry lump and grinned. "Scary."

He took a deep breath. Maybe the quietness of the night-shrouded room would make it easier for her to hear what he had to say. He sat back and turned so he could see her face. "Your father's really into those sweepstakes, isn't he?"

She gave a harsh bark of frustration. "Is he ever."

"Well, when he and I were clearing off the kitchen table for dinner, I noticed among all the sweepstakes paraphernalia four overdraft notifications from the bank. The first was for over one hundred dollars; the total amount was 537 dollars. All came within the past two weeks."

Cass stared at him. "How can that be?"

"Who handles their finances?"

"Dad. He's always been meticulous about financial things. They're far from rich. Dad was a mailman, but they have enough money coming in each month from Social Security, Dad's pension, and their investments that they should never have overdrafts."

"Living expenses continue to rise. Maybe daily expenses have gotten beyond them. Maybe they need to delve into their savings."

Cass shook her head vehemently. "Before they sold the family place and bought the house on Scallop, we went over their finances very thoroughly. They can live comfortably without having to touch the principal of any of their savings. Those moneys are for the possibility of catastrophic health problems and possible nursing home costs."

Which are probably right around the corner, he thought grimly. "Maybe your father forgot to deposit some checks?"

"They're all direct deposit."

"Have they taken any trips recently or bought anything big?"

Cass frowned. "They live quietly and haven't gone anywhere for several years except my brother Hal's in Colorado, and they'd saved up for that."

"Maybe he's gotten caught in some scam that panders to the elderly. Or maybe he's giving large sums to some TV evangelist or something."

"No, I don't think so." She pulled her knees up and rested her chin on them, her robe spilling over the cushions. Her movements dislodged a very unhappy cat who wasn't hesitant to express her feelings, though why she hissed at Dan was anyone's guess.

"Hey, cat, I didn't do it," he said, hands up in a gesture of innocence.

Cass put out a hand and rubbed Flossie's head. Purring replaced the pouting as the animal collapsed on the sofa between the two of them, leaning against Cass's hip.

"He's spending it on the sweepstakes; I know he is." Her voice shook. "He's buying stuff through them."

"But isn't it illegal to require you to buy stuff to enter?"

She nodded. "But he's told me that he feels he has a better chance to win if he buys something or gives something if the sweepstakes sponsor calls itself a charity. I showed him the printing that says you don't have to buy to enter, but he has his own logic. 'Of course they treat you better if you buy,' he says." Her sigh was part affection, part frustration. "He's one stubborn old man. And the brothers take after him."

They sat in the deep gray silence, and Dan worried on her behalf. She had Jenn on one hand and her parents on the other. Sandwiched. That was a lot for one woman. "What are your brothers doing about all that's going on?"

Cass closed her eyes and rested her head on the back of her seat. She didn't speak, just shrugged.

"Nothing?" Though that's what he had gathered from earlier conversations, he was still appalled.

She tried to defend them. "I'm the single one in the family. I'm the girl. And I think they think I have all this free time."

"With a business like yours? And why shouldn't sons help care for their parents as much as daughters?"

She smiled at him so warmly that his mental gears did nothing but spin for a few moments. He forced himself to look away and cleared his throat.

"If you want, I'm willing to look into the financial thing with your father. Conduct a sort of due diligence on his financial situation. Not that you couldn't do the same thing, but we can talk man-to-man and all that."

"You think he won't listen to me."

He threw an apologetic look her way. "I'm afraid so."

She gave a ladylike snort. "Don't be afraid of hurting my feelings. I know you're right; he won't. But, Dan, you don't have to get involved in our family crises. You're here on vacation. You're our guest."

"Are you saying you don't want me to help? That I'm butting in, and it's none of my business?" Life would certainly be simpler if she felt he was intruding, but it would also be lonely, barren, antiseptic.

She dropped her feet to the floor and leaned toward him, all intensity. "No, I'm not saying that at all. Don't put words in my mouth." She waved her hand. "It just seems unfair to you. You hardly know us."

He gave a short burst of laughter. He knew more about her and her family than he'd known about anyone in years, even his own family, he was ashamed to admit. Surface relationships abounded in the business world; personal problems rarely intruded and were looked at askance when they did. He'd come to think that's how all life should be. Strange how not being busy every moment gave you time to reevaluate.

"Believe me," he said, "you'll be doing me a favor if you let me help. I'll actually have something specific to do. I'm going nuts waiting on the Lord."

"Waiting on the Lord?" Her eyebrows rose, and even in the dimness he could see the questions sparkle in her eyes.

Rats. He should have kept his mouth shut. It was the darkness. Things slipped out that he'd never say in the light of day. Or maybe, just maybe, it was her.

"Come on," she cajoled. "Tell me all about it. You know all sorts of ugly things about me. It's only fair you tell me something about you."

He looked into the darkened library, torn between feeling awkward and wanting to tell her all about it. "It's a long story, and you need your sleep."

She settled back on the sofa. "Like I could sleep even if I went to bed. Come on. Distract me."

He turned back to her. "You know that I conduct due diligence on companies, right?"

"Yeah, you're a vet."

He grinned. "An unemployed vet."

"Unemployed? You?" She all but hooted with laughter. "What'd you do? Try to take over for the CEO, and he got nervous?"

"I was the CEO."

"Ah." She nodded. "Now that I can believe."

He narrowed his eyes at her. "You can believe I was CEO but not that I'm unemployed?"

She leaned toward him. "Dan, a man like you doesn't lose his job. If you aren't working at this time, it's by choice."

A man like you. He wasn't exactly certain what that meant, but if he heard right, it was a compliment.

"Come on," she coaxed. "Give."

So he told her all about it.

"You actually saw the Towers go down?"

He nodded. "I was coming from an overlong breakfast meeting, already half an hour late. I was heading for a meeting with a company we were investigating, a company with offices in the north tower of the Trade Center."

She stared, mouth open. "If you'd been on time…"

He felt his heart pound even so many months after the event. "I ended up hiding behind a car when that black cloud roared down the street, sure I was going to die after all. When it became obvious that I wasn't, all I could think about was that if I had died, what would I have left behind? The terrible answer was just money." He stared at his hands and said quietly, "It shamed me. It still does."

They sat in silence for a short time. When he next spoke, it was because he didn't want her to think he was still all about money. He needed to explain himself more fully.

"By any standard I'd found success."

"Mr. CEO," she said softly.

"Yeah," he said, knowing she had no idea just how successful he'd been. And how proud. "But I realized that in spite of all my hard work, I'd accomplished nothing of lasting significance. I knew very clearly from the examples of my parents and Andy what a life of real worth looked like. I wanted to find a life like that, the life that God patterned for me. I started my search for true meaning with long talks with the Lord—'What do You want of me, Lord? Where do You want me? What should I be doing?'— I'm embarrassed to say, I'd ignored Him for too many years. In the process of waiting for answers, I ended up coming to Seaside, to SeaSong, and I'm going stir-crazy with nothing to do."

She thought for a minute. "I can understand why you came to Seaside to wait, knowing your past history here. And I think it's wonderful that you're doing such a thing."

"You do?" He could feel his heart swell. "You don't think I'm nuts?"

"Not at all. I think you're wise. But why did you come to SeaSong when you could have stayed anywhere?"

"I don't know why I'm here," Dan said, though he was beginning to get an idea. "I just know somehow that this is where I should be for now."

She nodded. "So how much would you charge to check Dad's finances while you wait?"

He was insulted. "I wouldn't charge anything! You're letting me eat in the kitchen."

"You're waiving fees because you eat with the help in the kitchen?"

"And you shared Sunday dinner and your morning jogs. Come on, Cass. Helping your father would give me a goal for at least a few days."

She stood, gathering Flossie into her arms and grabbing a paperback. "When you put it that way, Dad's all yours. Now we just have to figure out how to get him to agree to talk to you without hurting his pride."

Eleven

"DO YOU HAVE a busy weekend coming up?" Dan asked at breakfast Friday morning. He'd lived at SeaSong for a week, but already it seemed part of him.

Cass smiled as she stroked Glossy Flossie who lay as usual on her place mat. "Full house. And it's supposed to be a very pleasant weekend weatherwise, too." There was nothing like being able to hang out a No Vacancy sign to make an innkeeper smile. "They start arriving this afternoon."

"Do I have to eat in the dining room with them?"

Cass studied his face. "Do you want to?"

"No. It's cozier out here."

"You'll get lousy service. The girls and I will be concentrating on serving in the dining room."

"I'll pour me some cereal," he said.

Cass gave him a disgusted look. "You will not. It's just that there'll be chaos in the kitchen, and you'll get stuff tossed your way as we have time."

"When do you eat?"

"Me?"

He nodded. "I'll eat when you do."

"We all eat when everyone else is finished."

"Okay. I'll get a bowl of cereal after my morning run and then eat with you after the dining room closes."

A warm feeling crept over Cass, and it scared her witless. She was beginning to enjoy their mornings a bit too much. They jogged together, sometimes talking, sometimes just enjoying the silence, always enjoying each other's company. At least she enjoyed his and hoped he enjoyed hers. And sitting at the table enjoying a second cup of coffee together after the kids left for school felt dangerously wonderful.

When she hadn't known how nice it was to have a man across the breakfast table, she had been happy, if occasionally lonely. Now she knew the pleasure of someone who listened to her as if her opinions were important, and it filled her with quiet joy. The loneliness she'd known in the past was the palest powder blue compared to the deep navy she foresaw after Dan left to return to his real life.

I should make him eat in the dining room on weekends just to remember what my real life's like. Maybe the distance would help me keep my balance.

Are you insane? asked her alter ego. *Give up such a good thing?*

But when he leaves!

So deal with it when he leaves. In the meantime, enjoy!

Brenna pushed the back door open and came into the kitchen. "Hi." She gave a halfhearted wave.

"Get a cup of coffee." Cass pointed to the carafe.

Brenna shook her head. "Mind if I get a glass of juice instead?"

"Help yourself. And while you're at it, inventory what juices we have. I'm going to the store as soon as breakfast is cleaned up."

"Do you want some company?" Dan asked. He even looked eager.

Cass snorted. "You really are desperate for things to do, aren't you?"

"Your father can't see me until Sunday afternoon. I'm about read out, and if I try one more crossword puzzle, I'll go nuts."

"Next thing you know," Cass said solemnly, "you'll be reduced to jigsaw puzzles in the common room."

"With the little old lady guests," Brenna added.

"Mock all you want." Dan leaned back in his chair and took another drink of coffee. "I am a man with a mission. I just don't know what it is yet."

Grinning, Cass put an unhappy Flossie on the floor and pulled out her list of things to be done before the new guests arrived. She and Brenna bent their heads over the paper and divvied up the work.

"When Jared gets home, he can give the lawn what may well be the last mowing of the season," Cass finished. Having the boy on site did come in handy, even if he ate nonstop, putting an unexpected crimp in her food budget. She handed Brenna her list of tasks for the day. "If either of us has an extra minute, we can deadhead the mums. I noticed when I jogged past this morning that some of them need tending."

"I can mow the grass," Dan offered.

Cass was horrified. "But you're our guest!"

"A bored guest," he reminded her. "Let me do it. It's been so long since I tended a lawn that it even sounds like fun."

"How are the mighty fallen," Cass said. "From CEO to lawn boy."

"Not to mention shopper's assistant." He grinned. "The day shows promise after all."

Dan proved himself invaluable as he lugged grocery bags, mowed the lawn, deadheaded the mums, swept the front porch and the sidewalks, and rearranged the library's nonfiction titles by topics and fiction section by author. He was standing in the front hall wearing jeans and a deep brown long-sleeved tee when the first guests arrived. When he saw them, he hurried down the porch steps to carry their luggage.

Cass mentally rolled her eyes as he ushered them to the registration desk.

"This is Mr. and Mrs. Novack," he told Cass. He turned to the Novacks. "Cass is the innkeeper at SeaSong, and she'll take good care of you." He stepped back and grinned at Cass over the Novacks' heads. The sound of slamming car doors had him running out front to play bellhop once again.

Cass ran Mr. Novack's credit card, gave the couple their room key, and turned to Brenna who had just entered from the kitchen. "Will you escort the Novacks to the third-floor turret room?"

Brenna smiled a greeting at the Novacks and reached for one of the suitcases.

Dan appeared in the lobby at that moment, the luggage of

another couple in his hands. "Leave it, Brenna. I'll bring the Novacks things up while the Mancinis register."

She grinned and dropped the suitcase, then turned to the Novacks. "Your room is right this way." She led them upstairs.

The next hour passed in a blur of new arrivals, registrations, and questions for Cass. Brenna escorted people upstairs, and Dan carried everyone's luggage. By 6 P.M. everyone was accounted for, a very unusual situation. Cass stretched her hands over her head as Brenna escorted the last couple to the third floor, Dan following with the bags.

When he returned, he grinned. "That was fun."

"Hey!" Jared stuck his head in from the kitchen. "Who mowed the lawn and when's dinner?"

"Dan did and in a half hour," Cass said. "How'd your day go?"

Jared looked at Dan in surprise. "Good man. Thanks. It went fine."

Cass flicked her thumb at Dan as she said to Jared, "He figured you'd be tired after practice."

Jared looked chagrined. "Well, practice on Friday is mostly reading and reviewing plays and the coach's pep talk for tomorrow's game. I've been at Paulie's."

"Hey, Ms. Merton." Paulie stuck his head under Jared's arm. "How are you doing?"

"Hi, Paulie. This is Mr. Harmon. I take it you're here for dinner?"

"Hey, Mr. Harmon." Paulie smiled, then turned to Cass. "Nobody cooks like you, Ms. Merton." His face clouded. "My mom sure doesn't."

"You'll eat with us too, won't you?" Cass looked at Dan. "You've certainly earned your food today."

Dan nodded, looking inordinately pleased. Well, of course he was pleased, Cass thought. He didn't have to buy dinner at a restaurant and eat staring at a wall. His pleasure was nothing she should take personally.

"Hey," Paulie asked, trying to look nonchalant and failing miserably. "Where's Jenn?"

Poor Paulie. "I think she's in her room." Cass pointed upstairs. "But she'll be down for dinner."

Paulie smiled, his teeth gleaming his pleasure.

"Jared, pull out an extra pack of rolls and get them ready for the oven. And an extra bag of salad. I'll be with you in a couple of minutes."

"Come on, guys," Dan said. "We can get dinner ready for the ladies." The three men disappeared into the back of the house.

Cass checked to be certain that all her paperwork and computer records were current, knowing how easy it would be to miss something in the flood of guests. She looked up as she heard Brenna come down the stairs. One look at the girl's face told Cass there was a problem. Tears sat at the edge of Brenna's lower lashes, like water on the crest of a dam about to overflow, and her chin wobbled.

Cass rushed to her. "Brenna, what's wrong?" It couldn't be more strange phone calls. All SeaSong's rooms were occupied, which meant Brenna couldn't use any upstairs phone, and Cass herself had been at the registration desk all evening. Cass gave Brenna a quick hug. "Tell me."

"The Novacks," she said, her voice all shaky.

Cass stiffened. "What did they do to you?" she demanded, feeling very protective.

"They're unhappy with their accommodations."

"What?" Cass stared, surprised. Nobody was ever unhappy with SeaSong. "But the third-floor tower is one of our best rooms. It's beautiful. What's not to like?"

"Mr. Novack found a hair on the pillowcase." Brenna's tears breached the lids and slipped slowly down her cheek. "He said he couldn't stay in a room that was obviously dirty."

Cass frowned. "A hair on the pillowcase?"

Brenna nodded miserably. "I made up that room. I must have been careless. I'm so sorry." She sniffed. "They insist on seeing you."

"You wait right here until I get back, okay?" Cass said as she started up the stairs. "Don't go anywhere."

Brenna sank onto the antique red velvet slipper chair that sat next to the grandfather clock and sniffed several times.

When Cass reached the third floor, she knocked quietly on the door of the tower room.

"Come in," Mr. Novack called.

She turned the handle and entered the apricot room. The quilt was turned partially down, the pillow closest to the door exposed. In the middle of the crisp pillowcase lay a long hair.

Mr. Novack pointed. "How can you ask us to sleep in a bed with sheets that have obviously been used before?"

Cass smiled sweetly at Mr. Novack as inside she fumed. There was absolutely no way that hair, so very long and curly, had been left on that pillow from a previous guest. As she walked to the bed to study the circumstantial evidence, she noted Mrs. Novack sitting in the alcove of the turret, looking out the window, ignoring the conversation behind her. She was an attractive woman in navy slacks and a royal blue sweater set, her long, light brown, curly hair hanging below her shoulders.

Cass took hold of the quilt, blanket, and top sheet and pulled them down, draping them over the foot of the bed. She gestured to the revealed bottom sheet.

"As you can see, Mr. Novack, this bed has not been slept in since it was changed. All our bedding is fresh, as are our towels and washcloths."

He looked at the pristine sheet and went, "Humph! I thought this was a bed-and-breakfast of impeccable reputation. I see now that I was wrong." He looked at Cass's blond hair. "It was probably that girl you have working for you."

Cass bit back her defense of Brenna. "Let me remake the bed for you, Mr. Novack. That way you will be assured of the cleanest, freshest bedding possible." Smiling even though it hurt, Cass turned for the door.

"I must tell you," Mr. Novack said, his voice sly and smarmy, "that I find it reprehensible that you would still charge us full price when such an avoidable and egregious mistake has been made."

Bingo. "Let me get the fresh sheets, Mr. Novack, and we can talk."

By the time the bed was remade and they were finished talking, Mr. Novack was satisfied with the 15 percent price cut Cass gave him. She left his room, fuming at his chicanery as she ran down the stairs. When she reached the front hall, Brenna rose to her feet, red-eyed and despairing.

"I'm so sorry, Cass." She sniffed. "I don't know how it happened."

"Was he unkind to you? Did he say anything offensive?

Because if he did, I'll ask them to leave."

Brenna shook her head, new tears falling. "He just made me feel like a complete incompetent."

"Well, don't you worry, honey." Cass gathered Brenna close. "It wasn't you, and it wasn't your hair. It was Mrs. Novack's."

Brenna stepped back, shock showing on her face. "Really?"

"Really. I just haven't decided yet why she cooperates with her worm of a husband. She sat facing away from me the whole time, as though she was distancing herself from the con or was terribly embarrassed by her husband's shenanigans."

"What did you do to calm him down?"

"I remade the bed and gave them a 15 percent price break."

Brenna frowned. "But why? You know he's lying. Now he thinks he's won."

"I have a house full of other guests, nice people who are paying a goodly sum for an enjoyable, relaxing weekend. I want them to have a great time here, a pleasant time. If I ignored Mr. Novack, he'd make all my other guests miserable with complaints all weekend. I'll take the loss for the sake of the honest guests."

Brenna nodded. "The customer is always right, even when he isn't."

Cass smiled wryly. "He's so transparent it's pathetic. I'm downright curious to see what he tries next, and be assured he will try something. I'd bet my life on it." Cass slung her arm over Brenna's shoulders and led her toward the kitchen. "I need to pass his name on to the B&B Guild members so they can be on the watch for him in case he tries something like this again."

Reminder: Be certain to mention that the B&B has no room if Mr. Novack ever calls again.

"You think he does this a lot?"

"Oh, yeah. You have no idea of the tricks, both clever and mean, that people try to pull without thinking about the person they're hurting."

Brenna gave a little noise like someone had punched her in the stomach. Surprised, Cass looked at her. The girl quickly lowered her head, but not before Cass saw a new surge of tears glistening in her eyes. She thought back over her words. Tricks? Clever and mean? Hurting people? Poor Brenna.

Cass gave the girl's shoulders a squeeze, and with a hand on the swinging door, said, "If you ever want to talk, I'm here."

Brenna froze for an instant. Then she nodded, head still bent. "Thanks," she whispered. "I'm—it's—uh—" She stumbled to silence and ducked out from under Cass's arm and almost ran to the back door "I'll see you tomorrow at seven-thirty."

Cass watched Brenna hurry out without acknowledging any of the people who were in the kitchen, no small feat since Dan, Jared and Paulie all called out good-bye.

"Come on, Cass." Dan drew out a chair. "Sit here. Dinner's ready."

Jared pulled the casserole and the rolls from the oven and put them on the counter. There was no room for them on the little table. Paulie poured iced tea into five glasses. Dan tossed the over-size Caesar salad.

"Jenn?" Cass asked.

"Here." She glided down the steps and into the kitchen, timing her entrance perfectly. No more work to be done, at least until clean-up time.

"Here, Jenn." Paulie held a chair for her, his face like that of an optimistic puppy that was ever hopeful of not being kicked.

With a grunt and a do-me-no-favors look that would have scorched most guys, Jenn flopped into her chair. She frowned when Paulie sat beside her, her brow so furrowed it resembled corrugated cardboard.

Poor Paulie.

Cass was pleased because the bell on the registration desk rang only four times with requests for advice about restaurants, theaters, and the weather. It was almost like eating undisturbed. When she returned to the registration area after dinner, Paulie was carrying dishes to the sink for Jenn to stuff in the dishwasher. Jared and Dan had disappeared. Almost immediately the sound of a basketball bouncing indicated a game of one-on-one out back.

It was nine-thirty when Greg Barnes of the Seaside police walked into the SeaSong lobby, followed by Joe Masterson, the owner of Dante's at the Dock.

"Gentlemen," Cass said with the instinctive clutch in her heart at an unexpected visit from a cop. She was glad that Jared and Jenn were watching a video in Jared's room, Paulie keeping them company. She offered Greg and Joe her hand. "What can I do for you?" Of course there was always Mom and Dad.

"Hey, Ms. Merton." Greg grinned as he shook her hand. "How are you doing? How's the B&B business?"

"I'm doing fine. How's the cop business?"

"Always interesting."

Cass liked Greg Barnes. He had been one of her students back in the old days at Seaside High. He had been a good kid then and had turned into a good cop. He'd married his high school sweetheart, a little bouncy redhead who had more energy than any ten people. "How are Ginny and the kids?"

Greg pulled out his wallet. "You should know better than to ask."

Cass oohed and aahed until Joe Masterson cleared his throat. His ears turning pink, Greg reverted to his professional persona, stuffing his wallet in his pocket and squaring his shoulders. "Do you have a Mr. Brian Novack staying here?"

Cass bit back a smile. She'd read Mr. Novack right. He was trying another con, only this one was going to get him into trouble. *Couldn't happen to a more deserving man.* "Mr. and Mrs. Novack are staying in the third-floor turret room."

"I need to speak to them," Greg said.

Cass climbed to the third floor once again, knocking gently at the Novacks' door.

"What?" Mr. Novack barked through the wood paneling.

"Someone to see you downstairs," Cass said sweetly.

The door opened, and Mr. Novack stepped out wearing navy dress slacks and a yellow oxford cloth shirt with a little pony over his heart. "Who?"

Cass would have enjoyed saying, "The cops," just to see his face, but she merely said, "I'm only bringing the message."

Mr. Novack snorted and surged past her and down the steps. She followed, filled with the anticipation of his comeuppance. *It doesn't say much about my character, but...* She grinned.

He stopped abruptly when he saw who awaited him.

"Mr. Novack?" Greg Barnes stood tall and Cass was impressed with how authoritative he could be when he put his mind to it.

"What do you want?" Mr. Novack snarled. Clearly charm wasn't the man's strong suit.

"Did you have dinner this evening at Dante's at the Dock?"

"The fancy side," prompted Joe Masterson. "That's important."

"Dante's at the Dock, you say?" Mr. Novack paused as if in thought. "Never heard of it."

"Then how come we have your name on our reservation list?" Joe asked.

All eyes fastened on Mr. Novack. He fidgeted. "What if I did eat there? Surely that's not a crime."

"You forgot to pay your bill," Joe said, his voice dripping dislike and more than a touch of anger.

"Is that true, Mr. Novack?" Greg asked, his face impassive.

"The waiter never gave it to me. How could I pay a bill that I didn't have?"

"So you just left?" Greg stared as if he were appalled by such actions.

Mr. Novack's cheeks flushed an unbecoming pink. "How do you know it's me who didn't pay?"

"You mean aside from the fact that you just admitted it?" Greg asked.

Joe stared at Mr. Novack as though he couldn't believe such stupidity. "Our reservation list shows you were assigned a certain table. My manager saw you leaving as soon as you finished your last swallow of coffee. He knew you had been a pain of a customer, harassing your poor waiter, so he was watching you. You didn't wait even two minutes for your bill, so he followed you. Then he called me to tell me where you'd gone, and I called the cops."

"He followed me?" Mr. Novack had the nerve to look angry. He turned to Greg. "Isn't that a violation of my right to privacy?"

Greg's cold stare dropped to frigid. "Pay Mr. Masterson. Right now."

"But I never got the bill. The service was lousy. The food was inferior."

Joe glowered at the insults. "Then don't leave a tip."

"Pay the man." Greg spread his feet and rested his hand on his gun. "Immediately."

Cass was still smiling long after Greg and Joe left, and Mr. Novack, minus a substantial number of dollars—it was, after all, the fancy side—returned to his room.

No one ever said inn keeping was dull.

Twelve

TUCKER STARED AT his grandfather in disbelief. One million dollars? He felt like knocking his hand against the side of his head to straighten out what must surely be defective hearing.

One million dollars!

"I put this money aside for you when you were born, Tucker, and for Sherri when your father married Patsi," the old man said. "Sherri was just a baby then. So sweet. So cute."

Tuck squirmed. The old man was right. Sherri had been cute and sweet, and from the moment she showed up, everyone forgot he was there. It was a clear case of along came the little princess, and the prince might as well have been a frog.

When his father remarried and presented Tuck with both a new mother and a baby sister, he didn't want either. He'd liked having Hank all to himself, being spoiled and indulged and catered to. But then, who asked him what he wanted?

Sometimes he wondered about the jealousy he'd felt toward Sherri from the moment he'd first seen her, an adorable two-year-old with dimples and a smile to rival the sun in luminosity. Often resentment and envy-induced spite seized him by the throat and shook him like a dog would shake a favorite toy. When that happened, he visited her room until he found the *zing*, showing her that she might be the favored one, but he was the one with the real power. Whether it was her favorite Barbie disappearing or her bike tires mysteriously going flat, he wanted her to suffer as he had suffered from her displacement of him as the favored and only child.

Such jealousy was supposed to be a character flaw, they all said so, whoever *they* were, but he'd decided they were all wrong. Jealousy made him strong. It gave him the strength to resent her, to withstand her charm, to begrudge any favor done her, to cause her as much subtle pain as possible.

But the frog-child was about to become a prince again. One million dollars!

Tuck looked at the old man with his paunchy belly, sad eyes, and skinny legs. He didn't look like a millionaire, but he'd made a great fortune by getting in on the California postwar building boom. The only guys richer than Grandpa Cal were some of the movie moguls.

Even so, why was he willing to give away such a good-sized chunk of change? Sure, he had plenty of it. Sure, when he died, it had to go somewhere, but while he lived, why wasn't he keeping it? It was a cinch Tuck would never part with a million for anyone.

Granddad Cal's sad eyes filled, and his jowls swayed as he shook his head. "Sherri. Your little sister. I still can't believe she's gone, even after all this time."

Yeah, yeah. Tucker put on his sad face. He had to bite the inside of his cheek to keep a smile at bay. One million dollars! *And she's not my sister, Cal. She's my stepsister. Big difference.*

"Anyway, I arranged it that each of you would get your money when you turned twenty-five whether I was still alive or not. Your twenty-fifth birthday is today, Tucker." He held out an envelope. "Here are the papers for the account opened in your name at the Wells Fargo bank downtown where I do all my business. You can move it wherever you want."

Tuck took the plain white envelope with a slightly shaking hand. He stared at it. One million dollars. Hank and Patsi sat across the room watching and listening, their gift on the floor beside him—the keys to a new Grand Cherokee. Not that anyone needed four-wheel drive in southern California, but it would be fun for the off-road tracks in the mountains.

Tuck swallowed and stared at the birthday cake sitting on the coffee table, its candles half burned. He'd blown them all out in one breath, and that meant his wish should come true. Of course, none of his wishes had ever panned out in the past, at least until last year. Wishing that Sherri would disappear from his life had finally paid off. She was good and gone. And Granddad Cal's million more than made up for all the other wishes that hadn't come true through the years.

Tuck arranged his features to look properly appreciative. "I'm overwhelmed, Granddad."

That statement at least was true. He'd expected something monetary. After all, the old fool had been hinting at it for some time. Tuck had been hoping against hope for one hundred thousand to bail him out of some bad debts and leave him some left over for fun. He'd been thinking too small. One million was the magic number!

Tuck looked across the backyard to smoggy L.A. in the distance. He allowed himself a brief daydream of white Caribbean beaches and turquoise water, slinky women and sleek boats. So long, congested freeways. Hello, warm winds and unpolluted skies. So long, nine to five. Hello, unlimited leisure.

Granddad Cal sniffed and used his handkerchief to dab at his weepy eyes. Tuck reached for the old man and gave his shoulders a squeeze. Who cared that the gesture was a lie? It ought to make Cal feel loved. Not that he hated Cal or wished him ill or anything. He just felt nothing for the old guy.

It occurred to Tuck that he felt nothing for anyone except himself, unless it was his hate for Sherri. There was undoubtedly a name for such a condition. Surely in all the years of therapy his father had put him through, he'd heard it. Narcissism? Whatever. All he knew was that he cared not at all for the people he was supposed to love—nor for anyone else either.

People existed to make him happy, to supply his needs, not to sap his emotions. Without even realizing it, Cal had fulfilled his purpose with flying colors. He had made Tucker very happy indeed.

Speaking of flying colors, Tuck'd get a yacht with those little pennants that rippled in the breezes. Yeah, a yacht, and one bigger than his father's. A picture of a huge white boat rose in his mind. He'd live on it anchored in some tropical port and lie in the sun with the women. He sighed in deep anticipation. Finally a life as he deserved.

"I've decided," continued Granddad Cal after he put his handkerchief away, "that the money earmarked for Sherri on her twenty-fifth birthday will go to you if she isn't found by then."

Tuck blinked. Another million? Life didn't get much cooler than this! He thought that he'd have to wait for Hank to die to have financial freedom, but Cal had preempted him. Tuck avoided looking at his father. Hank wouldn't approve of the first million, let alone the second. These days Hank didn't approve of anything much about Tuck.

"Of course Sherri's twenty-fifth is five years from now," Granddad Cal said. "A lot could happen in five years." He looked hopeful.

Tuck tried to temper his excitement at the thought of a second million. He couldn't show his excitement at the idea because that would mean he wanted Sherri to stay missing. Well, truth to tell, he did, but the family mustn't know that. "Don't give up hope, Granddad Cal. Don't give up hope."

Tuck's father spoke. "Dad, do you think it's a good idea to give Tuck so much at such a young age? Maybe you should funnel it to him a bit at a time."

I knew it. Shut up, Hank! "Dad," Tuck said, his earnest face in place. "I'll use the money well. I'll invest it carefully. And I'll keep working at the office because I know that I need structure and strong goals."

Hank, who had made his own mark in the world by getting in on the new and burgeoning electronics phenomenon years ago, nodded, but he didn't look convinced.

"And I hope Sherri comes home soon." Inspiration struck him. "Why, I'll use part of my money to find her."

Hank gave that little wry half smile that meant he didn't believe Tuck, but he said nothing.

So where was little Sherri? He hadn't been overly worried about her for months because he figured she was dead, her body and the body of her boyfriend Kevin hidden somewhere.

Then those strange phone calls started, and he was no longer quite so sure. Dear, departed Sherri might not be so departed after all.

Thirteen

SUNDAY MORNING DAN stood in the kitchen at SeaSong and tried not to squirm. He glanced at his watch once again and made a low growling sound in his throat. They were going to be late for church. He hated to be late for anything, but especially church. It probably came from being a pastor's kid with a mother who thought the pastor's family being late was tantamount to heresy.

Cass grinned at his frustration. "It's obvious you never had a sister. Jenn will be here in a minute."

"Maybe. If we're lucky." Jared pulled a box of Honeycomb cereal from the cabinet beside the refrigerator and began to eat it by the fistful. "But I'm not holding my breath." He appeared unmindful of the crumbs that fell in a gentle snowfall onto the front of his deep green rugby shirt with *Seaside* in discreet lettering over his heart, then rolled with the help of gravity to the floor.

"Hey!" Brenna said from the sink, pointing a finger at Jared. "Outside with that mess."

"Yeah, yeah." Jared just grinned at her and kept chomping.

"I'm not sweeping up your mess, buddy," she said, trying to look threatening.

"You need a dog around here, Cass." Dan glanced at Glossy Flossie slumbering on the back of a love seat in the sitting area. "A dog would lick all those crumbs up instead of sleeping his life away like someone I could mention."

"Hey, now." Cass put her hands on her hips and glared at Dan. Only the sparkle in her eye told him she wasn't serious. "Don't you denigrate my baby. Besides, what would the health authorities say about a dog in a serving kitchen?"

"Probably the same thing they'd say about a cat," Dan muttered.

Footsteps sounded on the back stairs, and everyone except Flossie looked up expectantly.

"See?" Cass said. "I told you she'd only be a minute."

Abruptly the footfalls stopped and a muted "Rats," could be heard. Then the steps echoed their way back upstairs.

"At this rate, we'll be in time for the final amen," Jared said cheerfully. "That's still in time to go out to eat."

The bell on the registration desk sounded at the same time Jenn began another descent of the stairs.

"That should be the Novacks checking out." Cass started toward the swinging door. "Let me take care of them. I'll be quick."

Dan grabbed her wrist as she passed. He held his watch in front of her nose. "Let Brenna take care of them."

Brenna nodded. "I'll be glad to. Mr. Novack doesn't scare me now that I know what kind of a man he is. In fact, it'll be good experience to see if I can sneer politely at him."

"Thanks, Brenna." Dan dragged Cass toward the back door. "Hurry, woman," he hissed. "Jenn is actually walking toward the car. This may be our one and only opportunity before she remembers something else she needs. Or thinks she needs."

"I've got my cell phone," Cass called over her shoulder to Brenna. "Call if there's any trouble."

When he finally got everyone in the car, Dan felt like activating all the baby locks so no one could get out again until he said they could. Instead, he cranked the motor and took off.

The congregation was on its feet when they entered, ready to begin singing. If the first song hadn't yet been sung, then maybe they weren't late. Maybe the image of his mother tapping her watch would fade and he could get over feeling he'd broken what amounted to the eleventh commandment.

Dan followed Cass down the aisle to join her parents while the kids sat with friends. He kept his face neutral, but inside he smiled. Something about following this particular woman into the pew pleased him.

It wasn't that she looked especially lovely in a beige knit outfit with cream at the neck and cuffs, though she did. It wasn't that her legs looked longer than ever in the tan heels she was wearing. As much as he enjoyed looking at her, there was more to her than that wonderful hair, those hazel eyes, and those great legs. There was an enthusiasm about her, a fine intelligence, a spiritual maturity, a naturalness that appealed to him. Sure she was shy at times, but running together, eating breakfast together, even welcoming guests together had broken down most of those barriers. She was simply Cass, unique and wonderful.

Suddenly the thought of *waiting patiently* didn't seem so bad after all. If God was in no hurry to reveal His plans, then Dan didn't have to be in any hurry to leave SeaSong, to leave Cass.

Yesterday a box of his forwarded mail had arrived, sent on to him by the couple staying at his apartment. He'd tossed out all the offers for credit cards, all the pleas for funds for this cause and that ministry, glanced briefly at his bills, and fallen like a starving man on the Morningstar Fund Investor and his other professional journals.

The pleasure he'd gotten, the satisfaction and contentment he felt reading those magazines as he sat in the turret in his little room amazed him. He expected that his love of and attraction to the shifts and currents of the business world, both national and global, would wane as God redirected his life. That was not the case at all. Even reading materials that were dated filled him with that sharp edge of appreciation for the complexities and connections of markets and moneys all over the world.

He read eagerly for information about the more than five hundred companies on which he'd conducted due diligence. Which ones were still healthy and growing? Which ones were showing losses? Which ones were holding their own, looking good to the uninformed investor but screaming warnings to those who recognized that status quo in any organization was in actuality the early sound of its death knell?

Why do I still feel so strongly, Lord? Is it because as yet I haven't anything to fill the void that leaving my work created? I know a vacuum can't exist in nature. It also can't exist in my life. If being a vet goes—he smiled as he thought of Cass—*where is what will replace it? And if it's to go, why do I still feel the challenge and stimulation of that world so intensely?*

Now he glanced at Cass, standing next to him at the Chapel, singing to the Lord. She knew who she was. She felt secure in her family and with SeaSong. Of course, she wanted that derelict of a house next door, but basically her life was what she wanted it to be, what she had made it.

She must have felt his gaze because she looked up, a question on her face. He gave her what he hoped was a great smile, and she smiled shyly back, her cheeks flushing slightly. With a little duck of her head, she returned to singing.

Dan's eyes slid past her to her parents, and immediately he conceded that her life wasn't so perfect after all. Not that anyone's ever was, but some people were more pressured or more confused than others. Cass was definitely one of the pressured, thanks to Charlotte and Lew. And Jenn.

He was the confused, something he'd never, ever imagined he would be. How many times had he seen confused CEOs and felt superior? How many times had he given them advice on straightening out their business problems? What if he were one such confused CEO? What advice would he give himself?

Whenever a company was in trouble, relational problems lay at the root of the difficulties, not financial issues like most people thought. It was the wrong person in the job, the unqualified man or woman making decisions education and experience hadn't prepared him or her for. It was leadership unwilling to hire the best and fire the weak.

Dan grimaced inwardly. He was here in Seaside because of relational problems. The key issue was his poor performance spiritually. He'd survived his early years in business by sheer hard work and grit. He'd become successful if success meant money, position, respect, which it did on one level. He could also term himself a success if by that he meant the satisfying feeling of reaching his goals. He had built the Harmon Group into the premier conductor of due diligence in the city.

Maybe there had been short-term significance when he investigated a company and found it flourishing and well worth investing in, or even when he found a paper tiger and warned clients away. But companies rose and fell. What was booming yesterday could be risky tomorrow. What was wise counsel today could become fool's advice next week.

It was becoming more obvious daily that significance was ultimately found in the eternal, and only two things were eternal: God Himself and people.

He glanced at Cass again. By that criterion, she was involved in much that was significant, given her care for her parents, for Jenn and Jared, for Brenna, even for Paulie. It was the messy involvement in people's lives that held real meaning and brought real praise to God who had invested in people enough to send His Son for them.

Dan was surprised to find the singing finished, and he hastened to take his seat with the rest of the congregation. He watched Pastor Paul step to the pulpit, and Dan opened his Bible to follow along as the pastor read from Habakkuk: "'But these things I plan won't happen right away. Slowly, steadily, surely, the time approaches when the vision will be fulfilled. If it seems slow, wait patiently, for it will surely take place. It will not be delayed. Look at the proud! They trust in themselves, and their lives are crooked; but the righteous will live by their faith.'"

Dan didn't hear anything else Pastor Paul said. Over and over his mind replayed *slowly, steadily, surely* and *it seems slow.* Did it ever! But the promise was there too. *It will be fulfilled. It will surely take place.* God had something of significance for him to do.

Lord, help me to not rail against the slowly, steadily, surely *part but remember the* it will surely take place *part.*

He took a deep breath, deep enough that Cass glanced at him to be certain he was all right. He smiled reassuringly at her. For some reason she felt like an anchor, holding him steady in his sea of uncertainties.

After church the same group crowded the same corner at Dante's, and this week they took Dan's presence as a given. Mrs. Merton sat across the table from him and asked perceptive questions about why he was here in Seaside.

"October is not the usual vacation time at the Jersey shore, at least not for extended vacations like you're taking."

"Yes, well." He scratched his head, knowing he probably looked as uncomfortable as he felt. It wasn't that he minded her questioning him. He didn't even care whether she was simply curious or trying to ferret out information about the man who sat next to her daughter in church.

"You're a very choleric young man, aren't you?" she asked after he fumbled his way through an explanation of *wait patiently.*

"Er, am I?" he asked, uncertain how to react. To him *choleric* meant angry and temperamental, but he didn't think that was what she had in mind. At least he hoped it wasn't.

She was as alert and aware as anyone could wish today, her comments cogent, her faculties unimpaired. For the first time he understood why the brothers had a difficult time grasping how bad their mother could be. If you didn't witness her incidents, how could you believe this vivacious and clever woman was ill?

"I mean that you're the type of person who is used to being in control," she explained. "You're used to calling the shots. A position of power comes easily and naturally to you. You've probably always had a feeling that you would achieve, a feeling of destiny even when you didn't know what that destiny was. Am I right?"

He nodded, impressed. "Defined that way, yes, I am choleric."

"Then this uncertainty must be driving you crazy."

"Right over the edge."

"That's not surprising. I have several sons who are just as driven as you."

"I'm trying to change driven to trusting and obeying," Dan said, resisting the urge to blow the paper from his straw at Cass, who was listening to the conversation with great interest.

"He's bored," Cass told her mother. "Desperate for something to do. He's so restless he played bellhop Friday. He did a pretty good job, too."

Dan grinned. "It was fun, though I don't see it as a viable career move. Besides, the night belonged to Cass," he said. "You would have been proud of her." He told the story of Mr. Novack and the hair. Cass took over on the Novacks and their Dante's bill, waving a forkful of coleslaw until Dan was certain it would end up in either her lap or his.

When the coleslaw finally made it to Cass's mouth, Dan relaxed and ate his hot roast beef sandwich with fries. He had just decided he wouldn't have any dessert when Will called down the table, "Hey, BB, happy birthday!"

As Dan wondered who BB was, a piece of cake with four candles in it appeared between his and Cass's shoulders. Their server put it in front of Cass. Everyone at the table began singing, "Happy Birthday, dear Cassandra." Dan sang along, though he hadn't known it was her special day.

Cass looked at the cake, shook her head, and grinned as they all sang. People at a couple of nearby tables joined in, and everyone clapped as she blew out the candles.

"I was trying to forget this, you guys."

"Like we'd let you," Will said. "The big four-oh. My baby sister is now officially a middle-aged lady."

Dan looked at Cass, then back at Will. "Middle age never looked so good."

Will looked momentarily startled. Then he said, "BB, you've got a fan."

Dan glanced at Cass again and saw her color. He grinned. "She does."

"What do you want for your birthday?" Lucy asked as she passed a small, brightly flowered gift bag stuffed with yellow tissue paper down the table. "Of course, it's too late to make much difference. As you can see, we've already gotten the gift. Still, I'd like to know. Tell me and I'll tell you what I wanted when I turned forty."

"In a minute." Cass took the colorful bag and set it on the table before her. "First things first." She pulled out the tissue paper, reached into the bag, and drew out an envelope. She opened it, and though she kept her smile in place, somehow Dan knew she was hurt. "Look, everyone. A gift certificate to Home Depot."

Dan kept his face bland, but he wanted to scowl. What kind of a present was that for a beautiful woman on her birthday? Surely she deserved a personal something when she hit forty.

"Here, Cassandra Marie." Her mother handed a small, gaily wrapped gift across the table.

"Thanks, Mom, Dad." Cass blew a kiss at both of them. She slit the paper and pulled out a box. She lifted the lid, and Dan felt the same little disappointment, the same little hesitation in her. She kept her smile and held up gift subscription notices to *TV Guide, Ladies' Home Journal,* and *Redbook.*

"Your father picked them out all by himself," Charlotte announced proudly.

Cass smiled at her father who squirmed slightly in his seat.

Jared, Jenn, and the cousins had crowded around the table to watch, and Jenn said, "We'll give you your gifts on your actual birthday since we'll see you then."

"So today's not the official date?" Dan asked.

She shook her head. "It's tomorrow."

Good. There was time for him to get something to show his appreciation for her kindness and generosity. What that should be he had no idea, but hopefully by tomorrow he'd have a brain-storm.

"Now before we all go, I have something for everyone," Lew said, rising and pulling a plastic grocery bag from under his chair. He started handing out boxes. Dan was startled when Lew stuck one in his face.

"Thanks, Lew. You didn't have to do this." Dan opened his box and found a thermometer lying in it. "Just what I need. If I put it on my windowsill, I'll know how to dress each morning for my jogging."

The thermometer's white tube with its black numbers both centigrade and Fahrenheit rested on a jaunty red backdrop. He lifted it and held it up for inspection. As soon as the thermometer was upright, the glass fell off the plastic backing. Dan grabbed for it, but it hit the floor with a *plink*. He picked it up, expecting it to be broken, expecting to have to chase mercury across the floor, and was relieved to find it intact. He quickly placed both pieces in the box before he did something else dumb. He'd get a tube of Krazy Glue tomorrow.

He looked up and caught Lucy in her smart gray suit with the soft pink knit top staring at a wildly patterned blouse in oranges and purples. Will was showing her a plastic mug that read Big Boy. Dan glanced at Cass and saw she had a pen with retractable points, one red ink, one blue, one black. Unfortunately, none of the points would stay down when she tried to write on her paper place mat.

He glanced at the kids' table where Lew was dispensing his largesse. A miniature soccer ball key ring, a compact that had exaggerated eyelashes drawn on it, a ring that was sized by squeez-ing the edges together, a ceramic statue of a quite ugly little girl holding a book, and another pen like Cass's, though on this one

118 ～ Gayle Roper

the red point seemed to work. The kids seemed underwhelmed.

Will held his mug aloft. "Thanks, Dad," he said in a voice devoid of inflection.

"Yeah, thanks," echoed everyone.

Lew preened. "You're welcome. Enjoy."

As Cass placed her certificates and pen in her gift bag, everyone rose and prepared to leave. In the quiet chaos of collecting purses, jackets, and coats, Lucy said, "Cass, you never told us what you really wanted for your birthday."

"Yeah, BB," Will said. "What is your deepest wish?"

"Yeah, Aunt BB," one of Will's kids said, the one who had gotten the statue.

Dan saw Cass's jaw tense. She remained in her seat for a minute without moving while everyone looked at her. Then she took a deep breath and looked up smiling. She gave the royal wave. "What I really want for my birthday is world peace."

Everyone laughed.

"And what did you want for your birthday?" Charlotte asked Lucy brightly.

"My wish was much more selfish and much easier to attain. I wanted a day at a spa with all the trimmings." She grinned. "I have to do something to hold the ravages of age at bay."

Dan looked at petite Lucy and saw not a single ravage. "Did you get it?" he asked.

"Oh, yes," Lucy said, smiling sweetly at her husband. "Will was wonderful."

"Especially since Mom told him what she wanted every day for a solid month," said the key chain boy.

Lucy shrugged. "Whatever works."

Dan's attention was drawn from Lucy by a hand on his arm. Lew Merton looked at him, clearly uncomfortable and slightly belligerent.

"So Cass wants you to look over my money situation."

Lew was obviously unhappy, and Dan didn't find that at all surprising. The man knew he was going to be told he was misusing his money, making wrong and unwise purchases, wasting his resources.

"I want to know how she found out about those overdrafts."

Dan ignored the question. "Lew, from what Cass has told me,

you shouldn't be getting notices like that."

"It's none of her business."

"She loves you guys, Lew. She's concerned."

"Let her be concerned about her mother." Lew watched Charlotte exit the restaurant, his eyes tortured. "I'm fine."

Dan nodded. "No problem there. Cass is very concerned."

"She's why I do it, you know."

"Cass is why you're overdrawn?"

"No, no, not Cassandra Marie. Charlotte. She's why I play the sweepstakes."

"She urges you to?"

"No." Lew ran his hand nervously down his navy-and-red striped tie, patted it, pulled on it. "I'm afraid for her," he finally said. "No, I'm terrified for her. I want the money to guarantee she's cared for like she should be." He blinked, scowling at Dan as if daring him to notice the tears.

Dan's throat constricted as Lew's pain wrapped around him. He turned Cass's father toward his silver car. "Come on. Let's you and me drive to your place without the ladies."

Numbly Lew nodded and let himself be tucked into the passenger seat of the BMW. He buckled his seat belt with shaking hands.

Dan opened the driver's door and, one foot in the car, looked for Cass. He saw her beside her parents' car, talking with her mother and Lucy. He caught her eye and pointed to Charlotte. "Drive with your mother," he mouthed.

She nodded, tucking her hand onto her mother's arm. "Come on, Jenn, Jared. We're driving with Grandmom."

Before anyone had a chance to question the arrangement, Dan drove off. He headed away from Scallop Street. He and Lew rode in silence for several blocks. Then Lew started to talk, and once started, he couldn't stop.

"Forty-nine years. I've been married to Charlotte for forty-nine years. I barely remember life without her except for my time in the service. D day. Battle of the Bulge. Korea. I remember that all right. I was never so cold and lonely and scared in my life. But within two months of mustering out, we got married. She was so beautiful." He sighed. "She is so beautiful. You might not understand this, not being married and all, but I love her more today than I did when I married her—and I was crazy about her then."

Dan thought of his parents and the quiet, deep river of affection that flowed between them. It had been the bedrock of his life from his earliest memories. Cass and the brothers had been equally blessed.

"We didn't have any money back then," Lew said. "I managed to get a job with the post office, no small thing with all the veterans looking for work. It's a good thing I got that job because Will was born ten months after we married. Then Hal two years later, Tommy two years later, Bud two years after that. And then came Cassandra Marie."

Lew's eyes crinkled at the memory of his baby daughter. "She was a Gerber baby, so beautiful it hurt to look at her."

"She's still beautiful," Dan said.

Lew's eyes sharpened on Dan for a minute before his memories claimed him again. "We had a good life, Charlotte and me and the kids. Not extravagant. Good. The Lord was kind to us. I saved a little bit, but putting five kids through college took all we had and more. Charlotte worked as a receptionist for a doctor from the time Cassandra Marie started high school until retirement. After everyone graduated from college, we saved all Charlotte's salary. When we sold the family house and bought the little place on Scallop, we invested the difference. We've been careful. By and large we've been healthy. We're on Medicare and we have Medigap insurance."

Dan parked in the empty lot at Seaside Chapel and gave his full attention to Lew.

"But I'm terrified it's not going to be enough," Lew said, his eyes filling again. "You've seen her at her worst." A sob choked his voice. "My lovely Charlotte. She doesn't even know me when she has one of her spells." He shut his eyes against the pain. "Somehow she knows Cassandra Marie, but she doesn't know me."

Dan wished there was something he could say, something he could do. There wasn't. All he could do was plead, *Father, wrap Your comforting arms about Lew. Ease his pain.*

"We were going to go to Hawaii for our fiftieth anniversary." Lew looked blankly out the window. "Not now. I've pleaded with God to make her well. On days like today I think maybe He's listening. But tomorrow or the next day I'll know He's not."

Dan stared at the cross that hung in the peak of the roof over the front door of the chapel. That cross was the symbol of eternal healing for believers but no guarantee of temporal healing for a hurting man like Lew.

"So you're entering all the sweepstakes with the hope of making a killing that will cover any care Charlotte may need in the future," Dan said quietly.

Lew nodded. "Dumb idea, huh?" His voice quavered. "Like I'd ever really win."

"Desperate maybe, but not dumb. You love her."

"Yeah, I do. What's happening to her is killing me."

"And you're buying things that the sweepstakes offer, like the magazine subscriptions you gave Cass, hoping to increase your chances of winning."

Lew frowned. "I got a letter last week that said I had won a hundred thousand dollars, and an armored truck was driving to our house from Atlantic City to give me the cash. *Thank You, God!* I thought and rushed to tell Charlotte. She was having one of her good days, and she took the letter, showing me the catch in the wording of the announcement. I think the phrase was 'when you mail in your winning number.'"

"Ah," Dan said. "And when you mail in your nonwinning number, which is the case for 99.999 percent of the people, you don't get the truckful."

Lew just sighed and continued to stare out his window at the cloudless sky. "I want to leave an inheritance to my kids, too. I want to leave them something to ease their financial pressures what with the grandkids' college expenses and all. I want to leave Cassandra Marie something extra because she's a woman alone, something to make certain she's cared for. I want to take them all on a cruise, even the grandchildren. I want to take them to Hawaii."

He swallowed hard and closed his eyes. "It's not going to happen, is it? None of it's going to happen, at least not without the sweepstakes."

Dan looked at the broken man and felt as if he were about to kick a cowering puppy, but he knew he had to speak. "I've got something sort of hard to say here, Lew."

The man turned to him with apathetic eyes.

"Have you ever thought that God just might want you to trust and obey instead of finagle?"

Lew closed his eyes and dropped his head to his chest. "Yeah, I know. But it's hard to trust when He lets something like this happen to you."

Fourteen

CASS WOKE UP on Monday with a giant headache. Forty today. She stared at the sloping ceiling above her and dreaded getting up. When she looked in the mirror, she'd see an aging woman, wrinkles furrowing her brow, crow's-feet creeping from her eyes, jowls hanging like a turkey's wattle. Well, it wouldn't be that bad, but still.

Forty!

Why forty bothered her so much when she wasn't an especially vain woman—the brothers had knocked any vanity out of her years ago—was a mystery to her. Maybe it was because her life was now half over, and it was all downhill from here. Maybe it was that forty represented the final nail in the coffin of possible childbearing. Maybe it was because of the void she felt more and more deeply in her personal life.

I'm so lonely, Lord. She felt tears gather. *And I'm so pathetic that I didn't realize how lonely until the kids came to stay. And Dan.* Goose bumps gathered on her arms and legs, and it wasn't from the cool morning air. *I know You should be enough for me, but what will I do when they all leave? When he leaves?*

Climbing out from under the warm covers into the brisk chill, she pulled on her navy sweats. She combed her tousled hair with her fingers and crammed the blond strands into a ponytail caught by a hot pink scrunchie that used to be Jenn's.

"I'll never wear that ugly color again," Jenn had said as she threw the scrunchie in the trash. "Derrick hates it."

Cass had reached in and claimed the offending circle of elastic and fabric. It had come in handy on many a morning, and it was certainly easier to pull out of her hair than a rubber band.

She went quietly upstairs to the bathroom where she washed her face and brushed her teeth, not looking in the oval hanging over the sink for fear of what she might see—dark pouches under her eyes, hairs growing on her upper lip, cheeks pleated with wrinkles. She sighed.

You'd better get over it, girl. You'll never be any better than you are now.

All the more reason to jog. She went downstairs and checked the thermometer that hung next to the kitchen window. Forty-three degrees. She went back to her little room under the stairs for a pair of light gloves. It wasn't until she'd disarranged everything in her three dresser drawers that she realized the gloves were upstairs in her real room, Jenn's room.

She quailed at the thought of going up for them and waking Jenn before her alarm went off. She'd just pull down her sleeves and hold them over her hands. How painful could a few minutes of nippy weather be?

The cold might not have been too bad if it hadn't also been so breezy. The wind flayed her, cutting through her sweatshirt, finding each little air hole in the weave of the fabric. When Dan, looking gorgeous and bright-eyed, joined her as she warmed up, she felt positively ancient.

"Happy birthday, Cass!" he said with such enthusiasm that she wanted to wrap her hands about his neck and squeeze. She didn't want to kill him—he was too gorgeous for that. She'd just strangle him a bit until he turned as grumpy as she felt. Instead, she bent at the waist to hide her aging face.

"Thanks," she mumbled.

They ran without talking, and Cass was glad. She knew she wasn't good company this morning. She who was never temperamental had a blue mood that would make woebegone Eeyore look like a cockeyed optimist.

They were briskly walking the last block toward home when the Seaside garbage truck rolled toward them. Its fragrance rose on the wind, and Cass couldn't help but wonder how anyone could stand being near the truck in high summer. Even though it was shiny, red, and almost brand-new, it reeked even in the cool fall air. Two of the most disreputable-looking young men Cass had ever seen clung to the back handrails.

The truck stopped and the cab window rolled down. Cass smiled her first genuine smile of the day as she looked at the driver. "Did you come to wish me happy birthday, Clooney?"

"Not me, darlin'," the man said as he rested an elbow on the window ledge. "You might just expect a present."

"You mean you haven't anything in your stash of ill-gotten goods that you'd be willing to share?"

"Lean times is all I can say."

Cass grinned, not believing a word from this man she'd known since forever. Clooney was a Seaside celebrity of sorts, a decorated and disillusioned Vietnam vet who refused to use his keen mind in any pattern that could be perceived as conformity to the system. He searched the beaches all year long with his metal detector, and there wasn't a Seaside kid who hadn't trailed after him, fascinated. There also wasn't a kid who hadn't gotten one of the treasures he dug up. Cass still had the key ring with the silver butterfly medallion and five keys Clooney had given her the year she was fourteen, all legs, bosom, broad shoulders, and self-consciousness.

She had gone with the brothers and their friends to the Twelfth Street beach one July Saturday. She was there because her mother made the boys bring her. She was the price for them to have use of the car. Unfortunately, the brothers weren't happy they'd been forced to bring her, so she sat on her beach towel slightly apart from the rowdy guys.

Clooney saw her, huddled over a book, constantly trying to pull her bathing suit neckline up to her collarbone. She still remembered making believe she didn't feel conspicuous and failing spectacularly. Then Clooney knelt beside her and held out the key chain and medallion.

"This is for you, Cassandra," he said loudly enough for the brothers to hear. "One of these days you'll be that beautiful butterfly." He tapped the embossed wings, ignoring the brothers when they began to hoot. To them, *beautiful* and *Cass* were not analogous, and sadly she agreed with them. Clooney rattled the dangling pieces of metal. "And these are magic keys."

She looked at the butterfly medallion, so pretty and shiny, so perfect. She would emerge from a chrysalis and become like that? She knew an impossible dream when she heard one, yet a little prickle of hope made her heart jump.

"What do the keys open?" she asked, her voice breathy.

"Ah." Clooney closed her hand over the treasure. "That's for you to find out." And he walked off, swinging his detector in arcs over the sand, stopping every so often to use a child's red plastic spade to dig a hole.

"Let me see," Tommy demanded, and the others echoed him as they gathered around her.

Cass dangled the keys for the boys to see but kept her fist clamped around the butterfly medallion. She knew the brothers too well to put her new treasure in their grubby hands. They'd probably use it to play keep-away or some such game and lose it.

"That opens a Honda," Tommy said, pointing.

"And that's a front door key," Bud said. "No magic there."

Cass had turned from the brothers and walked to the water's edge, holding the medallion so tightly it hurt, listening to the melodic jingling of her magic keys. She looked skyward as the wavelets washed around her ankles and her feet sank into the soft sand.

God, can You make me a butterfly? Oh, please God, if You can, do it! Please!

Even today Cass could taste the desperation in the young Cassandra's prayer.

Well, she might not have become the butterfly, but thankfully she hadn't remained the caterpillar either. Maybe she was a moth, solid and self-sufficient, if not butterfly beautiful.

Whatever, that day had made Clooney special and every time she saw him a delight. Remembering her manners, Cass said, "Dan, this guy with hair longer than mine is Clooney. He's Seaside's resident historian and beachcomber."

"And since neither pays anything, I drive the garbage truck to pay my rent," Clooney added amiably.

"Dan's a CEO from New York City," she said, "and he's staying at SeaSong."

Dan reached up to take Clooney's hand. "Retired CEO."

"Obviously early retirement. Lucky you," Clooney said. "How long are you here?"

Dan shrugged. "Life's up in the air right now."

Clooney nodded. "I'm with you. Finding yourself is hard work. I know. I'm still looking."

Dan's mouth quirked. "That's an encouraging piece of information."

Clooney looked from Dan to Cass and back to Dan, his thoughts obvious enough to make her blush and hold her breath over what he would say. He surprised her when he merely nodded at Dan.

Dan met his gaze and smiled noncommittally.

Cass, mortified, scowled at Clooney. He grinned and with a wave drove away, the guys clinging to the handrails looking so sleepy it's a wonder they could hold on. Cass and Dan walked the remaining half block to SeaSong. With a reminiscent smile Cass found herself telling Dan the medallion story.

"Do you still have it?" he asked after he'd listened carefully.

"I do, somewhere in my stored stuff in the back of the closet in Jenn's room." Suddenly finding that butterfly was of the utmost importance on this day when she felt so full of gloom. She would look for it as soon as Jenn left for school.

Which she did, finally finding the medallion and key chain in a box of souvenirs trapped beneath her high school yearbook. Clasping the medallion tightly and whispering her butterfly prayer as ardently as she had at fourteen, she ran to Dan's room and knocked on his door, though not before she had taken care to brush her hair and add a little color to her cheeks.

"Come in," he called, and she entered. She held out her hand. The silver medallion was smaller than she remembered. In her mind it had assumed the proportions of a large doughnut. In reality it favored a silver dollar.

Dan studied it, his finger tracing the butterfly. "Well, you certainly fulfilled Clooney's prophecy. In fact, you surpassed it. You are more beautiful than any butterfly could hope to be." He raised his eyes and smiled at her.

Cass couldn't move, couldn't breathe. People didn't say things like that to her, didn't smile like that at her, especially men. She felt a great wave of heat move up her throat, over her face, and into her hairline. For several seconds she just stared at him. Finally, with a clearing of throat and a licking of lips, she managed, "You don't have to say things like that."

His expression as he studied her face was part puzzlement, part sincerity. "Of course I do." He gave a mischievous grin. "It's my Christian duty to speak the truth."

The truth? Surely not. It was just empty flattery to make her feel good on her birthday. Wasn't it? She dropped her gaze back to the medallion, feeling a flicker of the hope she'd felt that long-ago July day.

"And, Cass, when someone compliments you, you're supposed to say, 'Thank you, kind sir.'" The gentleness in his voice took away any quality of reprimand.

"Thank you, kind sir. I've got to go." *Before I make a bigger fool of myself.* She turned to run as Dan's cell phone rang.

When he said, "Hi, Lew," she paused.

Her father. But she didn't actually listen to the conversation. It was just an excuse to linger and look at Dan out of the corner of her eye. As she did, she felt both absolute terror and intense longing. He said the most wonderful, outlandish things to her. How could she not respond to him emotionally? When he told her she was pretty, she could almost think she was. How she longed to believe he meant it, that he truly thought her special, that he wasn't just being gracious and kind.

The truth was that he would go back to New York and his regular life sometime soon. When that happened, she'd be alone again and forever, an old maid of forty with no prospects and no hope, for she knew that no other man would ever interest her the way Dan did. She knew it deep in her soul.

No, when he left, she wouldn't just be alone, as in being by herself. Alone and its companion solitude were good, giving you a chance to think, to talk to the Lord, to contemplate the issues of life.

She would be lonely, achingly so, hurting for companionship, especially the companionship of a particular person. She shut her eyes against the ache and the fear that this was her future.

And she thought she'd felt bad when she woke up this morning.

Dan clicked off his phone and said, "Your father's coming over in a little while. He's bringing his financial records."

She blinked, pulling her mind to the moment. "Wouldn't it be easier if you went over there?"

Dan nodded. "Much, but he doesn't want your mother to know what he's done. He's afraid it'll send her into an episode."

"An episode?"

"That's what he calls her bad times."

Cass rubbed her temples. Her headache was back with a vengeance. "You can spread your stuff out over the kitchen table."

That's what the men did as she and Brenna stripped the beds and turned the mattresses, cleaned the bathrooms, and washed the linens. Dan and Dad didn't even stop working for lunch, eating their tuna salad sandwiches while poking Dan's calculator.

At four when Cass took meat out of the freezer and prepared to defrost it in the microwave, Dan abruptly rose. "What are you doing?"

She stared at him. "I'm starting dinner."

"On your birthday?"

She gave a little huff of laughter. "Somebody's got to feed us, and I sincerely doubt it'll be Jenn."

He took the package of hamburger from her hands and slid it back into the freezer.

"*Dan.*"

He smiled. "Trust me."

Cass became aware of her father watching them, and she struggled to be casual. "Trust you, huh?"

He winked and turned to her father. "Tomorrow, Lew? I think we can finish what we need to do by then."

Dad nodded and began sliding all his papers into his soft-sided briefcase.

Dan reached out and grabbed a small stack of business envelopes, tossing them back on the table. "Leave these here, Lew. No use letting yourself be tempted."

Sweepstakes, no doubt. Dad looked from the envelopes to Dan and back, clearly torn.

"Trust the Lord, Lew. Remember? Trust and obey."

With a deep sigh, Dad left the envelopes on the table. He shook Dan's hand, kissed Cass's cheek, and left. She watched him climb into his car and drive away.

She turned to Dan. "How bad are things?"

"Hmm?" Dan was absorbed in the envelopes. The longer he studied the letters, the harder his jaw clenched.

"Look at this!" He thrust a letter at her. "Right here on the back it says, 'No purchase necessary; purchase does not increase chances of winning.' But here on the front it asks for your processing fee of $17.97. If they don't get your money one way, they get it another." He flipped through the envelopes. "There are ten letters here, and they all ask for a similar amount. That's over $170.00! And this is only one day's worth of letters!"

"What about the ones that ask you to put a special sticker on the envelope if you're ordering something?" Cass waved the sheet with a shiny gold circle sticker. "How easy it is to think that the unmarked letters get thrown out. So you buy. I think that's where Dad is getting into such big trouble. Before he knows it, he's spent twenty-five or fifty dollars several times over."

Dan continued to rifle through the papers. "They all ask for his phone number and want to know if he has a major credit card. It's a setup for telephone solicitations if I ever saw one. Look at the wording on this one offering twenty-five thousand dollars." He held out a page with an official looking seal in the upper right corner. "'Please be advised that this official document shall be deemed sufficient notification of unclaimed cash award. You have been authorized to receive this cash award simply by returning the cash claim form attached.' And listen to this at the bottom of the page. 'I do hereby declare that I am the person to whom this notification is addressed, that I have read the Cash Declarative on the reverse side, and that I demand immediate payment of my unclaimed check. I am returning this claim form pursuant to these instructions and understand payment will be made via check within twenty-one days.'"

"It sounds like a guarantee to me," Cass said. "What's the catch? I don't see it." She took the document from him and studied it closely. Eventually she saw, running up the side of the page, *DEADLINE: 7 days to respond.* "Seven days," she muttered, grabbing the envelope. "Look. The letter's dated September 19, and the envelope is postmarked September 24. By the time the notice is received, the seven days are already gone!"

Dan looked up from the letter he was examining. "When you

feel pressed for money, these promises seem magical, the answer to all your problems."

"But Dad doesn't need money."

"He thinks he does. He wants it for your mother so she'll always have the best care, and he wants it so he can leave you kids an inheritance."

"What? Oh, Dan." Cass thought her heart would break. "Like we want him worrying over something like that." She folded the letter she held and tore it across again and again until all she had was a handful of confetti.

"Feel better?" Dan held out his hand for the paper.

Cass gave it to him. "Yes, I think I do."

"Good." He tossed the scraps at her, letting them rain down on her hair and shoulders. One sailed into her mouth, open in astonishment, and she spit it out.

"Now, birthday girl, go get dressed for a nice dinner." He pointed upstairs. "The residents of SeaSong are celebrating."

Cass stared at him, her hand stalled halfway to her shoulder to brush off the confetti. "We're going out for dinner?"

"No."

"Oh." Talk about feeling deflated.

"But we are having a special dinner nonetheless. From Dante's at the Dock, fancy side." The front doorbell rang, and Dan made a face. "Not yet! It's too soon. Would you get that, Cass, while I clean up the table?"

She hurried to the door where she found a delivery man from Seaside Flowers holding a vase filled with a dozen of the most beautiful red roses she'd ever seen. She took the vase and, eyes sparkling, spun around to see Dan smiling at her.

"From you?" She scarcely dared believe it.

"Why don't you read the card?"

She set the vase on the desk and pulled out the card tucked among the deep green leaves. "Putting on the ritz for your birthday. Love, Jenn, Jared, Brenna, Mike, and Dan—the SeaSong clan."

Maybe not just from him, but close enough. She leaned in and breathed deeply.

"Now you have to get lost until six-thirty," Dan told her as he tipped the delivery boy.

She looked at him. "What?"

"You heard me. I'd suggest a nice relaxing bath followed by a power nap. Since Jenn's going to be reporting for duty any minute now to help with preparations, you can primp and polish in your real room upstairs. Remember, we don't want to see you until six-thirty, and then only if you're dressed in your best." He glanced at her faded jeans and turtleneck. "Lovely as you look, tonight's for putting on the ritz."

Cass knew she wore a goofy smile, but she couldn't help it. They were having a party for her! Caught between tears and laughter, she held the flowers close. "I'm taking my roses upstairs with me."

Dan smiled, his navy eyes alight with his pleasure at her delight. "Oh, and when you come down, come down the front stairs."

"The front stairs. Yes, sir." She raced to her cubby room, collected clean clothes, and flew upstairs. Free time! Wow.

Jenn had left a floral gift bag on her bed with a big Aunt Cassandra sign resting against it. Cass put her roses on the dresser, running a finger over the deep crimson velvet and smiling to herself before turning to the bag. Filled with anticipation, she reached inside. Several packages, each wrapped in pink tissue paper and tied with deep fuchsia curly ribbon, kept her busy. Bubble bath, bath gel, body lotion, a spritz bottle of cologne, a mesh sponge, and the latest Deborah Raney romance.

A little note inside the bag read, "For the perfect preparations for putting on the ritz. From all of us."

Carrying her roses and her bag of goodies into the just cleaned but now vacant guest Jacuzzi bath, Cass filled the tub, poured in the bubble bath, and climbed in. When the jets began pulsing along her spine, she sighed. She couldn't remember the last time she'd indulged in such luxury. She opened her new novel and settled in.

When she came downstairs at six-thirty smelling like a flower garden, carrying her roses, and wearing her floaty blue dress that she usually wore to the annual banquet of the local chamber of commerce, she found Jared, wearing a dress shirt and tie, waiting at the foot of the stairs.

"Wow, do you look handsome," she said.

"Well, you look pretty good yourself, all sort of glowy." He extended his arm for her to take. "If I may seat you, ma'am."

She rested her hand in the crook of his elbow and walked beside him through the common room to the dining room where several of the small tables had been strung together and covered with a deep gold cloth. Good china that looked suspiciously like Jenn and Jared's mother's sat at six places also set with their mother's sterling and crystal. Candles glowed on the table and on every available surface: tall candles, fat candles, slim candles, votive candles.

"Just like in the movies," Jenn said as a delighted Cass took in the golden scene and the smiling faces of her five hosts.

The air was redolent with the scent of fine food, and not one Dante's box was visible. Dan stepped forward to seat her at one end of the table. He took his seat at the other end with Jenn and Jared on one side and Brenna and Mike on the other.

Jenn served the appetizer, a warm spinach-artichoke dip with petite vegetables and crackers for dipping. At the same time Jared poured everyone sparkling cider.

When the only thing that remained of the hors d'oeuvres was a pair of miniature carrots, Jenn stood and pulled a piece of paper from the pocket of her Sunday dress.

"What I Appreciate Most about Aunt Cassandra," she read.

Cass felt her jaw drop. There was something the girl actually appreciated?

"Number one—I know she cares about me, even when her decisions make me angry."

Everyone laughed, Cass wryly.

Jenn continued. "Two, she took us in. Three, she's a good role model. Four, she makes me clean toilets—NOT! And last, she loves Jesus and shows me what that looks like." Jenn handed the list to Cass with a flourish, then bent to kiss her cheek. "Happy Birthday, Aunt Cassandra."

"Thank you, Jenn," Cass said around the lump in her throat.

Jared rose next. "Dan told us we could only list five things because otherwise this could go on all night."

Dan. Cass looked down the table at him, but he was watching Jared like a proud papa. She forced her eyes to her nephew.

"Number one." Jared grinned at Cass. "You like Paulie. Not everybody's smart enough to see what a great guy he is." He shot a look at Jenn who smiled sweetly, insincerely back.

Cass nodded. "Paulie's special. One of a kind."

"You can say that again," muttered Jenn who had the grace to blush when Jared and Cass both turned to look at her. "Sorry."

Jared cleared his throat. "Number two: You opened your home to us at great inconvenience. Three, you come to all my football games and cheer like crazy. Four, you keep the cereal shelf stocked with all my favorites. And last but far from least, you live as a Christian should both in your private life and in your business life."

"Oh, Jared, thank you," Cass whispered through tears. "That was wonderful."

Mike and Brenna excused themselves and headed for the kitchen as a pleased Jared grabbed the appetizer dishes and followed. They returned shortly with medallions of filet mignon topped with crab imperial, roasted potatoes, and green beans almondine.

The food was delicious, and conversation hopped all around the table. Cass listened in a rosy glow. No Home Depot cards tonight. No *TV Guide*. This was a real birthday party.

When they all sat before empty plates, Brenna stood. "I appreciate several things about Cass, too. One is that she gave me a job. Without it I wouldn't be eating this wonderful dinner tonight."

They laughed together, and Cass caught Dan's eye. She knew he was the finances behind this wonderful evening, undoubtedly even the small fortune Jenn had spent on candles.

Thank you, she mouthed.

You're welcome, he mouthed back, then winked.

Cass's heart leapt as she turned her attention back to Brenna.

"I also appreciate what a fine business Cass has built, all with her own grit and determination. SeaSong is wonderful. And last, I know she cares about me." Brenna blinked rapidly. When she spoke again, her voice was thick with emotion. "And that means more than you'll ever know."

With that, she sat abruptly, then jumped to her feet. She grabbed a pair of dirty plates and hurried to the kitchen. Mike rose quickly, grabbed a couple more, and followed her, a frown wrinkling his thin face.

Silence hovered until Dan rose. "I'm the dessert man. Would you like a cup of coffee, Cass?"

She nodded, overwhelmed by it all. She watched as Dan poured her coffee. Was he going to say anything about her? When Mike hadn't spoken, Cass hadn't been surprised. He barely knew her. He was basically here because of Brenna.

But Dan. Would he say something? If so, what?

Don't expect too much. Don't ruin the evening with unrealistic dreams.

Mike and Brenna resumed their seats, all peaceful between them for the moment. Dan excused himself and disappeared through the swinging door to return with a cake iced in white with white buttercream flowers rimming the perimeter.

"From Let Them Eat Cake." Cass smiled. "You couldn't have done any better than that."

"Jenn told me you loved this cake best." Dan placed the cake, alight with little candles, before her.

"Forty candles?" she groaned. "Did you have to?"

"We sure did," Jenn said.

"Reason number six." Cass smiled at her niece, enjoying their détente, even if the peace was only temporary. "I gave you a chance to be a pyromaniac for the evening."

Finally the cake and ice cream were gone, the coffee drunk. All that remained were six sated people. Then Dan rose.

He looked down the table at Cass, and she felt as though she'd never be able to look away. She wasn't exactly sure how he had done it, but in the short time she'd known him, he had become the most important person in her life. Her hand went to her heart as if to protect it.

"Cass," Dan said her name and stopped. He just looked at her, and the air between them vibrated. On either side of the table the kids grinned and rolled their eyes, but Cass didn't care. At this moment there was only Dan.

He cleared his throat. "I appreciate you for many reasons, some as substantial as your great legs, your beautiful hair, and your enchanting eyes."

Cass blinked. *Wow.* The kids giggled.

"But what I appreciate most is that you have generously offered yourself, your home, and your family to me during the most difficult time in my life. I was lost, but you found me and took me home with you. You have made these uncertain days a joy and reminded me that the Father does know what He's doing. I could not ask for more, and I thank you from the bottom of my heart."

He reached into his suit jacket's inside pocket. "And now." He pulled out a slim, padded, ruby-colored box with a gold string wrapped around it and tied in a bow. He held it toward her. "Happy birthday, Cassie. From all of us."

Cass watched as Jared took the box and passed it to Jenn who passed it to her. She looked down the table at Dan who was so handsome in his navy pinstripe suit, so Mr. CEO. He might have said, "From all of us," but Cass knew better.

"Open it," Jenn ordered. "Come on, Aunt Cassandra."

Cass's fingers shook only slightly as she slid the string off and lifted the lid. Inside on a bed of ivory satin lay a bracelet, a golden chain with one small, exquisitely etched medallion attached: a butterfly, wings spread for soaring. Dangling next to the butterfly was a tiny key.

The swell of joy Cass felt made speech all but impossible. She held the bracelet up for everyone to see. Dimly she heard Jenn say, "Very pretty butterfly, but what's with the little key?"

She didn't answer. She slid the gold chain about her wrist and with Jenn's help fastened it. She held her hand out so everyone could see. Then she lowered her hands to her lap and closed her hand around the little medallion, feeling it warm in her hand. She looked at Dan who looked back with a tiny half smile. He dropped one lid in a wink.

It was the best birthday she'd ever had.

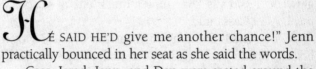

Fifteen

HE SAID HE'D give me another chance!" Jenn practically bounced in her seat as she said the words.

Cass, Jared, Jenn, and Dan were seated around the tiny table in the kitchen on Wednesday night enjoying Cass's special lasagna. Between Dan and Jared there was little room left under the table for Cass's knees. She wound her feet around her chair legs to keep them out of the way, just as she did at breakfast. At Jenn's excited words, she halted a forkful of lasagna on its way to her mouth and eyed her niece with suspicion.

"Who said he'd give you another chance?" But Cass was certain she knew the answer, and it didn't please her. She'd live happily ever after if that Smith boy never spoke to Jenn again.

"Derrick," Jenn breathed out his name like it was magic.

Jared looked at Dan and rolled his eyes. "Oh, brother."

Jenn blinked, focused, then snarled, "Butt out, Jared. My life is none of your business."

Seeing a family spat looming, Cass grabbed the basket filled with slices of crusty, garlic-adorned Italian bread. "Have another piece, Jared, Jenn. It won't keep well."

Jared, easily distracted by anything edible, took

two pieces of bread. Jenn sniffed and took one. Feeling like she'd just escaped a major war, Cass offered the basket to Dan.

"Thanks." He took a slice. "That was wonderful lasagna."

"I add slices of pepperoni." Cass looked at his empty plate. The man was a vacuum cleaner. He inhaled everything she served him at breakfast, too. "More?"

He nodded. "But I'll get it." He stood and walked to the pan resting on the stove.

"How about more for me, too?" Jared reached toward Dan, his empty plate in hand.

"He wants to take me to the movies Saturday night." Jenn glowed. "I said yes." She took a quick bite of salad. "Mmm. Great meal, Aunt Cassandra."

Cass stilled. Saturday night at the movies? Not if she could help it. But how could she keep Jenn away from Derrick without alienating the girl?

"What movie and where?" Cass asked, taking care to keep her voice curious, not censorious.

"Who cares?" Jenn looked dreamy again. "Anywhere with Derrick is okay with me."

"But not me. Until I know where you're going, I can't give my permission, Jenn." Cass felt her ingested pasta and tomatoes congealing into an acidic glob just below her ribs. "Surely you know that."

Immediately Jenn turned whiny. "You don't trust me."

Cass returned a suddenly unappetizing forkful of lasagna to her plate. "We've been there before, Jenn, and you're partly right. I don't trust him." She didn't think she trusted her niece either, at least not while she was under Derrick's influence, but she knew the wisdom of keeping that piece of intelligence to herself.

Dan and Jared continued to eat as if there was no life-defining conversation going on, their food disappearing at an alarming rate. Any minute now Cass expected them to pick up their plates and lick off the extra sauce.

Ill manners were so much easier to deal with than rebellious nieces.

"Why don't you and Derrick go to the movies with me and Jeannie?" Jared said around his last bite of bread.

Cass stared at him in amazement. She hadn't even thought he

was listening. Just proved that men could multitask after all.

Jenn blanched and made a face. Obviously the idea of double-dating with her brother was not to her liking.

Jared calmly ignored the mask of horror his sister wore. "I bet Aunt Cassandra would let you go that way."

Cass glanced gratefully at Jared. "You're right; I would."

"Can you stand spending the evening with three seniors, *little* sister?"

The girl's deer-in-the-headlights expression said it all. She was trapped, and she knew it.

"There are times, Jenn," Dan said, his last forkful of lasagna waving as he talked, "when it's wise to compromise." He shoveled in the last bite and chewed contentedly.

Jenn stared at her plate, deep in thought, undoubtedly looking for a way out of her dilemma. Finally, she sighed dramatically. "Oh, all right."

Nothing like a gracious loser.

"You do remember that you have a curfew of midnight, right?" Cass reminded her.

"What?" Angry color reddened Jenn's face.

"No problem." Jared put a hand over his sister's. "Midnight it is."

Jenn looked at her brother in disgust. He ignored her and scoured the table, then the kitchen for something more to eat.

"Thanks, Jared," Cass said, grateful all the way to her toes.

Jenn snorted. She grabbed her partially eaten dinner and dumped it unceremoniously down the garbage disposal. She stalked back to the table and piled Jared's and Dan's salad and dinner plates, then reached for Cass's plate. "Finished?" Her tone was belligerent.

Cass would have liked a second serving of the lasagna now that her stomach had uncoiled and if there was still some in the pan, which she doubted after watching Jared and Dan, but she just leaned back and watched her plate disappear into the dishwasher. Thank goodness for Corelle, or the abused dishes would have been a collection of shards littering the floor.

Reminder: Never let Jenn near the antique china when she's in a bad mood.

Jenn stomped back to the table and reached for Jared's glass. He stood and grabbed it first. "Why don't I take the glasses over? They might actually live until tomorrow that way." He quickly looped his fingers into the four tumblers.

Jenn growled something unintelligible and grabbed the silver. She dumped it in the basket, sloshed some detergent in the tiny cups, and slammed the dishwasher door closed. She locked it, pushed the correct button, and without a word headed to her room.

Off to sulk, Cass thought. Or to e-mail all her friends about how absolutely awful it was to be subject to someone like her old-fashioned, stick-in-the-mud aunt.

Cass looked at Dan. Poor man. Her dinner invitation was supposed to offer him congenial company to counter so much time spent alone. "Coffee?"

Dan nodded. "Sounds good."

"I didn't make any dessert." Cass grabbed the carafe from the coffeemaker and set it on a hot pad on the table. "I'll eat too much if I make it." She grabbed two mugs and looked questioningly at Jared who shook his head.

"No coffee for me. It'll stunt my growth."

"You get much taller, and you'll be bumping your head on doorjambs for the rest of your life," she said, turning toward the cupboard. She glanced over her shoulder at Dan. "I think I have some coffee cake left from breakfast if you want a slice."

"Uh, sorry." Jared opened the refrigerator and pulled out a liter bottle of Coke. "All gone." He reached over Cass's shoulder and took out a bag of pretzels. "I was hungry when I got home from practice."

Cass eyed him. "The snickerdoodles I made yesterday?"

Jared shrugged and grinned unrepentantly. "They were very good. Paulie thought so too. You should make some more soon."

"Only if you promise to leave me a dozen," Cass said.

"I'll try, but you know Paulie."

"Paulie, my eye."

He grinned again. "Got to hit the homework. See you." With books, Coke, and pretzels in hand, he disappeared upstairs.

Cass dropped into her seat and looked at Dan. "Did you eat like that when you were his age?"

Dan shrugged. "I don't remember, but I do remember my mother muttering about Andy and me eating them out of house and home."

They sat in silence, sipping their coffee. Then Cass's anger got the best of her.

"He's willing to give her another chance! Did you ever hear anything so, so…"

"Reprehensible?"

She looked at him and nodded emphatically. "Absolutely!" She stewed some more while he calmly sipped. "Why, look at Jenn. Any boy would be delighted to go out with her." Cass glared at Dan. "Right?"

He nodded. "She's cute as a bug's ear."

"Darn right she is. Cute and petite and pretty with wonderful hair and great eyes. She's just about perfect."

"Just about perfect." He took his mug to the sink and rinsed it. "What's a bug's ear look like anyway? Ever seen one?"

She ignored him. Derrick was the object of her ire, and she wouldn't allow herself to be distracted. "Stupid boy, too dumb to appreciate a treasure. I'd like to get my hands on him. Hurting my baby. Making her feel bad."

She felt Dan's gaze. "What?"

"Cass, it's only a temporary dating problem, not the end of the world."

"You've never been a sixteen-year-old girl."

"You've got *that* right."

"Believe me, it is the end of the world to be rejected, humiliated like she was."

He made a noise deep in his throat, and it sounded like disagreement to her. She glared at him, willing to spread the animosity around. "You're not still upset at her about her crack to me that first night, are you?"

He shook his head. "All forgiven and forgotten."

"Then what's wrong?"

"Nothing." He walked to the door leading back to the main part of the house. He turned. "I'm going for a walk. Want to come along?"

"Oh." Cass felt her cheeks go hot with pleasure and hoped it didn't show. Of course, she was sitting directly under the light over the table, so fat chance of that. "Trying to distract me?"

He nodded. "Is it working?"

She smiled. "Yes. I'd like to go for a walk." *With you.*

"Ten minutes?"

"Ten minutes," she repeated.

He gave a half smile, pushed the door open, then paused. He looked back at her over his shoulder, his eyes again intense. "You know, Jenn may be a cute little thing, but sometimes big is better."

Sometimes big is better?

Dan closed his eyes and considered batting his head against the wall as he went upstairs. Talk about inane! He pushed his arms into his jacket. *Will I ever get the art of compliments right?* He'd done okay at her birthday party; he was pretty sure of that. But tonight? That's what he got for feeling too confident.

Lord, conducting due diligence and advising about investments is a piece of cake compared to complimenting a woman, at least for me. Help!

One wonderful thing about figures, the monetary kind: You couldn't inadvertently insult them. They were what they were. But figures, the womanly kind, the beautiful kind, the Cass kind, well, that was a different story.

Sighing, he left his room and walked downstairs. He half expected Cass to stand him up. He deserved it; that was for certain. But she was there, bundled in a dark green fleece jacket that made her hazel eyes vivid and alive with deep, rich color. She'd put on some pink lipstick that made her smiling lips shiny, but otherwise her face was still free of cosmetics, still naturally beautiful.

He reached around her and opened the door. She stepped through; he followed. They moved down the front walk side by side. As always, Cass looked next door. Mr. Carmichael stood on his front porch in the dim light of a twenty-watt bulb by the door, glaring at the world. Both the man with his tatty suspenders holding up his baggy pants and the house with its cracked windows staring blankly gave Dan the heebie-jeebies.

"Hi, Mr. Carmichael," Cass called, waving, smiling.

He glowered her way but said nothing.

"Ready to sell yet?"

He moved his hand in a go-away motion. "Not to you, missy."

"Why not, Mr. Carmichael?" Dan asked, careful to sound

merely inquisitive instead of irked like the old wretch's attitude toward Cass made him feel.

Mr. Carmichael scowled, his wrinkled face taking on the look of a dried apple. "None of your business."

Dan nodded. Thoughtful, gracious answer. Typical of the man. "Well, maybe we can talk again later," Dan said easily and waved good-bye.

Mr. Carmichael snorted.

Sighing, Cass turned toward the boardwalk, away from the old man. "I wish I knew for sure what he has against me."

"You don't have any idea?"

"Well, I have an idea or two," Cass said. "Not that they make sense to me, but they might to him."

When she didn't continue, he prompted, "And they would be?"

"For one, maybe he's jealous of the time I gave the Eshelmans."

Jealousy and Mr. Carmichael were a mental stretch for Dan, but then he'd be the first to admit that he wasn't the best at understanding why people did things. He didn't even fully understand why he liked to hang around with Cass so much. If he couldn't figure out himself, how could he hope to comprehend a grump like Mr. Carmichael? "Who are the Eshelmans?"

"The old couple who used to own SeaSong back when it was just a big, old Victorian falling into ruin. When I was still teaching, I drove past the place every day driving to and from school. I stopped one day, introduced myself, and asked about buying the place. They told me no in no uncertain terms, but I liked them and hung around for two years as their friend." She smiled, pleasant memories obviously unrolling for her. "I'd stop in two or three days a week after school. Some days I'd bring dinner. I think those were the only days they ate properly."

He was struck by how deeply a part of her those care-giving instincts were. Not just her family but any in need benefited from knowing her.

"The Eshelmans didn't have any family and were very lonely, so they appreciated my visits. Mrs. Eshelman loved to talk. When she thought I might be coming, she'd watch the news all day so we could discuss it. She was this tiny, tiny lady who came to my waist and weighed about ninety pounds soaking wet. But she had heart and spirit and would have been an excellent foreign policy advisor for the president. Mr. Eshelman hated world affairs and loved to complain. When he wasn't yelling at her to speak up, he was ordering her to turn off the news." She laughed. "The first time he saw me, he said, 'Big one, aren't you? Flab or muscle?'"

Dan blinked. Hardly a polite or politic beginning to a friendship.

"He was this little man confined to bed, and he always said whatever came to mind. He drove his wife crazy, but I loved him almost as much as she did. And he loved me." Cass fell silent for a minute. "I miss them." She glanced back toward SeaSong. "I hope they'd like what I did to their home."

If they didn't, they were nuts, Dan thought. "What happened to them?"

"She fell down the steps and never regained consciousness." Cass's smile was sad. "I was with her when she died after three days in a coma. Mr. Eshelman died less than a month later. He had to go to a nursing home after her fall, and he just turned his face to the wall and died."

She glanced back toward Mr. Carmichael's place and sighed. "If he's not jealous, then maybe he thinks I somehow hoodwinked the Eshelmans into leaving me their house. He thinks I'm dishonorable."

"You? Never. He's just putting his own behavior patterns on you. He imagines you in there browbeating the Eshelmans until they signed on the dotted line because that's what he would do."

Cass shrugged. "Maybe. But I never knew their intentions concerning the house until after they died. When their lawyer called, I couldn't believe it. I am so grateful to them for their generosity. I certainly don't expect the same from Mr. Carmichael. I've offered him a fair price."

Dan looked at her, saw the frustration and sorrow that washed over her. "You really want that place, don't you?"

"I'll live if I don't get it, but I'd rather get it and live in it."

"What? You want to live there?" He turned and studied the place again, walking backward a few paces. He saw not one saving feature on the whole ugly building. "Why, for Pete's sake?"

Cass stuck her hands in her jacket pockets. "A bit more privacy, but I'd be close enough to handle any problems that might arise at SeaSong. It'd also open up the back bedrooms at SeaSong that I've kept for my use."

"More privacy and more income." He nodded. "But will the extra income pay for the house and its renovation? And where would you start with a place that's so derelict? Or do you want to tear it down and build new? I think I'd tear it down."

"You wouldn't!" Cass looked at him, appalled.

"Cass, be practical. The place is a wreck. Carmichael hasn't done anything on upkeep for years!"

"That doesn't mean there's not a fine house buried in the ruin."

"Tear it down."

Cass shook her head. "Absolutely not." Her look turned dreamy. "I've got all kinds of sketches of what I'd like to do with the place. And estimates of cost. I'm collecting furniture for the place at estate sales and flea markets. I've already refinished some of it. I found the most wonderful old headboard at a place up in New Hope. I know I paid too much—after all, it's New Hope— but it's wonderful."

Dan, who knew nothing about New Hope and had never gotten excited about a headboard in his life, nodded. He decided to keep this conversation practical. "What happens when old Carmichael dies? Has he got family who might be sympathetic to your cause?"

"No one. He's absolutely alone, just like the Eshelmans. That's one of the reasons I try to be nice to him." She sighed. "He's going to die intestate, and some builder will probably come along and offer the bank or whoever a stupendous price that I could never match."

Dan thought she was probably right, but he wisely didn't say so. "If that's the likely scenario, did you ever think that you might be wasting your time with all your planning?"

She shrugged. "Sure, but why not? I enjoy it. Then, too, there's my secret weapon."

He looked at her, raising an eyebrow.

She gave a humorous little snort. "Mr. Carmichael might not know it, but he's the target of a prayer campaign, one I've been waging for four years."

"Four years? You've been praying for that grumpy old man for four years?"

"Sure," she said easily. "I don't know God's timetable."

A terrible thought struck Dan broadside. *Lord, I don't know Your timetable either. Please tell me that slowly, steadily, surely doesn't mean four years!*

They reached the boardwalk, moved up the ramp, and turned north, the far lights of Atlantic City visible in the distance.

"Oh, look. There's Johnson's Popcorn," she said, just like she'd made a great discovery. "Let's get a tub."

He followed her, ordered the big tub, and paid for it. The man behind the counter handed it to Cass who eyed with delight the mound of caramel corn, heaped well above the rim of the tub. The man gave Dan the lid. Cass all but purred as she took her first fistful. They began walking again.

"Think you'll share?" he asked with a smile.

She wrapped both arms around the container, her expression possessive. "Do I have to?" Then she grinned, her enchanting face lighting up. She held out the tub. He took a handful of the caramel corn, still warm and crisp.

"Dessert," he said as the rich taste filled his mouth. "Delicious."

They walked in companionable silence for a while, their only noise the crunch of the popcorn. Dan thought about the things he'd learned about Cass. She was a single woman who had followed her dream—developing, marketing, and running SeaSong. That was quite a feat for anyone. She took in her niece and nephew at no small inconvenience, and she seemed to have most of the family responsibility for watching over her parents.

Their hands bumped as they both reached for more popcorn. Dan grinned at her. "You're one smart lady, you know that?"

She looked at him in surprise, her skepticism as obvious as the sand on the beach. "What brought that on?"

He watched her for a minute as she ate the popcorn. "You don't do well with compliments, do you?"

Cass, looking self-conscious, shrugged. "I'm not used to them."

Dan thought of her family who obviously loved her but treated her with a casualness that bothered him. "Your family doesn't compliment you very often, do they?"

She wouldn't look at him. "They love me."

"Yes, they do, but they don't compliment you or encourage you, do they?"

Her "no" was such a soft, sad whisper that the wind almost blew it away. She walked to the railing and stopped, looking out at the ocean, at the ripples of white indicating the breaking waves in the night-blackened water.

Dan took the popcorn from her and snapped the lid on. He rested his arms on the railing beside her and waited to see if she'd say more. He counted fifteen waves breaking before she spoke.

"I think a lot of my problem comes from being the youngest. The brothers were always telling me what I should and shouldn't do, teasing me, making my life fun and miserable in equal measures. And they were always so big!"

Dan imagined a little blond girl, ponytail flying, trying to keep up with the big boys, trying to measure up to their standards.

She wrapped her hands around the railing and leaned back, her arms stretched straight. "We were all athletic, playing any sport we could. I was one of the first girls to play in the local Little League. The brothers always told me I was as good as the boys my age or better." She shrugged. "That was true most of the time because I was always so big, so developed, especially in junior high where the girls mature faster than the guys."

Now Dan saw a lithesome blonde, legs stretching to the sky, racing down a basketball court, shooting over the heads of the short guys and barreling over the slight ones.

"I hated being so big." Again, if Dan hadn't been listening carefully, the words would have been lost, this time in the muted roar of the sea. "If I'd been thin like a model, it might not have been so bad, but I was built then like I am now."

"What's wrong with the way you are now?"

She slanted her eyes at him but didn't answer.

"I happen to like the way you are now," he said. "I probably would have liked the way you were then, even if I'd needed a stepladder to talk to you."

"What?"

"I was a runt," he said. "I hated that. My memory of junior high is turning around and bumping into all the girls' knees, I was so little."

Cass stepped back and looked at him in disbelief.

He raised his hand. "True, so help me."

"Well, you certainly caught up."

"But not until my senior year in high school. I was five four in September and six two by June. That whole year I never had any clothes that fit, and my legs ached all the time. And I was so skinny they could have put me in one of those pictures for starving children. All I needed was a fly sitting in the corner of my eye. That was undoubtedly the year my mother said I was eating her out of house and home."

"Did they make fun of you?" she asked in a tone that let him know they'd made fun of her.

"Did they ever. *Runt* was one of the kinder names."

"*BB* was mine."

He nodded. "Your brother called you that on Sunday. What does it stand for?"

She looked out at the ocean again and cleared her throat before she spoke. "Big Bottom."

He flinched. "Ouch."

"Double ouch. My brothers started calling me that when I was about eight. They wouldn't tell me what it meant for years. They finally confessed when I was thirteen. Thirteen! I was devastated."

Still are, Dan thought, and he couldn't blame her. "Next time one of them uses those initials, think of them meaning Beautiful Blonde."

"Right." Her tone was dry.

He grinned. "If that won't work, then tell them to stop."

Her look was pure incredulity. "My brothers? Stop?"

"Cass, they're not going to stop seeing you as their little sister until you make them. You've got to speak up for yourself."

She snorted. "A lot you know." She turned back to the boardwalk and home. "Can I have some popcorn, please?" She took the tub and started walking, the tub tucked under her arm like a football.

He walked beside her, thinking about the intricacies of family.

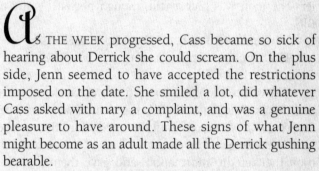

 $\mathcal{C}$ s THE WEEK progressed, Cass became so sick of hearing about Derrick she could scream. On the plus side, Jenn seemed to have accepted the restrictions imposed on the date. She smiled a lot, did whatever Cass asked with nary a complaint, and was a genuine pleasure to have around. These signs of what Jenn might become as an adult made all the Derrick gushing bearable.

"Derrick looked so nice today in that bright blue sweater that made his eyes sooo blue," Jenn burbled as she set the dinner table Thursday. "And he walked me home, Aunt Cassandra! All the way to my corner, and he lives in the opposite direction!"

Cass tried to look properly impressed and was certain she was failing. Jenn didn't seem to notice, thank goodness.

And Friday evening as she looked at herself in the small mirror hanging on the inside of the door to Cass's understairs bedroom, Jenn said, "Derrick passed me a note in the hall, and it said I looked pretty today!"

Cass nodded. "You always look pretty, sweetheart."

Jenn nodded absently as she leaned in to check her impeccable eye makeup. "Thanks, but you're supposed to say that. You're my aunt. But Derrick…" The sentence dwindled away as Jenn's eyes lost focus over thoughts of the object of her affections.

"When do I get to meet this wonderful person?" Cass watched with interest as Jenn blanched.

After a minute of what could only be described as panic, Jenn blurted, "I've gotta go up and do my homework. Bye!"

"On a Friday?" Cass called after her.

The bell on the registration desk rang, and Cass put her innkeeper's welcoming smile back on. She pushed open the door, and there was Dan, luggage in hand, making small talk with the couple waiting to register. He was looking up as he spoke, an experience that must be very unusual for him. The woman was at least four inches taller than his six-four and several pounds heavier. The man was bigger still, though not fat by any means. Just BIG.

"Mr. and Mrs. Patchett," Dan said to Cass.

The Patchetts smiled sweetly at Cass, their faces open and excited.

"We've been looking forward to this weekend for a very long time," Mrs. Patchett said. "We heard such wonderful things about SeaSong that we waited until we could afford the very best."

"We're so glad you can be with us." Cass returned their smiles, took their credit information, and gave them their keys, all the while disoriented at feeling like a pygmy, and an underfed one at that. "If there is anything we can do, don't hesitate to ask."

Cass pointed to the binder resting on the breakfront in the common room. "That's the notebook listing all the local restaurants and activities that are open this time of the year."

"Thank you," Mr. Patchett said. "Your husband has already been telling us about all the things here in Seaside." He nodded at Dan who looked only slightly surprised at his elevation to husband status.

Cass smiled through her blush, knowing an explanation of her relationship with Dan would embarrass the Patchetts more than Dan and her. "Yes, he enjoys helping folks." Besides, how was she to explain a guest who played bellhop?

As the Patchetts turned toward the stairs, Dan looked at her, startled by her comment. "I do?"

"Sure you do," she said softly. "You're always helping around here."

He shook his head like he was having trouble with the idea.

"And I thought I was just bored."

"Well, there's no denying that, too, but lots of bored people never help. They gripe. They turn griping into an art form. You don't gripe. You help. You've got the gift of helping."

He still looked shell-shocked at the thought. "No one's ever told me that before."

She shrugged. "That doesn't mean I'm wrong." She grinned. "It means that others weren't as perceptive as I am."

He grinned back. "Maybe." He grabbed the two large duffels and trailed the giants upstairs.

As Cass watched the Patchetts ascend the steps, both of them turning their feet sideways to fit on the treads, she felt something close to panic. These people, nice as they were, were too big for the beds. Even one of them was too big, let alone both of them. All SeaSong beds were queen-sized; none of the rooms was large enough for a king. How would the Patchetts ever fit? How would they ever manage to sleep? How would the beds ever make it through the night?

Reminder: Pray all night that nothing breaks.

Dan came downstairs, a bemused expression on his face. "I have never as an adult felt so small."

"Did they like their room?" Cass asked anxiously. "Were they expecting a larger bed? The website says queens. So do the flyers."

"They seemed very pleased. She said the room was beautiful, even lovelier than the pictures. She sat on the bed and said it was very comfortable."

Cass shook her head. "Dan, you know I'm sensitive to size, being so big myself, and I'm sure the Patchetts are lovely people, but—"

"You don't think they'll fit," Dan finished for her. "I often have that trouble myself."

"Yes. That's it exactly. They're longer than the bed is. They're wider than the bed is, especially together." Another terrible thought crossed her mind. "Will the tub and the toilet hold them? What if they crash through the floor and get hurt? What if their weight somehow causes a water line to rupture? What—"

She slid to a stop for two reasons. Dan was laughing so hard his eyes were tearing, and four weekend guests came through the door. After the Patchetts, they seemed like Lilliputians, though

Cass was fairly certain they were regular-sized people.

Cass felt great relief when she awoke the next morning and realized the Patchetts had passed the night without any unfortunate situations developing. As she prepared breakfast, she made half again as much coffee cake as she'd planned, and she automatically gave the Patchetts two orders each of eggs Benedict drenched in her own famous hollandaise sauce. All through the meal she kept listening for the thunder of a dining room chair giving way, causing a Patchett to tumble. The idea of such an accident upset Cass for several reasons, the primary one being the potential embarrassment or hurt to her oversize guests.

When Brenna reported an empty dining room, meaning breakfast was over, Cass sighed. She collapsed into her own chair for coffee and eggs Benedict with Dan and the kids.

"Only eight more hours," Jenn said dreamily.

Cass started. She had actually forgotten about Derrick for a time. For that alone, she ought to offer the Patchetts a free weekend.

Brenna looked at Jenn's fatuous expression. "Jenn, don't be so obvious. It's not a good move. Don't fall into his arms too easily. Let him think he's got to work for you."

Don't fall into his arms at all! Cass thought as she chewed her last bite of eggs. *Please. I don't think I could take it. I'm not used to this mothering stuff.*

Jenn looked at Brenna with great interest. "Did you make Mike work for you?"

Brenna nodded. "We were friends for three or four months before I agreed to date him."

Jenn looked horrified. "Three or four months? That's forever!"

"Important decisions need time," Brenna said. "And sometimes you still wonder if you did right." She said the last quietly and to her plate.

"What?" Jenn squeaked, her acute hearing having no trouble with Brenna's muttered comment. Her Seaside green and gold fingernail pointed at Brenna. "Of course you did right! I know you did."

Brenna looked amused. "You do, huh?"

Jenn grabbed Brenna's hand. "Tell me you're not thinking of breaking up with Mike. You can't! He loves you."

Brenna studied Jenn with interest. "Why do you say that?"

Cass rested her chin in her palm, fascinated by the girls' conversation. Even Dan awaited the answer to the last question.

Jenn looked stumped for a minute, but only a minute. "He looks at you."

Brenna leaned back in her chair and crossed her arms. "He *looks* at me?"

"Yeah, you know. Like he follows you with his eyes."

Brenna frowned.

"At Aunt Cassandra's party, whenever you got up from the table, he watched you the whole time. It's like he can't let you out of his sight. It's so romantic! And he's always touching you, holding your hand, putting his arm around your shoulders, patting your leg." Jenn sighed. "It's wonderful."

More than once Cass felt like rolling her eyes at Jenn's overly romanticized view of love, but she had to agree that Mike did watch Brenna. He did touch her all the time. That Sunday when the pair had sat in front of her in church, Cass had noticed his preoccupation with Brenna, his attention to her rather than the Word. Did all this caring mean affection or an unhealthy desire to control? Or maybe he was just concerned over her recent melancholy, much as Cass herself was, and he showed it in his own way.

"It's wonderful," Jenn repeated dreamily.

Brenna fell quiet at Jenn's words, her face a study of conflicting emotions. She began to rub her arms like she was chilled in spite of the denim shirt and navy cardigan she wore with her khakis.

Suddenly Dan spoke. "He's a very nice young man, Brenna, but don't stay with him if you're not certain."

All three females turned to him as one. He looked from one to the other, obviously unnerved by the unanticipated scrutiny. "Well, marriage is forever. If she doesn't love him, now's the time to bail." His voice was mildly defensive.

"But he loves her," Jenn wailed.

Dan shrugged. "The question is: Does she love him?"

They all turned to Brenna who looked as unnerved under the stares as Dan had.

Cass decided it was time to change the topic before Brenna felt pilloried. "Brenna, I wrote your work assignments down. I think the paper is lying on the counter by the refrigerator."

Brenna jumped from her chair and hurried to grab the list.

"Start with the Patchetts' room," Cass continued. Brenna smiled though the smile didn't reach her eyes. "They're such nice people. When I served them, they were always thanking me. When they weren't thanking me or eating, they were staring at each other."

Jenn bounced with enthusiasm. "Like Mike stares at you! Like I hope Derrick will look at me."

Cass shuddered at the thought, though she wasn't against a few such stares for herself from Dan.

"Do you think they're on their honeymoon or something?" Brenna asked.

"Well, I think they're just lucky to have found someone their own size," Jenn said as she grabbed all the dishes from the table, slapped them in the dishwasher, added detergent, and banged the door shut. The muted rush of water into the machine sounded. With a furtive glance at her aunt, she dashed upstairs before Cass could give her any more jobs.

"Brenna." Cass looked over her shoulder as she wiped the kitchen counters, a part of cleanup Jenn routinely ignored.

The girl paused at the swinging door.

"If anyone needs me, I'll be out in the patio area getting things put away for winter."

"Need some help?" Dan asked. He looked gorgeous in his jeans and navy long-sleeved T-shirt.

Cass didn't know what to say. Sure, she wanted help, especially his, but he was a guest. "I'm going to have to start paying you instead of the other way around. You don't have to do anything. You're our guest."

"Your bored guest." He held his hands out in appeal. "Please. After all, someone told me recently that I like to help." He gave her a goofy grin as he rehearsed her words back at her.

Cass shook her head at him. "Guy, you've got to get yourself a real job!" She pulled her rattiest sweatshirt over her head.

A flash of emotions passed over his face—frustration, anger, impatience, resignation. "Tell me about it." Then he grinned. "But you can keep me off the streets today."

Cass pulled the back door open. "If you want to work, who am I to turn down the help? Sure, come on."

She gave him the pressure sprayer filled with a strong solution of detergent and bleach. "Every nook and cranny," she ordered, pointing to the four shower stalls used by guests for rinsing sand and seawater off after a day at the beach.

Dan eyed the first stall with its wooden door and its slatted floor for runoff. "Looks pretty clean to me."

Cass gasped and clutched her heart. "Pretty clean doesn't cut it, sir. This is SeaSong."

Dan grinned. "Yes, boss."

"And if you splash yourself, rinse off right away. The solution's awfully strong. And rinse down each stall with clear water after the bleach spray."

Cass herself took a sudsy solution and washed down all the outdoor furniture. Then she carefully rinsed it with the hose and dried it with old towels. She was carrying a wicker rocker to the shed when Dan lifted it from her arms.

"Just show me where."

By noon work that would have taken Cass multiple days was done.

She glanced at Dan, his navy shirt sporting a couple of quarter-sized bleach spots as well as several smaller ones. His hair stood on end where he had run a wet hand through it. His sneakers were drenched, as were his socks and the bottoms of his jeans, from hosing the showers down after the bleach. He looked wonderful. He *was* wonderful.

"Thank you!" She looked at the clean showers and glanced at the locked shed with its cache of furniture. "I can't believe we got so much done."

Oh, how I could get used to help like this.

Yeah, if you're an idiot. He's not staying.

Maybe he will.

In your dreams.

Maybe the Lord won't tell him his new plans for a long, long time.

A long time or tomorrow, it doesn't matter. If you don't watch yourself, you're going to be hurt big time. I repeat. He's not staying.

Cass shut her eyes for a brief moment to let that unpalatable truth sink in. Jesus, she reminded herself. He was enough. He had been for years, and He would be again.

So why did she feel so hollow inside?

Dan rubbed his hands together. "I haven't had a chance to do much physical labor in years, so it was fun. What do we do this afternoon?"

"Go watch Jared play."

Cass smothered a smile as Dan manfully swallowed his dismay. "Sure." He even attempted a smile. "Why not?"

Knowing she had essentially trapped him, she said, "Come on. The least I can do is give you a sandwich."

Jared played well, and Seaside won by ten points. Cass cheered and screamed and had a wonderful time. Dan sat quietly beside her at first, but as the game heated up, so did his involvement. Before the end of the first half, he was hollering as loudly as she was.

When they left the football field after congratulating Jared and Paulie and the other team members, they turned toward the boardwalk. They didn't talk, content just to enjoy the crisp autumn day.

Cass had on her deep green fleece jacket over a cinnamon sweater. She held her face to the brisk breeze, a smile on her lips. "I love autumn."

"That's because it's your birthday time, and you get presents."

Cass smiled wryly. "Magazine subscriptions and Home Depot gift certificates. So personal."

He grinned sympathetically. "Poor Cass. But don't forget the flowers and the dinner party."

"As if I could." She still felt like singing every time she thought of all he—they—had done. "And there's my bracelet." She held out her arm so he could see it. As the sunlight glinted off the butterfly disk, she didn't bother to tell him that she hadn't taken it off since she'd gotten it.

"So why else do you love autumn?"

"I love autumn because it's a time for dreams," she said. "A time for wondering and longing and stretching." She looked at him. "I first approached the people about SeaSong in the autumn."

He nodded. "And look at me. Here I am in autumn, waiting for God's leading."

"Do you dream about where He's going to take you?"

"I don't even have enough imagination to know where to start wondering, let alone feeling anything as magical as a hope and a dream."

"Nothing's so sweet as autumn dreams," she said. "They're the ones that come true."

"Always?"

She was suddenly uncertain. "I first thought of buying the house next door in the autumn. That's one dream that might not make it."

They angled across the boardwalk and sat on one of the benches that looked across the beach to the ocean. On the horizon, great ships looking like bathtub toys carried their cargoes on mysterious journeys, their smokestacks sending gray plumes into the brilliant blue sky.

"Where do you think they're going?" She pointed to the ships.

But Dan was looking at her, not the ships, his gaze intense.

"What?" she said, suddenly self-conscious. "Spinach in my teeth?"

"Have I told you how lovely you look today? That jacket makes your eyes so green."

"Dan!" She couldn't believe he'd just blurted such a thing out. She stood, looking everywhere but at him. "You've got to stop that."

"Stop what?" He stood and leaned on the rail beside her.

"You can't go around saying things like that."

"Like what?" He cocked his head at her, daring her to answer the question.

She flushed. "You know. What you just said."

"What did I just say?"

"You know."

He furrowed his brow as if in thought. "I've said a lot of things."

She finally looked at him, her exasperation overcoming her shyness. "You're going to make me say it, aren't you?"

He grinned. "Yep."

She looked away, frowning. "It's not nice to embarrass people."

"It's not nice to dismiss people's compliments either." He spoke quietly, but his words were full of emotion.

Her mouth dropped open, and she spun to him. "What?"

"You heard me. When someone pays you a compliment that he clearly means, you are not supposed to brush it off. You're supposed to smile and say thank you."

She flushed again, her eyes skittering away from his. "So you told me before."

"I'm new at trying to say the right thing, Cass. If I can learn to speak, you can learn to accept." He reached his hand to her chin and made her look at him. "Believe me when I say this: You are beautiful."

Cassandra looked at him, confused, stunned, amazed. She searched his eyes. *He means it. He honestly thinks I'm pretty. Dan thinks I'm pretty.*

No one had thought her pretty in years, if ever. Oh, the nephews dutifully said, "You look very pretty, Aunt Cassandra," at the wedding of yet another person years younger than she. Sometimes one of the brothers said, "Very handsome, Cassandra."

Handsome. Like one of the guys. Now there was a compliment.

But Dan had just said, "Cass, you are beautiful."

The wind had been playing wildly with her hair, her nose was bright red from the sun, and she weighed more than she should. Still, when he had looked at her, his eyes darkened, his lips parted, and he said the magic words, "You are beautiful."

And suddenly, she felt beautiful. "Thank you," she whispered, wondering if he saw the joy that leapt in her eyes.

He dropped her chin and stood close, his shoulder pressed tightly against hers as they leaned on the rail

"Why have you never married?" he asked, his eyes on shops across the boardwalk.

His unexpected question shocked the truth out of her. "No one has ever asked."

He shook his head. "The men in New Jersey certainly are a foolish bunch."

Her pulse raced and her mouth went dry at this new, oblique compliment. *Dear Lord, I'm too old for this, too inexperienced. Not that I'm complaining.*

"You're telling me there's never been a man wise enough to love you?"

Cass shrugged. "There was Glenn in college. I thought maybe he was the one."

"But you decided he wasn't?"

"I think it was mutual. I decided he was a wimp and he decided I was a tartar."

Dan grinned. "You're that all right."

Somehow he made it sound like another compliment. She

grinned wryly. "To my mother's everlasting dismay."

"Listen, Cassie, there's nothing wrong with being a strong woman."

"No." Cass spoke without thinking, the bitterness and hurt seeping out. "It's being a *big,* strong woman that's the sin."

Dan reached out and put an arm around her shoulders, giving her a hug. "I personally like a woman of substance, both in character and size. I've never understood men's attraction to cute little things or anorexic models. When I hug someone, I want to feel a real woman in my arms, not a skinny, little person who will break if I squeeze her."

Cass ducked her head. "Well, I won't break, that's for sure." It was barely a whisper. All she could think was how much she wanted him to hug her, really hug her. Right now. Right here on the boardwalk.

They stood quietly, she tucked to his side, the air between them charged. Cass's heart galloped, and her shoulders tingled where his arm rested on them. When he leaned down and kissed her temple, her eyes slid shut. The longing for more from this man was a physical ache in her chest.

A pair of seagulls squawked overhead. Cass and Dan blinked and looked up to watch their fight for position on the lamppost nearby, and the tension between them was broken. He removed his arm and gave her an awkward little pat on the back. She smiled self-consciously. They both became busy watching the people walking on the boardwalk.

"Hey," Dan said. "Isn't that Brenna?"

Cass followed his line of vision and saw the girl go to a public phone at the top of the boardwalk ramp. She dialed a number, listened for a few moments, then hung up without speaking.

"Look! She's done it again!" Cass couldn't believe it.

"I'd like to know what she's listening to," Dan said. "Somehow I don't think it's the correct time or a prayer for the day."

They watched from across the boardwalk as Brenna walked slowly from the phone, head down, wiping ineffectively at the tears washing her cheeks.

"Tears like falling leaves," said Cass. "Shattered autumn dreams. But why?"

Seventeen

HOW MANY TIMES recently had he picked up the receiver and heard nothing? Five? Ten? At first he'd assumed it was some pervert breathing hard, but he changed his mind. The calls didn't come in the middle of the night like the nutty ones usually did. They came at odd hours with no pattern, and they all came from the same 800 number, displayed in digital numerals on the caller ID he kept in his room. No pervert had an 800 number.

Against all good sense, he'd begun to consider Sherri. In fact, he'd called the mysterious number two days ago to see what he could learn.

"SeaSong Bed-and-Breakfast," some chirpy lady answered.

Bed-and-breakfast? What would Sherri be doing there? And where was there?

"Hello. I saw an ad for the SeaSong, but I can't remember exactly where it's located," he said. "My wife and I are thinking of coming, but we need directions."

"Seaside is very near Atlantic City," the woman said. "Where are you coming from? Philadelphia? New York?"

"Near Atlantic City? New Jersey?" Visions of Miss America rose.

"Yes." She sounded as though that was more than obvious.

"Then I'm fine with directions. All I need is my trusty map. See you." And he hung up.

Seaside, New Jersey. No way was a pervert going to call California from New Jersey just to breathe hard. Sherri? And why didn't she say something? He pondered the riddle and could find no satisfactory answers.

He'd had a late night last night and slept in. He had only a slight hangover headache, thank goodness, but his stomach gurgled with need. He couldn't remember if he'd had any dinner last night, or if he'd just drunk the night away. He shrugged carefully, not wanting to jiggle his head. Who cared anyway? He pulled on jeans and a T-shirt and left his bedroom without bothering to shave or brush his hair. Saturdays were for relaxing, even if Hank did call it indolence. He was a millionaire now. He could be and do anything he wanted. Scratching his empty stomach, he wandered into the dining room, late for lunch.

Was it Sherri who was calling and not speaking? It was the question of the hour. As if his thinking caused it to happen, the phone on the sideboard rang.

Patsi, semialert for once, picked up before Tuck could beat her to it.

"Hello?" She waited. "Hello. Is anyone there?" She pulled the receiver from her ear and stared at it as if she could tell by looking who was calling. She glanced at Hank. "The line's open, but no one's talking." Then her face blanched, and her eyes went wide. "Sherri." Patsi's voice was a whisper, half hope, half fear.

A chill climbed Tuck's spine. Why couldn't it be a pervert? He'd rather have a pervert any day.

Patsi slapped the phone back on her ear. "Sherri? Is that you? Sherri? Speak to me, darling. Tell me you're all right. Tell me where you are. We'll come get you. I-I love you, Sherri. We love you. Please come home." She started to sob so hard she could hardly talk. She shook from head to foot.

Hank rushed to his wife, his face taut with concern. "Don't do this to yourself, Patsi." He reached for the phone, but Patsi stood, stepping away from him.

"No, Hank. It's Sherri. I know it is."

"Patsi, don't." Hank looked about to cry.

"Sherri," she screamed into the receiver. "Don't go! Please, don't go!"

Tuck watched Hank and Patsi, his heart accelerating. His eyes narrowed as he saw what he now considered his second million disappearing.

Stay lost, Sherri! Stay dead!

Hank trailed Patsi, the phone still clamped to her ear, until she was backed against the wall. Then he grabbed the receiver and held it to his ear, listening. He shook his head and set it in the cradle.

"She was there. I know she was!" Patsi covered her face with trembling hands.

Hank reached for his sobbing wife. He grasped her hands and pulled them down, winding them around his own waist. Her face, already bloated from antidepressants and lack of exercise, was blotched from crying, and Hank looked old and haggard. He gathered her in his arms and held her while Tuck watched with dispassionate curiosity.

"I've got to take her to the bedroom and get her a sedative," Hank told Tuck as he led her away. He never took his eyes off her.

Tuck watched them leave. Then he raced to his room and checked the Caller ID.

When Sherri first disappeared, the police tapped their phones, ready to trace any calls that asked for a ransom. Hank was a wealthy man, and a ransom demand seemed a logical expectation. To everyone's surprise, no such calls came, and Tuck became convinced that Sherri and her boyfriend had been waylaid by some crazy and killed.

At times he found it in himself to wonder what she might have gone through, though when he carefully examined how he felt, it was more curiosity about what might have happened than distress that she might have suffered.

He checked the readout on the Caller ID that he'd bought after the police had moved out, taking their equipment with them. It wasn't the 800 number. It was a new number with the 609 area code. Making certain his door was closed so his father couldn't hear, he dialed the number. It rang and rang. Finally someone answered. "Yeah, what do you want?"

"Is this the SeaSong?"

"Huh? What's a sea song?"

"I may have a wrong number. Can you tell me who I've reached?"

"This is Ricky, man. I was just walking by."

"Walking by what?"

"The phone." Ricky was getting peeved. "What'd you think I was walking by?"

Tuck could hear noise in the background, but he couldn't distinguish anything specific until a voice yelled, "Come on, Ricky! We're not waiting any longer."

"Shut up," Ricky roared back. "I'm coming."

"Hey, Ricky," Tuck yelled before Ricky hung up on him. "Tell me exactly where this phone is. Please, man."

"Well." Ricky was silent for a minute.

"Yo, Ricky! Are you still there?" Tuck asked, afraid he'd lost his connection.

"I'm looking for the street sign, man. Give me a break here. I'm trying to help."

"Oh, sorry," Tuck forced the words between clenched teeth. He hated to apologize to anyone, let alone a buffoon like Ricky. He could just imagine the body piercings and tattoos.

"This is the phone at Tenth and the boardwalk, and I gotta go." The receiver slammed.

Tuck hung up. Tenth and the boardwalk where? Seaside where the SeaSong was? Tuck went to his computer and called up the Seaside, New Jersey site. He scanned the list of B&Bs in town; they all had the 609 area code.

He lay on his bed thinking. Was Patsi right? Was it Sherri calling? He sat bolt upright as a terrible premonition barreled into him. Sherri was getting ready to come in out of the cold. She missed her mama, poor little girl, and wanted to come home.

Well, not if he could help it, she wasn't. He began planning an immediate trip to Seaside, New Jersey.

To the SeaSong.

Eighteen

JENN WAS SO excited and nervous that she felt sick to her stomach. Derrick would be here any minute now. She closed her eyes and breathed deeply.

How did she get to be so lucky?

He was the handsomest guy in the senior class. He was funny and popular and smart. All the girls wanted to go out with him. She still couldn't believe he had picked her, especially after the party mess. Aunt Cassandra hadn't made this date any easier either.

"She wants to meet you." Jenn had told Derrick yesterday at school.

He looked at her as if she was crazy. "No way. I'll beep the horn so you know I'm there. That's what I always do."

Jenn's palms went all sweaty. She wiped them on the seat of her jeans. "You have to come to the door."

He did not look thrilled, and Jenn thought she might hyperventilate. After all, he already had more than enough reason to resent Aunt Cassandra.

"It'll only take a minute." She felt like she was begging.

Derrick watched Marge Jacobs walk by with more than a little interest.

"Hi, Derrick," she purred.

Jenn looked away, knowing this was his way of reminding her that she was the fortunate one. There were lots of others if she became too much trouble.

Derrick turned back to her. "Look, Jenn—"

She broke in. "She's just not used to being a parent." Jenn's eyes pleaded for his understanding. Even though he was absolutely the most wonderful guy in the world, he was also very touchy. "Please. Do it for me. It's only this once."

He just looked at her for a long minute. He hadn't exactly sneered at her request, but it had been close. His nod had been abrupt and unenthusiastic. "I don't like being told what to do."

He was so annoyed, she hadn't been able to bring herself to tell him about Aunt Cassandra's other requirements for their date. With only minutes until he arrived, Jenn stood with her hand pressed to her stomach to ease the swirling discomfort. What would he do when he found out they were going with Jared and Jeannie? Or that she had to be home by midnight?

She shuddered and pushed those worries to the back of her mind. She would concentrate on how she looked. This problem she could control.

She glanced in the little mirror on Aunt Cassandra's door. Maybe she should change again. Maybe the red sweater with the falling leaves knit in it was too dressy with her jeans. Maybe she should go put on that plain black shirt and her black stretch slacks. Or was that too edgy, like she was going to dye her hair blue or something? How about the yellow top? It was bright and happy but not too wild.

Jared thudded down the back stairs and into the kitchen wearing his jeans and a Seaside sweatshirt.

"Ready, kiddo?" he asked Jenn. "You look nice."

She was thrilled he thought so, even if he was only her brother. She nodded, not certain she could speak without sounding breathless.

The doorbell rang.

Jenn froze. She swallowed convulsively. So much was at stake in the next few minutes. It had to go right. It had to!

She felt a gentle push from behind.

"You need to let him in," Jared said.

Jenn nodded, forcing herself forward. She had to get to him before Aunt Cassandra. She pushed the swinging door open and went into the entry hall. What she saw made her blood run cold.

Derrick stood there, handsome and solemn, surrounded by Aunt Cassandra and Dan. At least it looked like surrounded, they were so big. Derrick was slight and not quite as tall as Aunt Cassandra. Jenn thought of him as lean and elegant, like a tiger prowling the jungle. He didn't need bulk like Dan and Jared and her father. He commanded just by his presence.

"I've been looking forward to meeting you," Aunt Cassandra said to him, offering her hand.

"Yeah, me too," he said as he shook. Jenn was proud of him. He managed to look as if he actually meant it.

"I'm sure Jenn told you she has a midnight curfew," Aunt Cassandra continued.

"Uh, sure." Derrick threw Jenn a bland glance, but his left brow was raised like it was when he was scornful or mocking.

She closed her eyes in embarrassment.

"But then I know you and Jared will see that she gets here on time." Aunt Cassandra gave an insincere smile. Dan just stood beside her and loomed.

"Jared?" Derrick said, frowning.

"We'll be waiting up for her, of course," Aunt Cassandra continued.

"Right there." Dan pointed to the common room.

Let me die right now, Jenn thought. *I can't stand it!*

"Of course," Derrick agreed, eyeing Dan uncertainly. Jenn could almost hear him wondering who in the world Dan was.

"Hey, Derrick," Jared said easily, pushing Jenn before him.

"Ah, here she is now." Aunt Cassandra slipped an arm around Jenn's shoulders.

Jenn smiled at Derrick, ignoring her aunt's arm as best she could. "Hi." She tried to sound perky, no easy task when she'd never been so mortified, so terrified in her life.

Derrick opened his mouth, but Jared took that moment to slap him on the back. "We'd better get going. Jeannie's expecting us."

Derrick stumbled a bit under the blow but recovered quickly. "Jeannie?"

"Jeannie Stanley. You know her, don't you?"

"Well, sure. With the names Smith and Stanley, we always sit near each other. We have since kindergarten."

"Good." Jared jingled the keys to Aunt Cassandra's car. "Let's go. We don't want to be late. We might miss the coming attractions. I love the coming attractions."

"We're double dating," Jenn said, trying again for perky. "Won't that be fun?"

She shouldn't have asked. The thundercloud eyes he turned on her made it very clear what he thought. She fought to keep her chin from wobbling.

Aunt Cassandra and Dan walked out onto the porch with them, watching as she and Derrick climbed into the backseat of Aunt Cassandra's car, waiting for them at the front curb. Jared took the driver's seat. Derrick's wheels sat abandoned.

The Patchetts chose that moment to leave for dinner. They joined Aunt Cassandra and Dan for the big send off.

"Have fun!"

"Enjoy the movie."

"Drive carefully." This from Aunt Cassandra.

"Hands in your own laps," called Mr. Patchett who proceeded to roar with laughter at his wit. His wife laughed loudly too.

Jenn had never felt so humiliated.

It only took a couple of minutes to get to Jeannie's house, minutes that passed in silence except for Jared's tortured rendition of "The Gambler." It was bad enough that he was a fan of country western instead of rock, but did he have to sing Kenny Rogers, for Pete's sake? He could at least do Tim McGraw or Garth Brooks. The evening had barely begun, and she was already ready to fold 'em and walk away, maybe even run. Her only happy thought was that things couldn't get worse.

Jared parked the car, climbed out, and went to Jeannie's door. Silence filled the car, deep and brooding, the kind that ate you alive.

"I'm sorry," Jenn finally forced herself to say. She felt like crying. She had wanted things to go so well tonight.

For a few minutes Derrick said nothing, his head turned away as he stared out the far window. Then he tilted his head and turned to her with an utterly charming, quite cocky smile. "You know, it just occurred to me that there's something to be said about having to ride in the backseat." He reached for her and pulled her close. He leaned down to her ear and said softly, suggestively, "No one can see what we're doing."

Jenn's eyes went wide. "Wh-what will we be doing?"

Before he had a chance to answer, the front passenger door opened, and Jeannie climbed in. She turned immediately and said, "Hi, Jenn. Hey, Derrick."

Jenn shifted away from Derrick, self-conscious about being so close to him in front of Jeannie and Jared, who now took his place behind the wheel.

Jeannie bounced in her seat. "This is going to be such a fun night."

"Oh, yeah." Derrick's sarcasm was so sharp that Jeannie's happy smile faltered.

They drove off.

Jenn wasn't paying attention to where they were going because Derrick had hold of her hand and kept running his thumb over her knuckles. She concentrated on the thrill of his touch. When the car slowed, then stopped, she said, "Are we there already?"

"Nah," Jared said as he beeped the horn. "We're picking up one more."

One more? Derrick looked at Jenn, dropped her hand, and scowled. She held out her hands to show she had no idea what was happening. Suddenly the door next to her was pulled open, and Paulie climbed in, all six feet, two inches and 240 pounds of him.

No, not Paulie. Please, God, not Paulie!

Caught between Derrick and Paulie, Jenn felt as squeezed as any orange about to become juice. She could imagine all too clearly what Derrick was thinking even before she heard his snort of derision. She wanted to die, and she knew for a fact that Jared would die as soon as they got home. She was going to murder him herself.

Oh, God, what are You doing to me? Can't I just have a nice normal date like everyone else?

"Hi, Jeannie, Jared," Paulie said, grinning like the idiot he was. "Derrick." He didn't smile at Derrick. He finally looked at Jenn and said, his voice low and warm, "Hi, Jenn."

Jenn stared straight ahead, ignoring the puppylike enthusiasm of her brother's best friend. She knew he had a crush on her, but she usually managed to stay away from him whenever he came to the house. Now here he was, sitting so close that his huge shoulders were pressed against hers.

The evening went downhill from there.

Nineteen

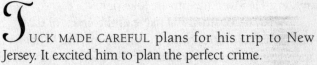

TUCK MADE CAREFUL plans for his trip to New Jersey. It excited him to plan the perfect crime.

Ah, the *zing* of upping the ante.

Knowing he didn't want to get near Sherri, didn't want her to see him and recognize him, shooting was the obvious choice. All those years of target practice would finally pay off. He grinned. Wouldn't Hank be pleased to know that Tuck was making such good use of one of the skills he had passed on to his son?

Knowing how intense airport security was, Tuck carefully packaged two of his guns, a rifle with a great scope and a .38 handgun, in a sturdy cardboard box filled with foam peanuts. He wound packing tape around and around and around. He took the box to the UPS store in a mall forty-five minutes away and mailed it overnight to himself at a Mail and Such store in Seaside that he'd found on the Internet.

"It won't get there until Monday," the clerk said. "Tomorrow's Sunday."

"Exactly when I need it," he said, paying cash. As he waited for his change, he brushed the bushy mustache he wore glued to his lip.

He didn't use his own name for his ticket purchase. He'd lifted the license and a credit card from the wallet of the guy in front of him at the bar in a dark, crowded taproom last night. The guy had been about his height and coloring, so his license picture matched Tuck's appearance well enough, and he was drunk as a skunk, feeling no pain. Bump, lift, slip out the license and card, bump, replace. The guy would be none the wiser until it was too late to do anything about it. Tuck repeated the action at another dreary, dark bar, stealing another identity.

Again considering security, Sunday he brought nothing suspicious with him on his cross-country trip, just a backpack full of a pair of jeans, a sweatshirt, a heavy rugby shirt, and three changes of underwear. He wore a heavy jacket over his sweater and jeans and carried a paperback he lifted from Hank's library, a murder mystery. He loved the private joke of it.

When he boarded his plane at the crack of dawn, he held out Ken Whalin's license and the ticket in Ken Whalin's name. The attendant smiled and passed him through. As he walked down the jet way, Tuck smirked. Served Ken Whalin right, wherever he was. Such identity theft was exactly why they told you not to put your wallet in your back pocket, especially in a crowd.

Tuck landed at Philadelphia International Airport with no trouble. The parents thought he was on a short vacation trip to Hawaii, and so did everyone at the office. He expected no one to call to check on him. He smiled. No one cared enough. As he passed a trash receptacle, he tossed Ken's IDs and his return tickets inside.

At the airport car rental counter Tuck showed the second license and the MasterCard belonging to a Carl Filbert. He couldn't imagine what it was like for Carl to face the world named after a nut. Carl's IDs went into the trash container in the men's room. He'd steal a new identity for his trip home, even though it meant buying another round-trip air ticket. What was another ticket to a millionaire?

He left the airport and pulled into the first motel he found. Bushy mustache firmly in place, he walked up to the counter.

"Hey," he said, just like he'd talked with the girl in the navy blazer before. "Can I borrow a phone directory for a minute? I need to look up an address, and I hate to go back to my room."

She passed the thick city directory to him and he found what he wanted, a costume rental business whose ad said it was open seven days a week and which his map indicated wasn't too far from the airport. With a smile he handed the directory back and drove to the shop where he purchased some props with cash.

Driving down the Atlantic City Expressway, he went over his plans. First, he needed to find out who was calling. If by some fluke it was Sherri, still alive and kicking, part two of his plan would kick in: Deal with her.

He grinned as he swung south onto the Garden State Parkway not far from Atlantic City. He had his own version of the final solution in mind, though he'd need to make another purchase to carry it out. He'd been unwilling to mail bullets, and he certainly couldn't carry them onto a plane these days, so he needed to buy some. No biggie.

If it wasn't Sherri calling but some lunatic, he'd leave whoever it was to it. She could call to her heart's content. If the pressure made Patsi lose what little mind she had left, so what? She wasn't his worry. The two million was.

Tuck drove over the Ninth Street Causeway and into Seaside. He couldn't say he was impressed. The island was all stores, restaurants, and houses from what he could see as he searched for SeaSong. He took it on faith that there was probably a beach out there somewhere, and if he had time, he'd search it out. He liked to watch the ocean. It reminded him of himself, all motion and hidden depths.

There it was. The SeaSong. He pulled to the side of the road a block past the big, old Victorian, then strolled back to study it. He wasn't worried about Sherri recognizing him. He was wearing his fake mustache and a baseball cap with a wig attached that gave him a ponytail, just one of the new props he'd gotten at the costume store. Besides, the last person she expected to see in New Jersey was Tucker Best.

There were lots of lights on in the house. Even in the dark Tuck could tell it was a first-class operation. How was Sherri able to pay for staying there? He knew for a fact that she hadn't used any of her credit cards. Nor had she withdrawn anything from her rather substantial bank accounts. Hank had always been generous with her, and she never seemed to spend it all, something he never understood. Money was for spending. But she hadn't touched any of her money for the whole year. That was one of the major reasons the authorities thought she was probably dead.

It never failed to amaze him how thoroughly she had disappeared along with that boyfriend of hers, Kevin Grayson. Not a trace! The police had searched for days all over California and found nothing, nada, zip. False sightings had Sherri and Kevin in Las Vegas for a quickie wedding, in Yellowstone camping, up in the San Juan Islands boating. Someone even reported seeing them on a Caribbean cruise. All leads petered out. Sherri and Kevin had vanished as completely as the dodo and the passenger pigeon.

Tuck had always believed they were dead because he didn't think either she or Kevin was smart enough to pull off so clever and complete a disappearance. Besides, why would they disappear of their own free will? It made no sense.

When they vanished more than a year ago, Tuck was as surprised as everyone. When the police began their questioning, he was more than relieved to have an airtight alibi. He had been in Chicago with three others from the Best Electronics sales team. His every hour was accounted for, even the hours he was alone in his room because of the X-rated videos he rented when he had trouble sleeping.

Kevin's car had been found abandoned in downtown L.A., its motor cold, his and Sherri's school papers in a mess on the backseat, their laptops and other personal paraphernalia gone. Immediately everyone thought abduction and ransom. After all, Granddad Cal and Hank were wealthy men. The police as well as the family waited for the ransom call, but none came. When the search finally sputtered to a halt, Tuck thought murder.

Only Patsi kept hanging on to the hope that Sherri and Kevin were alive. Wouldn't it be ironic if basket case Patsi was right?

Tuck walked back to his car from the SeaSong. He'd come back tomorrow when he could see. He drove absently around the island for a while. He entered an area called the Gardens, if the sign was to be believed. Here the houses seemed less like B&Bs or boarding houses but more like single homes. The lawns were still small, but they were nicely landscaped and tended.

He pulled to a stop when the road ended at what was obviously the beach. He climbed out of the car and walked along a narrow path between a couple of sand dunes. In the light of a quarter moon he saw the black water, the waves limned in white foam. In the distance the lights of a city—Atlantic City?—shone in the dark.

Smiling, he walked to the ocean's edge. He let the roar of the water fill his ears and the scent of the sea his nostrils. A brisk wind tugged at his baseball cap, pulling it askew. He tugged it down lower on his head. The last thing he wanted was for the hat and the attached ponytail to go blowing across the beach, even if there was no one to see.

He took several deep breaths to let the crisp sea air cleanse the L.A. pollution from his lungs. When he settled on his Caribbean island, he'd never again have to worry about smog and its effects on his body.

He glanced over his shoulder and jumped when he realized he wasn't alone. A guy with a white ponytail was swinging a metal detector over the sand, but his eyes weren't watching the machine. They were watching Tuck.

Nonchalance. That was the key.

He walked to the man. "Hi. I'm Ken Whalin. What are you doing?"

Twenty

$\mathcal{D}$AN WATCHED JENN in amazement in the aftermath of her disastrous date, at least disastrous to her. Never having been around a teenaged girl who felt herself wronged, to say nothing of deeply embarrassed, he couldn't believe her ability to hold a grudge. She stormed to bed on Saturday night without a word to anyone, face set, fists clenched, hurt and resentment pouring off her in waves. Then he watched on Sunday morning, fascinated, as she deliberately turned her back on Jared when he entered the kitchen.

"Imagine my surprise when I learned that a double date wasn't four people but five," she said to the room at large as she poured herself a glass of orange juice. She then pointedly returned the juice to the refrigerator when Jared reached to take it from her.

Jared just rolled his eyes and got out the juice again.

"What can a person say when her own brother plots to ruin her life?" she asked as she locked the doors to the backseat of Dan's car so Jared couldn't sit next to her on the way to church.

Jared just smirked and moved to the front seat, forcing Cass into the back, much to Dan's displeasure.

"I don't think it's too much to ask that a girl have a nice evening with her date without unwanted company tagging along, do you?" she asked the cousins quite loudly at dinner after church.

The cousins all laughed and spread their sympathy along sexist lines, the boys sitting at a table apart from the girls, the girls leaning in and whispering who knew what calumnies about men in general and Jared and Paulie in particular.

It was a relief to Dan to escape to his room when they returned home. He refused to consider that it might also be cowardly. After all, Cass had given her blessing to his retreat.

"Go upstairs," she'd said, resting a hand on his arm, the golden chain with its butterfly and key shining on her wrist. "There's no reason you should have to put up with her moods. After all, you're our guest."

He realized as he booted up his laptop that he was getting to hate that line of Cass's. Surely he was more than a guest, wasn't he? He'd sat up with Cass last night waiting for the kids to come home, not that it had been a hardship. None of the other guests sat with them.

Feeling disgruntled, he checked his e-mail more for something to do than because he expected to find anything in particular. The amount of daily electronic correspondence had shrunk drastically when people realized he was serious about closing the Harmon Group. Conducting due diligence to determine companies that would make good financial risks had been the sole mutual concern of Dan and his clients. If he couldn't talk business with them, what could he talk about? Nothing. He had learned over the past year or so how few friends he actually had.

A message from Andy captured his attention. He smiled. For the past couple of weeks, ever since the day he'd opened that portfolio for Andy, he and his brother had been writing frequently. Not that Andy knew about the money set aside for him and his kids. Rather, it was that Dan had taken the time to respond to his brother's e-mails promptly. In return Andy had answered quickly too, and suddenly they were talking more than they had since they lived under the same roof as kids.

Dan knew the emotional distance that had developed between him and Andy over the years was his fault, unintentional as it had been. He'd been too busy, too preoccupied with business, too obsessed with making the Harmon Group the best on the Street for there to have been time for something as mundane as writing his brother.

Just another sign that the problems in his life were relational. Just in case he was too dense to figure it out by himself, God had set Cass in his life. She threw his failings into sharp relief with her love and concern for her family, a family that didn't appreciate her nearly as much as they should, in his opinion. A family that took her for granted. Yet her love never faltered. Her involvement never lessened.

In that moment he understood what a great gift it would be to be loved by Cass Merton. She would be constant, her love never wavering, her commitment absolute. He also understood that he, selfish and self-absorbed as he'd been, didn't deserve her love. Not that her family did either, but they were family. That relationship alone was enough to warrant her affection. He was nothing but a rudderless, former due diligence whiz, an unemployed vet.

The phrase made him think of her, and he couldn't help but smile. She was something else. Warmed by thoughts of her, he turned to Andy's e-mail.

Dan,

Do you remember when I told you that Go and Tell International now had a new director, a friend of mine from college, Adam Streeter? Adam's a good man, the former president of an insignificant little Bible school that he built into a school of excellent reputation. GTI wooed him big time, and he accepted the job of filling Dr. Newmeyer's shoes.

Well, Adam's found an organization in chaos. Dr. Newmeyer is a wonderful man of God, a man of vision, but apparently not an administrator. He came home from the Korean War all those years ago with a burden for the Koreans due to the hardships of the war and the hopelessness he saw. He was committed to giving them the opportunity to know Christ.

From that small beginning he grew a mission with 525 missionaries serving all over the world, and he grew it with the passion and conviction he communicated to others like Muriel and me.

Since Adam assumed the directorship three months ago, he has used me as a sounding board because of our longtime friendship and my longtime association with GTI. I don't know all the problems he's found or if/how they can be fixed. I do know a lot of them are financial, some personnel. Not that GTI is about to go under, but it's close.

We both know you got all the financial and business genes in the family. I'm just a small-time teacher of the Word, trying to save souls and build a strong church here in Cognin. I'm going to ask you for a really big favor, Dan. I know I'm imposing, but I have to ask. Do you have time to consult with GTI? I realize you're in flux personally, but this is crisis time for us. With the current financial situation, I don't think GTI can pay you at all, let alone what you're worth.

Anyway, think about it, will you? Pray about it. Whatever you decide, know I appreciate you, big brother.

Andy

Dan stared at Andy's letter for a long time. Five hundred and twenty-five missionaries, including Andy and Muriel, at about twenty thousand dollars each a year, give or take. Over ten million a year in funds passed through GTI, and that didn't count the salaries of the home office workers or special funds like those for vehicles and home leave and emergency illnesses.

That was a lot of money to mismanage, a lot of administrative challenges to meet.

Dan shrugged. It wasn't as if he had lots to do, though he had promised Cass he'd help paint the front porch as long as he didn't have to do the spindles. She'd just smiled, and he'd known he'd do the blasted spindles too. What mattered here was that GTI and his brother needed help.

Andy,

Let the home office know that if they are willing to work with me, I'll see what I can do. In the meantime, don't you two worry. I'm sure the Lord will work everything out.

One thought: The Board of GTI—and the missionaries serving under its aegis—shouldn't expect Adam to fill

Dr. Newmeyer's shoes. He will never be another Dr. Newmeyer. What they should expect and pray for is that he take the work that Dr. Newmeyer developed and move it forward in new ways.
>
>   Dan

Andy's response was immediate.

Dan,
>   Adam will take your call anytime.
>   Andy

Andy,
>   Tomorrow at 10 A.M.
>   Dan

Dan spent the rest of the afternoon thinking about GTI. Having done due diligence on over five hundred companies in the course of his career, he knew what made a company sound. He went to GTI's web page and studied it, especially their mission statement. He made lists of questions for Adam, lists of things he needed to think through himself. When he finally checked his watch, he was surprised to find it was time for dinner.

He hurried downstairs, anxious to see Cass. He wanted to tell her about the opportunity to help GTI. It seemed to him that it was just the type of thing she'd be taken with. He was right.

"Oh, Dan, how wonderful that you can help here!" She blessed him with one of her glorious smiles. "Just think. You'll be helping with the spread of the gospel around the world. How special is that? If the Harmon Group were still going full-bore, you wouldn't have the time to give."

If the Harmon Group were still going, Dan thought, *I wouldn't be eating dinner with you.*

Jenn looked from Dan to Cass and back, and it was obvious that she was not impressed with Dan's opportunity. She looked at Jared. She took a couple of bites of her barbeque sandwich, then stood. "Call me when it's time to do the dishes. I'll be in my room. The company here is giving me a stomachache." Grabbing her plate and her drink, she clomped upstairs.

Jared watched her go, shaking his head. "I sure hope she grows up someday."

Dan very much agreed, thinking that she was like the hurricane that the weather service said was churning its way up the East Coast, all fury and flash, *Sturm und Drang*. He shoved a forkful of potato salad into his mouth to keep from saying so.

Cass placed a hand on Jared's as he reached for the bowl of fresh fruit. "Taking Paulie along wasn't the wisest thing you've ever done," she said gently. "You can't make her like him."

"At least Paulie's honorable." The depth of his concern for his sister was clear to see, and Dan, already impressed with Jared's maturity, liked the boy even more. "I wouldn't have to worry about her with him. But Derrick—"

Cass released Jared's hand and patted it a couple of times. "I wish she liked Paulie too. Well, quite frankly, I wish she didn't like anyone. It would simplify all our lives. But if she's got to like anyone, I'd prefer Paulie over Derrick any day, too."

Since they were all in agreement on that issue, there seemed nothing more to say. They ate in silence for a minute. Then Cass spoke.

"Poor Dan. He's got this wonderful opportunity to serve the Lord, and what do we do? Get sidetracked. Tell us more about it, okay?"

"Yeah," Jared said, looking glad for the change of topic. "How come they got in trouble in the first place?"

"I don't know yet. That's part of what I'll have to find out." Dan eyed the platter of sloppy joes, debating with himself about taking another.

"Well, if money's a problem, they have to cut expenses somehow, don't they?" Jared took another roll full of hamburger barbeque, his third if Dan was counting correctly. "Isn't the best way to let people go? That's what they did at Dad's company a couple of years ago. They cut 10 percent of the workers across the board. Dad had to decide who in his department went. It almost gave him an ulcer."

Dan watched the boy devour his sandwich in four bites. Amazing. Had he taken time to chew, or did he just swallow it whole, sort of like a dog did? "Most people think you make cuts in a situation like GTI's, but I disagree. It's too easy to lose good workers that way. What you really need to do is increase income."

"But if they knew how to do that, they wouldn't be in this problem." Cass poured herself another glass of iced tea.

Dan held his glass out, and she filled it for him. He smiled his thanks. "My guess is that their problems aren't really financial, though that's what presents itself as obvious. The problems are more likely relational and psychological. By that I mean that they may have to get rid of some programs—and maybe some people—that they are attached to but are no longer doing the job they were designed or hired to do. Conversely, they may have to initiate some programs they've been loathe to establish. They may also have to hire some new highly qualified people."

"The old hire one, fire one," Cass said.

Dan looked at her in surprise.

"I might have been an English major, but I have a business minor. I've also taken several courses on running a B&B." She smiled sweetly and took a forkful of fruit salad. "I am not a dummy."

"No, you're anything but." Dan started to reach for the last sandwich and sighed as Jared beat him to it. That's what he got for hesitating.

When Cass called Jenn to come do the dishes, the girl came down with obvious reluctance, the great burden of unfair labor practices draped over her slim and undeserving shoulders. She did the dishes as noisily as she could manage.

Dan winced at every slap and slam of china and cutlery. The crash of the pans rattled the windows. "Are girls always like this when they're miffed?" he asked Cass *sotto voce* as the two of them lingered over their coffee.

"Just some girls. We happen to be living with a master."

Dan shook his head. Guys were so straightforward. If he'd had a gripe with Andy when they were young, he either pounded his brother into the ground or had it out verbally. "I never knew girls were so good at wringing every last dram of drama out of a situation."

"You poor sheltered man." Cass laughed softly at him.

"I bet you weren't like that when you were a kid." She was too straightforward to have ever been so. He knew it to his bones.

"I don't think I was. Neither my mother nor the brothers would have tolerated it. Besides, I'm a pleaser. Always have been."

He looked at her. She sure pleased him. "And she isn't?" He jerked his head toward the sink and Jenn as a particularly loud crash of pots sounded.

"Well, she doesn't like to purposely make people mad at her, but if things don't go as she likes, she's—" Cass searched for the right word.

"A pain in the neck?"

"Dan!" Cass said, but she was laughing.

Jenn turned to glare at them with a how-dare-you-be-happy-when-I'm-not stare.

Jared loped down the stairs and into the kitchen, a basketball tucked under his arm. "Hey, Dan, want to play some one-on-one?" He bounced the ball, making the whole room shudder. Jenn's glare intensified, something Dan found astounding. He wouldn't have thought she could look any angrier.

He looked at Cass. Much as he wanted the exercise and the challenge of beating the kid, he hated to abandon Cass to the irate Jenn. "Want to play too?"

She smiled. "Go ahead. I've got some things to plan for next week."

"You're sure?"

"Yes."

He nodded and turned to Jared. With a quick swipe, he stole the ball midbounce. He was just petty enough to enjoy the boy's startled look and Cass's admiring smile. At least he thought it was admiring. "Let's play, guy. I feel the need to whup someone."

"Yeah, right. Like you could." Jared grabbed the ball back and was out the door before Dan stood up.

Jared was good. He was quick on his feet, had a good eye, and had perfected a three-point shot that invariably slid through the hoop with barely a ripple of the net. When the kid learned not to whoop so loudly after each score, he'd be the consummate player.

"Do you play on your school team?" Dan asked, puffing more than he liked from chasing the kid all over the apron of Cass's drive.

Jared nodded as he feinted and drove for the basket. Only an inglorious lunge on Dan's part knocked the ball off its trajectory.

"Jared," Cass called from the back door. "Jeannie's on the phone for you."

The boy arched his eyebrows and grinned. Dan laughed as he retrieved the ball, dribbling it automatically.

"I'll only be a couple of minutes," Jared said as he passed Cass and went into the kitchen. He pulled the door closed behind him, leaving Cass on the outside.

She shook her head. "They're good for at least a half hour."

Dan agreed. "They've got last night and today to discuss."

Cass walked to the driveway and watched as he bounced the ball from hand to hand. After a minute, her hand lashed out and the ball was hers. She dribbled for the basket and jumped for as pretty a layup as he'd ever seen. She caught the ball as it dropped through the net, turned, and smiled at him in blatant challenge.

At first Dan checked himself as he played, not wanting to hurt her, but it soon became apparent that she had no similar qualms. She bumped him, elbowed him, and blocked him like she was one of the boys. His height and weight didn't intimidate her in the least.

"Four brothers," she said after throwing her hip and knocking him off-stride and out of bounds. The ball went flying. She reclaimed it with a grin and was at the basket before he was even back on the court.

From then on he played as if he were facing one of the guys. They both worked up a sweat, and Dan realized he hadn't had so much fun playing basketball in years. She wasn't as quick as Jared—twenty-two years was bound to slow someone—but she made up for any lack in speed with skill and smarts. If he didn't stay on his toes, she'd beat him, something he had no doubt she'd love.

He scored, and she took the ball, dribbled to the back of the court, and began her move. She drove straight for him, feinted at the last second, and broke to her left. The first two times she'd tried that move, he fell for it. This time he was ready for her. She hit him hard, bounced off his chest, and started to go down. He grabbed for her, snaking an arm about her waist. She in turn clutched at his sweatshirt.

They ended up facing each other, mere inches apart. Somehow his second arm ended up around her, and he held her in a loose embrace. She felt good in his arms, substantial but definitely feminine. If he tightened his grip, he wouldn't have to worry about snapping her spine. If he kissed her, he wouldn't give himself a stiff back from bending low. She was just the right height, just the right size. Just the right person.

She looked up, startled to find herself held so close. He wasn't certain what she saw in his face, but her surprise vanished, replaced by a soft little smile that made his heart swell.

In the spotlight mounted on the corner of the garage, he could see little tendrils of hair, loosened from her ponytail by their vigorous game, curling around her lovely face. Her nose was red from the nip in the air, and her upper lip was moist with perspiration. Her cheeks were rosy, and those wonderful eyes had a slightly dreamy look. Her breathing was accelerated. Just from the game? He knew his own heart was beating fast, and it wasn't all from exertion. Not by a long shot.

"You are so beautiful," he whispered.

She sighed, and the hands gripping his sweatshirt uncurled and slid to his shoulders. His arms wrapped more tightly about her. He leaned down and brushed her lips, his touch tentative. He hovered a moment, testing her reaction. He thought she leaned even closer. She definitely did not pull away.

Smiling inside, he kissed her again, a true kiss this time, one that stopped time, at least for him. At first she was hesitant, not pulling back, but not fully participating. Then suddenly her arms were around his neck and she kissed him back with an enthusiasm that matched his own.

When they finally pulled apart to take a much needed breath, he kept his arms tight so she wouldn't escape. When had he felt like this, kissing a woman, holding a woman? Had he ever reacted so strongly?

She laid her cheek against the hollow between his neck and shoulder, snuggled in, and took a few deep breaths. He smiled into her hair. He'd like nothing better than to kiss her again and again, but he knew he mustn't. It would be too much too quickly. Also, they were literally standing in the spotlight with Jenn and Jared mere feet away. He knew being a good example to them was important to Cass. And most important, as a Christian, he knew there had to be limits to physical expressions of affection, even the relatively safe and totally delightful action of kissing.

The back door slammed open, and Cass jumped like she'd been hit with a cattle prod. She pulled from him, eyes wide, looking like she was guilty of a terrible crime. He had to smile. All Jared had to do was look at his aunt, and he'd have a very good idea what she had been doing and with whom.

"I'm back," Jared announced as he grabbed the basketball, forgotten and lying at the edge of the drive. He dribbled to the basket and shot without looking at them. "Miss me?"

Cass almost ran to the door. "I-I'll just get back to my work."

Dan watched her go, and just before she pulled the back door shut behind her, she turned and looked at him. She gave a slight smile, then ducked her head and was gone.

He was still staring after her when the basketball hit him hard in the stomach. His air whooshed out, and he spun to Jared even as he rubbed his middle. What was the matter with the kid, throwing the ball that hard and without warning?

Jared stood, hands on hips, staring belligerently. "It's your turn."

It didn't take much to realize that Jared had seen the kisses and was feeling very protective of his aunt.

"I wouldn't hurt her for the world," Dan said, deciding to tackle the resentment head on.

Jared looked skeptical. "Do you love her? Are you going to marry her?"

Did he? Was he? Dan didn't know the answers to those questions yet. "I think she's marvelous. I like her immensely and enjoy her company."

"That's not what I asked."

"It's all I can tell you at the moment. I repeat, I won't hurt her."

"You're going to leave."

Dan sighed and nodded. He was, whenever God told him what He wanted from him, and implicit in his leaving was hurting Cass. He didn't even want to think about how much he might be hurt too.

"I don't think I want to play anymore tonight." Jared grabbed his basketball and headed for the house.

"I didn't force her to kiss me," Dan said. "And you're just afraid I'm going to whip the pants off you."

Jared froze. He turned slowly. "In your dreams. And all I want is her happiness."

Dan held his hands out for the ball. "On that we are agreed. And you just can't handle the idea of being beaten by an old man like me, can you?"

Jared's anger at Dan transmuted itself into aggressive play. In no time Dan's lungs burned as the boy raced around the court, and he was forced to follow. He also felt an interesting crop of bruises develop from Jared's very pointed elbows. When they stopped playing an hour later, Jared had trounced him soundly.

The good thing was that Jared had worked off his mad, and when they went into the kitchen and Dan suggested sharing the pitcher of iced tea, Jared joined him with all good humor.

The bad thing was that Cass was nowhere to be seen.

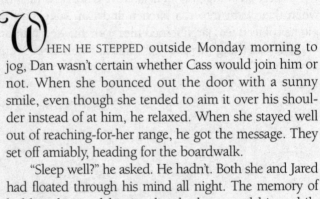

Twenty-One

WHEN HE STEPPED outside Monday morning to jog, Dan wasn't certain whether Cass would join him or not. When she bounced out the door with a sunny smile, even though she tended to aim it over his shoulder instead of at him, he relaxed. When she stayed well out of reaching-for-her range, he got the message. They set off amiably, heading for the boardwalk.

"Sleep well?" he asked. He hadn't. Both she and Jared had floated through his mind all night. The memory of holding her and kissing her had warmed him while Jared's hard questions had worried him.

"Never slept better," she answered in spite of the bruised-looking circles under her eyes.

"Have any good dreams?" *Of me?*

She shot him a look that let him know she realized he was on a fishing expedition. "I never remember my dreams. I'm not even sure I dream at all."

"What? I thought everybody dreamed."

She looked at him askance. "I," she said quietly, "am not everybody."

He couldn't help grinning at her as they turned north on the boardwalk, running easily together. She wasn't going to let him bait her no matter how hard he tried. Her ponytail bobbed with each step, and the exertion of jogging put roses in her cheeks and a sparkle in her eyes. Lovely, both inside and out.

He simply couldn't understand her singleness. She wasn't the kind of woman who rejoiced in being alone. She loved family and would make a wonderful wife and mother. Why there had been no takers was beyond him, not that he was complaining.

Of course, he didn't doubt that she scared a lot of guys because she was so strong in opinions, ability, and spiritual maturity. She needed a man with a lot of self-confidence, a man who didn't see her strength as arrogance, her abilities as a threat, and her opinions as bossiness. He guessed tall, assertive men with hearts for the Lord weren't a dime a dozen in South Jersey any more than they were anyplace else.

They reached the end of the boardwalk and turned for home.

"I won't be at SeaSong tomorrow night," she said suddenly. "I wanted you to know."

"Oh?" His step faltered. Where was she going? And with whom? That was the real question. He made a noise that he hoped conveyed friendly interest, not the stab of jealousy he felt. He blinked. Jealousy? Certainly not.

Cass continued, thankfully unaware of his reaction. "I'm making one of my reconnaissance trips."

He frowned. "What's a reconnaissance trip?"

She swiped a hand across her forehead. "It's my form of industrial espionage."

"What?" She never failed to surprise him.

She grinned. "A couple of times a year, I go spend a night at a top-notch B&B to see what my competition's doing."

"Alone?" As soon as the word left his mouth, he wanted to kick himself. Did he really think she'd go with a man? Such a suggestion would make her justifiably angry, and all because of his newfound tendency to jealousy, one of the seven deadly sins.

She nodded. "I can't take Jenn and Jared out of school."

The tension left Dan's shoulders. She'd misunderstood his question. *Thank You, Lord.*

"Brenna's agreed to spend the night with the kids," she said. "Not that they really need or want a babysitter. Still, I'm not comfortable leaving them alone, especially with Jenn in her current state of mind. Then, too, there's Rodney coming."

"Rodney?" Who was he?

"The hurricane."

"Oh." Of course. He felt like a fool. "As for the kids, I could watch them." After all, he was right there on site. Brenna wasn't.

"Dan!" Cass sounded much too surprised at the suggestion. "I couldn't ask you to babysit. You're our guest."

"You're our guest." While he understood what she meant and why she felt that way, today for some reason he was more than miffed at that response. It was as if she were trying to keep him a safe distance away from her and her family. "Is that your not-too-subtle way of telling me to butt out?"

Cass stopped and stared at him. "What?"

He ran a circle around her. He was an idiot. Cass hadn't an unkind bone in her body. She'd gone out of her way to include him time after time. "You heard me."

He blinked at himself. Surely the devil had made him say that.

"Yes, I heard you, but I don't understand." Her eyes couldn't open any wider if she tried. He could see concern and confusion in them.

He jogged to the rail and looked out over the beach. What was the matter with him, jumping on her like that? So she thought of him as a guest, a business acquaintance. Just because he got to eat with her family a few times and have breakfast and dinner with her every day, even lunch most days, just because she kissed him back enthusiastically didn't mean she felt anything but the polite, considerate innkeeper toward him.

He frowned. She was more than the innkeeper to him. Lots more. She was his friend, for Pete's sake. His good friend. His *very* good friend. His chest heaved as air huffed in and out of his lungs. He heard Jared's questions: *"Do you love her? Are you going to marry her?"*

Did he? Was he? He gripped the rail and stared at the sand, blown all wavy by the strong autumn winds. *Like an old lady with marcelled hair,* he thought.

He closed his eyes. Surely he was more to her than a guest. After all, she didn't kiss any of her other guests or let them play bellhop. She liked him as much as he liked her. She did. She must.

She came and stood beside him at the rail, staring straight ahead. Neither said a word. After a time she bumped him with her elbow and looked up, frowning. "I'm not sure why you're upset, but please know I wouldn't hurt you for anything."

He studied her earnest face and felt that swelling in his heart that was quickly becoming the norm whenever he looked at her. He slipped his arm across her shoulders and hugged her gently. He forced himself to smile. "Low blood sugar must be making me cranky. I'm sorry."

What he really wanted to say was, "Let me go with you on your spy mission," but he couldn't bring himself to ask. What if she didn't want his company?

She smiled sweetly, and his breath caught. Very good friend, my foot.

"Come on, then," she said. "Let's go home, and I'll get you a glass of orange juice."

"Freshly squeezed?"

"Absolutely."

Because I'm your guest? Your friend? Your what? But he wisely kept his mouth shut this time.

A block from SeaSong, Cass and Dan stopped at the curb for the shiny red Seaside garbage truck. She glanced at the pair of disreputable-looking men hanging off the back. They looked like the same two as last week, their dirty jackets gleaming in the thin sunlight where the filth had turned the original color a shiny black.

The truck stopped, the driver's window rolled down, and Clooney stuck his head out. "Still running, I see."

Cass grinned, glad to see her favorite eccentric. "It's good for you."

Clooney shook his head. "Anything that takes that much effort can't be good for you." He turned his attention to Dan. "And you're still here, I see."

Dan nodded. "For the foreseeable future."

Clooney pulled off his baseball cap, ran his hand over his head, and resettled the cap, pulling his ponytail out the hole in the back. "The foreseeable future could be a very long time."

Dan looked Clooney calmly in the eye. "Could be."

He and Clooney stared at each other for a moment. It was some kind of man thing, Cass decided, this sending and receiving of signals they didn't want her to intercept. Did they think she was dumb? She couldn't figure out that she was the subject of their stare-down?

She wasn't certain which one of them blinked first, but Clooney finally returned his attention to her. "Listen, darlin', this may mean nothing, but I met a strange guy last night."

Cass bit her tongue to keep from saying something smart-alecky. If the guys hanging off the back of the truck were any indication, Clooney knew lots of strange guys.

"I was down on the beach in the Gardens," Clooney said, "in front of one of the new glass houses. They had a big party over the weekend, and people kept wandering outside to walk the beach or sit in the sun in spite of the chill. I figured they might have dropped a few things, don't you know, and I didn't want such treasures to be damaged by the elements."

Cass grinned. "And you're kind enough to care for any treasures you find with all the dedication of the previous owners."

"More dedication. I don't lose them once I find them." Clooney fingered the huge diamond stud in his left ear. "Anyway it was almost midnight, and this dude comes walking along, taking deep breaths like he's cleansing his lungs or something. We start to talk, and he asks a lot of questions."

"How appropriate," Cass said. "You're a guy with a lot of answers."

Clooney nodded acknowledgment. "Thing is, most of his questions had to do with you or SeaSong."

Cass shrugged. "People ask questions about SeaSong all the time. I want them to. That's one of the reasons for the web site and the PR material. Maybe people will vacation with us if their questions are answered to their satisfaction."

Clooney shook his head and grimaced. "He wasn't asking the way people do when they're looking for a place to stay. You know, how much does it cost? What are the meals like? That sort of thing."

Cass pointed a finger at him. "You didn't like the guy, did you? I can tell."

Clooney gave a short laugh. "You got that right. I didn't. I get these feelings about people sometimes, and they're always right. He's a bad one."

"What kind of questions did he ask?" Dan growled. He obviously didn't like the idea of a "bad one" inquiring about anything that had to do with her. She'd seen the brothers get all protective of their wives before, but this was the first time anyone had shown an inclination to shield her. She thought she liked it.

Clooney waved his hands as he talked. "Who runs SeaSong? Did I know Cass? What kind of a person was she? How old was she? Had she been here in Seaside long? Who else lived at SeaSong? Anyone new show up recently?" He made a disgusted sound. "I just looked at the dude on that one. 'Anyone new?' I said. 'This is a resort town, and that's a bed-and-breakfast. Of course there's someone new. Lots of someones. She'd go out of business if there wasn't.'"

"So a lot of his questions were about Cass personally?" Dan's voice was hard.

"At first. Then when he learned she'd lived here all her life, he lost interest. That's when he started the nonsense about anyone new." Clooney twirled the end of his white ponytail where it draped over his shoulder. "You don't have a guy with a funny looking ponytail staying with you, do you?"

"You mean a ponytail like yours?" Cass asked innocently.

Clooney grinned. "No, not like mine. Mine's quite excellent. This guy's was crooked."

"Crooked?" Cass and Dan said together.

"Yeah. You know how girls sometimes think it's cute to wear a ponytail on the side of their head? Well, his wasn't quite that off center, but something was wrong. It was too dark for me to make out exactly what the problem was, but I've wondered if he wasn't wearing a rug."

"There's no guy with a wig or a ponytail at SeaSong." Cass glanced at Dan. "He's my only guest right now, male or female."

Clooney looked Dan up and down, nodding. "Good. In case this guy is as weird as I think, I feel better that you're with her."

"Me too," Dan said.

"Jared and Jenn are with me too."

Clooney heard her but kept talking to Dan. "Well, Jenn won't do her any good, but Jared's one big boy." He pulled back into the cab. "Just keep an eye out for a young guy with a strange ponytail."

Dan nodded. "Will do."

Cass felt like waving her hand to remind them that she was

still here, that she had been taking care of herself all her life. She didn't because she knew they'd listen as much as the brothers did, which was to say not at all. There were days when she despaired of men.

Then she remembered last night's kisses and knew that men—correction, one man in particular—could also delight. She'd been both astonished and more-than-slightly giddy at discovering how much. All night she'd lain in her dark cubbyhole reliving The Clinch. She had been surprised when he actually kissed her. She thought that such an idea was only in her dreams. Was his grumpiness this morning because he regretted it? If that were the case, she never wanted to know. It would be too mortifying!

And don't forget, she reminded herself. *He will be leaving sometime in the not-too-distant future. He has never indicated in any way that Seaside, SeaSong, or Cass Merton is perceived as anything more than a temporary part of his life.*

Well, she had lived forty years without him. She could live without him for forty more. The Lord was enough.

So why did she suddenly feel like crying?

Clooney started rolling up his window. "I know it's probably nothing, but I feel better for telling you about the guy."

Again he spoke to Dan, but Cass responded. "Thanks." She forced herself to be upbeat as the truck rolled slowly down the street.

As she and Dan walked the last block home, Dan was quiet. She might still be trying to understand his distress on the boardwalk earlier, but she knew exactly what he was thinking now. He was worrying about the strange man on the beach.

What was it with men and their protective instincts?

Cass sighed. A man with a strange ponytail didn't spell trouble. Bad hair maybe, but not trouble. Trouble was Derrick Smith. Just thinking of him made Cass sweat. A sudden thought struck her and she grinned. Thinking of Dan made her sweat too, but with pleasure, not fear.

They reached the corner where SeaSong held sway at the same time that Mike's car pulled up to the curb, and Brenna climbed out. She blew him a kiss and waved him on his way, but when she turned, Cass saw the dark circles under her eyes and the lost look in them.

"Good morning, Brenna," she called, wondering once again what she could do to help the girl. "How are you today?"

Brenna wore jeans, a UCLA sweatshirt, and a pair of ratty sneakers. Her shiny brown hair was pulled behind her ears and allowed to hang free behind a denim headband. She was such a pretty girl, even with her haunted eyes.

Brenna gave a little wave as she walked toward Cass and Dan. She forced out a small smile. "Did the Patchetts' room survive the weekend?"

"As far as I know," Cass said. "When we start cleaning, I'll do that room with you just to check that everything's to my satisfaction."

Brenna nodded. "How would you ever fly anywhere if you were that big?" she asked apropos of nothing. "I've been thinking about that all weekend for some reason. Even first class seats aren't that big."

Cass grinned but made no comment. She didn't like to talk about her guests unless necessary for business, and airplane seats were hardly crucial to the running of SeaSong. "About tomorrow night, Brenna. Do you want the third-floor turret?"

"A guest room?" Her face lit up.

"Why not? I certainly can't ask you to sleep in that closet under the stairs."

"Sure you could. It's only for one night. And you sleep there."

"Only for the duration. Then back to my decent-sized room."

Brenna spread her arms wide and turned in a circle, her eyes to the sky. "I love this place," she announced to the trail of cirrus clouds gliding by. "There is not a better place in all the world to be."

"Seaside or SeaSong?" Cass asked as she watched Brenna twirl. In truth she thought Brenna's comments were strange in light of the girl's sorrow. Of course, it was possible to like a spot geographically even if you were unhappy over something while you were there.

"Both," Brenna said. "Definitely both."

Grinning at the girl's diplomacy, Cass stepped aside to make room for a man with a bushy brown mustache as he jogged by. The man kept his eyes fixed on the sidewalk as he passed, intent on some private world of his thoughts.

Cass smiled slightly as she watched Dan follow the man's

progress. Even though he didn't wear a funny ponytail, the man was an unknown and therefore suspicious, at least to Dan. Cass shook her head at the absurdity, but it was nice to know Dan cared.

When the man turned up the neighboring walk and knocked at the front door of the derelict house, Cass blinked. She and Dan exchanged glances and watched with interest, waiting for Mr. Carmichael to send the caller packing in no uncertain terms.

The front door opened, Mr. Carmichael peeked out, and the man began to talk. In the blink of an eye, Mr. Carmichael nodded and held the door open. The man with the mustache walked right in.

"Did you see that?" Cass demanded.

Brenna stopped her twirl and turned startled eyes to her. "What?"

"He let him in!"

"Who let who in?" Brenna looked at her with that alert, questioning interest that signaled that there was more to Brenna than met the eye.

"Mr. Carmichael let some man in next door." Dan waved at the now shut front door.

Brenna turned to the neighboring house. "But he never lets anyone in."

"Tell me about it." Cass felt as though she'd been betrayed, strange as that seemed. As long as the old man was uniformly hateful to people, she didn't have to take his nastiness too personally, and she could hold out hope that he'd change his mind about selling to her. But if he started being nice now and then, she'd have to acknowledge that his antagonism was personal, and the danger existed that someone might charm the house from him just because he felt spiteful toward her. The thought was enough to make her feel ill.

"You don't suppose he's going to sell to that guy, do you?" Her voice was small and sad.

Dan narrowed his eyes as he studied the house. Then he turned to her with a big smile that was probably supposed to be reassuring but was as phony as a telemarketer's happy talk. "Don't go jumping to conclusions, Cass." He patted her shoulder. "Your dream house is safe. I'd bet the farm on it."

"Easy for you to say." Cass eyed the house next door with yearning. "You don't have a farm."

Dan laughed as they went inside. He didn't know another woman like Cass. Humor, looks, a good and godly heart, and a penchant for fixing up broken-down things. With a wry smile aimed at himself, he acknowledged that he was probably just the kind of project she loved—a lost cause, a foundering ship, a wheel-less car up on concrete blocks, an athlete up for trade with no team to take him, a company whose stock had tanked. An ex-CEO. An ex-vet.

It struck him suddenly and hard that he didn't want her to think of him as a broken-down anything any more than he wanted her to think of him as her guest. He wasn't a loser. He was just a man in search of a new path. There was a huge difference. Surely she was intelligent enough to appreciate that fact. Still, the idea that she looked on him much as she looked at Mr. Carmichael's derelict house continued to niggle, eating away his peace of mind.

After they finished breakfast and he helped her clean up the kitchen, he took her by the shoulders and turned her to face him. He glanced around to make sure Brenna wasn't in sight. The kids were at school, so he knew he need not worry about them.

"I'm not a loser, you know," he said, looking into her beautiful hazel eyes.

Cass stared back at him like he was several million sand granules short of a beach. "Of course you're not."

"I'm just waiting on the Lord."

She nodded. "I know, and I think it's wonderful."

"I'm not a rudderless drifter." He noticed with satisfaction that her hands had found their way to his waist.

"You're anything but."

Her calm manner made him think he wasn't getting the depth of his concern across to her. He gave her shoulders a little shake in frustration.

In response she dug her fingers into his waist, making him jump. She smiled. "Ticklish, are we?"

"Cass!" She didn't understand.

"Shh," she soothed as she rubbed her hands up and down his sides. "It's that guy thing about the lost feeling you get when you don't have a job to identify yourself by, isn't it? If you're not Dan Harmon of the Harmon Group, then who are you? How do people perceive you?" She paused. "How do I perceive you?"

He just stared at her, emotions tumbling. She did understand.

"Four brothers," she said by way of explanation. "And no one in her right mind would ever see you as a loser or a drifter." She smiled shyly. "I certainly don't and never did."

Relief rolled through him. He pulled her close, wrapping her in his embrace. He was delighted to feel her arms slide to his back and tighten. He rested his cheek on her hair and wondered at the confusion she could rouse in him without trying and the benediction she could pronounce that set all his fears to rest. He leaned to kiss her.

"Cass!" Brenna's voice drifted from upstairs. "I'm ready to tackle the Patchetts' room."

Cass jumped and stepped away. "I'm coming!"

As she started toward the swinging door, he grabbed her arm and pulled her back. She looked up in surprise, and he kissed her before she could escape again. She blushed and smiled and hurried through the door. He followed slowly, enjoying once again her rear view.

He was still smiling when he reached his room, already cleaned and tidied by Brenna. He sat in the chair in the turret and pulled out his Bible and his laptop. On his Bible software he typed in *wait patiently* and watched the references scroll up.

With a sigh he noted that none of the verses had magic answers for how long the wait was to be. He thought of the Old Testament story of Elijah waiting three years by the stream, fed by ravens.

Three years, Lord?

He hoped not, but at least Cass didn't think him a shirker. And he had time for his brother's problems. He glanced at his watch. Time to call Go and Tell International.

Within minutes, Adam Streeter, the director of GTI, was on the phone.

"The precarious financial position and organizational chaos of the mission were surprises to me," he told Dan. "When I interviewed for the position of director, everyone was very careful to keep the desperate situation from me because they wanted me so much. They knew what I had done for the college, and they wanted me to do the same thing for the mission." He sighed. "At least when I went to the college, I knew what I was getting into."

"And now that you've found out the truth about GTI, are you going to stay with the job?" Dan asked.

"I'll admit that I was ready to resign at first. I felt duped. But I had a strong sense of God's call when I originally said I'd accept the job. Just because things were in lousy shape didn't mean God's call was any less. I'm staying. If the mission goes down, we go down together."

Dan liked the crisp, authoritative way the man spoke, the way he was committed to taking on a huge challenge. It was always a pleasure to work with someone used to taking charge, willing to take the risks required to lead.

"Adam, I have some questions for you, and I want you to think about them carefully."

"Shoot."

"First, what is *your* dream for the mission? What difference do *you* want to make? I went on-line and read what's there on the web site. That's Dr. Newmeyer's program and position. I want to know what you think."

"Got it. What else?"

"What do you see as the three greatest roadblocks to fulfilling your dreams?"

Streeter laughed. "That's easy. Money, people, and the time to accomplish all I want to."

"In broad strokes, that's typical," Dan said. "Let's shoot for GTI specifics. How much money? Which people? What's eating up your time that you can drop or delegate?"

"Okay. Be specific." The sound of computer keys being pressed came down the wire.

"I also want you to help me understand your board. What kind of men and women are they? Are they there because they're friends of Dr. Newmeyer or because they're qualified to advise a ten-million dollar operation? Is the guy that asks all the questions simply a detail man or an obstructionist? Things like that."

"Whew, you don't ask much, do you?"

"Wait. I've got more. If things are tight financially, it's important to raise money. Wisdom tells us that it's easier to raise money from large donors than small. It takes much less time, and they have more discretionary monies. I want you to develop a wish list of what you would do with a gift of five thousand dollars, ten thousand, fifteen, twenty, twenty-five, etc. When you and I—and Dr. Newmeyer if he's willing—go visit potential donors, you'll need that list to prove to these people that you'll use their hard earned and carefully tended money wisely."

"I can do that," Streeter said. "We had a great financial development guy at the college. I learned a lot from him."

"Don't hesitate to call him for advice," Dan said. "Take advantage of everyone you know who might be able to help you out."

"GTI doesn't have a wills and annuities program. Should we think about starting one? A couple of the men on the board are pushing for it, and the college benefited greatly from its program."

"I don't think it's a wise idea to go after that right away. Maybe down the road two or three years. It takes thirteen years on average before you see any real benefit from wills and annuities. What you need are three things that can be done in the next ninety days that will make a 50 percent difference for the mission."

"Whoa," Streeter said, his frustration evident even through the phone. "I'm suffering from option overload here. I'll never sort it all out."

"Sure you will. I'll help. If you don't mind, I'd like to meet with you sometime soon."

"You do understand that we can't pay you?" Streeter's voice was apologetic. "I'm not even sure we can pay our office workers next week."

Dan felt sorry for the man, forced to admit to a problem he hadn't created. "I'm not expecting payment. I'm doing this for Andy."

"Well, then come anytime," Streeter said, clearly wanting him there in the next five minutes.

Dan laughed. "I think it would be a wise idea to give you time to answer your questions before I come. How about next Monday?"

"I'll be expecting you."

Dan hung up and punched the air with excitement. What a great call. He had to find Cass and tell her all about it. Oh, and write to Andy too.

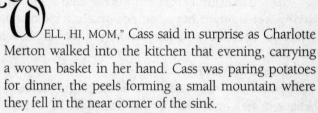

Twenty-Two

"WELL, HI, MOM," Cass said in surprise as Charlotte Merton walked into the kitchen that evening, carrying a woven basket in her hand. Cass was paring potatoes for dinner, the peels forming a small mountain where they fell in the near corner of the sink.

"Hello, Cassandra Marie." Mom held out her old-fashioned market basket, an antique that Cass coveted. It was made of sturdy saplings, a deep basket with flowers painted on one side beneath the coat of varnish that gave the thing a faint shine. "I brought you some goodies."

"Wonderful!" Cass grinned as she rinsed the last potato and put it in the pan. She set the pan on the stove to boil. "Is there a reason for this largesse?"

Mom shrugged. "Does there need to be a reason?"

Cass reached for a paper towel from the roll hanging on the wall beside the sink. She dried her hands. "Of course not."

"Well, I'll give you two anyway. One, I love you. Two, you work so hard, I thought I'd give you a hand."

She pulled a plastic quart container from the basket and held it out for Cass to see. "Applesauce." She set the container and the basket on the table and shrugged out of her coat. She tossed it on one of the love seats in the sitting area.

"Applesauce?" Cass's eyes lit, and she reached for

the container. "Your own? Oh, it's still warm."

"Of course it's my own." Mom looked insulted. "Why would I bring you anyone else's?"

"Good question," Cass murmured, feigning remorse. "It just slipped out. Sorry."

Mom nodded, mollified, and placed four more identical containers on the counter. Next she pulled out a pie covered with aluminum foil. She looked at Cass. "Apple. My own," she said, but a small smile robbed the words of any sting.

Cass grinned, still hugging the warm container of applesauce. "Why would you bring me anyone else's?"

The women grinned at each other, and Cass felt the joy of having her mother, her genuine, unadulterated, intellectually aware mother, here in her kitchen with her. It was a sweet moment.

"Is Dad with you?"

Mom shook her head. "He's home starting dinner. If you can believe it, he's gotten it into his head that he wants to learn to cook. Now I ask you, why should a man his age want to become the next Emeril?"

"I don't know," Cass said, though she did know, visions of seared hamburgers and burning Bakelite reminding her. "But if I were you, I'd let him have at it. After all your years of cooking, I'd think it would be wonderful to be relieved of the duty every so often."

Mom nodded. "There is that. And I guess it will be better if he ever gets the hang of it. I've eaten more scorched eggs and undercooked hamburgers recently than ever in my life." She peered at the mountain of browning peels in the sink. "Why in the world are you peeling so many potatoes?"

Cass stared at the peels and the pan full of cooking potatoes and shrugged. "Because they eat a lot."

"What? You're cooking dinner for guests these days?"

"If you can call Jared and Jenn guests. Jared eats like no one I've ever seen. He puts the brothers to shame, and I remember them always feeding their faces." Cass wasn't about to mention Dan's name. She knew her mother's shameless matchmaking tendencies too well. If Mom knew he now ate dinner with them every night, there'd be no peace in the valley.

"It's that football," Mom said. "I never did think it was good for a boy to get himself jumped on and knocked to the ground by other big boys who want to hurt him if they can. Then he does it back to them. And they all do this to each other for two hours or so." She shook her head. "It's a man thing, and it doesn't make sense."

Cass, who loved to watch football, kept quiet. The subject of the wisdom or foolishness of the sport had been debated to death in the Merton house as the brothers and Cass grew, and Mom always lost. She never let that little fact influence her opinion one iota.

Cass lowered the heat under the potatoes and opened the oven door to check on the rump roast inside. As soon as the potatoes were parboiled, they'd go in with the roast to brown. Carrots and onions already circled the meat, adding their aroma to the delicious scent filling the air.

The back door burst open, and Jared and Paulie exploded into the room.

"Whoa! Does it smell good in here." Paulie sniffed the air with pleasure.

"Hey, Grandmom!" Jared gave Mom a bear hug.

Mom batted ineffectually at his back. "Let go of me, boy. I like to breathe."

Jared stepped back, grinning. "You remember Paulie, don't you, Grandmom?"

Mom smiled at Jared's friend. "Certainly. It's good to see you again, Paulie."

"Hi, Ms. Merton." Paulie's eyes brightened, and he looked from Mom to Cass. "Hey, Ms. Merton and Ms. Merton!"

"So clever," said a sarcastic voice from the stairs. "So very clever."

As everyone swung toward Jenn, Paulie's face turned scarlet.

"Jenn," Cass said, warning in her voice. Jenn could be as peeved at the boys as she wanted, but she couldn't be nasty, hurtful.

When every eye was fixed on her, Jenn looked first at her brother, then at Paulie, sniffed with utter disdain, turned, and went slowly upstairs.

"Well!" said Mom, staring after Jenn. "I can see she hasn't gotten over whatever was bothering her yesterday."

"Don't worry about it, Grandmom," Jared said, investigating the containers on the table. He lifted the aluminum foil off the pie and nudged Paulie. "Apple. The best. Jenn's mad at Paulie and me because she thinks we ruined her date Saturday night."

"Did you?" Mom reached into her basket and pulled out two large plastic zipper bags bulging with chocolate chip cookies.

"It needed to be ruined," Paulie said earnestly, his eyes on the cookies. "The guy's a jerk."

Mom looked at Cass for confirmation.

"A jerk," Cass agreed. "Big time."

Mom looked at the two bags of cookies. "I brought these two to give one to Jared—"

"Yes," he said, extending his hand.

"—and Jenn. But I think I've changed my mind." She put one bag in Jared's outstretched hand and offered the other to Paulie. "For helping stave off the jerk."

"For me?" A huge grin filled his face. "Really?"

"If you don't take them," Jared said, "I will."

Paulie took the bag and held it to his nose. "They smell wonderful! Thanks, Ms. Merton."

Cass enjoyed the boy's delight. "Want to stay for dinner?"

"Can I?" He looked toward the stairs. "I mean, should I? Jenn might not be willing to sit at the same table with me."

Cass shrugged. "That's her problem. As far as I'm concerned, there's room and food for all."

"Then, sure. I'm in."

Mom reached into her magic basket and pulled out another bag of cookies. "Now where's that nice Dan? He's still here, isn't he?"

Cass peered into the basket. It was empty. "None for me?"

"Don't change the subject," Mom said.

Jared and Paulie, hands inside their cookie bags, grinned at Cass. They each pulled out a cookie, nicely browned, full of chocolate morsels and, if Cass knew her mother, crispy all the way through, just the way she liked them.

She eyed the boys, trying to make them feel guilty because they had cookies and she didn't. They munched away, untouched by so much as a thought of her suffering. Conceding defeat, she held out her hand, going for overt pressure. "Aren't you going to offer me one?"

"Oh." Jared grimaced at what was obviously a new and unpleasant idea. "Sure." He extended his bag with all the enthusiasm of a kid forced to share his blue M&M's. "Have *one*."

"Oops, sorry, Ms. Merton." Paulie held out his bag. "Take as many as you want."

Cass took two from each bag, knowing they wouldn't make a dent in the supply.

She set them carefully on the counter, saving them for dessert. She glanced at her mother and said with mock seriousness, "At least some people are kind enough to care for my sweet tooth."

Mom ignored the comment and repeated, "Where's that nice Dan?" She glanced around the kitchen and sitting area as if she expected him to pop out from behind the love seat or from under the table. "He's such a handsome man, don't you think, Cass?"

Cass turned to the refrigerator and blindly pulled out the first bag of frozen vegetables she touched. She grabbed a pan from the cabinet under the ovens, making as much noise as she possibly could, and filled it with water. Her theory—if you ignore the question, it will go away—had never before worked with her mother, but it was always worth a try, especially since she couldn't think of any other way to change the subject.

The last thing she wanted to do was discuss Dan in front of Jared and Paulie. The next to the last thing she wanted to do was discuss him with her mother under any circumstances. Her feelings for him were too tender, too complicated.

"They run together every morning," Jared told Mom with a sly smile at Cass.

"I should have taken five cookies," she told him.

"He gave her roses for her birthday," Paulie added helpfully.

"Everybody gave me those roses," Cass corrected.

"But they were his idea," Jared said. "So was the bracelet."

"What bracelet?" Mom wanted to know.

With a sigh, Cass held out her arm. "This one."

"Very pretty," Mom said as she examined the butterfly and key. "And very expensive."

"Mom!" Cass protested, pulling her arm back.

"Bet you haven't taken it off since you got it. Bet you even sleep in it."

Cass rolled her eyes. Mom was incorrigible.

"He winked when he gave it to her," Jared said. "She blushed."

"When was this?" Mom asked.

"On her birthday." Jared pulled another cookie from his bag. "He had dinner sent in from Dante's, the fancy side."

"Filet mignon with crab imperial," Paulie offered, glad to be able to contribute.

Cass looked at him. How did he know? He wasn't even here.

"Tell me more, boys." Mom pulled out a chair and sat at the table.

"They played one-on-one last night after dinner," Jared told her.

"In the dark," Paulie added. "Just the two of them."

"Someone has a really big mouth." Cass stared at Jared who grinned unrepentantly back.

"In the dark," Mom repeated, looking at Cass with eyes full of speculation. "Just the two of them."

"He guarded her very closely," Jared offered. "*Very* closely."

"Jared!" Cass knew her face was scarlet and her privacy gone forever.

"He came to the football game with her on Saturday," Paulie said. "And he doesn't even know anyone from Seaside but us." He pointed to Jared and himself.

"They go for walks on the boardwalk." Jared bit into another cookie. "Lots of walks."

Mom pointed to the cookie. "You'll ruin your appetite."

"Fat chance," Cass said.

"And," Jared said, his tone implying the best was about to come. "He eats breakfast *and* dinner with us. For all I know, they eat lunch together too."

"Well, I never!" Mom flopped back in her chair as though she couldn't believe her ears.

Three sets of eyes fixed on Cass who kept from squirming only by sheer force of will. "I hope you like Brussels sprouts, Paulie."

Paulie wrinkled his nose. "Anything you fix will be fine, I'm sure," he said politely and with obvious untruth.

"I like them," a deep voice said as Dan pushed open the swinging door and poked his head in the room.

Cass jumped and stared nervously at him as Jared, Paulie, and her mother grinned like conspirators with secret information. It was bad enough that she had to worry about them blurting out what she'd thought was privileged information. But what if he had actually heard some or all of the conversation before the Brussels sprouts? If he had, she'd never be able to look him in the eye again.

"You eating with us again, Paulie?" Dan asked as he let the door swing shut behind him.

"Us, huh?" Mom said as she peered around Paulie to see Dan.

Dan leaned for a better view of Mom and said, "Good evening, Charlotte. How are you today?"

"Fine, just fine."

Cass felt a keen relief. He gave no sign of having heard anything.

Mom held out the last bag of cookies. "Here. These are for you."

"Yeah?" Dan was obviously pleased. "Thanks. That's very nice of you."

Cass grinned to herself. He had no idea how special it was to be included in one of Mom's baking frenzies. Nothing spelled acceptance quite as clearly.

Mom shrugged. "Nice things for nice people."

Dan unzipped the bag, took an appreciative breath, and held it out to Cass. "Want a bite?" He smiled at her, one corner of his mouth quirking higher than the other.

She smiled back, the pan of potatoes she'd just taken from the stove forgotten as their eyes locked.

"You're going to spill," Mom warned, her voice dry.

Cass started, pulling her attention from Dan to the tilting pan. Blushing, she turned to the sink and drained off the water. When she finally turned from placing the potatoes in the roasting pan, she felt she could deal with all the grinning faces.

Then Dan held a cookie out for her to take a bite. One bite was already missing, and blushing at the heady intimacy of sharing in front of everyone, she took a delicate nibble.

"I said a bite." Dan continued to hold the cookie. "A big one." He gave her a little lift of his chin, a go-ahead signal, and waved the cookie beneath her nose.

Cass grabbed his wrist to hold it still and bit, her teeth just missing his fingers, enjoying his momentary look of alarm.

With half the cookie in her mouth, she closed her eyes to savor the wonderful taste. "Mmm. Wonderful, Mom." She opened her eyes and smiled at Dan. "Thanks." That was when she realized she was still holding his wrist. She released him quickly while Jared snickered and Mom preened like the proud mama she was.

Cass grabbed one of the containers of applesauce and upended it into a dish. She sprinkled a dash of cinnamon on it.

"Dinner looks good and smells better," Dan said as he zipped his cookie bag shut. "Can't spoil my appetite. Cass is too good a cook."

With a happy sigh, Mom walked to the love seat where she rescued her coat from beneath Glossy Flossie and slipped it on. "I've got to go home and see if Lew's burned down the house yet."

At Dan's look of surprise, Mom said, "He's teaching himself to cook. He even watches the food network, if you can believe it."

Cass linked her arm through her mother's. "I'm going to walk Mom to her car." She looked at Jared and Paulie who looked innocently back. "In the meantime, you guys set the table and put on beverages for everyone. Don't forget the napkins." She smirked. "It's the least you traitors can do."

Dan grinned at the unenthusiastic boys. "It'll all be done before you return," he promised. "Right, guys?"

"Right," Paulie said. Jared just shrugged.

Cass and her mother closed the door and walked companionably to Mom's car, parked in front of Cass's garage.

"He's a wonderful man, Cassandra Marie." Mom kissed Cass on the cheek. "I'm so happy for you."

Cass merely nodded. She still had no intention of talking about Dan with her mother. Anything she said would be family fodder well before bedtime tonight. She shuddered when she thought of Mom's version of the evening's earlier conversation zinging over the phone lines from here to Colorado. Tommy and Rhonda would get an e-mail version.

Mom slid into the driver's seat. "It's a good thing I've got my spies to tell me what's going on, that's all I can say."

"Thanks for the applesauce and pie. Nobody does it better than you."

"When Jenn's over her pique, I bet she'll be an even better source."

Cass hesitated a minute, then caved in to the inevitable. "Mom, he's wonderful, all I could ever want. But he's not staying." She waved her hand at SeaSong. "And I'm not going."

Mom looked thoughtful but said nothing.

Cass shrugged. She felt brittle, fragile. "I've lived without him for forty years, and I—" She swallowed and forced herself to say it. "I can live without him for forty more."

Mom looked at her with much too much understanding. "Cassandra Marie, the question isn't *can* you live without him. Of course you can. People live without those they love all the time due to illness or catastrophe or death. You are very competent and have proven yourself many times over the past forty years. You can live without Dan. The real question is do you *want* to live without him."

Cass gave a weak smile. "What I want isn't really the issue either. We're not talking about a unilateral decision. Besides, Jesus is everything I need, right?" She hoped Mom didn't hear the wobble in her voice.

"Oh, my dear." Mom climbed out and gave Cass a hug. She stood back and looked at Cass. "Listen carefully, Cassandra Marie. What I'm about to say is very important. Of course Jesus is enough in one sense. He's enough spiritually, providing salvation, offering peace of heart and mind, surrounding us with His grace. He never leaves us or forsakes us." Mom smiled slightly. "He's not about to move to New York City and leave you behind.

"But—and it's a big but—He's put us in families and Christian community because He knows we need each other. We need people to talk to, to hug, to do things with and go places with. We need people to encourage us and worship with us, to tell us off when we need it, and cry with us when we sorrow. Why do you think the Bible is full of verses that tell us to take care of one another? Jesus has chosen to let us represent Him to each other."

Cass nodded. *Hopefully when Dan goes back to New York City, the family will be there to sorrow with me. I'll certainly need them.*

Mom climbed back into the car. "Don't be afraid to admit that you need another human being, in this case a special man." She shut the door and rolled down her window. "More prayer," she said, looking directly at Cass. "Don't you worry about anything. I'll tell the girls."

The brothers' wives. Family fodder. But the aching yearning in her heart made Cass glad for the spiritual intervention on her behalf, especially since she knew she'd never have dared to ask for it. Her feelings about Dan were almost superstitious, though she was definitely not a superstitious person by any stretch of the imagination. *If I talk about him, he will go.* Ridiculous, but there it was.

"Pray for courage for me, Mom, whatever happens. For God's will."

"Right." Mom slipped the car into reverse. "God's will."

Cass knew the prayers would be much more explicit than the generic, "God's will." Cass knew for a fact that Mom had prayed very specifically about the brothers when they started dating their wives.

"Lord, she's just the right woman for Hal," or Tommy or Will or Bud. "You know, Lord, that I started praying for all my children's spouses before the children were even born. I asked for just the right mate to help make them the best people, the godliest people they could be. I think he's finally found her. Let's bring her home, Lord."

Cass always thought it sounded like reeling in a nice, fat fish.

Now Mom'd be praying, "Let's bring Dan home, Lord." Let's reel him in.

"Don't you worry about things. Now, good-bye, Cassandra Marie." Mom glanced over her shoulder, checked the alley for traffic, then stepped on the gas. Nothing happened. She opened her door and stepped out. "Am I up against something?"

Cass walked behind the car. She shook her head. "There's nothing here."

Mom frowned. Then, "Ah. I put on the emergency brake. I usually don't because the handle is broken off. You have to lean under the dash to release it." And she reached below the dash.

"No, Mom!" Cass lunged to stop her mother, but she was too late. The car, still in gear, began to move backwards as soon as the brake released. With amazing speed, the open door slapped Mom in the side and knocked her facedown right in the path of the accelerating car.

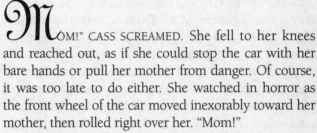

Twenty-Three

$\mathcal{M}$OM!" CASS SCREAMED. She fell to her knees and reached out, as if she could stop the car with her bare hands or pull her mother from danger. Of course, it was too late to do either. She watched in horror as the front wheel of the car moved inexorably toward her mother, then rolled right over her. "Mom!"

The front fender brushed Cass's hand with surprising force as it slid past, knocking her off balance. She fell on her side, her elbow scraping across the tiny pebbles and sand that lay in the drive, her hip slamming hard against the cement. Vaguely she felt her turtleneck sleeve give way under the force of her fall and knew the sting of a colossal brush burn.

Her mother lay unmoving, her head turned toward Cass, as the car continued to drive itself, rolling down the alley and out into the street, stopping only when it came up against the curb on the far side.

Cass scrambled to her knees, fear a cold hand about her heart. "Mom!"

Oh, God, please! Please!

She reached a trembling hand to her mother's neck to check her carotid artery. The thought that she might find no pulse made it difficult to draw a breath. She glanced frantically around, but there was no one in sight, no one to help her. She was on her own.

Oh, God! Oh, Lord! Please!

She didn't know whether she meant please let Mom be alive, or please help me do the right thing, or please send someone to help me, or all three. Probably all three. She placed her fingers lightly on her mother's neck below the ear. She went weak with relief as she felt a faint but steady heartbeat.

Still, the possibility of internal injuries scared her spitless, and she needed to get help and fast. The house, the phone, and Dan were just yards away, but how could she leave Mom long enough to avail herself of that help? What if someone whipped around the corner of the alley and didn't see her lying by the garage?

Her mother groaned.

"Mom!" Tears pooled in Cass's eyes as she lay on the ground beside her. "I'm here, Mom. I'm here." She was afraid to touch her, afraid not to. She laid a tentative hand over Mom's, flung out to the side. She gave the lightest of squeezes.

Mom groaned again, and Cass jerked her hand back like she was recoiling from the touch of a hot iron. "I'm sorry, Mom. I'm sorry. I didn't mean to hurt you." She pushed to her knees. "I've got to go get help, Mom." Cass stood. "I'll be right back."

Had Mom heard? Who knew? She turned and ran for the house, aware of a sharp twinge in her hip from her fall. *Please, Lord, don't let her think I'm deserting her.*

Breathless with haste and fear, Cass yanked open the back door and burst into the kitchen. "Call 911! Call 911!"

Dan, Jared, and Paulie froze where they were. Paulie had one of his chocolate chips submerged to his fingertips in a glass of milk. Jared had his hand in his cookie bag, pulling out one. Dan had his coffee mug raised to his mouth. On the table sat dinner, waiting only for her appearance to get the meal started. Poor roast. Who knew when it would get eaten now.

She turned back toward the alley, calling over her shoulder as she ran, "Mom's hurt! We need an ambulance."

"Jared!" she heard Dan order. She glanced back and saw Dan was right behind her. Jared, who had been running after her too, stopped in the doorway, reached back, and grabbed the phone off the wall.

When she got to the alley, she skidded to a halt, astonished. Dan bumped into her, his hands going to her waist to steady both of them. Cass barely noticed. She was too busy staring at her mother.

Mom was sitting up, leaning against the garage.

"Mom!" Cass knelt before her mother. "You shouldn't have moved."

"I'm fine," Mom said, raising a shaky hand to brush back her hair. "Just help me stand up."

Cass put a gentle hand on her shoulder to prevent her from moving any more. "Don't you dare think of standing. It's bad enough you're sitting. We don't know how badly you're injured yet."

Mom rested her head against the garage and shut her eyes. "I'm fine. Just a little winded, a little tired. Now give me a hand, and help me up."

Dan came down beside Cass. "Charlotte, Cass is right. You can't stand, not until the paramedics check you out. In fact, you probably should lie down."

"Paramedics?" Mom looked aghast. "I don't need paramedics. I just need my own bed for a nice nap. Do you hear me, Cassandra Marie? No paramedics. I mean it."

Cass ignored her mother's foolish order. "Where do you hurt? Can you tell me?"

"I don't know." Mom frowned as she thought about the question. "I can move everything." She flexed first one leg, then the other, twirled one hand at the wrist, then the other. She winced slightly, glancing up to see if Cass had noted. "See? All okay."

Cass, who had not missed the flinch, bit back a sarcastic *yeah, right.*

"What happened, Charlotte?" Dan asked. "Cass?"

"The car door slapped Mom and knocked her down. Then the car ran over her."

"What?" Dan looked at Mom with incredulity.

Mom made a disgusted noise. "I ran over myself. How's that for stupid? When Lew hears that, he'll never let me have the car keys again."

"It was an accident," Cass said as Jared, Paulie, and a very pale Jenn appeared from around the garage. "Dad'll understand." In fact, he might be relieved since this incident had nothing to do with dementia.

Paulie clutched a throw that he'd grabbed from the back of the love seat. "Put this around her so she stays warm," he said as he handed it to Cass. "You need to keep her warm."

"Thanks, Paulie. That was good thinking." Cass draped the covering lightly over Mom's shoulders.

"I took a first aid class over the summer," Paulie said. "Always keep the victim warm. It's important to help prevent shock."

"Thank you, Paulie." Mom pulled the edges of the throw closed. "You're a good boy."

Paulie flushed with pleasure, his red face visible even in the low light of the alley. "I took the class because I hate to be in a situation and not know what to do, you know?" He glanced toward Jenn. "It makes me feel weird."

As she adjusted the throw, Cass felt the tiny shivers that seized Mom. She looked into her mother's eyes to see if she was fading into shock. Both pupils looked normal, but her level of expertise at assessing such things was nil.

Jared cleared his throat, doing his best not to look scared. "The ambulance is coming. The 911 people tried to get me to stay on the line, but I didn't. I had to see how Grandmom was."

"Grandmom," Jenn whispered and started to cry. "Is she going to die?"

"Don't ask your aunt," Mom said in an amazingly strong, tart voice. "She doesn't know the answer. Ask me."

Jenn sniffed, her eyes wide with fright. "Are you?" she breathed.

Jared socked Jenn in the arm, knocking her off balance, and Paulie said in an appalled voice, "Jenn!"

"Let her be," Mom said. "It's a legitimate question to ask when someone's hurt." She looked at Jenn. "I'm not going to die, not for a good long time, and certainly not from this foolishness. So you can dry your tears." She patted the ground beside her. "Why don't you come sit beside me and help keep me warm?"

"Oh." Jenn looked at Cass for guidance, and when Cass nodded, she gingerly lowered herself beside her grandmother. "I don't want to hurt you."

"Don't worry. You won't. It'll take a lot more than you to do me in." With her left arm Mom reached to pull the corners of the throw more tightly about her neck and gasped.

"Mom?" Cass felt the blood drain from her face.

"Something's wrong with my arm." Mom studied the offending limb. She moved all her fingers carefully and again twirled her wrist. She shook her head. "That wasn't bad." She tried to lift the arm again and gasped at the pain.

A police car drew up to the curb, lights rotating but siren silent, and Greg Barnes climbed out. He strode to the group huddled around Mom, and Cass felt great relief that help was here. Almost immediately they heard the siren announcing the approaching ambulance.

Mom heard the ambulance too and frowned. "I told you. I don't need to go to the hospital. Just take me home."

"No, ma'am," Greg said as he knelt beside Mom. "You're going in the ambulance. Police orders."

Mom shook her head vigorously. "Greg Barnes, you're a very nice young man, and I'm certain you're a good cop, but I don't have to take any orders from you."

"Care to debate that?" he asked, a slight smile on his face.

Before Mom could muster her arguments, the ambulance pulled into the alley. A pair of paramedics climbed out. Tactfully but firmly they moved Cass, Dan, and the kids back and went to work on Mom.

"I don't want to go to the hospital," she protested. "I can't go to the hospital."

The paramedics ignored her.

"My husband will be upset."

"Your child will be upset if you don't go. And I'm here. He's not."

Mom shot Cass a dirty look.

"Now stay still," one paramedic said. "I'm going to immobilize your neck."

"There's nothing wrong with my neck. The car didn't touch my neck."

And I thank You, God! Cass thought as she watched.

When they slid Mom into the ambulance, she was still protesting to no avail.

"Come to the emergency ward at Shore Memorial," the paramedic said. Then she climbed into the back with Mom and they drove off, lights flashing but siren silent, announcing a serious situation within but not one which was life threatening.

As the ambulance disappeared around the corner, Greg returned from his perusal of Mom's car across the street, its nose sticking out into the road, forcing cars to drive around it.

"Can I move it?" Dan asked. "Park it here by the garage?"

Greg nodded. "I've got all I need for my report." He turned to Cass. "Do you want me to go tell Mr. Merton for you?"

"No," Cass said. "I'll tell him." And the brothers.

"Let me get Charlotte's car out of the road, then I'll take you to your dad's," Dan said.

Cass nodded and turned to Dan's car in a daze. The kids followed her, and Dan found himself with a car full. Greg led the way to Scallop Street with his lights turning, clearing any traffic from before them.

They found Dad in the kitchen looking at a very overcooked piece of steak.

"Where is she?" he demanded. "Look at my dinner! Ruined because she didn't come right home. She promised she would."

In spite of her worry, Cass couldn't help but smile. He sounded just like a frustrated homemaker whose family ignored her calls to the table. Then she sobered.

"Dad, we have some bad news, but it's not nearly as bad as it could be." *At least I don't think so.*

Immediately Dad forgot the steak. "She had one of her incidents? She hurt herself?"

Cass shook her head. "No incident."

"She got run over!" Jenn blurted, eyes huge.

"What?" Dad grabbed the back of a chair for support.

"Shut up, Jenn," Jared hissed. "Just keep your mouth closed. Let Aunt Cassandra tell. She was there."

Jenn started to cry. Paulie patted her on the back, his desire to comfort her palpable. She flinched at every pat.

"Mom did get run over," Cass said, and continued quickly, before her father could speak. "The front car door knocked her down and the front wheel rolled over her. She's on her way to the hospital right now, and we came to take you. She'll want to see you, and I know you'll want to see her."

The next few hours passed in a blur for Cass. There was the ride to the hospital and the wait in the emergency room. While they waited, she called Will, Hal, and Bud.

"Should we fly home?" Bud asked from Colorado. "We can be there by noon tomorrow."

Cass sagged against the wall as she held her cell phone to her ear. "I don't think you need to come. I don't think she's hurt nearly as badly as she could have been. Dad's with her now, and I'll call when I know more."

"We'll put her on the church prayer chain right away."

"Thanks," Cass mumbled and thought about her own church prayer chain. Pastor Paul ought to be notified too.

The doors to the waiting room flew open and Will and Lucy rushed in, followed by the three cousins.

"I called Pastor Paul and got Mom on the prayer chain," Lucy said. "Pastor said he'd be here as soon as he could make it."

"Now what's this about Mom running over herself?" Will demanded.

Cass hadn't finished telling the story before the door flew open again and Hal and Ellie, minus their kids, came in. Cass told the story a second time. Then Pastor Paul arrived and the story was rehearsed again with lots of prompting from all those who hadn't been present at the event.

As the family settled in to wait for any news about Mom, Will put his hand on Cass's shoulder and squeezed. "You did good, BB."

"Thanks, Will." Cass collapsed in one of the molded plastic chairs, Dan taking the one beside her.

He shifted his weight, trying to find a comfortable position. "Whoever designed these didn't have a man my size in mind."

"Poor baby." Cass patted his arm.

He grinned at her for a minute, then turned serious. He took her hand in both of his. "You doing okay, Cassie?"

She gave him a weary half smile and reached to push her hair off her face. She winced but ignored the cause. "Poor Dan. Another family emergency. You'll be so glad when it's time to leave Seaside and get back to your normal, uneventful life."

He didn't comment, just brushed the hair back for her. Then he turned her arm so he could look at her elbow. "When'd this happen?"

She glanced at the torn shirt and the brush burn. "I think the car knocked me over."

He stood and pulled her to her feet. "Come on. This needs to be cleaned and treated." He led her against her will to the desk. "Miss Merton hurt herself slightly in the same accident that her mother's being treated for."

The next thing Cass knew she was sitting on a gurney, Dan standing behind her with his hands on her shoulders, while a nurse cleansed and dressed the wound.

"There, all done," the nurse said. "And look, there's Dr. Wirshup. She can tell you all about your mom."

It was a great relief to learn that Mom suffered no internal injuries, only a broken clavicle. She had to remain in the hospital for two or three nights to be certain she was as fine as the doctor thought. After all, she wasn't a young woman.

"While we move her to her room, why don't you all—" the doctor indicated the family spread around the waiting room—"go to the cafeteria and get something to eat. Give us thirty minutes, then come up to Room 215."

"I can't stay with her while you move her?" Dad asked.

"Not for the next half hour. Go. Eat. We don't want you getting sick. Then you can stay with her as long as you like. We can even put a cot in the room if you want to spend the night."

In the cafeteria the adults clustered around one table, joined by Pastor Paul, and the cousins and Paulie sat at another. Warmed-over pizza and premade sandwiches were all that was left to eat, and Cass thought longingly of the roast left sitting on the kitchen table. Maybe tomorrow night. But wait. Tomorrow night she was supposed to go to Cape May on her reconnaissance trip. And on Wednesday at noon seven people were due to arrive for a three-day planning retreat for their software company. If Hurricane Rodney didn't keep them away.

Immediately guilt and indecision gripped her. Should she forget her trip? Send the seven people to another B&B? Certainly if Mom were seriously hurt, she wouldn't go out of town, even though she was only talking a little over an hour to Cape May. If Mom were in a life-and-death situation, she'd gladly send her guests elsewhere. But what was required for the present situation? Would she be a terrible daughter if she wasn't at the hospital every waking moment?

At that instant Will looked over at her from his seat across the table. "It's a good thing you're around to take care of Mom. She's going to need help."

"Yeah," Hal agreed. "It's a godsend that you've got the time to give her."

Cass felt Dan stiffen beside her as she digested the brothers' comments. She had lots of free time? Her eyes narrowed. She worked just like they did, maybe even harder since it was her own business, not some large, faceless corporation that employed her.

Even if she didn't go to Cape May, time was an issue. Seven people were coming the day after tomorrow. Seven single rooms. Food to buy and prepare. The dining room to rearrange so they could eat together. Lunches thrown into the deal for a very nice increase in her usual price. Dinners for Dan and the kids. Rodney coming and the need to prepare SeaSong to ride it out with seven guests plus Dan and the kids.

Dad frowned at Will and Hal. "I think taking care of Charlotte is my job, not Cass's."

"Well, sure, Dad," Will said. "But Cass will be available to you day or night if you need her." He smiled at her. "Right, BB?"

Dan leaned toward Cass and whispered for her ear alone, "It's up to you. I'll back you, but it's up to you."

He was right; she knew it. She wanted to stand up for herself; she truly did. She had to if the brothers were ever to understand that she was one of five siblings, all of whom owed Mom and Dad their time. She took a deep breath but didn't know how to begin without sounding selfish.

Pastor Paul studied Cass for a minute. "Maybe Cass doesn't have any more available time than you do, Will. Maybe you're putting an unfair burden on her."

Will blinked, clearly startled at the idea.

"After all," Pastor Paul continued, "she runs her own business, and everyone knows that running a B&B takes over your life. Then she's got Jared and Jenn living with her on top of that."

"And me," Dan said. "Plus she's got a business trip scheduled tomorrow night and seven guests arriving on Wednesday."

"She won't mind postponing her trip, will you, BB?" Hal smiled and took a bite of his ice cream Popsicle. He clearly thought the issue settled.

Maybe it was Hal's assumption that she'd do as he wanted. Maybe it was hearing the hated BB another time. Maybe it was the residual adrenaline from witnessing Mom's accident. Whatever, the dam broke.

Cass stood and stuck her finger in Hal's face. Her voice was low and angry. "Don't ever call me BB again."

Hal blinked, his face frozen. He turned to Will with a where-did-that-come-from look. "But we've called you that all your life."

"Well, I've hated it all my life." Her voice shook. "I know you didn't mean anything nasty, but it is still a terrible thing to call someone, meaning what it means."

"It doesn't mean anything anymore," Hal protested.

"It does to me. Every time I hear it, I cringe inside. I'm telling you both." She looked from brother to brother. "Never again. I mean it. Never again."

"I hate to say I told you so, Will, but I told you so," Lucy said. "I've told you for years it hurts her feelings."

"But she never said," Will defended.

"All you ever had to do was look at her face," Lucy told him.

"Then what do we call her?" Hal asked in a tone that just missed whining.

"Cass," she hissed. "Call me Cass. After all, it is my name." And she sat down before her shaking knees gave way. She was appalled at herself. What kind of a daughter made a big deal out of a stupid nickname while her mother was being admitted to the hospital?

In the ensuing silence everyone avoided Cass's eyes as they gathered their trash and quickly left the table until only Cass and Dan remained.

She turned to Dan. "Did I just make an idiot of myself?"

He gave a little laugh. "It wasn't quite what I expected you to say."

"It wasn't what I expected me to say either." She covered her face with her shaking hands.

"Hey, don't let it worry you." He pulled her hands from her face and held them. He leaned close to her until their faces were only inches apart. "You said what needed to be said. This may not have been the best time, but it wasn't the worst either."

She let her forehead drop to rest on his. "Thanks. What would I do without you?"

When they finally stumbled home after the nurse made everyone but Dad leave Mom's room, Cass rescued her dried roast and wrinkled vegetables and stored them in the refrigerator to resurrect another day. She sent Paulie home, Jenn and Jared upstairs, and reveled in a comforting hug from Dan. Somehow his hug made the unbearable bearable. What would she do without him? It didn't abide thinking about, especially when he was holding her like she was precious. She told herself to just enjoy the moment. The future would come soon enough. Finally, he kissed her good night and took himself upstairs too.

Cass stumbled into her little room beneath the stairs and pulled on her nightshirt, the one that read *She sells seashells down by the Seaside.* She stuffed her feet into cozy socks. Glossy Flossie might keep her warm through the middle as the animal cuddled against her, but her feet were constantly freezing without the socks. Not very classy, but then who would see?

Cass sighed as she climbed into her little bed. She burrowed under the covers, Glossy Flossie purring comfortably in her arms. She buried her face in the cat's soft fur and let the rhythmic rise and fall of Flossie's contented purr and the sensuous feel of the silky coat comfort her.

She'd been so sure she'd seen her mother killed.

Thank You, God. Thank You!

Then she'd taken her stand against BB.

And thank You, Lord, for loving even us idiots.

And what had she been thinking when she assumed taking in the kids would mean just a couple of extra bodies around? Talk about ignorant! And talk about feeling overwhelmed!

Add Dan to the pot, and life was a full rolling boil. Dan. She felt such an aching, such a yearning that her throat hurt. How she loved him.

Her breath caught. She loved him.

The realization burst over her like the Fourth of July fireworks, all color and enchantment, filling her with wonder that the magic had finally exploded for her.

She loved him with all her heart.

And he would leave her.

The bright swirls of color filling her heart fizzled and died.

Lord, I'm terrified and full of awe at the same time. I'm so afraid of when he leaves. Before when my heart wanted a soul mate, it was just a vague feeling of longing for what I saw so many others have, including the brothers. I felt left out, out of step, but there was no one I focused on, no unrequited love. Now my longing has a name. I can't believe that such a wonderful man exists and that he seems to choose to be with me. Me!

And then he'll choose to leave, just as soon as You tell him what it is You want him to know. And I'll be worse off than before because I'll have had a taste of a man I could love for the rest of my life.

And tears fell, much to Cass's surprise. She wasn't a weepy woman. She toughed things out. She didn't cry. But her cheeks were still wet when she fell asleep.

She awoke to the raucous blast of the smoke alarm and a choking cloud of smoke.

Twenty-Four

*A*T THE SOUND OF the alarm, Cass sat bolt upright in bed. Immediately she smelled smoke, lots of it. In the darkness of her little cell, she couldn't see it, but she *felt* it in the heaviness of the air around her. Smoke. Terrible sulfur-smelling smoke! Fire!

Get out! Get out! Grab Flossie and get out. Get the kids out. Get Dan out.

She reached for the light on the tiny table by the bed. In her haste and fright, she knocked against the lamp, and it went tumbling over the far side of the table to crash in the tiny square of space between the bureau and the wall. Even over the blare of the alarm she heard the pop as the bulb shattered.

In blackness she slid from bed onto the narrow alley of floor, barely registering the chill in the November air. She knew she had to be low to stay under the worst of the fumes, to find air that was safe to breathe. Keeping her head down, she reached up, feeling for Flossie who lay sleeping somewhere in the blankets, oblivious of the bleating alarm. Cass had thought the animal was going deaf, but now she knew for certain. No creature with working ears could miss the cacophony of the alarm.

She felt all over the comforter without finding Flossie. She took a deep breath, rose up on her knees, and threw the comforter over the foot of the bed, no easy task in her position. She skimmed the blanket with her hands. No Flossie. She threw it back too and felt wildly about. She was running out of air and time. Her hand smacked into a pile of warm fur that grunted at the slug she'd inadvertently given it. Cass grabbed the startled cat, tucked her under one arm, and dropped back to all fours to crawl out of the room.

She'd taken no more than two steps when the door to her room burst open. Dan rushed in, bringing very dim light from the kitchen and setting the thick smoke to swirling wildly in the new air currents.

"Cass! Cass!" he yelled, then tripped over the foot of the bed. With a yelp of pain he sprawled full length where a minute or two before she had slept.

She could hear Jenn and Jared calling her name from the smoke-shrouded kitchen. She yelled, "I'm coming! Go outside! Go!"

"Cass!" Dan was flailing around in the bed, searching for her, and she realized he couldn't see her down on the floor.

"I'm here," she shouted over the bleat of the alarm, reaching up and slapping at the bed. She connected with his leg, stinging her hand.

Dan growled something and rolled off the empty bed right on top of her. As his weight hit her, she collapsed facedown in the tiny space between the bed and the dresser, her hip, already sore from the fall by her mother's car, catching one of the dresser knobs as she fell. Pain. Then all the air whooshed from her lungs as Dan landed on top of her, his feet dangling in her face.

Flossie, caught beneath Cass, let out a fierce howl at the indignity of being squashed and began to claw her way free. The animal had only her rear claws, but her desperation made them more than enough.

"Ouch, ouch, ouch!" Cass yelled as fiery scratches burned down her arm. She managed to lift her upper body enough to free the cat who streaked from the room. She collapsed immediately as Dan squirmed, trying to turn toward the door in a space not meant for anyone his size to move.

"Out!" Dan swatted at her.

"Off," Cass gasped, elbowing him in the solar plexus.

Dan groaned and shifted to the side as much as he could,

which wasn't much. "Just get out," he yelled. "The smoke is gathering in here." He coughed, a deep, ugly rasp, and scrambled to turn himself around, kicking her a couple of times in the process.

Cass pulled herself forward on her elbows like a soldier under fire. When she was free from the bulk of his weight, she got back to her knees and began crawling. Her head spun, her lungs burned with the effects of the smoke, and her stomach heaved at the noxious rotten egg smell.

"Hurry." Dan's hand found her rump and pushed. He coughed some more.

Cass crawled into and across the kitchen and out the door the kids had left open behind them. Once outside she got to her feet and headed for the sycamore. The clean, cold air washed over her. Sinking to her knees, she pressed her hands to her aching chest and breathed it in. Wonderful!

"I called 911," Jenn said, holding her cell phone in Cass's face. "I called them as soon as I got outside."

Cass looked up at Jenn, who had on a fuzzy blue robe and white bunny slippers.

"Good girl. Thanks, Jenn." She reached out and patted a bunny slipper. But was a cell phone the first thing to grab in case of fire?

Beside her, still on his hands and knees, Dan inhaled and coughed, inhaled and coughed.

"Are you okay?" She laid her hand on his back as, head down, he struggled for breath.

"Yeah, I'm fine." His voice was raspy, but he was obviously breathing more easily all the time. He turned and sat, leaning his back against the tree. She turned and propped herself against the tree beside him. They stared at the house as they waited for the fire engines.

Poor firemen, Cass thought. All volunteers, pulled out of bed in the middle of the night.

"Where's the fire?" Jared asked after a few minutes. "There's no fire."

"What do you mean?" Cass stared at SeaSong. As far as she could see, Jared was right. "But all the smoke—" It poured out the back door and out the window over the kitchen sink.

Jared, wearing only old sweatpants that looked as if they'd lost all their elastic or their drawstring and threatened to slip off his narrow hips at any minute, walked to one side of the house and then the other. "Something's weird here." He disappeared down the side yard.

"Be careful!" Cass called after him. A gust of chill wind whipped by. She wrapped her arms about herself in a futile attempt to keep warm. She wanted the throw that Paulie had brought for Mom. She looked down at her *She sells seashells down by the Seaside* nightshirt and shivered. If it wouldn't keep her warm in bed under the covers unless the cat cuddled against her, there wasn't a ghost of a chance it'd do much good out here. At least she had her heavy socks on. Poor Dan's bare feet must be freezing. He sat beside her dressed in a t-shirt and jeans.

Cass shuddered, and Dan slid his arm around her shoulders. "Lean in. We'll keep each other warm."

Cass leaned, angling so her back rested against part of Dan's chest. Immediately his body heat eased her shivering. He rested his cheek against Cass's head, and she closed her eyes to enjoy his nearness.

"I'm just glad there aren't any other guests," she said, thinking of the chaos and danger if there had been. "And thank goodness the insurance is paid."

Dan's arm tightened about her. "Don't ever do that to me again," he said softly. Then his voice turned rough. "You scared me to death."

She turned and looked at him. "Do what?"

"The kids were both out in the yard when I hit the kitchen, but you weren't anywhere in sight. All that smoke, so dense in the kitchen, and your closed door. I thought my heart would stop."

"Yeah?" Sorry as she was that he'd been worried, she definitely felt toasty at that revelation. "And that's when you crashed into my room?"

"That's when I came to save you," he corrected, kissing the top of her head.

Jared reappeared on the far side of the house. "Still no fire. And there's only smoke in the back. Could be the way the wind's blowing or something. I went up on the front porch and peered in the door and windows. No smoke."

Dan hauled himself to his feet, and Cass felt the loss of his heat immediately. Sighing, she climbed to her feet too. She could hear the sirens drawing closer by the second.

"You're right, Jared," Dan said. "Now that I'm thinking more clearly, there was no smoke until I pushed the door open to the kitchen. Then there was plenty, and it smelled like rotten eggs."

"Reminds me of a chemistry experiment gone bad," Jared said.

Cass studied SeaSong. Jared and Dan were right. Something was weird here.

Jared pointed. "How'd the kitchen window get broken? Did any of you break it?"

Cass, Jenn, and Dan shook their heads as they followed Jared and stood staring at the kitchen window, or rather the place where the window had been. All that remained in the lower sash were a few shards sticking out at varying angles like transparent knives.

"Maybe the heat from the fire blew it out?" Cass suggested.

"What heat?" Dan shuddered with the cold. "There's no heat, just like there's no flames." He started toward the kitchen door.

Cass grabbed his arm. "Where are you going?"

"If there's no heat and no flames, there's no fire. I want to see what's going on."

"Yeah, me too." Jared was excited, ready to race into the house with Dan.

Cass grabbed Jared with her other hand. She glared at them both. "Let the firemen go in first! They're almost here."

Even as she spoke, Greg Barnes pulled up to SeaSong for the second time that night. The fire department was right on his bumper. Men in their heavy coats, boots, and hats filled the yard. One shooed Cass, Dan, and the kids back out of their way. Others grabbed the hoses and attached them to the nearby hydrant. Neighbors who had begun appearing at the sound of the blaring alarm gathered in little groups, whispering among themselves. All the commotion almost drowned out the still bleating alarm.

Reminder: Thank the company that had hardwired the system through the whole house for her. It worked very well.

Cass looked at the heavy hoses and imagined the destruction to SeaSong under the pressure of the water that would explode as soon as the nozzles were opened.

"Wait!" she cried, rushing up to the first man on the hose. "We don't think there's a fire. See?" She waved her hand at the house.

"No flames. Please don't make water damage! I've got irreplaceable antiques in there."

"Lady," the fireman said politely, "if we don't find fire, we won't shoot water. I promise."

Feeling like an idiot but still glad she'd spoken, Cass stood with Dan and the kids and watched as the firemen swarmed in and out of SeaSong.

"You were right," Greg told them after conferring with the fire chief. "There's no sign of fire. Just the remains of a smoke bomb in the sink."

"A smoke bomb in the sink?" Cass could hardly believe her ears. A smoke bomb? "Are you sure?"

"The paper lying in the sink is clearly the remains of the wrappings of a spent smoke bomb. We all recognized it right away because we use bombs like that in training drills. Someone broke the window and dropped the lit bomb in the sink."

"But why?" Cass stared at the broken window where wisps of white smoke still appeared.

"Random malicious mischief," Greg offered. "That's our best guess. That is, unless you've got a secret enemy out there trying to harm you." He smiled at the absurdity of that idea.

Enemies? Her? Cass shook her head. "It makes no sense."

Greg shrugged. "This kind of vandalism rarely does."

"You mentioned an enemy harming her. How would the smoke bomb harm her?" Dan asked. "Aside from scaring us all and forcing us out into the night."

"The smell," Greg said. "It could drive away the guests at a B&B easily."

"But I don't have any guests but Dan." Cass shivered and not just from the cold. An enemy?

"We'll do our best to find those responsible," Greg said, "but hit-and-run nastiness like this is hard to trace." He patted Cass awkwardly on the shoulder.

And that's supposed to make me feel better? Cass wanted to ask but didn't. She was afraid she was feeling more than a bit whiny, but then she'd never had her personal space invaded in such an act of vandalism before. She rubbed her arms, trying to get the goose bumps to go away. SeaSong, the castle she'd built by the sea, had been breached.

Dan moved to stand behind her, his hands on her shoulders just like in the emergency room earlier that same night. Immediately she felt safer, which was foolish because the invader was still out there.

"Where does someone get a smoke bomb?" Dan asked Greg. "It's not something you pick up at your local Wal-Mart."

"A fire supply store that sells to fire companies," he said promptly. "Anyone could buy one. Businesses use the bombs sometimes to trace the effectiveness of heating and cooling systems. Light the bomb and see where the smoke goes. Oh, by the way, Cass, whoever slept in the little room under the stairs shouldn't go back there tonight. It'll be the last place free of the smoke."

Finally the weary firemen left to return to their warm beds, and Greg drove off on his appointed rounds. The neighbors went back home, and the street fell quiet again. After a quick bowl of ice cream, the kids went off to bed, Jared taking the remains of his bag of chocolate chip cookies with him for sustenance through what remained of the night.

After she grabbed her smelly robe from the floor where it had fallen when she almost stripped the bed looking for Flossie, Cass walked through the whole house, checking each room thoroughly for possible damage.

"Do you smell that rotten egg smell up here?" she asked Dan who trailed her to the third floor.

"I don't think I do, but then we both smell so bad, I really can't tell." He took her by the shoulders and turned her toward the stairs to the second floor. "Tomorrow we'll be able to tell much better. For now, grab one of the guest rooms, take a nice hot shower, and climb into a decent-sized bed for a change."

"Flossie!" Cass yelled so loudly that Dan jumped. Guilt washed over her when she realized she hadn't given the cat a thought over the last couple of hours. It was the mention of bed that finally made thoughts of Flossie's warm presence spring to her mind. "We've got to find her and make sure she's all right."

"It's a cinch she wouldn't go outside. She's probably hiding under one of the love seats in the sitting area," Dan said.

Cass blanched at the thought. "What if she was overcome by smoke?" She raced down the stairs and rushed through the swinging doors. She came to a halt as she saw Glossy Flossie draped over the back of a love seat, her chest rising and falling in sleep.

"Told you," Dan said from directly behind her.

She grabbed the cat who gave a startled squeak. "Are you okay, baby? You don't have to be afraid anymore. Mama's here." As she hugged the animal, Flossie responded with a contented purr that made Cass smile. "Come on, sweetheart. We're going upstairs to bed."

Weariness washed over Cass as she and Dan climbed to the second floor. He opened the door of a room across the hall from his. She walked in and put Flossie on the bed. Then she came back to the hall. "Thanks, Dan, for everything. I—I don't know what I would have done without you."

He smiled and wrapped his arms tightly around her. She rested her head on his shoulder.

"Just know I'm here for you, Cassie. I won't let anything bad happen to you or the kids."

She knew he couldn't guarantee that he'd be able to keep that promise. No one could. Life was too uncertain. But she delighted in the fact that he cared enough to try. He kissed her good night, and went to his room. As his door closed, she rubbed at her arms against a sudden chill that had nothing to do with the weather. Unsafe in her own house!

She showered, washing away the smell of the night but not the lurking fear. She slept fitfully in her guest room, clad in an old sweat suit of Jared's that was only slightly too big. Even with Flossie tight against her, she couldn't get warm. It was 5:30 A.M. when she finally gave up trying and got up.

She went downstairs to the kitchen and turned on the coffeemaker. A fine gritty dust lay over the entire back of the house. While she waited for the brew to drip through, she wiped down the counters and the table.

She felt edgy as, mug of coffee on the table beside her, she snuggled on the love seat, feet pulled up and under the throw Paulie had brought for Mom. She wished she had the quilt from the bed she'd just slept in to fend off the cold seeping around the cardboard that Jared and Dan had tacked over the gaping window. Her own quilt stank too much to use without a thorough cleaning. The love seat didn't smell too good either.

"Couldn't sleep?" Dan stood in the doorway, wearing jeans

and a sweatshirt, tall, handsome, and sleep-rumpled. Cass's heart thumped at the sight.

"Help yourself to some coffee," she said. "I was just going to turn on the Weather Channel and get the bad news about Rodney."

Dan filled a mug and walked to the love seat. "Slide over a bit."

She slid away from the arm, her feet falling to the floor. Dan sat where she had been, twisted to rest his back against the arm, and slid one long leg behind her, letting the other fall to the floor. "Now turn and lean back on me. I'm freezing."

Cass turned and slowly, carefully rested her back against his chest. Her knees were bent, her feet resting against the other arm. She spread the throw haphazardly over them.

She held herself stiffly. It was bad enough she hadn't expected to see him for at least an hour, and therefore hadn't washed her face or combed her hair. She was also afraid he'd find her too heavy leaning her full weight on him.

He reached over her and adjusted the throw so that it covered her legs and was pulled up to her chin. "Relax," he whispered in her ear. "I won't bite, and already I've stopped shivering."

So had she.

By the time they finished their coffee, she had relaxed to the point of resting her head on his shoulder as she watched Heather Tesch talk about Hurricane Rodney. It was a category two storm and had 110-mile-an-hour winds as, traveling north by northwest, it bore down on the coast of Virginia. It would make landfall around Virginia Beach in a couple of hours. Whether it would blow itself out as it hit land was anyone's guess.

There was a small possibility that Rodney would continue its north by northwest trajectory and travel up the Chesapeake Bay instead of following the coast. If it did so, Maryland, Delaware, southeastern Pennsylvania, and New Jersey would get a real beating. Traveling over the vast expanse of water that comprised the Chesapeake could help it sustain itself at strength instead of blowing itself out. If it continued at its present rate of travel, estimated time of arrival at the Jersey shore was sometime late Tuesday night or early Wednesday morning. There would be heavy rain and high tides no matter what Rodney did or became.

"Will the folks from Software Solutions still come, do you think?" Dan asked.

Cass shrugged. "Who knows? I sure hope so. They're the type of clientele that I'd like to develop for midweek off-season. I bought a small business mailing list and sent a specifically designed brochure to several hundred companies, describing SeaSong as the ideal place for a planning retreat. Software Solutions was the first response, and I've got two more companies booked for early next year. If a few businesses come and like it here, the word will get around, and bingo! I'll have a full house most of the winter."

Cass watched as the TV showed on-site pictures of the surf at Virginia Beach. Blown by the high winds, huge waves rolled in, covering the beach and rolling right into the streets. A piece of a metal roof flew by followed by a Stop sign.

"They could decapitate a person," Dan said as he too watched the flying debris.

"Ever been in a hurricane before?"

He shook his head. "Never had the privilege. You?"

Cass nodded. "You get this you-and-me-against-the-elements feeling. You know there's danger, and you respect the power, but it's also exhilarating. " She pointed at the TV. "See? That reporter's got it."

The TV reporter was hunkered inside a hooded raincoat, water streaming down his face. His expression reflected a mingling of fear for what the elements can do when they explode and exultation at standing unbowed by the wind and fury.

"But if there's an evacuation order, we will follow it," Cass added.

The station switched to taped shots of the Carolina Outer Banks taken yesterday. The video showed a house on the beach slowly collapsing as the waves pounded it, falling in slow motion into the furious sea. Cass was suddenly glad that SeaSong was two blocks from the water.

The station switched back to Virginia Beach. The reporter showed a tape from yesterday as the folks of that town prepared for the onslaught. Merchants shuttering show windows and home owners putting plywood over sliding doors reminded Cass.

"We've got to get that broken window fixed today." She

glanced toward the boarded-up opening. "I hope the glazier can come."

"I can do it for you," Dan said and seemed to stop breathing as he waited for her answer.

"Good with windows, are you?"

"Yes."

"But—"

"If you say, 'But you're our guest,' I think I'll toss you onto the floor."

Cass blinked and twisted to look at him. He stared back without expression, but she felt a suppressed anger rippling from him. Then it clicked.

"So that's what yesterday's little diatribe on the boardwalk was all about." *You're our guest.* She'd said those very words when he told her he could watch the kids. How many other times had she said it to him?

"It wasn't a diatribe."

She sat up and swung her legs to the floor. She turned to face him fully. "I'm sorry. I never meant to seem unkind." She took one of his hands as she looked into his eyes, searching for some clue that she was on the right track. "I've just been trying to save you from being caught in the cyclone that my life has become."

"What if I want to get caught?" he asked. "Ever think of that?"

She nodded. "Boredom can make you do all sorts of things you wouldn't normally do, I suppose."

"So can other emotions."

She stopped breathing. Other emotions? The same ones she felt? Her mouth went dry at the possibility.

He stared at her for a moment longer, unblinking. Then he grinned, reached out a finger, and pressed her nose. "So, do I have the job?"

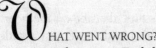

Twenty-Five

WHAT WENT WRONG?

At midmorning Tuck looked out his bedroom window in the ratty room in the house next to SeaSong. He was careful not to brush against the filthy curtains that hung in near tatters. The dust cloud they'd raise would surely asphyxiate him. Dirty as they were, though, they weren't as bad as the pillow he'd had to use last night. He'd covered the gray case with one of his T-shirts, but he still got the whim-whams when he laid his head down. Fortunately, he hadn't spent much of the night in bed.

He couldn't let himself think too much about his surroundings, or he'd hyperventilate at all the dirt and crud. The germs and little creatures that shared his room made his skin crawl. The smelly old man who owned the place, crazy as a coot, hacked and coughed all day and all night, spewing who knew what latent epidemic into the air, but he had one saving grace. He didn't ask questions. He was too busy hating the world to wonder about a guest willing to pay an exorbitant sum to stay in his abominable place. If the stakes weren't so high, Tuck wouldn't stay here on a bet.

But the stakes were high. Two million high. Not that two million went all that far when one lived as he intended to. And that brought up the issue of Grandad Cal's will, not to mention Hank's. One heir for all that green stuff was so much better than two. Tuck smiled at the thought of that money. He stared through the dirty window and thought of his Caribbean island, its clean air, its pristine beaches, and its lovely women.

All that stood in his way was Sherri.

So where had she been last night? He didn't understand it. Several people had rushed outside, but not Sherri. Did she and that idiot Kevin sleep so soundly that they couldn't hear smoke alarms? He'd worked under the assumption that in a public building like SeaSong, if one alarm sensed smoke, they all rang.

Maybe the alarms were individual battery alarms instead of ones hard wired into the electrical system. If they were individual, they wouldn't have sounded unless the smoke reached them. It was possible to sleep through the noise under those circumstances if you were, say, on the third floor with a fan or air conditioner on. But it was November. Who had cooling units on this time of year in this locale? The furnace was more like it. And certainly the people who lived in SeaSong with them would make certain they escaped.

Today was Tuesday. Time was becoming an issue. If he had found SeaSong's number, so could Hank. If he had come to Seaside, so could Hank and Patsi. He had to make certain there was nothing for them to find if and when they arrived. He had to be certain, too, that he was long gone.

Smiling to himself, he leaned on the window frame and studied SeaSong. What he wouldn't give to be able to stay there instead of in this garbage pit. He loved class, and SeaSong had it in spades.

The back door opened and the tall blonde stepped out. Pretty lady. A bit overblown for his taste, so tall and round and all, but still very attractive. She dumped a green trash bag full of stuff— probably dirty rags and paper towels from cleaning up his mess— in the big trash bin behind the garage.

He'd watched with fascination last evening as the comedy of errors with her mother had unfolded behind the garage. He shook his head. How did you manage to run over yourself without killing yourself?

He hadn't seen Sherri at the car accident scene, but he hadn't really expected to. A guest wouldn't necessarily be involved in a situation like that, probably wouldn't even know about it. It was the blonde and her family—the two kids and that big guy who was her husband. No way did Tuck want to tangle with him. Not only was he huge; he was also in shape, a bad combination if ever there was one.

The back door opened again, and he blinked as Sherri walked out. She had a large green plastic bag in her arms too, and when she met the returning blonde halfway to the trash, the blonde turned back and opened the lid of the trash bin for her.

What was Sherri doing helping the blonde clean up? Sure, she'd always had an unhealthy addiction to helping people, but this was extreme. He studied the blonde. He couldn't believe that someone who ran as classy a place as SeaSong would let guests help. It wasn't like the damage from the smoke was all that great.

He hadn't wanted to burn the place down or anything. Arson wasn't his thing. He'd dropped the smoke bomb through the kitchen window he'd broken, taking care not to cut himself on the shards of glass sticking up in the frame. He wasn't about to leave his DNA on the windowsill.

The bomb had done a great job, loosing billows of white, nasty-smelling smoke that swirled through the kitchen. He'd watched it pour out the broken window for a minute before he ran back to his vantage point at the window in his room.

There he waited for everyone to rush outside so he could have a shot at Sherri, maybe even Kevin. He had a great angle on both the front and back of SeaSong. But Sherri hadn't appeared.

Now here she was, and he was leery of shooting in the daylight. He'd be too vulnerable.

Sherri and the blonde stopped just outside the back door of SeaSong as the big guy pulled into the parking area in front of the garage and got out of his BMW. Tuck eyed the silver car with appreciation. Running a B&B must bring in better money than he'd thought, if that car was any indication.

The guy leaned into the backseat and lifted out a pane of glass, which he proceeded to mount where the broken kitchen window had been. The blonde and Sherri watched for a minute. Then the blonde pointed to the window and made little back-and-forth motions with her hand. Sherri nodded and disappeared inside. She reappeared in a few minutes with a big bottle of blue liquid and a roll of paper towels.

The big guy climbed down from the stepladder he'd been using, and Sherri scrambled up. She began washing the window.

Washing the window? Sherri? Suddenly he began to laugh, and he couldn't stop. She was the help, not a guest.

Tuck had rarely been so surprised in his life. Sherri Best, Miss Apple of Hank's Eye, was working as a chambermaid or house-keeper or something like that. She who never had to work a day in her life, she who had grades in school that would more than set her up for a good position in Best Electronics—she was doing grunt work.

What was wrong with her?

Not that he cared. She had to go regardless. At least he now knew why she hadn't come outside last night. She wasn't staying there. So where did she live? He'd have to keep watch for when she finished work and follow her home. This new development made only a slight ripple in his plan. He'd scope her place out and act tonight, maybe even with the same plan as last night. In the meantime, he'd better contact his alter ego staying at the Marriott Suites in Hawaii.

He dialed the number, let it ring twice, hung up, then dialed again immediately. He waited impatiently for Lonnie to answer.

The phone was picked up on the fifth ring. "Tucker Best here."

That was supposed to sound like him? It's a good thing he'd told the creep not to answer the phone unless it was his special ring.

"Lonnie, it's Tuck. How's it going?"

"Let me tell you, Tuck, I love this place."

Tuck could practically hear the guy smiling as he looked out over the Pacific paradise. He'd done right in picking this poor schlep for the job.

Lonnie continued to rhapsodize. "I love this hotel, you know? They got room service like you wouldn't believe! I'm running you up a bill, man."

"Don't worry about the money. Just enjoy yourself." He might as well. It'd be one of his last undertakings, if not the last. "You're not letting them see you, are you? You're staying in the room like I told you to?"

"Yep. But I gotta ask you. What's the good of being in Hawaii if you can't go to the beach and watch the girls in their bikinis?"

"Just a day or two longer, Lonnie. Then you get paid, and you can get your own room anywhere you want."

"Cool!"

Like he'd live that long. Even a dumb jock like Lonnie would figure things out when Sherri's murder made the papers. "Don't forget to order the dirty movies at night so they know you're there." Tuck laughed. "So they know *I'm* there."

"I did it just like you said the last two nights. I gotta tell you, being you is way cool. All I want to know is, what's her name that you're sneaking off to see, and why don't Hank like her?"

Tuck laughed. Wouldn't Lonnie just blow a gasket if he did know her name? "Uh-uh, Lonnie. No lady's name. I'm too much of a gentleman."

Lonnie snickered, and Tuck shook his head. The guy was an idiot, a gen-u-wine brass-plated idiot. As he hung up, Tuck felt a familiar rush of power slide through him. There was nothing in the world like being the most clever. Nothing.

Except maybe some clean sea air to blow away all the beasties and crawlies that he no doubt had clinging to him after a day in this hole. He grabbed his jacket and left.

Twenty-Six

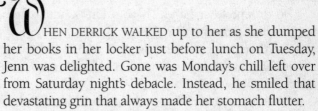

HEN DERRICK WALKED up to her as she dumped her books in her locker just before lunch on Tuesday, Jenn was delighted. Gone was Monday's chill left over from Saturday night's debacle. Instead, he smiled that devastating grin that always made her stomach flutter.

"Guess what happened last night?" She was eager to tell him of the smoke bomb adventures.

"Want to go for a ride with me?" he asked.

"I'd like that." She wished she could be cool, but she could feel the flush of pleasure that stained her face.

He held out a hand. "Let's go."

She blinked. "Right now?" Leave school in the middle of the day? The clock on the wall read 11:05. She couldn't imagine such a thing.

"Sure, right now." He leaned in and kissed her nose. "Why not?"

She was flustered and confused. She felt all warm and cherished from his kiss, but his invitation made her feel odd, almost like she was on trial or something. "But school—we can't leave school."

"Sure we can. We just walk out the door."

She stared, both appalled and impressed with his daring.

"Just a little drive around the block over lunch."

"But we're not supposed to go off campus."

He raised that awful eyebrow at her. "Are you scared of bending the rules, Jenn?"

Yes. Yes, she was. When you left school, you got in trouble. Big trouble.

His grin faded, and he stared at her in disappointed disbelief. "I thought you liked me."

"I do," she hastened to say. "I really do." But her chest hurt, and her heart pounded.

He grinned, happy again. "Then come with me. You won't get in trouble. They'll never know you're gone."

"Can't we go for a ride after school?" Her voice was breathy, pleading.

He dropped her hand. "If you don't want to come with me now, I'll find someone who does."

She thought of all the girls who wanted to be with him, and her stomach cramped even more. "I-I want to go with you," she managed, "but—"

Derrick shrugged. "But nothing. You'll be back before anyone notices." He smiled that wonderful smile again, rested one hand on her waist, and leaned in close. "Come on, sweetheart," he whispered in her ear, making goose bumps rise all over her arms and neck. "Do you think I'd let you get in trouble? Now do you?"

Not trusting her voice, she just shook her head. If she liked him, she had to trust him, didn't she?

He gave her a little squeeze. "Grab your coat and let's go."

Jenn glanced up and down the hall and found it empty. All the kids were either at lunch or in their next class. More important, all the teachers were busy elsewhere too. Before she knew it, she was running down the hall, her hand in his. As they raced outside, she kept waiting for someone to yell, "Get back here!" No one did.

He led her to his car, opened her door for her, and shut her firmly inside. Feeling brazen, excited, and conscience-stricken all at the same time, she watched him climb in his seat and turn the key in the ignition. Her hands gripped each other in her lap.

Derrick Smith was taking her for a ride in broad daylight on a school day. Wow!

She forced a wobbly smile and thought she'd be sick to her stomach with nerves.

If her father ever found out, he'd ground her until she was

thirty—not that he'd ever know. When he and Mom deserted her, she became free to make her own choices. Derrick grinned over at her, and she smiled back. He was her choice.

He fingered the fall of hair that rested on her shoulder. "You are so beautiful. We're going to have a wonderful time together."

She settled into her seat, enchanted that he said such things to her. Her smile faltered a bit as he reached behind the seat and pulled out a bottle filled with clear liquid. His hand covered the label.

"What are you drinking?"

"Water," he said, taking a swallow.

"Really?" The bottle wasn't like any water bottle she'd ever seen.

He pointed a finger at her. "You are too suspicious." Again that charming smile. "You need to trust me, Jenn. Trust me."

She nodded, but a little piece of her remained skeptical. She tried to brush it aside. She'd been listening to Jared too much.

They drove south on the island into the area of town that was largely summer homes. The streets were quiet and empty. When Derrick pulled into an alley, she thought nothing of it until he pulled into the parking space beneath a home one block back from the beach.

"What are we stopping for?" she asked as Derrick took another drink. He held the bottle out to her, and she shook her head.

As he took another swallow, two other cars pulled into the parking area. Several kids she knew vaguely from school climbed out. She watched them, frowning slightly. They weren't kids she would have normally picked to be with.

She looked at Derrick. "I thought we were going for a ride, just you and me."

"Disappointed?" He leaned over and kissed the tip of her nose again. His lips were wet from his drink, and she had to stop herself from wiping the kiss away.

She shrugged. "I thought maybe we'd finally have some time alone." At his suggestively raised eyebrow she hastily added, "To talk, you know?"

The others surged past their car, several banging on the windows as they passed. The girls waved at Derrick with a tad more

240   Gayle Roper

friendliness than Jenn thought appropriate with her sitting beside him. She wanted to stick a huge Hands Off sign on him.

"It's Mark's house," Derrick said, pointing to one of the guys. "We're just stopping here for a minute." He climbed out, taking his bottle with him. "Come on."

Jenn followed because she didn't know what else to do.

The crowd gave a small cheer when the door opened. They climbed the stairs behind Mark and poured inside. Derrick took Jenn by the hand and pulled her inside too.

"Hey, look!" Mark pointed to a cabinet against the living room wall. Through a small window on either door of the cabinet a row of bottles showed. "Booze!"

Jenn watched the kids cheer and head for the cabinet, her eyes wide and distressed. "Derrick, I think we should go," she whispered.

"Not now, sweetcakes. The fun's just starting."

"But you said a ride around the block."

He shrugged. "So we drove a bit farther."

She tried to tug Derrick toward the door. "If we stay, we're going to get in trouble!"

He took another swallow, set his bottle on an end table, and smiled. "Trouble? Nah. Nobody knows we're here."

"Then they'll miss us at school." Jenn had never felt so desperate.

"Hey, Mark," Derrick called. "They gonna miss you at school today?"

Mark made a face. "You kidding? I'm home sick in bed. I got the flu."

"I got a terrible cold."

"I'm going to a funeral."

"I have a college interview."

"I got terrible cramps."

"Hey, Mark, I've got the flu, too," Derrick said. "Whaddya know about that? I bet I caught it from you."

Everybody except Jenn laughed as person after person called out their excuse for not being at school. Jenn turned cold all over. She was the only one who was going to get in trouble because she had been at school.

Derrick, still pulling Jenn by the hand, called, "Who's got a knife?"

Three penknives were immediately thrust into his palm. He grabbed the biggest and pulled the blade out with his teeth.

"Watch this, darlin'," he said to Jenn, pulling her right up to the liquor cabinet.

"Derrick, don't!"

He grinned at her distress. "Relax, beautiful. Trust me."

To do what? she wanted to ask but didn't. She turned to Mark. "This isn't your house, is it?"

He looked bewildered. "Whatever gave you that idea?"

Jenn spun back to Derrick in time to see him insert the knife blade into the lock on the cupboard. The lock held, but the wood splintered, and the doors swung open. Everyone but Jenn cheered as they surged forward and grabbed the bottles. She fought the nausea rising in her throat. She tried to pull free of Derrick's grip, but he merely squeezed her hand tightly enough to hurt.

Derrick grabbed one of the bottles from the cabinet and held it out to Mark. "Open it."

Mark complied, and Derrick grabbed it back. He turned to Jenn and smiled. This time there was no charm in the grin, but a strange combination of challenge and mockery. "Have a drink, Jenn."

She shook her head desperately. "No, Derrick. Please, no. I want to go."

Around her people started chanting her name: "Jenn, Jenn, Jenn." Their eyes were all avid with an unhealthy need for her to become like them. Jenn shuddered.

"Drink, Jenn." It was an order. Derrick put the bottle to her lips and tilted it. "Drink, or it will pour all down your sweater. What will you tell your precious aunt when you come home smelling like a brewery?"

Jenn kept her lips pressed together.

Derrick jerked her arm, and she gasped in astonishment and pain. Liquid poured into her mouth. She swallowed the large mouthful automatically and immediately began to cough as the liquor burned its way to her stomach. She clapped her free hand over her mouth, afraid she'd retch. That would be the ultimate humiliation.

"Water," she managed as everyone laughed at her. She felt herself go from frightened pale to embarrassed red. "I need water."

Derrick released her hand and gave her a push. "The kitchen's that way. But hurry back."

She ran to the kitchen, threw open cupboards until she found glasses, and filled one. She swallowed the water, trying to cut the taste in her mouth and the pool of fire in her stomach. Maybe it wouldn't feel so weird if she'd had some food in her, but she didn't. What had she swallowed? Whiskey? Scotch? She didn't know much about alcohol since her parents didn't drink. Neither did Aunt Cassandra.

Tears burned her eyes. *God, what am I going to do? I've got to get out of here! Help me!* But no great plan of action occurred to her.

With a strong sense of mortification she realized that Jared, Aunt Cassandra, Dan, and even Paulie had been right about Derrick all along. *How could I have been so dumb?* She shivered and filled the glass again. She had seen only what she wanted to see. Stupid, stupid girl!

She set the glass on the counter and turned toward the living room. She had to talk Derrick into taking her back to school. She had to. She paused just inside the kitchen door to calm herself.

"The fun's just begun," she heard Derrick say. He laughed, and the sound made her flesh crawl. "Look here."

"What are they?" Mark asked.

"Roofies."

"You're kidding!" There was respect and excitement in Mark's voice.

"I drop one in her Coke, and she'll never know what hit her." He gave the nasty laugh again. "Magic pills. No odor, no taste."

Jenn pressed herself against the refrigerator because she wasn't sure her legs would hold her up anymore. Roofies! She knew what they were.

And she thought she'd been afraid before!

She blinked, trying to take in the magnitude of Derrick's betrayal. He planned to give her Rohypnol, the date rape drug.

God, I've got to get out of here! she prayed.

Derrick appeared in the doorway. "Look what I found, Jenn. Coke." He held out a filled glass and a can. "If you don't want to drink, you don't have to." He smiled that utterly charming smile, the one that used to override any of his nastiness by its sheer appeal.

Jenn stared at the glass as he walked to her and placed it in her hand.

"Hey," he said, concern in his voice. "You're trembling."

If she hadn't just heard him talking with Mark, she'd believe his worry for her was real.

"I don't feel so good," she managed, an understatement if ever there was one. She held a hand in front of her mouth like she might become sick and wrapped the other around her waist. "I'm not used to drinking, and I swallowed that awful stuff on an empty stomach." She made a gagging sound. "I need to go to the bathroom."

She pushed the Coke back into his hand. "I'll get this when I come back. It'll probably help settle my stomach."

Anger flared in Derrick's eyes, but she didn't care whether she upset him or not. Not anymore. She made a little urping sound and hurried down the hall until she found the bathroom. She shut the door behind her and turned the lock, her hands shaking so badly that she could barely make the little button move.

She put the toilet lid down and sat. She wiped wildly at the tears that now flowed.

Oh, God, I'm sorry! I should have listened. I should have been nicer. I should have asked You what You thought. Please, just get me out of here!

She took a deep breath and tried to think. *Get out. Door.* She looked at the door and knew who waited on the other side. *Get out. Window.* She stood and looked out the lone window, located between the toilet and the vanity.

Her stomach rolled worse than it had when the liquor hit it. The ground was so far away. The house was built so that the first level was merely pilings, and the house really began on the second floor. She'd never realized before just how far from the ground a second floor was.

A roar of laughter came from the other side of the door. Jenn thought about the people out there and the plans they had for her. Suddenly the drop to the ground didn't look so bad after all. And if she broke something and lay there in the drive, certainly Derrick wouldn't come out and attack her in broad daylight.

Anything was better than Roofies.

A knock sounded on the door. "You okay in there, sweet-cakes?" Derrick.

Jenn jumped and stifled a scream. "Sure." She made a gagging sound. "I-I just need a minute more." She gagged again.

"Take you time, Jenn. Take your time." She could almost see him stepping back, his face full of distaste.

"Thanks," she called, trying to sound wobbly and weak. It wasn't hard, since that was exactly how she felt, though for a different reason than he suspected.

When she heard him walk away, she went to the window and lifted the lower sash. A screen blocked her, and she pinched together the tabs on the bottom and lifted, listening for the catch, not wanting it to fall on her or her hands as she climbed out. A crisp breeze blew in her face, and she shivered. She was leaving her coat, but she didn't have a choice. Hopefully Aunt Cassandra wouldn't notice that she was suddenly wearing her old one everywhere.

At least she had her purse. She threw the strap of her shoulder bag over her head and stuck one arm through until it lay across her chest like a bandoleer. She pushed it to rest across her back.

Okay, Lord, please help me. And please don't let me fall and break something.

Taking a deep breath, she climbed onto the vanity, turned backward, and stuck one leg out the window. Carefully she slid her second leg out and balanced, her hips on the sill, her upper torso and head inside. She gripped the inside edge of the windowsill as tightly as she could and pushed herself out. She used her feet, braced against the siding, to keep herself from losing control.

Don't look down. Don't look down.

Slowly she lowered herself until she was hanging with her arms fully extended.

Oh, Lord!

She let go.

Twenty-Seven

"AUNT CASS! AUNT CASS!" Jared raced up the steps and through the front door, Paulie hard on his heels.

Heart pounding, Cass came running from the kitchen, Dan right behind her. What was Jared doing home from school in the middle of a school day? "What happened? What's wrong?"

"It's Jenn."

Cass grabbed Jared's hand, her heart kicking. "How badly is she hurt?"

Jared blinked. "She's not hurt."

"Then what's wrong?"

"I was looking out the window in the cafeteria, see, when all of a sudden I saw Jenn."

He stalled and Cass, her hand over her pounding heart, prompted, "And?"

"She was walking down the street with Derrick." Jared looked green around the gills. "They got into his car and drove off!"

"I saw them go too," Paulie said. "I was standing right beside Jared."

Jenn and Derrick? In his car? In the middle of the school day? Cass felt the blood drain from her face, and she became light-headed. She grabbed the banister to steady herself. Brenna, who had hurried downstairs at Jared's raised voice, placed her hand comfortingly over Cass's. She turned her hand over and gripped Brenna's.

Oh, dear Lord, help!

Quietly Dan came and stood close behind her, his strong hands resting on her shoulders. Immediately some of her fear dissipated.

Jared started pacing the entry hall. "Two other cars drove off after them." He looked at Cass, his face full of anguish. "Aunt Cassandra, those guys have such bad reputations. Everybody knows what wild men they are, but Derrick's got Jenn snookered. She thinks that he's so hot, and she likes all the attention he pays her. She has no idea what he's really like, no idea what she's getting herself into by going off with him. None."

"That's why we couldn't let her go to the movies with just him," Paulie said. "We don't trust him an inch. The man is evil."

"Why didn't you tell me he was so awful?" Cass asked. "I'd never have let her go."

"Then she might have tried to sneak," Jared said. "And we'd never know what was going on. We thought that if we kept a close watch, we'd be able to keep her safe." His shoulders slumped. "Not."

"They've done this type of thing before," Paulie said. "Bagging school, I mean." He buttoned and unbuttoned, buttoned and unbuttoned the top of his jacket. "Not Jenn. Derrick and his gang."

"Where do they go?" Dan asked, his voice calm.

Cass held her breath as she waited for the answer.

Jared looked as sick as if he'd gotten another large whiff of last night's obnoxious smoke. "I've heard them talking before, bragging, you know? They like to break into empty summerhouses and spend the day hanging out."

Cass flinched. Breaking in was bad, but... "How do you define hanging out?" She already knew the answer, but she needed to hear the words. Maybe then it wouldn't seem so unbelievable.

Unhappily Jared stared at his feet. "They drink and smoke." He hesitated. "And stuff."

"Drink heavily?"

Jared nodded.

"Smoke what?"

"Anything. Everything."

Cass closed her eyes. It was the party all over again, only

worse, much worse. The thought of what Derrick might talk the infatuated Jenn into doing made her want to throw up.

"Just a sip, Jenn. You'll like it." Or *"Come on, Jenn. Just a puff. It'll make you feel good."*

Dan's hands on her shoulders, hands that gently massaged the tense muscles, were all that held Cass together. That and the knowledge that God loved Jenn even more than she did. Otherwise she'd explode from tension, little pieces of her raining down all over Seaside. She took a deep breath.

"You said, 'And stuff.' Tell me. I've got to know." Her voice shook.

Jared swallowed uncomfortably, looking out the still open front door rather than at Cass. His young face was a study in misery. "Sex. Lots of sex."

Cass brought her hand to her mouth as she swallowed against the nausea. She dimly realized that she was leaning against Dan and hoped he didn't mind because she was afraid she wouldn't be able to stay erect on her own.

"Some of the wild girls always go along," Paulie said, his usually happy countenance pinched with dread. "But the latest idea is for one of the guys to con a virgin into going. When she leaves, she—" he swallowed convulsively—"she isn't a virgin anymore."

Cass had read and heard about such things happening, but to Jenn?

"Do they use force?" Dan asked quietly, and Cass shuddered.

Jared and Paulie looked at each other. Paulie looked ready to cry.

"Tell us," Cass said. Rape? Beautiful, willful Jenn? *Please, God, no!*

"Some of the guys were talking at football practice about Roofies being available in town," Jared said.

"Roofies? Rohypnol, the date rape drug?" Cass couldn't believe it. In quiet little Seaside? "And Derrick's gotten hold of some?"

"I don't know for sure."

"But you think so."

Jared nodded unhappily. "I know lots of the kids are easy as far as sex goes, but it's with their dates or their steadies. But these guys—Aunt Cass, Jenn can't take care of herself with these guys. She's too—"

"Naive," Cass said.

Jared made a face. "I was going to say stupid." He looked as though he wanted to cry right along with Paulie. "She knows better. She may be innocent, but she's not ignorant. She knows what's what."

"Okay." Dan's voice was steady and strong. "So we've got to find her before she's hurt. Derrick drives what?"

"A black Explorer. Two other cars followed them, a dark green Jeep, and a yellow VW Beetle."

Dan nodded. "We should be able to find them."

"But what if they go off island?" Cass asked in despair.

For a moment no one said anything. If the kids drove off island, there was no way they could find them.

Dan spoke to Cass. "Do you want to call the police to help us search?"

She closed her eyes and let herself lean even more heavily on him, absorbing his strength. She tried to think around her fear. Breaking and entering. Underage drinking. Drugs. Illicit sex.

Oh, Lord, let me make the right choice!

"You say they usually stay in Seaside?" she asked the boys.

They both nodded.

"Let's try by ourselves first. They only left school, what? Ten, fifteen minutes ago? It'll take some time for them to find a house to break into, won't it?" Unless they already had one staked out, she thought but didn't say. "If Jenn doesn't have to have a police record, it'd be better."

"Okay," Dan said. "We'll look ourselves. Agreed?"

Everyone nodded, and Dan continued. "They have to park somewhere. There aren't many garages in the south end of town where most of the summer homes are. Cars are in the open. We can drive around until we spot those three cars. The island isn't that big. When we find them, we'll rescue Jenn."

"Whether she likes it or not." Jared looked ready to fight anyone or anything.

Brenna spoke for the first time. "We can help. I'll get Mike—it's his day off—and we can look too."

"Jared, why don't you take your Aunt Cass's car? Paulie, you go with him. Cass and I can go in mine, and Brenna and Mike will make a third team."

Cass listened to Dan organize the hunt and was grateful. She herself could scarcely think. She was too afraid for her pretty little niece whom she planned to kill as soon as they'd saved her. And they had to save her. How could she face Tommy and Rhonda if they didn't?

"Do you each have cell phones?" Dan asked.

Brenna and Jared nodded.

"Trade numbers. Here's mine." Dan recited it. "Jared, you start at the south end and drive east-west patterns, ocean to bay. Brenna, you and Mike start in the Gardens and drive east-west patterns until you meet Jared in the middle. Then start again. We'll drive north-south. Whoever finds the cars, call the rest of us immediately."

Brenna and Jared nodded again.

"Then wait until we get there," Dan said as they both turned to leave. "Don't go running in alone. It might be dangerous. Wait for Cass and me. And now, Father God, help us locate Jenn. Keep her safe in Your care."

Oh yes! Oh, God, keep her safe! Don't let her get hurt. Please!

They ran for their cars, and in minutes, Cass and Dan were driving, looking, hoping, praying.

When Cass sniffed, Dan glanced at her. He reached for her hand and squeezed it. "Shh, Cass, it'll be all right. We'll find her. Don't cry."

At his words she became aware of the previously unnoticed tears on her cheeks. She rubbed at her face with her jacket sleeve. "Dan, she's so young!"

"She's not that young. And she knows right from wrong. After all, she has you as her model."

There was little comfort in that. All she could imagine was the Rohypnol being used, maybe slipped into a drink when Jenn wasn't looking. It didn't taste or smell, so she'd never know she'd been drugged until she woke up, and then it would be too late. "But what if—"

Dan gave her hand a shake. "Don't go there, Cassie. You're making it worse for yourself."

She nodded and sniffed again. "You're right." She stiffened her back. *Oh, Lord! Please!*

They made their way slowly up and down the length of the narrow island, first one street then another, then another. They scanned every car they saw, moving or parked. None matched the descriptions Jared had given. Cass felt panic rising.

"The alleys, Dan. Drive the alleys. They might park behind a house they wanted to get into rather than at the curb."

He nodded and turned down the nearest alley.

"Look! A yellow car!" Cass's heart leapt with hope.

"But it's a Honda, not a VW." Dan's voice was full of regret.

"What if they're in a garage?" Cass's words quivered in the air as they drove past the yellow Civic. "We'll never see them then."

"There were three cars according to Jared. That's a lot to find convenient garage space for."

They drove from the north end of the island to the south, turned, and drove back on the next alley. They passed a dark green Explorer and a black Jeep, neither the correct combination of color and vehicle.

"It's my fault, isn't it? I drove her to it with my hard line on Derrick."

"Cass! Jenn's doing what she knows is wrong, and it is not your fault. And you weren't too hard-line. You always gave her an alternative, a way to be with Derrick, but a way that kept her safe."

"And all he wants is to corrupt her."

"It sounds that way."

"Oh, Lord, please!" Derrick's thinking and plotting was so beyond Cass's experience that her mind balked. She couldn't imagine purposely hurting someone. She couldn't help but feel she was taking part in a movie, a very evil movie. The cameramen and director were just invisible.

As they turned to begin another pass, Cass spied a girl limping along the sidewalk, head down, arms hugging her middle. The girl's shoulders shook, and her long auburn hair hung down her back in a tousled mane.

"Dan!" Cass pointed, her heart in her throat.

"I see her." He pulled to the curb, and Cass threw the door open before they were even stopped.

"Jenn!"

The girl whirled, her face full of fear, her body bent in a protective crouch.

"Jenn, it's me." Cass spread her arms.

Jenn blinked her tear-swollen eyes, and her face lit up in relief. "Aunt Cassandra!" She raced into Cass's arms and glommed on. Great sobs tore from her throat.

Cass hugged her back. "Shh, sweetheart. It's okay." She ran one hand soothingly up and down Jenn's back. "It's okay. We've got you. You're safe."

"It was awful, Aunt Cassandra! I was so scared!" Jenn's whole body shook. "We were just going to drive around the block, but they hadn't even been to school." She shuddered. "Derrick only stopped in to get me."

Cass wasn't sure she understood everything Jenn was saying, but she hugged the girl and repeated, "It's okay. You're safe now."

"They were drinking." Jenn's voice grew disbelieving.

"Derrick, too?"

"He started as soon as we pulled away from school. He said it was water." She sniffed. "I think it was vodka. He offered me some, then told me how beautiful I was."

Just what any young girl wanted to hear. He was so clever. Cass shuddered as she led Jenn to the car. They leaned against the silver fender as Jenn continued her story. Cass kept an arm about her niece's waist.

"I'm so dumb. I thought the house belonged to one of the kids. Then one of the guys found a liquor cabinet, and they broke in." Jenn stared at Cass in a mix of disbelief and horror. "They took a penknife and forced the doors apart. The wood cracked and splintered, and they all laughed. That's when I knew I was in deep trouble."

"Ah, baby." Cass kissed her temple.

Jenn gave a weak smile. "Derrick wanted me to drink. I didn't want to, but he forced me," she wailed.

"Shh, honey. It's all right." But Cass knew it wasn't.

"It made me cough, and it burned! It tasted terrible." She made a face. "Everyone laughed at me, especially Derrick."

Cass could see the pain of betrayal in her eyes. The boy she thought was wonderful, the boy who kissed her and told her she was beautiful, had mocked her instead of protecting her.

Jenn sighed and put a hand to her mouth like she was trying to control the wobble in her lower lip. "I felt like my throat was on fire, and I thought I'd never breathe right again. I ran to the kitchen for some water, which only made them laugh harder." She swiped at her runny nose with a crumpled tissue. "I was coming back to the living room, trying to figure out how to get out of the mess I'd gotten myself into, when I heard Derrick laughing with the guys, a nasty laugh, you know? It made the hair on my arms stand up." She rubbed her arms at the memory.

Dan tapped Cass's arm and held out his jacket. For the first time she realized that Jenn was without her coat. She refrained from mentioning the fact, took Dan's jacket, and draped it over her niece's shoulders.

"R-roofies," Jenn said as she pulled the jacket close. "He had Roofies. 'She'll never know,' he said."

Jenn sniffed and wiped at her nose again. "Do you know what R-roofies are?"

Cass nodded.

"H-he was going to use them on m-me." Large tears washed Jenn's cheeks.

"Ah, sweetheart." Cass held her as she cried, rocking her gently.

"I w-wish my mom was here," Jenn whispered.

"I'm sure you do." Cass ran her hand down Jenn's fall of hair. She wished desperately that Rhonda were here too. Rhonda would know just what to say to make it all better. Mothers were like that.

"So how did you get away?" Cass made her voice brisk to help counter Jenn's tears.

Jenn straightened and sniffed. "I told them I felt sick to my stomach from the drink and had to go to the bathroom. I even managed to make gagging noises." She slumped again. "I felt sick, all right, sick with fear. I locked the door, prayed like crazy, and climbed out the window."

Cass gave a puff of laughter. "You climbed out the bathroom window? Good for you, girl! I'm proud of you."

"I was scared stiff."

"I'm sure you were." Cass looked at the house in front of them, raised on pilings. Her heart broke a bit more. "First floor?"

Jenn shook her head. "Second."

Second. "Onto concrete or dirt?"

"Dirt."

Cass closed her eyes, thankful beyond measure for that strip of dirt in the sea of concrete that ran beneath most houses built on pilings. She could imagine the terrified girl opening the window, scrambling over the sill, lowering herself by her hands, and dropping, dropping to the ground, all the while expecting Derrick to break in and grab her.

Thank You, Lord. How easy it would have been for her to break her legs. "Is that how you hurt your ankle?"

Jenn nodded and studied her foot. "It's swelling."

"Some ice will take care of it." Cass hoped she was right, that it wasn't any more serious than a sprain.

Brakes squealed as a car whipped around the corner. Jenn jumped and huddled closer to Cass. Dan stepped near them both. The car screeched to a stop, and Jared and Paulie leaped out. Jared raced to Jenn. He reached for her as she held out her arms to him. Their hug was fierce and full of love. Cass had to blink away her tears.

Then Jared stepped to the side, and Paulie gave Jenn a quick, awkward hug. For once Jenn didn't pull back.

"I'm glad you got away," Paulie said, holding Jenn by her shoulders. "I'm glad you're okay." He frowned. "You are okay, aren't you?"

She nodded. "I'm okay. Ashamed, maybe, but okay." One tear rolled down her velvet cheek.

"Where are they?" Jared's face was hard, his jaw muscles bunched.

Jenn opened her mouth, but Cass spoke first. "No, Jared. It's not your job to get them."

"Yes, it is." His hands were balled into fists. "She's my sister. Mess with her, and you answer to me."

"To me, too," Paulie said, his usually open face as set as Jared's.

If the situation weren't so serious, if Jared and Paulie weren't so determined, so intent in their desire to right the wrongs done to Jenn, Cass would have smiled at their vigilante spirit. It was so unlike either of them. They were the quintessential good guys.

Dan spoke for the first time, "I don't blame you, Jared, Paulie, for wanting to get those guys. If someone did something like that to Cass, I'd want to get them too."

Cass stared, staggered at the vehemence in Dan's voice. Over her. She caught Jenn's astonished and impressed glance and flushed.

Dan continued, "But we can't go around beating up guys, no

matter how much they deserve it. That's taking the law into our own hands. We'll call the police. We'll let them take care of the problem for us."

"But, Dan—"

"No, Jared." Dan held up a hand, palm out in a stop signal. "No. Besides, I'm pretty sure the cops'll do a much better job than we would. Fines, some time in a holding cell, a trial, community service or jail."

"Names in the papers?" Paulie asked hopefully. "Nice and embarrassing?"

"Probably," Dan said. "They're old enough, but no guarantees."

"Will Jenn be mentioned?" Concern colored Paulie's voice as he looked at her, his heart in his eyes.

"I doubt it," Dan said.

"Because I'm a minor, right?" Jenn asked.

"I think it's more that Derrick won't mention you because of the testimony he knows you could give. It'll be bad enough for them without some sweet young thing saying they were going to give her the date rape drug."

Jenn shuddered at the memory, and Cass stepped close, running her hand in circles on her niece's back.

Jared and Paulie looked at each other, then nodded in resignation. "Okay, call the cops."

"So where are they, Jenn?" Dan asked.

She made a choking noise and looked scared. "I can't tell."

Cass sympathized. When the house was raided, all the kids would know who had ratted. Still, there was the issue of responsibility. Cass looked Jenn in the eye. "If you don't tell, some other girl is going to go through the same thing you went through, and she might not be lucky enough to escape."

Jenn wrapped her arms around herself as tightly as she could. She started to cry again. "I thought he liked m-me."

Cass watched in mild surprise as Paulie gently laid his arm around Jenn's shoulders and pulled her close to his side, and in deep surprise when she didn't pull away.

"I'm such a f-fool," she blurted. "Such a fool."

"Now don't talk that way about one of my favorite people," Paulie said, giving her a squeeze. "Besides, I think you're a heroine."

Jenn blinked and looked at him, so big and tall beside her. "What?"

"You escaped. Talk about clever and brave."

"Oh." Obviously she hadn't considered things from that viewpoint. "Oh." She brightened a bit.

"Where are they, Jenn?" Dan asked again.

She looked at her brother who nodded, then at Paulie who nodded and gave her a thumbs-up.

"You two are going to have to be my bodyguards, you know," she said, only half joking.

Paulie grinned. "Okay by me."

She took a deep breath and straightened her spine. She turned to Dan and gave the address of the house where the party was going on. He nodded his thanks and pulled out his phone.

Brenna and Mike pulled up as Dan made his call. Brenna ran to Jenn and hugged her, dislodging Paulie's arm. Resigned, he stepped back, his moment of glory over.

"I'm so glad you're safe!" Brenna cried. "I was so worried."

Jenn looked at the six people surrounding her. "You all were looking for me?"

They nodded as one.

Cass watched as it struck Jenn that she was well and truly loved. The girl blinked rapidly as more tears threatened.

"I-I don't know how to thank you. Especially since I've been so horrible lately."

"Yeah, you have," Jared said.

"Jared!" Cass glared at him.

He shrugged. "I'm just being honest."

"Sometimes it's best to just be silent."

"It's okay, Aunt Cassandra." Jenn smiled at Jared. "He's got no tact, but he's still the best brother a girl could have."

Jared reddened and grabbed his sister in another bear hug.

Cass looked at Dan to see if he appreciated what a sweet moment this was, especially since he'd lived through Jenn in high dudgeon. He winked at her, and her heart swelled. He understood.

"We'd better get back to school," Jared said as he released Jenn. "Before we're really in trouble."

Cass looked at her niece, eyes still red, face flushed. "Do you want to come home for the rest of the day? You can put your ankle up and keep it on ice."

She shook her head. "I've got to go back. People have to see me. It's the only way I can save some of my reputation."

Jared looked thoughtful. "You know, I think you should walk around holding Paulie's hand for the next few days."

"What?" Jenn and Paulie said together.

Jared leveled his forefinger at Jenn. "Just listen. We want to put as much distance between you and Derrick as possible, right?"

"Well, yeah."

"The best way is to make it look like you have a new boyfriend."

"Okay by me," Paulie said, smiling broadly.

Jenn looked less convinced.

"And when people say they thought you were going with Derrick, just say that you decided that he was too wild for you. That's not a lie."

"But saying Paulie's my boyfriend is."

"Now wait," Paulie said. "I'm a boy and I'm a friend, right?"

Jenn nodded.

"Well, there you are." Paulie stuck his hands in his jeans pockets and waited for her response.

"But everybody knows I try to avoid you."

"So tell them you changed your mind," Jared said. "Think Derrick, and Paulie ought to look pretty good."

Cass rolled her eyes at Jared's less-than-flattering pronouncement, but Paulie seemed untroubled.

"Sounds like a plan to me, Jenn," Brenna said. "It's not like Paulie's ugly or anything. In fact, he's kind of cute in a shaggy dog kind of way." She grinned at Paulie who flushed to the tips of his ears. "And believe me, Derrick isn't going to pick a fight with someone Paulie's size. You and your reputation will be safe."

Jenn thought for a minute longer, then nodded. "Yeah, okay. It's worth a try."

Cass's shoulders relaxed. She glanced at Dan who looked amused by the whole idea. Jared looked satisfied, and Paulie was floating three feet off the ground.

"Do you want notes to get back into school?" Cass asked.

The kids nodded, and Cass pulled a tablet from her purse.

"Family emergency ought to do it except for Paulie."

"Put it for me too," he said. "I'm practically family."

When the notes were written, Jared, Jenn, and Paulie climbed into Cass's car.

"Don't worry, Aunt Cassandra," Jared called as he slipped the car into drive. "We'll take care of her." He smiled at his sister. Then his face took on a fierce look. "As long as she promises never to do such a stupid thing again."

Jenn scrunched her nose at him. "Do I look that dumb?"

"You look beautiful," Paulie said. "As always. Here, let me hold your hand so we can practice."

Jenn rolled her eyes.

Twenty-Eight

Cass COLLAPSED INTO a kitchen chair. Tremors like an earthquake's aftershocks rolled through her. She held out her hand so Dan could see it shaking. "I'm a wreck."

"And you're surprised at this?" Dan put a glass of water on the table in front of her.

"Thanks," she whispered but made no move to pick the glass up. She'd slop it all over herself; she knew it.

Dan pulled his chair close to hers. He reached for her hands. "Reaction shivers. That's all." He rubbed his thumbs over the backs of her hands.

"Mmm." She closed her eyes and tried to think happy thoughts, tried to forget what might have happened if Jenn hadn't escaped. It didn't work. The shivers continued. "So close, Dan. So close!"

"But she saved herself, Cass. Be proud of her."

"I am—when I'm not still terrified. Or furious." She scowled at him. "How could she have been so stupid?"

Dan gave a half grin. "She's sixteen. Do you remember how mature you were at that age?"

She gave him a small wry smile and felt it wobble. "I haven't thanked you yet for all you did to help. I don't know what I would have done without you." She blinked against sudden tears. "You were wonderful."

Dan's eyes became bright with emotion. "You were the one who was wonderful." He leaned over and kissed her cheek. "You handled those kids just right."

"Strictly the grace of God." Cass sighed. "I never realized how hard being a parent is, especially without the first sixteen years to set the pace."

They sat in a comfortable silence until Cass glanced at the clock on the wall.

Twelve thirty-five. She blinked and pushed to her feet.

"Yikes! Look at the time!"

Dan studied the clock. "Lunch."

"Lunch, my foot. It's time to get to work. There's so much to do before tomorrow. I've got to visit Mom, finish getting ready for Software Solutions, and call and cancel tonight. And then there's Rodney."

Dan frowned at her. "Why are you canceling tonight? Go. It'll be good for you."

She sighed. "I can't leave Jenn. Not after today. "

He picked up her glass and took a drink. "Sure you can." He downed the rest of the water.

Cass shook her head. "She'll need me around. I'll just go some other time."

"Cass, honey, she'll be fine. Jared and Paulie aren't going to leave her side for quite some time. They'll take care of her. And Brenna will be here."

Cass closed her eyes. She had been looking forward to being away from the kids, much as she loved them, to being accountable just to herself for a few hours. "I'd feel like I was deserting the ship."

"Miss Responsibility." Dan gave her a warm, tender smile. "You need to get away, even if it's only for one night."

She looked at him out of the corner of her eye. "Trying to get rid of me, are you?"

Dan put the empty glass in the dishwasher. "Just the opposite. I was going to offer to drive you down to Cape May."

Drive her? "I couldn't let you do that. It's too far. Besides—" she paused and saw him stiffen—"you're our guest."

"Cass!" He looked like a thundercloud ready to unleash a wild and woolly lightning bolt.

She grinned. "Gotcha."

He growled at her as he grabbed her in a bear hug. "Terrible woman."

Her grin broadened, then disappeared. "Seriously, Dan, it's too far. It's not like driving me a couple of blocks to my parents'."

He frowned. "I wasn't planning to just drop you off, you know. I thought I just might try that B&B too."

She stared at him. "W-what?"

He fidgeted uncomfortably. "I thought I could, um, you know, go along and sort of help you with your industrial espionage and all."

Help her with her spying? "You want to go to Cape May with me?"

He nodded.

"But why?" Was he so bored here that even a quick trip to Cape May looked exciting? Or did he think she couldn't manage by herself, especially with Rodney coming?

He shrugged. "Why not?"

"Not reason enough. Why?"

He looked directly into her eyes. "Because I want to be with you."

She stared. People didn't go places simply to be with her. At least men people didn't. Her voice sounded breathless when she said, "You'd better call for a reservation."

He looked slightly embarrassed. "I called yesterday. After our 'discussion' on the boardwalk."

"What?" She couldn't believe it. "And you didn't tell me?"

"I was going to tell you after dinner last night, but things got a bit wild."

Well, that was certainly true. Still, she couldn't believe he wanted to go to Cape May with her. Just to be with her. Her! She felt warm and cozy inside, especially since she knew she'd never have had the nerve to ask him to come along.

"I think we should leave in time to be there for their high tea this afternoon," he said. "How about two?"

Cass nodded, dazed. "I've still got to visit Mom, and make certain we're ready for the Software Solutions group tomorrow."

"Well, then let's get to it. Where's your checklist of things to be ready for Rodney?"

—⚏—

Russell House was a lovely old Victorian painted yellow with navy, royal blue, and white trim. It had been built in the 1880s after the great fire in 1878 destroyed Cape May's entire hotel district with its tightly packed wooden structures. Warren Islington Russell of Philadelphia, who made his fortune in canned goods, built the place for his wife and eleven children to spend their summers in the healthful climate of the seaside. He commuted weekends from Philadelphia on the train that ran right through Seaside on its way to Cape May on the southern tip of New Jersey. The Russells were long gone, and the present owners had done to the grand old house much the same thing Cass had done to SeaSong.

"You'll love it," she assured Dan as he drove south on the Garden State Parkway.

She still couldn't believe he was seated beside her. What a wonderful memory the trip would make after he left. Firmly she pushed aside the empty feeling any thought of his departure brought. She was going to enjoy this special interlude to its fullest.

Warm and welcoming, Russell House was filled with marvelous antiques. After they were shown to their rooms, Cass and Dan wandered through the common rooms and studied the wealth of history present in the pieces of furniture, the paintings, and the objet d'art.

"Look at this wonderful hand-painted chocolate set." Cass lightly skimmed her forefinger over the tall, narrow china pitcher covered with clusters of bluebells tied with golden ribbons. Small cups, also covered with the bluebells and ribbons, sat on tiny saucers edged in gold leaf. "It must be at least a hundred years old."

Dan squinted at the cups. "The trick must have been to drink a lot of water before you came for chocolate because one of those little cups would never satisfy anyone, especially not a guy my size."

"They didn't have guys your size back then."

"It's a good thing because how could someone with large hands ever hold the delicate thing? There's no way my finger would ever fit that handle."

Cass looked from the slim golden handles to Dan's massive

hands. High tea ought to be very interesting. Dainty cups with fragile handles would be all that was available, though the teacups would be larger than chocolate cups.

An hour later, Dan stood with a steaming cup and saucer in Spode's Billingsley Rose pattern in one hand and a matching dish filled with petits fours, slivers of cucumber sandwiches, a thin slice of nut bread spread with an equally thin layer of cream cheese, a pair of small raisin scones topped with clotted cream, two meringues, and a small pile of cashews, carefully selected from the mixed nuts available. Cass held pale blue Wedgwood ringed with white flowers and a bit less food. She spotted a vacant pair of balloon back chairs with beautiful petit point seats and headed for them, Dan trailing. They sat.

Cass carefully set her plate of food on her lap and took a sip of her Earl Grey. She thought again how glad she was that she had come. With life going nonstop at the moment, it was delightful to sit and sip a cup of tea that someone else had prepared. She looked forward to sleeping in a bed someone else had made, eating a breakfast someone else had cooked, and leaving all her mess for someone else to clean up.

"Isn't this great?" She turned to Dan, only to find him sitting stiffly with both hands still full.

"There's no place to put this stuff down," he hissed.

She grinned. How many times had she seen the brothers with both hands full and no place to put something down? "That's because you don't have a lap," she said. "You have to sit with your knees together."

He looked horrified. "Not me. The only way I sit with my knees together is when I stretch my legs out with my ankles crossed." He demonstrated and immediately another guest almost tripped over him. With a quick apology, Dan pulled his legs back.

Cass tried not to laugh. "Don't want to try balancing a dish on your kneecap?"

"Laugh all you want," Dan said, feigning sorrow. "I'll just sit here and suffer."

Cass glanced around the room and found every flat surface covered with something—a Royal Doulton figurine, a miniature painting on a little easel, a bouquet of fresh flowers, one of an unending collection of vintage candlesticks of all sizes and materials, a hand-painted porcelain dish or pitcher.

Reminder: Make certain there were plenty of spaces at SeaSong for people to put things down. She might not do elegant high tea, but she often offered iced tea or lemonade in the late afternoon with crackers and cheeses.

"I need a TV tray." Dan looked ready to lick the food off his plate if he didn't soon find a solution.

"Not in a classy place like this." Cass held out her hand. "Here. Give me your tea."

He handed it over and began working on his plateful of food. "But what about you? Now both your hands are tied up."

"It'll take you about ten seconds to eat that food. Then you can put your teacup and saucer on top of the empty plate."

It was more like a minute and a half before all the dainty tea food disappeared from Dan's plate and he took his cup and saucer back. Cass gave him full marks for sipping his tea instead of swallowing it in a couple of gulps like the brothers would have done. When he finished, he waited patiently in the chair that was really too small for his bulk while she took her time savoring the experience.

After tea they wandered hand in hand through Cape May, peering into shop windows until closing time, looking at all the beautiful Victorian mansions for which the town was famous, and walking on the beach in the early evening darkness.

"Surf's high," Dan said as the wind ruffled their hair. "You can hear it."

"Rodney's almost here. If it keeps coming up the Chesapeake Bay like it is, the tides won't be as high as if it were hitting from the sea. We'll still have lots of rain but much less flooding."

"I've never heard of a hurricane following a path like this one. Inland in Virginia, up the Bay."

"Usually once a hurricane makes landfall, it blows itself out," Cass said. "But coming up the Chesapeake seems to be keeping this one strong. All that open space and water, I guess. The question becomes will it keep traveling north and smash Pennsylvania, or will it curl east back toward the Atlantic."

"And you have no prognostication?"

She shook her head as she watched the moon disappear behind dark clouds. A soft drizzle began to fall, blown in their faces by the ever-increasing wind. Cass pulled her Indiana Jones hat from her pocket and put it on.

Dan grinned at her hat. "I like."

I like too, she thought. *Oh, how I like.*

They enjoyed dinner in a lovely little candlelit restaurant that Cass thought was the most romantic place in which she had ever eaten. Of course, the handsome man seated across from her might have had more to do with the ambience than the candles. As she stared at him as he studied the menu, she felt incandescent, lit from within. She suspected her joy glowed on her face since she couldn't stop smiling.

Dan glanced up, his nose wrinkling. "Cass, do you smell something burning?"

She blinked. "Umm?"

"Burning." He gulped and pointed. "Your menu!"

Cass stared in horror at the little flames eating away at the edges of her oversize bill of fare. While she had been staring at Dan, the heavy paper had dipped to rest against one of the candles on their table, eventually igniting. She dropped the menu onto the table and began squashing the flames with her napkin. Dan reached over and helped. The small blaze was extinguished in seconds, but it left Cass's menu looking like a replica of an old document whose edges were singed and darkened by time.

When she handed it back to the waiter after placing her order, she smiled sweetly, acting like nothing was amiss. After a momentary facial tic at the sight of the burnt paper, so did the waiter. Cass and Dan were still laughing when their salads arrived.

Dan broke off a piece of roll and buttered it. "I'll be driving to Philadelphia on Monday to meet with Adam Streeter of Go and Tell International."

Cass nodded. "It's so wonderful how you're helping him." She took a bite of her crab cakes. "How long will you be gone?"

He speared a piece of his filet mignon. "I'll probably spend two days with Adam. Then I thought I'd run up to New York to see how things are going at home."

Home. He was going home. What if he got there and decided to stay? Cass felt her glow dim dramatically. She busied herself with her food so he wouldn't see her face.

"I should be back on Thursday in time for dinner."

He was coming back! Surely she could live four days without him. She'd already managed forty years. She probably glowed again. He was coming back. She decided to celebrate by having crème brûlée for dessert.

After dinner they walked some more, Dan's arm slung over her shoulders, an oversize umbrella hovering protectively over their heads. The wind from the approaching storm picked up some, causing Dan to struggle for control of the umbrella and the drizzle to intensify into a light rain. They paused to watch a shopkeeper taking down the sign that normally swung over his door and admired the plywood he'd nailed across his plate glass windows. Chilled, yet exhilarated by the strong weather, they returned to Russell House to sit in the living room and talk quietly together when they weren't watching the Weather Channel with the rest of the guests.

"It's going to get us," Cass said as the set was flicked off after the third rerun of the same information. "It'll be from our backside, but it'll get us."

"As if being with you wouldn't be enough to make tomorrow interesting," Dan whispered in her ear as they went upstairs to their rooms.

As she got ready for bed, Cass mentally reviewed the precautions already taken at SeaSong to prepare for the storm. Everything outside had been put away: the swing that hung on the front porch, the flag that flew on the front lawn, even the SeaSong sign itself. Extra water had been drawn, filling three twenty-five-gallon containers; flashlights were ready in every room with fresh batteries in each one and extra batteries beside them; and the pantry held a more-than-adequate supply of nonperishable food and drink to feed the expected guests. All her important documents were in a waterproof pouch in the third floor linen closet just in case.

Given all the buildings between SeaSong and the sea, it would take a mighty tidal surge to even reach the house, let alone reach the third floor. All her preparation was more in case of wind damage causing breakage, downed wires, and loss of electricity. Flooding was always a slight possibility, but SeaSong was built up on pilings elegantly enclosed by latticework.

Wearing her heavy socks and her navy cardigan as a bed

jacket over her polished cotton gown, a Lands' End special that she often took on trips because she hated to lug a bathrobe along, she walked to one of the two antique sleigh beds in the room. She ran her hands over the beautiful white on white duvet cover, patches of lace, narrow satin ribbon, and eyelet rippling beneath her fingers and palm. She counted eight pillows propped against the headboard, all with crispy white cotton cases trimmed with more lace and eyelet, each case unique. Her favorites were the ones that looked like fabric envelopes with the eyelet flaps embroidered with seed pearls and delicate satin ribbons and with satin loops that fitted around covered buttons to hold the flaps in place and the pillows inside.

The Russell House might not have room to set down your teacups, but it was beautifully appointed. In fact, it was almost as lovely as SeaSong. Cass grinned. Almost.

Reminder: No need to feel threatened.

She pulled back the covers and climbed into the bed. She sank into a feather mattress that rested on top of the real mattress. Plush and luxurious, provided you weren't allergic to feathers. Had anyone asked her about allergies? She didn't think so. Fortunately, it wasn't a problem for her. Still, it was a question that should be asked. SeaSong would ask it.

Feeling slightly superior, she plumped the two biggest pillows against the headboard so she could lean on them while she read for a while. The selection of books available all over Russell House made her mouth water, and she'd brought three to the room with her. She pushed herself up against the headboard, trying to decide which of the three resting on her night table she would read.

The bed shifted under her, and she gave a little scream as she fell.

I broke the bed! The Patchetts didn't, but I did!

She jolted to a halt without slamming to the floor. She stared wide-eyed at nothing, trying to assess what had just happened. Well, maybe she hadn't actually broken the bed. Rather she'd just bent it. And it had certainly bent her. She found herself wedged tightly, her back still flush against the headboard, and her feet, rather than resting in front of her making a comfortable L as she bent at the hips, were above her head. The mattress had somehow dipped beneath her bottom and flipped almost upright at her feet, trapping her in a deep V position.

Thank goodness no one was here to see how ridiculous she looked, no one meaning especially Dan. She put her hands down on either side of her hips to push herself free, but there was nothing to put her hands on. The mattress that should have been beneath her was pointing one end to the floor while the rest reared up in front of her, pointing to the ceiling.

Box spring, she thought. *I can push on that.*

However, when she managed to peer over her shoulder and look down—no easy feat wedged as tightly as she was—all she saw were black shadows. No box spring. In a flash she realized what had happened. The antique bed was still using wooden slats to support its mattress just as it had for untold years. These supports ran under the mattress from side to side at intervals up the length of the bed. Unfortunately for her, there was no support slat at the head of the bed. When people lay down to go to sleep, there was no need for a support at the head. Not enough weight rested on that area to cause any problems. But if you leaned against the headboard with no wooden slats beneath you, down you went and up flipped the mattress.

Am I the only one who has ever read in this bed? Cass stared in amazement at her elevated feet, clad in their heavy socks. There was only one explanation. This was a new bed, at least to Russell House.

They're trying to impress me. Not!

She felt both laughter and panic bubbling up. How was she to get out of this position before the chambermaid came in to clean tomorrow morning and found her making like a turkey's wishbone? If she didn't figure out something, she would be stuck all night with her knees in her chin and her bottom nearly on the floor. She wiggled and squirmed and wiggled and squirmed and only succeeded in wedging herself more tightly. As the minutes ticked by, her crab cakes began to complain about the pressure on her stomach, and her lower back began reminding her that at forty she was no longer as supple as she used to be. At least the pillows protected her backbone from the headboard.

She noticed a large bruise on her right shin, which hovered less than two feet from her face. She probably got it last night in her scramble to escape the smoke. She rubbed it absently as she considered her options for escape from tonight's calamity.

She could call for help. 911. *Help, I'm trapped.* She brightened momentarily until she remembered that her cell phone was in her purse over by the door on the overstuffed chair with the upholstery that matched the wallpaper. No help there.

She could opt to stay here until morning, braving the pain. She glanced at the night table. She had three books with which to distract herself and help the time pass. She reached out and pulled a book from the pile. She opened it and realized that she was wedged in such a tight V that she couldn't hold the words far enough from her face for her eyes to focus. She sighed. So much for reading the night away.

There was a third possibility. She could scream bloody murder until someone came and broke down her door. She imagined all the guests exploding into her room like a SWAT team into a crisis situation, clad in their jammies instead of bulletproof vests. She wrinkled her nose. She wasn't overjoyed at the idea of making a fool of herself that publicly, but at least her Lands' End nightie wasn't translucent or transparent.

She stared at the wall to her left. Dan was just on the other side. If he could quietly rescue her, maybe she could be saved the embarrassment of everyone knowing of her dilemma. Surely he was strong enough to pull her free. But what if he wasn't? Would they have to call 911 after all? Did the Jaws of Life cut through mattresses as easily as through metal?

"Dan," she called softly.

No response.

"Dan." Her voice was normal volume.

Nothing. He was probably asleep already, making so much noise snoring that he couldn't hear her.

"Dan!" she yelled. "Dan!" For once she regretted the thick walls found in old houses like this one and the modern insulation that had undoubtedly been added when the place was rewired. At least insulation had been put in place at SeaSong, both for blocking noise and ease of heating in winter. "Dan! Help!"

"Cass?" came faintly through the wall.

Relief washed through her. "Dan! Help me! Please!"

She heard nothing and was beginning to despair when her doorknob rattled. Then came knocking on the door and Dan calling much too loudly, "Open up, Cass. Unlock the door."

"I can't."

"What?"

"I can't."

"You can't?"

Cass stared at the door. It was maybe fifteen or twenty feet away across the large room, but it might as well have been miles. "No, I can't!"

"What's wrong? Are you hurt?"

She could hear the anxiety in Dan's voice. "I'm not hurt. I'm, ah, stuck."

"Stuck?" The word *incredulous* was invented to describe Dan's reaction. "Stuck how?"

Cass heard a door open across the hall. "Quiet out there. We're trying to sleep."

Another voice called, "What in the world is going on out there?"

And another. "What's wrong? Who's stuck? Stuck where?"

Cass grimaced. So much for a private rescue. Wait until they got the door open and saw her, fuzzy-socked feet flying high. She pulled her sweater tightly across her chest. She'd look like an idiot, but at least she could be a decent one.

"I'm going to go look for another key," Dan called through the door. "Don't worry; I'll be right back. Just stay still." She heard him running down the stairs.

Just stay still. Hah! As if she was going anywhere. She wiggled a bit and felt herself slide down a couple more inches. She stilled before her knees met her ears.

A guest called from the hall, "The extra keys are in a drawer behind the registration desk."

There was a little pause during which Cass heard the whispers outside her door without being able to decipher words. Then came the thud of heavy footfalls returning and Dan calling, "I got it!"

A couple of guests actually cheered.

The key slipped into the lock, turned, and the door burst open. Dan rushed in. And slid to an abrupt halt when he saw her. The other men, tight on his heels to help with the rescue, bumped into him, knocking him forward a few steps.

"If you laugh, I'll—" Cass couldn't think of anything dire enough to threaten him with. She ignored the other men and the wives who now peered in the door curiously.

"I wouldn't think of laughing," Dan assured her as his lips twitched. He pressed them together to keep them still, but the corners kept turning up, and his eyes danced suspiciously.

"Is she okay?" The other guests tried to peer over and around Dan. "Any blood? Do we need an ambulance?"

Cass gave them all the royal wave. "I'm fine," she called, trying to act like getting wedged in a bed was an everyday matter.

Dan walked to the bed and stood studying her. She propped an elbow on her knee, her chin in her palm, and studied him back.

"Oh, my," said one of the guests, censure in his voice. "She broke the bed."

"I did not," Cass protested. "It collapsed under me."

"What's the difference?" he asked.

Dan reached out a hand, grabbed one of hers, and pulled. Nothing happened.

"Good grief, Cass. You really are stuck."

"Tell me about it."

He gripped both her hands and heaved. Cass didn't actually hear a pop, but she flew through the air like an ice cube exploding from a plastic tray. The mattress fell crookedly across the support slats with a loud thud, and she crashed full speed into Dan.

He caught her as she bounced off him, holding her steady. He looked down at her, she looked up at him, and they both began to laugh. They laughed until tears came, and they gasped for breath. Soon the awakened guests were laughing with them as they called good night and wandered back to their rooms. Cass knew they were thinking about what a great story this was to tell their friends.

Still chuckling, Cass and Dan realigned the bed slats, making sure one was at the head of the bed so she could sit up and read. They realigned the mattress and straightened the bedding.

Cass walked Dan to the door. They grinned at each other.

"You know," he said as he draped an arm over her shoulder, "I used to live an ordered and orderly life before I knew you."

"Ha!" Cass countered. "What about me? I *never* got in trouble before I knew you."

He caressed her cheek. "Our lives must have been pretty boring, and we didn't even notice."

"Oh, I noticed all right, but I didn't know how to fix it." *Until now. Until you.* Suddenly afraid her dopey, love-struck face revealed too much, she looked away.

He put a hand under her chin and turned her face to his. "And now you know?"

The air between them crackled, and she knew they were talking about much more than fixing boring lives. She stared into his handsome face and nodded, her heart in her eyes. "I know," she whispered.

He nodded. "Me, too."

His good night kiss touched her all the way to her toes.

Twenty-Nine

HE HAD FOLLOWED Sherri home from work. He stared in disbelief at the tacky apartment building where she and Kevin lived. It was a big house divided into four units, and the entire structure looked even more unstable than the place where he was staying. If this beast of a hurricane didn't blow that place down like the big, bad wolf blew down the pigs' houses of straw and sticks, he'd be amazed.

All that Best money at her fingertips, and she chose to live in a collapsing dump, her stuffed checking accounts and credit cards untouched. It made no sense whatsoever.

At six o'clock last evening Sherri and Kevin went out as he watched, slumped down in the seat of his rental car. He tailed them to some cheap restaurant that would probably give them ptomaine poisoning. He shrugged. It'd save him a lot of trouble.

While they were eating, he went back to his room and collected what he needed, then took himself to eat in an elegant restaurant on the bay where he enjoyed superior service and marvelous food. At ten he returned to Sherri and Kevin's and hid himself behind a particularly large and unruly hydrangea, its dried flowers still clinging to the branches and providing good cover. He settled to wait until all the lights were out.

The boredom wasn't too bad, but the rain was an

unexpected bother as it progressed from soft shower to mature downfall. In no time he was soaked, and with the whipping wind constantly increasing in vigor, he also became thoroughly chilled. His nose began to run, and he coughed with a rasp that made him think that a near death experience was just waiting to grab him.

Two million dollars, he reminded himself. And all the rest of the Best money eventually. What was some discomfort, even pneumonia, in light of that prize? There were always antibiotics. He sneezed and wiped his nose on his saturated jacket sleeve. *It's worth it.*

It's worth it. It's worth it. It's worth it became his mantra.

Finally the lights were out in all four apartments. He waited another half hour, then sneaked to the house, climbing carefully onto the front porch. As quietly as possible he broke one of the panes in a front window. He was glad for the noise of the howling wind to help disguise the fall of glass.

He unwrapped the smoke bomb from the three plastic bags he'd carefully wrapped it in to protect it, thankful that he'd had enough foresight to buy more than one bomb at the fire supplies store. The Blue Tip safety matches, protected in the same bags, didn't want to stay lit in the wind. Finally, he huddled against the house and made himself a strong enough wind block for the flame to last long enough to light the bomb.

Thick white smoke enveloped him, choking him with its sulfur and rotten egg smell. He gagged and tossed the bomb through the broken window. He stood still, breathing the rain-freshened air hungrily to clear his lungs, listening until he heard the fire alarms kick in. Then he ran to the hydrangea and grabbed his rifle. He lay on his stomach like a soldier, trying to be the smallest, most invisible target possible. He raised the rifle and sighted.

Residents streamed out of the house into the rain. An old couple in bathrobes had remembered to bring an umbrella. They huddled on the front sidewalk. A young couple with three little kids in tow dashed out and across the street to stand on the porch of a deserted summerhouse. Tuck could hear the kids crying through the wind's howls. A young couple ran out and stopped on the sidewalk. Tuck had sighted in on the girl before he realized she wasn't Sherri. He felt like shooting her anyway and might have if it wouldn't have been a warning to Sherri.

Finally Kevin, wearing boxers and a T-shirt, raced out. He joined the young couple on the sidewalk, all of them getting wetter by the second.

Where was Sherri?

A police car pulled up, and the same cop as last night climbed out. Right behind him came the fire company. Tuck lay under the hydrangea, gnashing his teeth, afraid to move, rain dripping down his neck.

Where was Sherri?

He watched them bring out the remains of the smoke bomb and the undamaged paper casing it came in. He watched the renters, including Kevin, go back inside and the policeman and fire fighters drive away.

Where was Sherri?

By the time he finally made it back to the rat hole he was staying in, his fury consumed him. He punched the wall again and again, his fists bouncing off the plaster. The old walls were so sturdily built that he couldn't even have the satisfaction of making holes in the walls. Finally the pain in his hands became so intense that it broke through the red haze.

In agony he staggered down the hall to the bathroom where he held his bloody hands in a sinkful of cold water. As the water slowly turned red, he shook with the intensity of his hatred for Sherri.

She should be dead, having bled out as she lay on the sodden ground. Instead, he didn't even know where she was.

Thirty

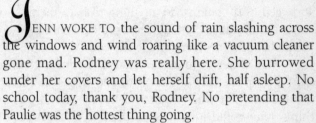

ENN WOKE TO the sound of rain slashing across the windows and wind roaring like a vacuum cleaner gone mad. Rodney was really here. She burrowed under her covers and let herself drift, half asleep. No school today, thank you, Rodney. No pretending that Paulie was the hottest thing going.

A momentary pang gripped her heart as she thought of her disappointment in Derrick. She had thought he was wonderful, misunderstood by others not as perceptive as she was. Instead, she had been the deceived one. How could she ever trust her own judgment again?

She'd heard last evening that Derrick and the others at the house had been arrested for breaking and entering and other lesser charges. They had all pleaded guilty. What else could they have done? They were caught inside the house, locks broken, liquor consumed, marijuana present. She'd heard nothing of the Roofies. Maybe they had been flushed. Maybe there had only been enough for the glass of soda that was supposed to be hers.

All the kids had been released on bail but had to report for sentencing in a couple of weeks. Jenn would be on edge the whole time. Would someone mention her presence? She knew she deserved it if she got dragged into the mess, but, *Oh, dear Lord, can You keep me out of it?*

A loud crash shook the house as something struck it. She tensed, waiting, but didn't hear any breaking glass. No windows taken out. Good. The last thing she wanted was to try and cover a gaping hole as the rain beat her up and tried to insinuate itself inside.

She turned her head on her pillow and looked out the back window. Through the heavy gloom she could see the sycamore whipping and shuddering as the fierce winds savaged it. She hugged herself, enjoying the sweet pleasure of being dry and warm inside while the rain and wind roared outside. She wondered idly what street people did during a hurricane, then shrugged. She couldn't do anything to help them, so why worry about them? She had enough real problems not even counting the possibility of someone ratting to the cops.

What if her parents learned of her misadventure? Jared would keep his mouth shut, but she wasn't at all certain about Aunt Cassandra who might feel honor bound to report everything. Jenn could just imagine the letters she'd get if Mom and Dad found out how stupid she'd been. She stilled. Maybe if they knew, they'd come home. Maybe there was a silver lining to her stupidity after all.

Like that would happen. Dad had signed a contract for a full twelve months. He couldn't come home, so Mom wouldn't come home. But she didn't doubt for one minute their ability to put her through the wringer if they were mad enough. And a person could be grounded and allowances withheld by a word from Saudi Arabia as well as one from Seaside.

Sighing, Jenn tossed back her covers. She really should get up and see if there was anything she could do to help get ready for the guests coming today. With Aunt Cassandra away until later this morning, Brenna might need her help.

Jenn pulled on a pair of jeans and a Seaside sweatshirt. She pulled her hair back in a ponytail and carefully applied her makeup. It might be a no-school day, but a girl should still look nice. You never knew when a tall, kind senior might drop over. Not that she liked Paulie, but if she was to act like his girl, then she had to look nice for him. It was only logical.

Her eyes lost focus as she thought about how wonderful he'd

been to her yesterday. He could have decided she was stupid and trashy. He could have wanted nothing to do with her anymore; lots of guys would have. But not Paulie. He stood proudly beside her, holding her hand as she explained to a group of girls why she didn't like Derrick anymore.

"I thought you were going with him when he bagged school today," one said. "At least that's what he said."

"He asked," Jenn said with a dismissive air.

"And you didn't go?" All the girls looked like they couldn't believe what they were hearing.

"Do I look like I bagged school?"

Obviously there was no argument with her standing there in person.

"Besides, Derrick is too wild for me." She grimaced. "I mean, do I want to drink my life away? Or get in trouble for taking off school? Sure, he's good looking, real hot. And he can make you feel special. But if you don't agree with everything he says, look out!" She glanced at Paulie. "I prefer people who like you even when you're dumb."

At that comment, a grinning Paulie dropped her hand and slung his arm across her shoulders. "I like you any way you are," he said with utter conviction.

And what a gift that acceptance was, Jenn finally realized. As she padded around her room making her bed and picking up her clothes, she thought about the events of yesterday and the difference between Derrick and the other people close to her—Paulie and Jared and Aunt Cassandra.

Of course Jared loved her. He was her brother and he was supposed to. Yet when he left school without permission yesterday to help save her, he'd risked a lot. They could have taken away football, which would have meant not only hurting the Seaside team but taking away Jared's potential college scholarship opportunities as well. Thankfully, the lady in the school office accepted Aunt Cassandra's family emergency note without question, though she looked strangely at Paulie when his read the same as hers and Jared's.

Jenn shook her head, knowing she loved her brother for caring so much, especially since she knew he was mad at her for liking Derrick in the first place.

And there was Aunt Cassandra who dropped everything to

search for her, even though she was worried about Grandmom and about Rodney and the new guests coming today. As Jenn thought about how nasty she'd been to her aunt the past several weeks, she flushed. She'd always prided herself on being a nice person, but she certainly hadn't been recently. She'd been snippy, rude, and uncooperative. It wasn't Aunt Cassandra's fault that her parents had gone away for a year. She'd make up for being so rotten by helping her any way she could. Aunt Cassandra was really pretty cool and very wise. Embarrassing as it was to admit, she had been right about Derrick all along.

A new idea wiggled in the back of Jenn's mind, and she frowned. Was Aunt Cassandra right about Paulie too? She seemed to like him as much as she disliked Derrick. Jenn lifted her eyes as if she were looking at the six-foot-three-inch Paulie.

Well, Paulie was different from Derrick in any way you could imagine. He was like an eager-to-please puppy, completely lacking Derrick's polished, sophisticated charm. He was tall, a little over-weight with his body still lacking a man's definition where Derrick was slight with a strong chin and a firm build. Paulie was clumsy where Derrick was smooth. He was also sweet where Derrick was edgy, caring and giving where Derrick was demanding. He treated her like a queen instead of a servant, like someone to be cherished instead of someone to be taken advantage of in the worst possible way.

Jenn smiled at her reflection in the mirror over the dresser. All in all, Paulie wasn't too bad for a pretend boyfriend.

Boyfriend. The word made her think of Dan, and Jenn's smile broadened. He sure had it bad for Aunt Cassandra, and Jenn felt certain that Aunt Cassandra had it just as bad for him. Look at how he'd said he'd want to get anyone who hurt Aunt Cassandra. His face had been so fierce when he said it.

Jenn blinked as a new thought hit her. Men who loved you wanted to protect you, not ravish you. They wanted to take care of you, not get you in trouble.

A knock sounded on her door just as Jenn prayed, *Lord, don't let Dan leave.*

"Up and at 'em, Jenn," called Brenna.

Jenn grabbed the door and pulled it open, startling Brenna.

"Whoa, girl, I thought you'd still be fast asleep."

Jenn flipped off the lights in her room and followed Brenna to the kitchen. Here all the lights were on to ward off the dark gray world outside, but the flashlights were lined up on the counter, ready for loss of electricity, which Jenn was surprised hadn't happened already, given the way the wind was whipping.

"How are you doing this morning?" Brenna asked, eyeing Jenn. "Did you manage to sleep?"

"I'm fine, and I slept like a baby." Jenn smiled.

Brenna looked skeptical.

"Really, I'm fine. After all, nothing happened yesterday except I behaved like a fool. But the bad stuff didn't happen."

"Thank God." Brenna wrapped her arms around Jenn and hugged her.

"I've been thanking Him every time I think about it." Jenn hugged Brenna back.

"Okay, then." Brenna rubbed her hands together. "I was afraid you might have had nightmares or something."

Jenn laughed and shook her head.

"So you didn't mind that Cass wasn't here?"

Again Jenn shook her head. "If anything, I was glad she was gone when I came home from school. I felt dumb enough without facing her. Do you—" Jenn hesitated. "Do you think she'll tell my mom?"

"I don't know." Brenna poured both of them a glass of orange juice. "But even if she does, I have to tell you, I was impressed by the love your family showed yesterday."

Jenn grinned over the rim of her glass. "They were pretty great, weren't they?"

"You should have seen their concern when Jared and Paulie came running from school." Brenna looked very sad, Jenn thought. Personally, the thought of how everyone had come through for her made her grin from ear to ear.

"I couldn't believe that they left school." Jenn rinsed her glass and stuck it in the dishwasher. She grabbed Jared's Cheerios and poured herself a dishful. "They could have gotten in so much trouble."

"They cared more about you than the trouble they might have found." Brenna turned her back suddenly, but Jenn still heard the catch in her voice. "I'm just realizing how much the people left behind suffer when they don't know what's going on."

"Well, sure," Jenn said. "I was left behind by my parents and I hate it, and I even know what's going on. I can't imagine being left and not knowing."

She reached in the refrigerator for the milk and slapped the door shut with her hip. She glanced at the row of ice chests on the floor in the family area. "Are they full of ice?"

Brenna didn't answer.

Jenn pulled the oversize freezer door open and there sat bag after bag of ice cubes, ready to go in the chests along with the milk and other necessary perishables as soon as the electricity went. That way they wouldn't have to open the refrigerator door and bleed off the cold. That way fewer things would spoil.

"Did you make up all those bags? You did a good job."

Again Brenna didn't answer. Jenn set her cereal and the milk carton on the counter. "Brenna?"

Still nothing. It was weird, like Brenna had turned into a pillar of salt like Lot's wife. She didn't move and she didn't talk.

Jenn leaned around Brenna and saw her face crunched up as in pain. Jenn's breath caught. "Brenna, what's wrong?"

Brenna shook her head as loud footsteps sounded on the stairs and Jared ran into the kitchen. "Hey, girl, you're eating my cereal!"

At the same moment the back door burst open, letting in a great blast of wind and rain as Mike blew into the room.

"Mike!" Brenna forced a smile. "What are you doing here?" She checked the clock. "Aren't you supposed to be at work?"

Mike kissed her cheek and settled an arm on her shoulders. "I'm on my way, not that I expect many customers in weather like this. But that's not why I came. Guess what, Bren?" His voice was very excited.

Dumb question, Jenn thought. How can she possibly guess?

He waited a beat, then said, "We had a smoke bomb at our apartment last night."

Jenn and the others spun to him. "What?"

He nodded. "Just like you guys. And I've been thinking about what's the common link between our place and SeaSong. There's only one."

He, Jenn, and Jared turned to stare at Brenna just as the lights flickered once and went dead.

Thirty-One

TUCK TURNED A bleary eye to the clock and read nothing. It wasn't pulsing, spitting out its seconds, clicking off its minutes. He grimaced. No electricity.

He had no idea what time it was. It was so dark in the room, it could have been midnight. Rodney. Tuck pulled himself from his disgusting bed and looked out the crusty window at the deluge pounding against the house. What else could go wrong?

He sneezed and shivered as damp wind leaked in around the warped window frame, making the dusty curtains shudder and billow like dirty, green wraiths. Before this trip was over, he was going to end up with pneumonia. He just knew it. How would he explain getting pneumonia to people when he was supposedly lying around in sunny, balmy Hawaii?

He swiped at his running nose with his hand and winced at the unexpected pain. He held his hands out and stared in bewilderment at his swollen, bent, and bloody knuckles. He tried to straighten his fingers, but the pain that roared through him was too intense.

What had happened? How had he sustained such a monstrous and terrible injury? And to both hands. He replayed last night up to the frustrating and highly disappointing conclusion of no Sherri and still had no idea what had happened. Had someone attacked him on his way home?

The black space between realizing there would be no Sherri and wakening this morning in his revolting room was frightening. Nothing like this had ever happened to him before. He shuddered and promised himself he'd not think about it anymore. It was too distressing.

This whole trip had been distressing. Where was Sherri? Even this morning he didn't *know* where she was. He could only assume she was at work at SeaSong, all safe and warm in a clean, lovely place while he was forced to wallow in this repulsive, disgusting, filthy place.

Rage gripped him. *She will not win*, he promised himself. *She will not win! I will not let her.*

He took a long, hot shower to calm himself. Just as he began to feel the tension seep from his shoulders, the old man beat on the locked bathroom door.

"Turn off that shower, you idiot in there!"

"Yeah, yeah," muttered Tuck, not answering.

"Without electricity we can't heat any more," the old man shouted.

"Like I care," Tuck screamed back. He climbed out when the water turned cool and he was all pruney. He felt much better. Even his poor hands didn't hurt as much.

It was time to call California and see how things were there.

The phone was answered on the second ring. "Best residence. May I help you?"

Tuck rolled his eyes. No one sounded as stuffy and self-important as Mr. Beauchamps, the family butler. "Hey, Mr. B.," he said with deliberate disrespect, "it's Tucker." He loved to hear the old man's voice go extra frosty.

Instead of the expected cool acknowledgment, Mr. Beauchamps positively bubbled as he said, "Oh, Tucker, I've the most wonderful news. They think they may have found her!"

Tuck went cold all over. "What?"

"Your parents think they may have found her. They think she's in New Jersey! They tried to call you last night to share the good news, but you didn't answer. They left you messages, but I guess you didn't get them."

"No, I didn't." But Lonnie would have. *Good-bye, Lonnie. You haven't got a chance now. Enjoy your last hours of life.*

"They've flown to check it out," Mr. Beauchamps said.

"What?" Tuck felt the words like a punch to the chest. "Already?"

"Mr. Best had the plane brought out last evening as soon as they traced the number that kept appearing on your caller ID gizmo. They flew out to see if it's really Sherri who had been calling."

Tuck flinched. Hoist by his own petard, whatever a petard was. He should have hidden that little electronic troublemaker. Or destroyed it. "But there's a hurricane hitting New Jersey right now."

"Is there?" Old Beauchamps sounded surprised. "I didn't know that."

Tuck could have kicked himself. How would he, vacationing in Hawaii, know about New Jersey's weather? Why would he be interested? "Yeah. I saw it on the Weather Channel." Did Hawaii get the Weather Channel? "What I meant was that I don't think they could land."

"Well, maybe they will land at New York or Boston and drive to Seaside."

Seaside! They really did have it pegged. "It's great news about Sherri, if it is her," Tuck forced himself to say with what he hoped was heard as excitement. Then he hung up and began to sweat and plot in earnest.

He simply had to find her.

Thirty-Two

CASS AND DAN arrived at SeaSong close to 11 A.M., racing each other from the garage to the back door.

"I beat you," Cass yelled as she dashed in the door holding her Indiana Jones hat on with one hand so the wind didn't steal it from her head.

"Only because I'm polite enough to let you go first," Dan countered.

"Yeah, yeah." Cass grinned at him. "It's a good line."

"Now, children, be nice," Jared said, hugging Cass and shaking Dan's hand. "Hard driving?"

"Very nasty," Dan said. "The wind kept trying to push us off the road, and the driving rain made visibility very poor."

"He did great," Cass said, grabbing a couple of dish towels and mopping up the water they'd brought in. She looked from Jared to Jenn to Brenna. "Have we heard anything from the software folks? Have they canceled? Or called to say they've been delayed?"

"No one's called, so we're acting as if they'll be here for lunch as planned," Jenn said as she threw herself into Cass's arms. "Welcome home."

Cass kissed her niece, delighted with the warm greeting. The kitchen looked toasty and homey with a pair of Coleman lanterns hissing softly, but the hugs were what filled Cass's heart.

"Are you doing okay, sweetie?" She studied Jenn's face carefully.

Jenn nodded. "I'm fine." Both she and Cass ignored the fine tremor that flashed across her face. "Really. I still can't believe how stupid I was, but I'm fine."

Cass gave the girl a quick hug. "Of course you're fine. I don't know why I even asked. You're a Merton, for Pete's sake."

Dan wrapped one arm about Jenn's shoulders and the other about Cass's. "And Merton women are pretty special, let me tell you." He smiled from one to the other.

Cass felt warmed as she watched Jenn turn pink with pleasure. She dropped her head briefly to Dan's shoulder, snaked her arm around his waist, and squeezed. "Thanks."

"How about Merton men?" Jared asked, his hand in the Cheerios box.

Jenn blew him a kiss. "They, as we all know, are big bozos—not!"

Brenna glanced over her shoulder from the counter where she stood blinking away tears as she cut thin, thin slices of onion. "You want to check that I'm doing this right, Cass?"

Cass moved to the food preparation area. Tuna mixed with mayonnaise and a touch of salt and pepper sat in a bowl. Several crisp Gala apples lay in a cluster, waiting attention. Two bags of Pepperidge Farm thin whole wheat bread rested against the bowl of tuna. "Looks like you guys don't even need me. We should have stayed in Cape May, Dan. We never did get to use their hot tub."

"Hot tub," said Brenna in a yearning voice. "I can't remember the last time I soaked in one."

"Humph," Jenn said. "I don't know that I ever did."

"Don't feel too bad," Dan said to Cass. "I checked, and it was on the roof under a lattice sunshade. We'd have been pounded with cold rain while we tried to relax in the bubbly warmth—that is, if we weren't blown away trying to cross the roof to get to it. Didn't sound appealing to me."

Cass laughed as she walked to the stove. Her nose told her the chicken corn soup she'd made several days ago and frozen was heating gently.

"Three cheers for gas," Cass said as she lifted the lid of the soup pot and stirred. "If we had an electric stove, we'd be in trouble."

"You know, Cass, I've been thinking." Brenna sliced another paper thin sheet of onion. "These software guys are supposed to eat dinners out, right?"

Cass nodded.

"But will there be any restaurants open tonight? No electricity? Flooded roads?"

"You're right. Jenn, pull three containers of my spaghetti sauce with meatballs from the freezer, please." Cass gave the soup another stir. "Then check in the pantry to be certain we have three boxes of spaghetti."

Dan leaned over her shoulder and sniffed appreciatively at the simmering pot. "Talk about smelling wonderful!"

She lifted out a spoonful and held it to him. "Careful. It's very hot."

He blew on it for a minute, then tasted. His eyes closed in appreciation. "Deeeelicious!"

"That's because I use creamed corn," Cass said. "It makes the broth extra rich."

He grabbed the spoon from her hand. "I'm going to stay at SeaSong forever, Cass Merton. I want to eat food this good the rest of my life." He dipped the spoon for another taste.

Forever, eh? Fine with me. She smiled sweetly and said only, "I'm glad you like it. It's my grandmother's recipe."

She turned to Jared. "I take it the tables are grouped in the dining room as I asked? And set?"

He nodded. "All done."

"Good. I'll just go check." She grabbed a large flashlight and walked into the dining room where smaller tables had been pushed together to seat seven, three settings on each side and one at the head. The crimson tablecloth looked smart with the white dishes and the crimson, gold, and deep green napkins. A fabric pumpkin sat in a nest of Spanish moss while small gourds spilled down the table in both directions. She fiddled with the gourds a little until their conformation pleased her, then placed votive candles at each place. A Coleman lantern stood ready for duty on the hutch.

Satisfied, she went back to the kitchen.

"Where's Dan?" she asked.

"He went upstairs to change into dry stuff and unpack," Jenn said.

Nodding, Cass turned to the counter where Brenna had moved from the onions to the apples, slicing them as thinly as she could and placing the slices in a dish containing orange juice to stop the browning of the tender fruit. "Looking good."

Cass turned to Jenn. "Get the medium-sized basket down, the one with the green strands woven through it, and line it with a napkin to match the ones on the table. Get several kinds of crackers from the pantry. Don't open them though. They'll lose their crispness by the time we serve if you do."

Jenn disappeared into the pantry, and Cass opened the loaves of bread. She laid the slices out before her and spooned some tuna mixture onto each, spread it, and topped each with a gossamer thin onion slice. Next she fished apples slices out of the orange juice, blotted them dry and arranged a fan of them on top of the onion. She went to the refrigerator and took out a package of thinly sliced Swiss cheese. Carefully she separated the slices and placed one over the apples. As she finished each sandwich, she placed it on a cookie sheet, ready to slide in the oven for a quick melting of the cheese.

"Will these guys appreciate something this creative?" Brenna asked as she eyed the open-faced sandwiches. "Computer geeks aren't known for culinary awareness."

Cass shrugged. "We'll just try to teach them class while they're here."

Jenn reappeared with the basket and boxes of crackers. "I'll put them on the serving hutch in the dining room."

Jenn returned to the kitchen and came to stand beside Cass. She watched Cass build a couple of sandwiches without saying a word.

"What?" Cass finally said, unnerved by Jenn's stare.

"I need to say thank you and tell you how much I appreciate you." Jenn sniffed, and Cass looked up to see tears in the girl's eyes.

"Now, don't cry, Jenny. It's all over. You're safe and sound. Just know I love you very much, and I'd hug you, but I can't." She held out her messy hands.

"Then I'll hug you," Jenn said and did.

The back door opened and Jared and Paulie cannoned in, water dripping from the bills of their baseball caps. They both wore big black plastic bags over their jackets, holes cut in the tops for their heads. Their jeans were soaked from the knees down, and their shoes squished when they walked.

"I didn't even know you went out," Cass said to Jared. She bit her tongue so she wouldn't give a lecture about hurricane safety and the wisdom of wandering about in wind and weather like this. "Where've you been? Besides Paulie's, I mean."

"We went down to the boardwalk to see the action," he said, taking off his hat and shaking his head like a great Saint Bernard. Some of the flying drops landed on Flossie, asleep on the back of her favorite love seat. She hunched her back, hissed, scowled malevolently at Jared, and flopped back in the same position.

"It's great out there!" Paulie said, his eyes sparkling. "I've never seen the waves so big."

"Didn't you two ever hear of a tidal surge?" Cass demanded.

"No tidal surge here," Jared said. "The wind's blowing out to sea, not in from it."

"The wind blew me right across the boardwalk," Paulie said. "Blew me right up against the railing."

"I want to see," Jenn cried.

"You'll blow away," Cass protested.

"Get your rain stuff," Jared said.

Jenn ran upstairs, moving faster than Cass had seen her move in weeks.

"Is this safe?" Cass asked, wishing she, too, could go get blown across the boardwalk and watch the wild sea. It sounded wonderful.

"It's fine," Jared said. "No danger. Rodney's only a class one."

"Only a class one," Cass said as some shingles from someplace flew past the window.

Paulie started waving his hands. "And the wind's blowing away, out to sea. The huge waves crest, and *boom!* The wind blows all the spume and lots of the wave backwards so it falls down behind the waves instead of rushing to the beach. There's the fun of seeing all the big waves without the worry of seeing them eat all the sand."

"That's good. We've got to keep those beaches to keep those tourists," Cass said. Losing them to major storms was a matter of millions of dollars of lost revenue.

Jenn clattered down in her red hooded raincoat and duck shoes.

Jared pointed to her feet. "They won't do you much good. The streets are full of water."

Jenn shrugged and pulled the back door open. Wind and rain poured in. "So my feet get wet. Yours are wet."

"Wait a minute," Cass called. "Are there electrical lines down?"

"Not that we saw," Jared, standing on the back step, yelled over the roar of the wind.

Cass frowned. "You could get electrocuted if wires are down in standing water, and you walk in that water."

"Well, yeah." Jared stared at her as if to say, *And you had a point?*

Cass grabbed a towel and wiped her hands. "If you're going out to brave the elements, I want a kiss from all of you before you go. In fact, I want a kiss from you before you go anywhere anytime." She walked into the stream of wind and rain.

Paulie leaned down for her kiss first. She bussed him on the cheek and then patted the same cheek. "Thanks, Aunt Cass." He kissed her back.

Aunt Cass, huh? "Thank you, Paulie."

Then she kissed Jared and Jenn. "Be careful, guys."

"We will." Jared jumped in a puddle at the foot of the back steps. "Don't worry, Aunt Cass."

"Yeah, Aunt Cass," called a waving Jenn. "We'll be okay."

Aunt Cass. She pushed the door shut, no small feat against the force of the determined wind. *Somehow I've become Aunt Cass.* She smiled. She liked the intimacy of the shortened name, the name Dan called her.

"You have such a nice family," Brenna said as she rinsed the knife she'd been slicing the apples with. "You care about each other so much."

Cass shrugged. "That's what families do."

"That's what families *should* do," Brenna answered, her voice thick with emotion. A large tear rolled down her cheek.

"Oh, sweetie."

Brenna sniffed and another tear appeared.

Cass opened her arms, and Brenna fell into them. She clutched Cass with a startling strength, an unexpected neediness. Her slim shoulders shook.

"Can you tell me what's wrong?" Cass asked, keeping her voice soft and encouraging.

Brenna drew a deep breath. In a voice that quavered she said, "I miss my mom."

"Of course you do. How long since you've seen her?"

"Almost a year."

Cass rubbed Brenna's back. "That's a long time."

Brenna sniffed and nodded. She pulled back and looked at Cass with a terrible ferocity. "I love her."

"I know." Cass smiled gently. "We all love our moms." Even when they're driving us nuts.

Brenna's red eyes filled with new tears. "You don't understand."

"You're right. So why don't you explain."

Brenna looked uncertain, even scared.

Cass reached out and stroked the girl's hair. "Does it have something to do with the phone calls you've been making?"

If anything, Brenna looked more upset. "You know?"

"I know you've made calls from here several times, and Dan and I saw you make a call up on the boardwalk. I know you listen to something and then hang up in tears, but you don't speak."

"My mom. I listen to my mom."

Cass took Brenna's hand and led her to the love seat. "Why don't you speak to her?"

"I can't. I'm afraid she'll hang up on me, and I couldn't bear it." Agony etched Brenna's lovely face as she huddled in the corner of the love seat.

"Why would she do that?"

"Because she hates me."

Cass blinked. "Your mother hates you?"

Brenna nodded.

"Do you know for a fact that she hates you, or do you just think this?"

"I think it." Brenna pulled a very used tissue from her pocket and blew her nose. Cass reached into her own pocket and pulled out a heavily wrinkled but clean tissue. She offered it to Brenna who took it gratefully.

"Why would you think such a thing of your own mother?" Visions of all types of child abuse flitted through her mind.

"It's because of the terrible thing I did," Brenna whispered, her eyes on her lap.

Paradigm shift, Cass thought. "It's not what your mother did but what you did?"

Brenna hunched her shoulders. "I ran away from home."

Not good, but not the end of the world. "Lots of people have done that." Cass rested her hand on Brenna's knee.

"But I never left a note. I never called." Her voice caught and she had to swallow. "Not once all year."

Cass stared at Brenna's bent head, a million questions leaping about her mind like a bunch of unruly kangaroos.

Why had Brenna run?

Why had she never told her mother she was all right?

Did she run with Mike or meet him later?

What of her father? Had she left because she feared him?

How could the girl have put her mother through the agony of not knowing where she was? Surely she was old enough to know better. Unless there was danger from her mother or father?

"Did they abuse you, Brenna? Did they hurt you in any way?" Cass was ready to call the police this very minute. "Is that why you ran?"

"Oh, no." Brenna looked appalled at the thought. "They're very nice people. They've always loved me."

Cass blinked. "But you ran away without letting them know where you were or how you were doing for a whole year."

"We'd been apart all summer and missed each other desperately. We thought being together always would be so romantic." Brenna's voice shook.

"We meaning you and Mike?"

Brenna nodded, her eyes still on the floor.

"So you knew him before you ran?"

She nodded again. "We've been together since our freshman year."

"In college?"

Brenna looked up, confused. "What?"

"Not freshman year in high school."

"Oh. Right." Brenna cleared her throat. "I met him the first day at orientation. He's from Idaho and I'm from California, so there was no way we'd be able to know each other before, is there?"

"I guess not." Cass waited. She didn't have to wait long.

"We fell in love right off, just like in all the books." She smiled at the memory. "He's such a great guy." Her smile faded, and great hurt filled her eyes. "Except he won't go home with me."

"Why not?"

"I think he's afraid of what my dad will say."

And so he should be, Cass thought. "Tell me about the running away before we get to the going home part, okay?"

"I love my mom," Brenna said. "And I love my stepdad. Hank's a wonderful man. He really is. He's been wonderful to me. It was Tuck who gave me trouble."

"Who's Tuck?"

"My stepbrother, Hank's son. He was seven when Hank married my mom. I was two." Brenna fell silent, lost in her thoughts.

"Tell me more about him," Cass prompted. "He's the reason you ran away?" A nasty man or boy living in the same house could make life miserable, to say nothing of dangerous for a vulnerable younger stepsister.

"Tuck's strange. He always has been as far as I know. Hank's had him in therapy most of his life, though I don't think it's helped him. I know he resents me, and sometimes he scares me. He likes to hurt me, not so much physically as by hurting my things. He'll steal something or damage it. Once he hurt my pet bird so badly I had to have him put to sleep."

Cass shuddered. Living with someone like that could drive anyone to run away.

Brenna took a deep breath. "But I have to be honest. I chose to run away. I wish I could blame it on Tuck—he's strange enough to scare anyone off—but I can't. I can't blame it on anyone but me." She dropped her head into her hands. "I'm only twenty, Cass, and I've ruined my life forever."

Seeing a good bout of self-pity just around Brenna's corner, Cass said, "So you just decided to disappear? *Poof.* I'm gone?"

"That's about it. See, I always felt like a useless, poor lit—" She broke off.

Cass waited.

"A poor, useless college girl."

Yeah, right. What had she meant to say?

"But Mike made me feel special. He liked me for me, not for

my—" Again that hesitation as she searched for a word to replace the one she decided not to use. "Um—my body. In fact, he didn't even know I had any." The last was an outburst, like she was defending Mike.

"He didn't know you had a body?" Cass raised an eyebrow.

Brenna flushed as she realized how foolish her comment was, but she didn't change it or clarify. "Mike and I planned it carefully. We made believe we were driving back to school from our homes after fall break our sophomore year. We left our cars in downtown L.A., walked to the bus station where we bought tickets separately so no one would remember a couple, paid cash, and took the bus to Saint Louis. From there we took the train to Philadelphia. I dyed my hair brown—I'm really blond—and Mike got his hair cut real short. We hitched rides across New Jersey to Long Beach Island and worked at the various shore towns, staying about two months at each place. We never stayed too long because we didn't want anyone to get too close to us."

"Just the two of you against the world."

Brenna winced. "It sounded so cool when we thought of it." She shrugged. "When we left L.A., all we took with us were a backpack each, our laptops, and several hundred dollars as a bankroll. We were going to live on love and odd jobs." She turned a tragic face to Cass. "It's not working, at least not any longer. And it's all my fault."

"Because you miss your family."

"Yeah." Brenna blew her nose again, "I'm so homesick I could die, and I'm worried about them, too. I've watched you with Jared and Jenn and seen how much you care. And they're not even your kids. Yesterday you were so worried about Jenn when she took off. I got all too clear a picture of what my mom must have gone through."

"Is still going through," Cass said.

Brenna buried her face in her hands and wept. Cass watched, her heart breaking for the girl and for her mother.

Brenna gave a ghost of a smile. "In a way it's nice that Mike won't take me home. It proves he loves me."

"Wait a minute." Cass had to challenge that thought. All it proved to her was that Mike wanted to avoid conflict. "What about his family? Shouldn't he let them know he's all right? And don't you think that if he truly loved you, he'd want to make you happy whenever it was within his power?" She thought of the brothers and the care they took of their wives, her father and his care for her mother and her. "Or does he think that if you go home, you'll ditch him?"

"I'll never ditch him. I love him," she said simply. "And because I love him, how can I go home without him?"

"Hasn't the boy ever heard the word *visit?*"

Brenna nodded. "I know. We talked about me visiting alone if he didn't want to come. But I don't want to go alone because, quite frankly, I'm scared. If I'm alone, I don't know if I can make people understand why we did what we did."

Cass thought there was a good chance nobody'd understand even if Mike was with her.

Brenna put a hand to her mouth to mask the deep sob that rose from her throat. "What if I have to choose between my family and Mike?"

Cass patted her hand. "I don't think that will happen, sweetie. But even if it did, you'd be all right. You could go back to school, get your degree, get a job you liked. We can all live on our own if we have to, and we can live full lives. Look at me and SeaSong."

Brenna looked and it was obvious she didn't want for herself what she saw. She was just too polite to say so.

Cass sighed. Some days she didn't want what she had either. "Granted, life is probably more fun when you have someone to share it with, but my point is that you can make it on your own if that's the way things fall. God will help you."

"God doesn't even like me."

"How can you say that? God loves you."

"Yeah, maybe He loves me, but He doesn't like me. How can He after what I've done?"

"Brenna, don't you think that if God is really God, He can forgive anything? Don't make the mistake of thinking of Him as if He were a regular person. He's not. He's God. He can forgive the worst sins because of Jesus' death. If we don't believe that, we're saying that Jesus' death was in vain. It wasn't good enough because some sins were beyond His redeeming power."

Brenna frowned. Clearly she'd never thought of forgiveness in that way.

"What you did to your mom and Hank was unkind—"

"Cruel. Selfish." Brenna wasn't going to be easy on herself.

Cass nodded. "Okay. But it wasn't the worst thing the world has ever seen."

"Well, no. It wasn't the Holocaust or anything, but *I* did it. Me." Despair filled her voice.

"But Christ did more."

They were silent for a minute, considering the depths of Christ's sacrifice.

"I think you need to make that visit, Brenna, honey, with or without Mike. Your mother needs to see you." In the distance Cass heard the front door open and slam shut. The software people?

"Do you know that she cries when I call?" Brenna picked at the seam of her jeans. "Somehow she's figured out it's me, and she cries. She says my name over and over and begs me to come home."

"There you are, sweetie. See, she loves you."

"But Mike."

"It's only for a short time. You're not leaving him. You're just going home to visit with the folks."

Brenna nodded. "I told him that. But he thinks I'm in danger."

Surprise rippled through Cass. "How are you in danger?"

"He thinks that the things that have happened to us the past couple of nights are aimed at me. Two smoke bombs at two disparate places."

"Two smoke bombs?" This was news to Cass.

"There was one at our apartment building last night. No one was hurt, but a lot of people spent a lot of time in the driving rain." She paused, then announced dramatically, "And I'm the common link between SeaSong and our apartment."

"The attacks are aimed at you." Cass mulled the idea over. "But why?"

"I don't know. I've thought and thought, but I don't know."

As they sat in silence for a moment, thinking, the swinging door to the reception area swung open. Mike's thin face appeared. Cass watched as he scanned the kitchen, then looked over to the sitting area.

"Brenna." He stepped into the room and came over to her.

She looked up and began to cry in earnest. "Oh, Mike!" She threw herself into his arms.

"Easy, baby. Easy." He held her tightly with one arm while he patted her on the back with the other.

"What are you doing here?" she asked, her voice muffled by his wet coat.

"It's my lunch hour, and I needed to talk to you." He took her by the shoulders and set her away. "I wanted to say that I've been thinking some more, and you're right."

"Yeah?" She blinked eyes heavy with tears. "About what?"

"Going home. You should go home."

"Just me?" She looked panicked. "Alone?"

He shook his head. "I should never have put you in the position where you have to choose between your mom and me. You need us both."

"Oh, Mike!" Brenna's teary smile radiated as she lunged for him again.

He returned her hug. "I still think you're in danger, but that's here in Seaside for some reason. And if I'm with you, maybe I can keep you safe in L.A."

"Hello? Anyone here?" a voice called even as the bell on the registration desk jingled.

Cass stood. Software Solutions had arrived.

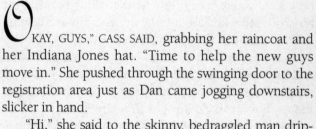

Thirty-Three

O KAY, GUYS," CASS SAID, grabbing her raincoat and her Indiana Jones hat. "Time to help the new guys move in." She pushed through the swinging door to the registration area just as Dan came jogging downstairs, slicker in hand.

"Hi," she said to the skinny, bedraggled man dripping all over the entry hall. He wore a bright blue plastic parka that read Software Solutions across the back in bright yellow, a light bulb dotting the *i* in *Solutions*. The hood was pushed back from his disordered hair, and from the looks of him, the parka hadn't been particularly effective. But then Rodney was no ordinary rainstorm. A category one hurricane carried winds up to ninety-five miles per hour.

The man must have read her mind because he looked down at his parka and said, "They seemed like a good idea when the ad man visited. Neither he nor we counted on a hurricane to test them out." He smiled wryly.

"You're lucky it wasn't blown completely off," Cass grinned back at him. She liked his attitude. "Welcome to SeaSong."

"I'm Connor McKee, by the way. VP at SS." He stuck out a wet hand and shook first Cass's hand, then Dan's. "Whew! Are we glad we made it. I didn't think driving would be this bad, but keeping that van on the road was murder. I think we're one of the last cars across the bridge. The police were about to close it."

"Really?" Cass was surprised. The Thirty-fourth Street Bridge arched far above the bay, unlike the causeway which was flat except for the section of bridge that could be raised for boats to pass.

"Yeah, the wind blowing up there makes it almost impossible for you to have any control. And you can feel the bridge shudder." He shuddered. "And the street just this side of the bridge is barely passable. The car throws up fountains, you know?" He made broad wave motions with each hand to illustrate. "Doesn't matter how slow you're going. It's like the wind's blowing the entire bay ashore." He looked around the dry comfort of SeaSong. "We're not moving until this thing is over!"

Cass understood completely. She'd been so relieved when she and Dan got home, and the wind seemed to have picked up in just these last few minutes. "Now let's get you all in and up to your rooms so you can get dry. Lunch is almost ready."

As she and Dan followed Connor McKee out the door, Brenna and Mike came from the kitchen to offer their assistance in getting the new guests settled. Brenna's eyes were still red, but she was smiling as she and Mike clasped hands. She looked at Cass and made a discreet circle with the thumb and forefinger of her free hand. Cass nodded and winked.

The wind slammed into Cass at her first step onto the porch, and she did a quick two-step to the side to catch her balance. Both Connor and Dan reached for her, but she had righted herself before they grabbed her. She put up a hand. "Thanks. I'm all right." She tied the scarf she'd looped over her hat even tighter.

They stepped down into the deluge, the rain slashing Cass across the face, the wind tugging at her hat. She pulled it down almost to her ears, trying to snug it enough that it stayed where it belonged. She tightened the scarf again. Already a stream of water poured from the brim.

The bright blue van at the curb sported the yellow words *Software Solutions* and the light bulb logo of the company just like Connor's rain parka. The vehicle's windows were so steamed on the inside that Cass couldn't see the passengers, but as she and the others approached, the doors popped open. Five men and one woman climbed out, all sporting identical blue parkas. Immediately the wind blew them up around everyone's ears, then tore the hoods free.

The woman grabbed the van handle to keep her balance, laughing as she did.

"This is so cool!" yelled one man who looked about sixteen but whom Cass assumed must be at least twenty-two and a college graduate. His glasses were so rain coated that his eyes shimmied behind them. He held his hands wide and turned his face to the sky. He opened his mouth and tried to catch the rain.

"They didn't drive," a disgruntled Connor shouted over the roar of the maelstrom. "They still have all their nine lives."

"New computer game," yelled another man. "Weather calamities. Hurricanes. Tornadoes. Tidal waves."

"Earthquakes," yelled another.

"Avalanches!"

"Cyclones!"

"How are cyclones different from tornadoes?"

"One goes one way and the other the other."

"Yeah?"

"Mighty Max and Midge!"

"Fighting against huge hailstones!"

"In a plane or a boat or on skis."

"Up in a balloon!"

"A flood from a dam break!"

"Like Johnstown!"

An aluminum chair sailed past, lethal in its force. The SS crew, holding on to the car or each other, watched it rocket toward the beach, bouncing off cars as it went.

"Cool," yelled one.

"Way cool," yelled another.

All this wild conversation flew as the back of the van was opened and everyone's luggage was pulled out. Every time Cass reached for a piece, someone snatched it first. Brenna was still empty handed too. Laughing, they lunged forward for the two remaining pieces just as Cass heard a loud *crack!*

"A gun?" said Connor McKee.

"Mighty Max and Midge holding off the world terrorists," one of the SS men shouted.

"In a hurricane."

"A cyclone."

"An avalanche."

But Cass ignored them as she heard Brenna cry in pain and felt the girl slump against her.

Tuck couldn't believe his luck, though he thought it was about time something went right. He'd looked out the window again, risking disease from the filthy curtains, just to see how violent the storm was in order to judge whether his father and Patsi could get through, and there was Kevin climbing out of his car and running into SeaSong.

Well, well. Where Kevin was, Sherri couldn't be far behind.

Tuck smiled, got down on his hands and knees, and pulled his rifle from under the bed. A hutchful of dust bunnies came along, and he had to dust the gun before he could attach the scope. His movements broke open some of the scabbing on his hands, and they ached worse than any toothache he'd ever had. Their swelling made his movements awkward and clumsy.

He opened the window a smidgen, just far enough that he could slip the barrel of the gun through. He ignored the rain that blew in the opening. For once, cold drafts were of no concern.

Which door should he watch? He thought a minute and settled on both, though he favored the front. That's where Kevin's car was. He thought Sherri would at least come out to wave him on his way. That's what Patsi always did when his father left, and personally Tuck thought it was pathetic. It was like saying *here I am; don't forget me; don't look at someone else; come home to me, please.*

As he knelt, nerves jumping in anticipation, eyes focused on the front of SeaSong, a bright blue van pulled up. He squinted, trying to read through the rain. Software Solutions. He frowned. A van of computer geeks. Now there was a party waiting to happen.

One guy jumped out of the driver's seat and raced inside the house. Tuck wondered idly if they were looking for a place to stay or if they had reservations. Not that it mattered. His eyes narrowed. What mattered was that they had gotten onto the island in spite of the flooding streets. If they could do it, so could Hank and Patsi.

His eye twitched. Time was running out.

"What do you think you're doing?"

Tuck swung to the door of his room and there stood the old man, a fleck of his morning egg still caught at the corner of his mouth.

Tuck ground his teeth in frustration. He had forgotten to shut the door when he came back from his shower. Dumb, dumb! Now he had to avert another catastrophe.

He lowered his rifle and turned to the old man. One punch ought to do it for now. Or a push down the rickety stairs.

"You're going to shoot someone!" The old man turned to run. "I'm going to tell!"

Tuck started after him, but a blur of movement stopped him before he took more than two steps. People were coming out of SeaSong and more people were jumping out of the van. Sherri? Kevin?

He fell back to his knees and searched for his quarry. He would deal with the old man later. He wasn't going anywhere in this weather.

And there she was, helping gather luggage. He lifted the rifle, looked through his very expensive, highly sophisticated laser scope, and homed in on his target. Humming to himself, he pulled the trigger.

Bingo!

"Brenna?" Cass turned and took the girl's weight in her arms, suitcases forgotten. "Brenna!"

"I'm okay," Brenna muttered, though clearly she wasn't. She couldn't even hold herself erect.

"What's wrong?" Cass asked. Then she felt a warm stickiness under her palm where she grasped Brenna's shoulder. She looked and saw a trail of crimson flowing from beneath her hand to wash away in the torrent of water beating on them.

Brenna's head fell back as she lost consciousness. Staring in horror, Cass tried to keep the girl from falling into the street where water ran to curb height. She could drown if she fell. "She's been shot!"

"I've got her, Cass. You can let go."

Cass stared at Dan blankly. Brenna had been shot! People didn't get shot, not people she knew. Lowlifes and TV characters got shot, not friends.

"Cass!" Dan kicked her gently in the shins. "Let go. I've got her."

Cass looked at him, affronted. "You kicked me."

"My arms are full," he explained. "Now let go of Brenna so I can get her inside."

Cass shook her head to clear it and stepped back. Connor, who had recognized the gunshot for what it was, raced ahead and opened the door for Dan.

Cass stood frozen, the rain beating on her back with a force that was painful. Brenna had been shot! An accident? Or on purpose? Mike thought she was in danger, but why? How?

Cass spun until she was standing where Brenna had been standing. Where had the shot come from? Behind her was the boarding house across the street on one corner and the tennis courts on the other. The house was closed for the season, and no one was on the tennis courts where the wind roared across the open space with enough force to blow a man off his feet.

No one could have shot Brenna from directly across the street without hitting Cass first, so that wasn't where the shooter was. On the other side was SeaSong itself, and no one there had shot Brenna.

That left in front. Sudden movement caught Cass's eye, and she looked up to see the curtains part at a second floor window of Mr. Carmichael's house. A man stood there, and if she wasn't mistaken, he held a rifle hanging muzzle down. He began to raise it, and Cass felt panic rise.

She'd found the shooter.

Dan laid Brenna carefully on the carpeted floor in the common area. Only he and Connor were still downstairs, the others having gone up to the rooms which Jenn and Jared were showing them. Connor had a cell phone at his ear as he told the 911 operator they needed an ambulance.

Dan stood and stripped off his raincoat. He watched Brenna's blood drip down the sleeve of her yellow raincoat onto the carpet, knowing that only a small portion of the hemorrhage was actually making its way through the hole torn in the coat by the bullet. He'd never felt so helpless.

"Does anybody here know first aid?" he roared. He dropped to his knees and began to undo Brenna's raincoat. He did know that they had to stop the bleeding, and that meant getting to the wound.

"Alma does. She runs with the ambulance in her township," Connor said as he raced to the stairs. "Alma! Get down here fast!"

Almost immediately there was a clatter on the stairs. "What's wrong?"

"Gunshot wound," Connor said.

Dan carefully slid Brenna's slack arms from her sleeves, flinching when he saw blood bubbling. He knew intense relief when the lone woman with the SS guests slid to her knees beside him. She was still dressed in her wet clothes, and her hair dripped onto Brenna, but she was all business.

"First aid kit?" she asked. "Scissors? Towels?"

Dan pushed himself to his feet, eyes still fixed on Brenna. "Jenn," he called. "Where's the first aid kit?" Dan knew Cass had an extensive one, but he wasn't certain where she stored it.

"Behind the registration counter."

Jenn's voice was soft and close, and Dan spun to see that the call to Alma had brought everyone running.

One of the SS group standing near the registration counter went behind it and passed the first aid kit forward. He also grabbed a pair of scissors that passed from guest to guest until they reached Dan, then Alma. Alma began cutting away Brenna's sweater and shirt. Jared ran upstairs to the linen closet and brought back several towels.

Mike and the SS man who looked sixteen came down the stairs laughing together. They stopped cold when they saw the crowd gathered and staring. Dan immediately moved toward Mike.

"What's going on?" Mike asked.

"The girl's hurt. Shot," said an SS man.

Mike looked surprised but not alarmed. "What girl?"

No one answered. Not that the SS people could, but Jenn and Jared kept quiet too. Dan couldn't blame them. He didn't want to tell Mike either.

Dan knew the moment Mike understood. His face went white. "Brenna?" He pushed the man with glasses out of his way as he surged forward. "Brenna!"

Dan caught him and held him as he tried to push his way to her side.

"Let Alma work on her," he said. "You'll just get in her way."

He struggled frantically to free himself from Dan's grip. "Let me go, Dan! I've got to get to her. She needs me."

"She's unconscious, Mike. She won't even know if you're there. We need to stay out of Alma's way."

"I could use an assistant," Alma called over her shoulder.

Mike strained against Dan's grasp, "Me."

Dan ignored him and looked around the room. "Cass, where are you?"

Silence.

"Cass!"

"I haven't seen her," Jenn said. "Not since you all went outside."

Dan's heart froze with fear. He forgot all about Mike and pushed to the front door. Cass!

When he saw her through the glass in the door, he felt weak with relief. The vise about his heart loosened, and his blood began to flow gain. She was just getting the rest of the baggage.

He looked around for his raincoat, grabbed it from under the feet of two SS men, and shrugged it on. A lot of good it would do him since it was as wet on the inside as the outside. Still, he snapped it, watching Cass through the door the whole time. He saw her look up toward Mr. Carmichael's house. His hands stilled on the snaps as he saw the panicked look on her face.

Then she began to run, but not toward SeaSong and safety. She ran toward Mr. Carmichael's.

Thirty-Four

CASS FLEW UP the sidewalk to Mr. Carmichael's house. That grouchy, impossible old man was in grave danger. Did he know he had a sniper in his house? Had the sniper harmed him somehow?

Cass turned the knob on the front door, expecting to find the door locked. She was surprised when it turned readily. She pushed gently against the frosted glass that filled the top half of the door, and the door squeaked open. She listened carefully. Nothing. So where was the man with the rifle?

Oh, Lord! Help!

She stepped cautiously inside.

"Mr. Carmichael?" she called softly. "Mr. Carmichael?"

"Go away," he shouted, his voice eerie in the darkness of the house. "Go away! Leave me alone!"

Cass stepped farther into the front hall. "Mr. Carmichael?"

"Go away! Go away!"

"Come with me," Cass urged, still trying to keep her voice soft so the man upstairs wouldn't hear her. "Come on. We need to get you out of here." She reached out her hand even though the old man wasn't in sight.

In a flash a hand came out from behind the door

and grabbed her wrist. She screamed automatically and felt her heart stop.

Reminder: Never again try to be a heroine like the dumb heroines in books. It's dangerous.

She stared at the hand gripping her wrist. In the gloom, it appeared disembodied, an entity in itself. Thing from the Addams Family flashed through her mind, and she knew she was in danger of hysteria. When a man wearing a baseball cap and a ponytail stepped out from behind the door, she was almost glad to see him. Clooney's man on the beach? At least she was glad until she saw the revolver he held in his free hand.

"Get away from the door." The man gestured with the gun to the center of the hall.

She got.

He kicked the big front door closed and twisted the lock without taking his eyes off her. "Go through to the kitchen," he ordered.

Cass didn't move. The farther she got from the door, the farther she was from help. Besides, she wasn't certain her legs would hold her if she tried to walk.

"Who are you?" she asked, her voice shaking. She swallowed and tried to sound more in control. "Why did you shoot Brenna?"

"Brenna?" He frowned in confusion. Then his face cleared. "Sherri. That was Sherri."

Now Cass looked confused. "Sherri?"

"My stepsister."

Cass was surprised he couldn't hear the click as the facts fell together in her mind. Tuck! The stepbrother who hurt things! Cass shuddered, and suddenly the brothers seemed like four of the most wonderful men in the world, stubbornness and all. Oh, what she wouldn't give to hear them calling her BB.

Tuck waved his gun. "The kitchen. Now."

Cass wrapped her arms around herself and again didn't move. If he was going to shoot her, he would do so regardless. Maybe she could keep Mr. Carmichael safe.

He studied her for a second, then lowered the gun and fired into the floor at her feet. Cass jumped as her heart leaped to her throat. She ran to the kitchen. There she found Mr. Carmichael, the phone at his ear.

"It's dead," he said, his wrinkled face distressed and drained of all color.

Cass's heart broke at his helpless fear. "Mr. Carmichael," she said, reaching out for him.

"Stop!" Tuck said, his voice cold. "Let the old fool alone. He's no threat to either of us."

A fist began pounding on the front door. "Cass! Cass! Are you in there? Open this door!"

A mix of hope and terror rose in Cass. Would Dan be able to save her, or would he be shot along with her?

Tuck looked at her. "Your husband?"

"My husb—? Oh, n-n-no, our guest. I'm not married."

"Um." Tuck grabbed a rifle Cass hadn't noticed lying on the counter. With the handgun in one fist and the rifle in the other, he gestured Cass toward the back door. "Outside."

Cass looked out the window at the raging storm. "W-where are we going?"

"Cass!" The front door began to shudder under Dan's attempts to make the lock give. "Open this door or I'm breaking the glass and coming in!"

Tuck raised his handgun.

"Dan, look out!"

Tuck fired.

"Dan!" Ears ringing from the explosion of sound in the enclosed space, she lurched toward the front of the house. "Dan!"

Tuck stuck out a foot, catching her in the shins. With a backward swing of his leg, he pulled her feet out from under her, tipping her forward. Her hands hit first, slapping the cracked linoleum, sliding, stinging. With a breathy huff, her chest hit the floor, then her chin. Her teeth clicked painfully. She lay stunned, gasping.

"Get up," Tuck hissed. "And don't ever try anything like that again."

Fighting tears of pain and fright, Cass climbed slowly to her feet. She hurt all over, but she couldn't pull her eyes from the front of the house. In the stormy darkness she couldn't see where Tuck's shot had gone, but she'd heard no shattering glass. At least the front door's frosted pane hadn't broken.

God, please! Let him be all right.

Tuck prodded her with his rifle. He wasn't a very tall man, but he was muscular, maybe a weight lifting fanatic. "Open the back door."

Cass moved slowly, all the while listening for noises from the front door. There were none. *Oh, Dan.* She reached the back door and turned the knob.

"Outside," Tuck ordered as he pulled the strap on his rifle over his head and centered the weapon on his back. He aimed his handgun directly at her.

Cass pulled the door open. Immediately wind and rain flooded in, slapping her in the face, making her eyes water. She ducked her head against the blast and stepped onto the back step. Tuck came right behind her, his handgun at the small of her back. All he wore for protection against the weather was a sweatshirt.

When Dan careened around the corner of the house and screeched to a stop mere feet from them, both Cass and Tuck flinched, startled. Tuck grabbed her about the waist and held her to him, his handgun at her temple.

Cass barely noticed, so intent on Dan was she. "You're okay?" She had to yell to be heard over the snarl of the wind. "He didn't shoot you?"

Dan took a step toward her. "I'm fine. Are you okay?"

"Get back, hotshot! You wouldn't want me to hurt her, now would you?" Tuck released her waist only to wrap his arm around her throat, tightening his hold until she began coughing at the pressure.

Dan stood still, impotent fury pouring off him in waves. "Are you okay?"

"She's fine," Tuck snarled. "But she won't be if you try anything heroic."

Dan raised his hands. "No gun. No tricks. Just don't hurt her."

"We're walking to my car, and you are not following." He took a step, dragging Cass with him.

"I am not following," Dan repeated.

"Move it, blondie. Walk under your own steam."

With one last desperate look at Dan, Cass did as she was told. She leaned into the wind and pushed herself toward the blue car in the back alley. A gust of wind struck and the man with the gun did a little dance to keep his feet under him. His baseball cap flew off, his ponytail flying off with it.

Definitely Clooney's midnight visitor.

They reached the car.

"Climb in the passenger side and through to the driver's side, blondie. You're taking us out of here."

She blinked. "You want me to drive?"

"Get in the car!"

She slid into the passenger seat and shivered with relief when the gun fell away from her temple. She climbed over the gear console, cracking her knee on the way. She kept stepping on her raincoat, making the process awkward and slow.

"Move!" He prodded her with the butt of his rifle. She glanced back and saw he'd pulled it off his back.

She fell into the driver's seat and had to rearrange her raincoat under her before she had enough freedom of movement. He climbed in after her. He rested his rifle against the console, butt down, but the revolver never wavered from its fix on her.

"The key's behind the visor," he said.

She pulled it out and slotted it into the ignition. She turned her head slightly for what might well be her last glimpse of Dan.

He wasn't there.

She felt an irrational sense of abandonment and isolation. In all the wet, wild world, there were only Tuck and her.

She gave herself a mental shake. Dan had gone for help. Somehow he was doing something to rescue her. She knew it, and hope flared.

Carefully, slowly, she drove down the alley. She looked in both directions and pulled out onto the street. As she did so, she heard a loud *crack!* Her first thought was that Tuck was shooting again, and her stomach turned over.

But no. He sat quietly, gun pointed at her, apparently unmoved by the crack of sound, at least until he saw the tree branch that had snapped and was hurtling right at them. Cass hit the brakes, throwing up her hands to protect her face while Tuck cursed. The car swerved wildly, but the huge limb missed them. Barely. Its leaves swiped across the windshield.

Cass sat shaking as she stared up at the great ragged tear where the branch had ripped from the tree. "That could have killed us."

"That is far from your greatest danger," Tuck snarled and

placed the revolver against her side. "Drive."

She gulped. "Where?"

He rammed the gun against her ribs. "I said drive."

"I'm not kidding." She hated that she sounded breathless with fear. "Where do you want me to go? We won't be able to get off island."

He stared for an instant. "I don't believe you! Just drive!"

She drove, her hands gripping the steering wheel as the wind buffeted the car. At one particularly strong gust, the car was blown across the road. Tuck flinched.

"Scary, isn't it?" Cass struggled to get the car back in its proper lane. Not that it mattered. No one else in his right mind was out driving in this weather.

She went four blocks before they came to a flooded intersection. Cass hit the brakes and stared at the dark water, its surface agitated by the gale.

"Drive through it," Tuck ordered.

Her hands turned slick on the wheel. "I don't know how deep it is."

"Who cares? Drive!"

"What if there's a sinkhole or something, and we fall in?" Cass had never heard of a sinkhole in Seaside, but it was always possible.

"Drive!" He pointed the gun at her again and started to tighten his finger on the trigger.

If she had been able to pry her fingers loose from the wheel, Cass would have slapped a hand over her mouth to hold back the bile rising in her throat. Slowly, slowly she moved through the water. As little waves eddied out from the tires, she asked, "How high does water have to be to short out the motor?"

"Who knows?" Tuck's free hand played a nervous tattoo on his thigh. "Who cares?"

Cass turned east toward the ocean as a great gust struck them broadside. The car shuddered and skidded.

"Where are you going?" Tuck's voice sounded tight with fear for the first time.

"The roads are less flooded this way. It's bayside that's the problem."

As she inched along, she glanced in her rearview mirror, then looked again in astonishment. She swallowed a hysterical urge to

laugh. Turning the corner behind her were a silver BMW, a blue
Software Solutions van, Mike's clunker, and her own car. She was
leading a parade.

She glanced at Tuck. He obviously had no idea they were
being followed. He was too busy playing the drums on his thigh
and shaking his foot in a colossal, jittery fit of nerves. His handgun
was now aimed at the dashboard while he scanned the road
ahead.

Cass drove steadily on, the curb-deep water rippling out in
waves as the car passed. A block from the ocean she turned right
as she pondered whether a highly nervous Tuck was better or
worse than the nasty one back at the house.

"Where are you going?" he demanded, turning the gun back
on her. "Why did you make that turn?"

"Because the ocean's there." She pointed. "We had to turn."

He blinked. "But why did you turn right?"

"I don't know. Do you want me to turn left?"

"I want you to turn the way that will get us off this island."

She swallowed. She knew what happened to bearers of bad
news. "I told you. We can't get off island."

He swung toward her and in a lightning-fast move grabbed a
fistful of her hair. He jerked her head toward him. She cried out in
pain and fear. She couldn't see the road! Their eyes met for an
instant, and Cass couldn't tell who was the more scared, she or
Tuck.

"I can't see where we're going!" she cried.

"Get us off this island!" He released her hair and shoved her
from him. She crashed against the door.

Talking to himself, he swiveled in his seat, seeking some clue
to the best route to take. In the driving rain, all street names were
obscured, all directional signs unreadable. Even if they had been
legible, Cass doubted they'd have helped him. She herself was
offering no help.

Tuck turned all the way around to look behind them, and
Cass felt him jerk when he spotted the procession behind them.

"What's that?" he shouted. "Who are they? What do they
want?"

She glanced in her mirror and watched as a police car fell into
the line, driving side by side with Dan.

Tuck saw too and hissed his distress. He raised his revolver, resting it on the top of his seat, aiming it out the back window. She heard the click of the safety releasing.

"No!" Cass screamed and swerved. Tuck lost his balance and slammed against his door. The gun went off as his hand jerked, and the bullet pinged as it flew through the roof.

"You little—" He pushed away from the door, his face crimson with rage.

Cass hit the automatic window buttons and the front windows whizzed down. Rain and wind poured in, inundating a surprised Tuck, drenching his already saturated sweatshirt.

"What the—" He reached for the button on his side, Cass momentarily forgotten, but before he could act, a plastic trash can, the kind that people often have in bathrooms, bounced against the car. He looked to see what had made the noise just as it flew in his downed window and struck him in the face. As he raised his hands protectively and yelped in shock and pain, his revolver fell to the floor.

While he struggled with the can, trying to push it back out the window, Cass grabbed his rifle, which was resting against the console. Heart beating frantically for fear he'd turn and see what she was doing, she pulled it across herself and heaved it out her open window. She grinned when she heard the splash. She looked at Tuck's revolver resting on the floor at his feet and knew there was no way she could reach it.

Finally, Tuck pushed the trash basket out the window and hit his window button. "Close your window, blondie, and I mean now!" He grabbed his gun from the floor, leaned over, and held it to her temple again. He vibrated with fury. With regret and a very shaky finger she raised her window.

He settled back in his seat, his foot tapping, tapping, tapping. Every few seconds his head jerked to check the cars behind him.

Cass kept her eyes straight ahead. "Why don't you give it up?" She was pleased that her voice was almost steady.

He looked at her, obviously scandalized at the idea. "I'm not giving up. I'm never giving up. We're going to the Caribbean." He gestured with his gun. "Keep driving."

To the Caribbean? As Cass thought of sun-swept beaches and

blue, blue waters, the rain stopped. At the same time, the wind became a mere whisper of sound.

"It's over!" Tuck was gleeful as he stared at the sky, squinting at the sun. "Now we can go."

"It's not over," Cass said. "It's the eye of the storm. "It'll start up again in just a little while."

They drove over a stretch of road that in Seaside was a hill, though anywhere else it would be the slightest rise. The result was that they drove out of the water flooding the streets, though a stream still flowed along the gutter.

"See?" Tuck pointed. "The roads are drying already. Turn that corner."

Cass did and a figure appeared, hand held out in a halt sign.

"Ignore him. Keep going," Tuck said.

"We can't. We have to stop and ask what's wrong." Cass slowed the car.

"I said keep going!"

"I can't!" Cass didn't have to feign the fear in her voice. "We have to find out what's the trouble."

Tuck made an indecipherable but distinctly unhappy noise.

Cass rolled her window down again. "What's the trouble?"

"Wire down," the man called. "We're waiting for the electric company. You have to go around."

She waved her understanding and raised her window.

She looked at Tuck. "We have to turn around."

"No, we don't. We can't. They're back there." He jerked his thumb.

"We can't drive through this water," Cass said, desperate.

"It's okay." Tuck sounded almost cheerful—which made Cass's skin crawl. "The downed wire is no problem. The tires will protect us."

Cass stared at him. "No, they won't! That's a myth."

He poked her in the ribs with the gun. "I am not stupid," he said quietly, grimly. "Don't try to be clever. You will not trick me."

"I'm not trying to trick you!" Each time she tried to pull farther from him, he and his gun followed until she was pinned against her door.

"Drive straight ahead or else."

Cass looked at his wild eyes, then at the deceptively innocuous water filling the street ahead from curb to curb. "No! I'm not driving into water that could electrocute me. You can shoot me if you want, but I won't do it."

He raised his gun and Cass closed her eyes.

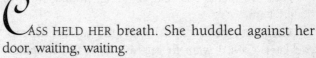

Thirty-Five

CASS HELD HER breath. She huddled against her door, waiting, waiting.

Lord, I don't want to die! I just found Dan! I can't leave the kids. And what about Mom?

When nothing happened immediately, she realized she was cowering, and she hated herself for that weakness. If she could tell the brothers off over BB, she could stand up to Tuck. She opened her eyes and gulped. He was staring at her, his face twisted with emotion, his hand shaking. It was obvious he was not a well man.

She straightened her spine and stared back. She was not going to make shooting her easy.

A rap sounded on Tuck's window. Cass's eyes widened at the sight of Greg Barnes standing there, his side arm drawn and pointing at Tuck. Tuck spun to the noise and stared openmouthed, his gun dipping in his surprise.

"Freeze!" Greg yelled, looking remarkably danger-ous with his two-handed grip on his revolver and his no-nonsense police face. Tuck froze.

At the same time, Cass's door flew open and Dan yanked her out and down. They landed in a puddle of water along the curb, but Cass didn't care. She was free! She wrapped her arms around Dan and held on. She buried her face in his chest and tried not to cry.

316 ~ Gayle Roper

As Greg opened Tuck's door and dragged him from the car, Dan helped Cass to her feet. At the same time three Software Solutions people poured out of their blue van, another from Mike's clunker, and one from Cass's own car. They gathered around the dripping Cass and Dan.

"Are you okay?" Dan leaned back, searching her face.

She nodded, still clinging to him.

"What's this?" He rubbed at her chin.

She flinched. "I fell."

Dan's face darkened and he glared at Tuck, now spread-eagled against Greg's car.

"But I'm okay," she said, sniffling, pulling from his embrace. "Really I am."

Greg put a handcuffed Tuck in the back of his car. "I'll contact you later, Cass. I want to get him back to the station before the storm starts again." With a wave he climbed in his vehicle and drove away just as the electric company truck arrived.

Cass leaned against Dan and looked at all her rescuers. "Thank you all so much!"

"Mighty Max saves the day," called one of the Solutions men.

"Rescues the beautiful damsel from the wicked ogre."

"Keeps her from getting electrocuted."

"Keeps her from being shot."

"Keeps her from being swept out to sea by the brutal storm."

Cass was struck by an urge to giggle. These Solutions people were consistent, if nothing else.

Dan carefully tucked Cass into his passenger seat, then paused. He leaned in and kissed her hard, a kiss of possession. They drove home as the wind began to roar once again and the heavens opened up.

The next morning Cass was at the breakfast table drinking coffee when Dan appeared. "Hey," she greeted, smiling broadly. She didn't want him to know how fragile she felt because she knew he'd worry. Post-traumatic stress syndrome. She'd slept with her light on all night, not that she'd slept much. She kept feeling guns pressed against her temple.

"Um," he muttered as he poured himself a mugful.

She cocked an eyebrow at him. She'd never seen him sullen before. "I called the hospital. Brenna's doing fine. She's going to hurt for a while, but she'll be up and about in no time. Isn't that great news? The police think she probably moved at the crucial time, and the shot got her shoulder instead of her chest."

"Um," he said again, burying his nose in his mug.

With determined goodwill, Cass continued. "Her mother and stepdad have arrived. Poor people. They're getting their daughter back on the one hand, but their son is going to jail for attempted murder."

To her surprise, Dan glared at her.

"What's the matter with you? I just gave you good news." She got up to refill her cup. "Get up on the wrong side of the bed?"

He ignored her and took a long drink of coffee. She could tell something was bothering him, and he was struggling to keep his emotions in check. Well, she was too. After all, she was the one who had the gun at her head yesterday, not him. She was the one forced to drive for a deranged man. But she wouldn't let such memories get the best of her. She decided to give perky another try.

"Isn't it a beautiful day? Sunshine and fluffy clouds. No rain. No wind. And no bad guys lurking."

He moved so fast he was on her before she saw him coming. He grabbed her by the shoulders and gave her a shake.

She blinked and batted at him. "What? Dan! Let go!"

He did. He took a step back, then another. "I had nightmares all night. Look." He held out his hand, and she was amazed to see it was shaking. "You did that." He glared at her again.

"Me? What did I do?"

"What did you *do*? You ran right into the middle of a murder attempt! That's what you did."

"Well, yeah, but I was trying—"

"I don't care what you were trying to do!" He leaned down, nose to nose with her. "Don't ever do it again!"

Cass's frayed nerves frayed a bit more. She narrowed her eyes. "Are you giving me orders?"

"What if I am?"

"You are not my brothers! No one gives me orders anymore!"

"You're darn right I'm not your brothers," he said from between gritted teeth.

Cass shivered at the heat in his gaze, feeling her anger drain. She grinned at him.

"But the fact remains," he continued, ignoring her friendly smile, "you obviously need a keeper."

Her resentment flared anew. "And that's you, I suppose?"

"It certainly is, lady. No one else. Ever."

If he hadn't hissed the words through those clenched teeth, his frown dark enough to make a puppy cower, Cass might have taken them better. Instead she yelled, "Ha!"

"Don't *ha!* me. I'm in no mood."

"You're in a mood, all right. And I can take care of myself, thank you. I've been doing it for forty years, and I don't need some bossy man messing things up at this late date!"

"You certainly need someone," he roared, reaching for her.

She ducked under his arms and ran out the back door, her heart beating so fast she thought it would shatter itself on her ribs. "Well, not you, big boy!" she yelled back over her shoulder, only to find him right behind her. She ran between her house and the derelict house next door, turned, and faced him, hands on hips. "Leave me alone!"

"Don't worry. I will as soon as I strangle you for being so stupid." He stalked toward her, the sun shining on his deep red hair and his steely navy eyes. She'd never seen anyone so handsome. Oh, how she loved him.

"Hey, Missy!"

Automatically Cass turned to find Mr. Carmichael standing on his front porch. He smiled and waved. Disoriented at his friendliness, Cass waved back.

"Are you ready to sell yet, Mr. Carmichael?" she called out of habit.

"Already sold," he called back, his whiny voice sounding almost happy.

Cass felt as if she'd been slugged. Sold? "What? When?" She walked toward him. Tears welled. "But you knew I wanted it."

"Got a great deal," he said as she stopped at the foot of his stairs. "No mortgage. Full payment." He chortled. "I'm going to Florida. Gonna buy me one of them condominiums on the beach. But hey, I wanted to thank you for coming over yesterday. It was nice of you."

She turned, wanting to get away before she disgraced herself by crying in front of the terrible old man. When she saw Dan behind her semaphoring Mr. Carmichael to be quiet, she went cold all over. For a moment all she could do was stare, hoping she had misunderstood. His guilty expression was all the proof she needed.

"*You* bought my house!" The pain of the betrayal sliced through her. "What are you going to do? Put a B&B right next to SeaSong? Is that what God has told you to do?" The idea of a B&B next door wasn't that upsetting. After all, Seaside was a resort town full of hotels, boarding houses, and B&Bs. What was one more? The duplicity was what devastated her.

"How could you?" she whispered, all the hopes and longings of the last weeks in her voice. "How could you?"

Needing to get as far from Dan as possible, she began to run, the tears streaming down her face. She didn't have on a warm jacket, but she didn't care. She needed movement, distance. She sloshed through leftover puddles, which became deeper as she neared the beach and absolute sea level. Without thought she ran up the ramp onto the boardwalk. As she raced across it, she could feel the heavy thud, thud, thud of footfalls behind her. Dan.

She doubled her speed, practically diving down the steps that led to the beach.

"Cass!"

He sounded so close, too close. She tried to run faster, but the sand, all soggy from the rain, slowed her. Then a hand grabbed her arm and whirled her around. She staggered, caught her balance, and found herself face-to-face with a winded Dan. He held her by both arms.

"What?" she demanded. "You want to abuse me some more?"

He just looked at her, and she knew what he saw. Her eyes were puffy from crying, her nose red and stuffy. Her hair was a tangled mess, hanging about her face like dirty blond snakes.

He shook his head slightly in amusement, and she stiffened. If he laughed at her, she'd kill him.

"Cass, sweetheart," he said, his voice catching and barely audible over the crash of the surf.

Cass, sweetheart. Yeah, right. Like he could sweet-talk his way out of this one.

"Oh, Cass, you are so beautiful." His hand pushed the straggly, windblown strands from her eyes and stayed threaded through her hair, cupping her head. "Sometimes I love you so much I can hardly stand the sweet pain of it."

She stared at him, openmouthed. "You love me?" How many times had she dreamed of hearing him say that? "But you think I need a keeper! And you bought my house!" She started to cry again, turning her face into the comfort of his palm.

He wrapped his free arm about her and pulled her to him. He kissed her, crushing her against him.

No, you idiot, she told herself. *Don't enjoy this! He betrayed you!*

But her heart wasn't listening. Her arms wrapped themselves about his waist and clung. Forty years she'd waited for a kiss like this, for a man like this, and she'd never imagined it could be so, so—she smiled, if you can smile with your mouth thoroughly involved in other activities. There were no words, she suddenly realized. No words at all. That was why God invented kisses.

"What are you smiling about?" Dan asked as his lips skittered to her ear. His warm breath sent a shiver down her back.

"Your kiss."

"Mmm." He sounded quite pleased with himself.

"But Dan," she said in a small voice. "How could you do that to me if you love me?"

"I did it because I do love you."

He took away her dream because he loved her? She pulled back and stared at him, rebuke in her eyes. "This had better be good," she said. "You're breaking my heart here, you know."

He leaned over and kissed her again. She couldn't help it; upset as she was, she kissed him back.

"Doesn't seem too broken to me."

She sighed. "A lot *you* know."

"I know you wanted that pile of debris with all your heart."

She nodded, uncertain whether she wanted to hear his justification for the hurt he'd given her, not sure how she'd deal with the treachery. Because she'd have to deal with it. She knew she loved him irrevocably, in spite of the hurt he'd dealt her.

"I know you've been saving for several years for when Carmichael finally put it on the market. So I approached him with my offer."

"You went to Mr. Carmichael? And he sold it to you just like that?" She stepped back, putting distance between them. She felt like a knife had been turned in her back. "But I've been asking him for years!"

Dan nodded "That's why he sold it to me."

Cass stared, the shaft of pain cutting to the core of her heart. She began shaking. Then she spun on her heel and walked. *I wanted it. They both knew I wanted it. Still Mr. Carmichael sold it to Dan, and Dan bought it!*

Lord, what am I to do? I'm dying here!

Dan caught her by the arm and stopped her. "I'm not doing very well here, am I?"

She looked at him, her eyes full of tears and hurt and love. "Dan, I don't think I can deal with all this."

He nodded, smiling.

The smile was what did it. The love and the anger overwhelmed her, and she lost control.

"Don't you smile at me, buster!" she suddenly yelled, punching him in the chest. Her hand bounced off his ribs and she had to force herself not to slug him again. "You've just taken my choicest dream and buried it!"

He smiled some more, rubbing the spot above his heart where she had connected. "Your choicest dream?" he asked with a knowing look and a raised eyebrow.

She closed her eyes, struggling to get a full breath into lungs suddenly unable to inhale. He was her choicest dream, and he knew it.

"But you bought my house!"

He pulled her into his arms again and rocked her against him, ignoring her halfhearted squirming for freedom. "That I did, Cass. That I did. But I bought it for you, sweetheart."

She stilled. "What?"

"As a wedding present," he said. "You weren't supposed to know about it until we got married and I could present you with the deed in a great romantic flourish on our wedding night. That way I would be the object of your undying affection for the rest of our lives."

"A wedding present?" It was a good thing he had his arms around her or she would have collapsed with shock. As it was, she grabbed his sleeves and held on, twisting his jacket hard in her fingers. "*My* wedding present?"

"*Your* wedding present, Cass." He smiled down at her. "There's certainly no one else I want to marry."

"You want to marry me?" Suddenly all the raucous gulls turned into glorious chimes, sounding the sweetest music she'd ever heard.

"More than anything I've ever wanted in my life. Cass, my sweet love, will you marry me and live with me in Carmichael's atrocity?"

"Oh, Dan, yes!" She threw herself at him with such enthusiasm that he was overbalanced, and they fell to the sand. He landed on his back and lay with his head in the drenched sand. She lay beside him on her stomach, her arm draped across his chest. He put his free arm under his head and looked at her, squinting against the brilliant sun. She looked back. They stared at each other for several minutes, smiling, delighted with themselves, with life, and filled with hearts of gratitude for the miracle God had sent them in each other.

"I hate to tell you this before you buy me an engagement ring," Cass finally said, "but you would have been the object of my undying affection without Mr. Carmichael's house. You know that, don't you?" She rested her chin on his chest. "But don't even think of returning the gift. You're committed now."

"Totally," he said, and she knew he meant more than just the house.

She grinned, then turned serious. "Do we have to wait until the renovations are done to get married?"

"I certainly hope not. I've seen the inside of that house, and it's going to take a long time to make it livable. A very long time."

"So we can do the deed soon?"

"As soon as you want. You're the bride."

She was the bride. Her heart swelled, and swirls of joy danced along her nerves. She had never felt so alive. A long-dead hope was being realized with the most wonderful man in the world.

"By the way," she said. "You do know that you can't order me around, don't you?"

"You're referring to our argument?"

She nodded.

"I do know. And I appreciate your independence. I was just so afraid I was going to lose you before I even had you, and it came out in anger. All night I kept remembering my fear, and I was in a state by morning. I'm sorry."

"I understand," she said. "I really do. If we hadn't gone to Cape May the night of Jenn's escapade, I probably would have said some harsh things to her, I'm sure."

"I guess anger is easier to articulate than fear." He pulled his hand from behind his head and took her by the chin. "Pointy thing. It's making a dent in my chest."

She pushed herself to a sitting position. It was the height of idiocy to lie on wet sand in November. She could feel the dampness all the way to her bones.

She sneezed. "Excuse me." She sneezed again.

Dan climbed to his feet. "Come on, sweetheart." He reached for her and pulled her erect. They started toward the steps to the boardwalk, hands clasped. As they hit the boardwalk, Dan started to jog. She followed his lead.

"We both need hot showers and dry clothes," he said. "I can't marry you if we're in the hospital with pneumonia. And, love, I do want to marry you. Soon."

Epilogue

Fourteen Months Later

CASS AND DAN stood at the front door of what was formerly the Carmichael place. It was now SeaScape, the newly refurbished home of Mr. and Mrs. Dan Harmon. Mike, their black lab, named not after Brenna's boyfriend as everyone thought but after Mr. Carmichael, quivered with excitement beside them. He'd been in this place many times during its restoration and loved it. Here he had the run of the house instead of being confined to the kitchen and family room like at SeaSong. Here there was no old cat to make his life miserable.

"Ready?" Dan asked Cass.

"I'm ready," she answered. "But are you certain you want to do this? I'm not exactly a featherweight."

"You're beautiful," he said. "I love you all fat and pregnant."

"Right. I glow."

He reached for her and lifted her in his arms. Cass was pleased to note that he didn't even grunt with the effort.

"All those months at the gym have paid off, haven't they?" she teased.

Dan grinned and stepped across the threshold into the front hall, Mike dancing beside him. "Welcome home, Cass." He set her on her feet, pulled her close, and kissed her. He barely flinched when one of the babies poked him. Twins. He couldn't believe it.

Mike bumped them with his nose.

"And welcome home to you, too, old boy." Dan ruffled the animal's ears.

Mike grinned and raced off to see what mischief he could get into.

"A puppy and babies? Are you sure you're up to this?" Dan had asked when Cass gave him Mike on Father's Day.

"We'll have several months to train him before the babies come," Cass said.

As they watched Mike rush to explore, Cass shook her head. "All I can say is that I hope the twins train more easily than he has."

She turned and leaned her back against Dan's chest. She looked around the lovingly refurbished place, at the shining hardwood floors, the sparkling windows, the crisp white trim, the wonderfully restored chandelier that sent shards of light shining through its crystal prisms. Granted, she hadn't been able to do quite as much of the work as she'd done on SeaSong, but there were enough of her brush strokes on the walls and varnish strokes on the woodwork to make her feel satisfied.

"Oh, Cassandra Marie." Her mother rushed up, arms spread wide. "Don't you love this pretty house? I'm so glad you could come and visit. We have lots of food." She gestured vaguely to the kitchen where Cass could see her sisters-in-law at work. "There are some, uh, people out there fixing, uh, things." She dimpled at Dan. "And you brought your friend."

"I'm Dan, Mom." He bent to kiss her.

"Dan." Mom drew back slightly and held out her hand. "So pleased to meet you."

Dan straightened before making contact with Mom's soft cheek. He extended his hand. "The feeling's mutual," he said, remembering the doctor's advice that they go to Mom's universe since she was unable to come to theirs. Correcting her, the doctor said, would only distress her.

Cass leaned in to hug her increasingly frail mother. *Thanks, Father, for letting this be one of her good days.*

"And Cassandra Marie, I hate to say this in front of—" She looked at Dan in question.

"Dan," he supplied again.

"Nice to meet you, Dan." Mom smiled sweetly at him, then skewered Cass. "You need to lose weight, dear."

Cass bit back the half groan, half laugh that threatened to bubble out. "You're right about that, Mom. Soon. I promise. Now why don't we go into the living room?"

"There are people in there," Mom whispered.

"I know. It's our family."

Mom stared into the crowded living room where everyone except Bud and Jane, the Colorado Mertons, had gathered. She frowned. "Are you sure? I don't see Mama and Daddy. Or Elsie."

"They couldn't come today," Cass said, taking her mother's arm. "But look. There's a wonderful seat for you next to Tommy."

"His name is Tommy? He's big."

"They're all big around here." Cass forced herself to smile. "Tommy's your son."

"Oh." Mom let herself be led to Tommy who assisted her to the seat beside him.

As Cass walked to the antique rocker that Dan had found for her at an estate sale in Hammonton, she wondered again how her father did the Charlotte thing twenty-four hours a day. At least he'd put their names on the waiting list at a very nice retirement community with excellent health care facilities, knowing it was only a matter of time before her care was beyond him.

As Cass sat, one of the twins poked her in the ribs. She absently rubbed the spot as she looked at Jared, home for winter break from his first year in college on a football scholarship. If anything, he was taller and broader than ever. She smiled. The boy had looks and a wonderful attitude toward life. The girls must be going crazy over him.

When she and Dan had gotten engaged, Dan felt he should leave SeaSong.

"You've only got one reputation, Cass, and I'm not going to sully it," he'd said.

Jared was the one who suggested that he and Dan live at Tommy and Rhonda's.

"The house is empty. Why not use it?"

The arrangement had worked very well for the month and a half until the wedding. Then Dan and Jared moved back to

SeaSong. At that time, Cass turned her understairs cubby back into a storage closet and moved into the turret room with her husband.

Now Jared smiled at her from across the room and patted his tummy. She grinned back and blew him a kiss.

Jenn sat on the sofa between Tommy and Rhonda. She obviously gloried in having her parents home again. She'd not only survived Derrick but grown ever more lovely in spirit as well as appearance in the past year.

Paulie, no taller than before but less bulky, sat at her feet. His face had firmed and matured, and he was becoming a very handsome young man. He, too, was a college freshman, but he had chosen not to play football, much to everyone's surprise.

"I decided I don't like it," he'd said. "Enough of getting the stuffings beaten out of me every day."

Jenn and Jared—and Paulie—had been gone from SeaSong for three months now, and Cass missed them. She knew Dan did too. Their time with the kids had been rich and wonderful, a gift from the Lord. Another kick reminded Cass that soon she'd have more than enough kid action to keep her busy, another wonderful gift from the Lord.

A knock on the door sent Dan to answer, and he returned with Sherri and Kevin.

"Happy housewarming, Cass," Sherri said, bending to give Cass a kiss and a gaily wrapped present.

"How was your trip?" Cass asked, thinking that she would be happy to have her lap back soon. She had nowhere to rest Sherri's gift.

Sherri and Kevin looked at each other and grinned.

Cass held up her hand. "Enough said. I know what those goofy smiles mean."

It had been a long, hard year for those two. Sherri's hospitalization, her recuperation at home in California, Kevin's discovery that she came from a very wealthy family, the repairing of trust between both Sherri and Kevin and their families, the hours spent in counseling. Now Sherri and Kevin were in Seaside to stay, newly married and just returned from their honeymoon.

Sherri was to be the assistant innkeeper at SeaSong while Kevin was back at school full-time, going for a degree in hospitality. It didn't take much imagination to know that SeaSong would have some very stiff competition in the not-too-distant future.

Another knock and Pastor Paul entered.

"Ah, the most important person," Dan said as he shook Pastor Paul's hand. "We couldn't do this without you."

Dan reached out a hand and pulled Cass from her chair, no easy feat these days. He slid his arm around her waist and waited until everyone fell quiet and the sisters-in-law joined them from the kitchen. Then he spoke.

"It's hard to believe that I didn't know any of you wonderful people a little over a year ago. God sent me here to find His will, and I found just how deep and wide His love for us is. He gave me Cass, another family, wonderful friends, and a new career. This being a dollar-a-year man consulting with Christian ministries has been more fulfilling than I ever imagined. I am a very happy man."

Cass, glowing with her own happiness, hugged her husband. "We asked you all here today for a very special ceremony. I did something similar at SeaSong, but then it was just me and the Lord. When I told Dan about it and suggested we do the same thing for SeaScape, we decided we'd like to ask your participation. A home can never have too much love and too much prayer."

"We've asked Pastor Paul to dedicate this house to the Lord," Dan said. "Cass and I found each other later than most, and maybe that's why we're so aware of God's place in our lives. We just know that we want the Lord to be always in this place as we live out our lives together and raise our kids." He laid a hand on Cass's belly and was promptly kicked.

Everyone laughed.

"Somehow, I think they're going to give you two a run for your money," Tommy said.

"Then we'd better pray extra hard," Cass said and bowed her head. The room fell quiet.

"Dear Father," Pastor Paul prayed. "We ask You to come dwell in this home. Fill each room with Your…"

Cass felt a wash of water flow down her legs. Pastor Paul's words faded as she glanced at her feet and the puddle surrounding them. Her water had broken. It was two weeks before her due date, but with twins, an early arrival wasn't all that unusual.

She pulled on Dan's sleeve. He glanced at her in question. She pointed down, and his eyes widened.

"Are you okay?" he mouthed as the pastor continued to pray.

She nodded. "Fi—" The word was cut off as a contraction gripped her. Her eyes widened in surprise at its strength. It made the Braxton-Hicks contractions she'd been enduring for a month seem like a single apple as opposed to an orchardful.

Dan lowered her to her chair. She grinned at him, tapping her watch. He nodded. He'd time the contractions.

"Towel?" she mouthed.

Dan nodded and left the room. He returned quickly with a white bath towel. *White. Why white?* Cass thought as he knelt and ran the towel over the floor.

When he rose, she thanked him with a smile, ignoring the smudges of dirt that streaked across the previously pristine towel. This time she felt the contraction begin its progress across her stomach and grasped the arms of her chair as it tightened like a vise. Her groan and Pastor Paul's amen sounded simultaneously.

Everyone in the room looked at her.

"The babies?" squeaked Jenn, her eyes bright with excitement.

"The babies," Cass confirmed as the pain receded.

"What babies?" Mom asked, wide-eyed.

"Cassandra Marie is having babies," Dad said, taking Mom's hand. "Twins. Remember?"

"Cassandra Marie?" Mom looked at Cass. "Then she needs to get married."

The kids giggled as Cass, her heart aching, said, "I am married, Mom. I've been married for almost a year."

Mom blinked. "Why didn't anyone tell me? To whom?"

"To me, Mom," Dan said.

"Who are you?" Mom asked.

"I'm Dan."

"I'm pleased to meet you, Dan." Mom held out her hand. "You're handsome. You should meet my daughter."

After that, things happened in a blur. More pain. A fast ride to the hospital with a caravan of relatives following. Greater pain. The *puff, puff* of breathing exercises. Dan's cheeriness when all she wanted was for the agony to go away, taking him along with it. The brisk professionalism of the hospital personnel. The incredible weariness between contractions. Dan's loving support. Then the unending haze of torture as the babies' heads pushed through the "ring of fire." Finally, that incredible moment of first one cry, then five minutes later, a second cry.

Her babies were here.

Early the next morning, Dan sat on Cass's bed. In his arms he held Dan, Jr., a red, wizened little gnome with no hair. A weary Cass held Tobi Lynn, a sweet-faced pixie with a shock of black hair that stood out like Tobi already had a close acquaintance with an electrical outlet.

"Dan after his daddy and Tobi because we met in October," Cass said, smothering a yawn.

"At least we'll always be able to tell them apart," Dan said as he studied Danny's little hands. He held his hand beside his son's. The miniature perfection of the baby amazed him. "Look at these fingernails. Did you ever see anything like them?" He looked at Tobi. "And did you ever see a more beautiful little one? She's gorgeous, just like her mother."

Cass shook her head at him. "You're besotted with them. It's very obvious that I'm going to have to be the firm one in the family, or these children will become wild little monkeys." She reached out and cupped Dan's jaw, her hazel eyes full of love. "I have to talk with your mother and find out her secrets of child raising because I want Danny to grow up just like his wonderful daddy."

Dan felt love welling in him like he'd never known, and he thought he couldn't love Cass more. As he tried to find words to articulate how he felt, Cass smothered another yawn. Dan leaned in and kissed her.

"Let me put the babies on their warming table, and then you can sleep." He put Danny down and took Tobi from Cass. By the time he came back to the bed, his wife was sound asleep. He gently moved her to one side of the bed, slipped off his shoes, and climbed in beside her. He adjusted the sheet and blanket over them both and settled into sleep too.

This business of waiting on the Lord was the best.

Dear Readers,

Dementia. Alzheimer's. These words strike fear into our hearts. Every time we forget a word or cannot recall someone's name, we are sure it's the first step to not knowing our own name. We pray, "Lord, while I'd like to keep the old body working as long as possible with as few complications and as little pain as possible, I beg You to protect my mind."

Unfortunately, my mother-in-law developed advanced Alzheimer's. Many of the situations that happened to Charlotte Merton happened to Mom Roper in her last years, even Charlotte's running over of herself. Our prize memory of that time is our son's song, "Grandmom Got Run Over by a Chrysler," sung for Mom at her eightieth birthday party three weeks after her accident.

I'd love to hear from you. I know some of you have stories like ours, some sad, some so ridiculous all you can do is laugh. Ah, thank God for laughter! Or maybe you have nothing to say to me but hello. Hey, some days hello sounds wonderful! Write me at gayle@gayleroper.com or visit me at www.gayleroper.com.

Gayle Roper

The publisher and author would love to hear your comments about this book. *Please contact us at:* www.multnomah.net/seasideseasons

Discussion Questions

1. Cass has been single for forty years. What do you admire about her as a single woman? Read 1 Corinthians 7:32–35. What are the advantages to being single?

2. When Cass finds herself falling in love with Dan and she fears it will come to nothing, she reminds herself that Jesus is enough. Her mother answers that she is both right and wrong. How do you react to that idea? Read Deuteronomy 6:5; Acts 4:12; John 13:34; Romans 15:7; Galatians 5:13.

3. Cass's family has fallen into the habit of taking her for granted, of expecting her to be there for everyone. What examples of this do we see in the story? In real life have you seen a family take one of the members for granted? How does Cass begin to reclaim her life? Read Philippians 2:3–4. How do these verses speak to this issue?

4. Why is Jenn so angry? Is she justified? Ephesians 6:4 says "do not exasperate your children." How do parents, or in Cass's case, a parental substitute, maintain standards for the children and still fulfill this verse?

5. Brenna is a prodigal. Did she have a valid reason for leaving home? What about her leaving is cruel? Read Luke 15:11–17. What causes the prodigal to finally return home? What causes Brenna to do the same? What does this truth mean to those who are the parents and loved ones of prodigals?

6. After the pain a prodigal puts a family through, what should be the response when one returns? Read Luke 15:18–32. What two responses do we see in this story?

7. The ultrasuccessful Dan has come to Seaside looking for significance in his life. What do you think are the things that truly count, especially in the eyes of God? Read Matthew 22:37–40. According to Jesus, what are the significant things in life?

8. Tuck is also looking for significance. Where has he made his mistakes? How does he compound them? Read Ephesians 4:31–32. What would Tuck say about these verses? What should we say?

9. Charlotte Merton is slipping further and further into dementia. How can God let a fine and intelligent woman like her suffer from a disease that robs her of her greatest assets? Read Philippians 3:10. Paul, the author, wants to know three things. Where does Charlotte's illness fit into this verse? How does your heart fit into this verse?

10. What are your thoughts about Lew and his sweepstakes? Read Philippians 4:19. What is the promise to Lew? But what about Christians who don't have enough to eat? A place to sleep? Who suffer for Christ like many believers do in other parts of the world today? Read Romans 8:28. What is God's purpose for us? Hint: read Romans 8:29.

YEARNING FOR SUNSHINE, ABBY FINDS DANGER, LOVE, AND LAUGHTER IN THE SUMMER SHADOWS

"A highly entertaining tale with just the right touch of mystery. I'm already looking forward to my next visit to Seaside."

—DEBORAH RANEY, author of *Beneath a Southern Sky*

Summer Shadows by Gayle Roper
Seaside Seasons, Book Two

The accident that killed Abby Patterson's husband and daughter has left her with a limp and chronic pain. Abby strikes out, determined to build a new life for herself. She finds the perfect home: a cottage on the beach. At least, it would be perfect except for one tiny irritant: Marsh Winslow, her landlord. But when Abby witnesses a hit-and-run accident and the trauma leaves her with amnesia, she finds an unexpected source of help: Marsh! When mysterious events make it clear that Abby is now a target, she and Marsh join forces to uncover a dangerous secret. Together they discover that God is in the business of putting broken lives back together so that they are more beautiful—and more perfect—than ever.

ISBN 1-57673-969-4

TEARS ARE FALLING LIKE SPRING RAIN...

Spring Rain **by Gayle Roper**
Seaside Seasons, Book One

Leigh Spenser, a young teacher and single mother of ten-year-old Billy, is thrown into conflict. Clay Wharton, the boy's estranged father, comes home to Seaside, New Jersey, to await the passing of his twin brother, Ted—now dying of AIDS. Threats against Billy's life ratchet the tension tighter, as Leigh wrestles with both tough and tender feelings for her old flame. Clay's own conflict, as he seeks to come to grips with his brother's lifestyle choices and the needs of the boy he fathered, underline the issue of God's forgiveness in the hearts—and lives—of this modern-day family. An emotionally gripping read!

ISBN 1-57673-638-5

DECISIONS COME HARD IN CONTEMPORARY MYSTERY

DATE DUE

"If you're looking for a contemporary mystery with wit and romance, Gayle Roper is the author you've been waiting for."

—ROBIN JONES GUNN

Rose Martin, fearless young nurse, cares for the critically injured. But when a car bomb explosion kills her cancer patient—rich widow and beloved mentor Sophie Hostetter—Rose faces a difficult question: Who could have done this? Was it Peter, Sophie's financial risk-taking son? Rose escapes into the arms of Jake, a man struggling with his past and his Amish heritage, yet decisions come hard in matters of love and forgiveness. Can the living find God's forgiveness for themselves and justice for the dead?

ISBN 1-57673-406-4